Dyad Love

DYAD CHRONICLES

ANN HINNENKAMP

An Ellora's Cave Publication

www.ellorascave.com

Dyad Love

ISBN 9781419965203

Edited by Shannon Combs.
Cover art by Dar Albert.

Electronic book publication September 2011
Trade paperback publication 2011

DYAD LOVE

Enjoy!

Dedication

For Leon, Ted, Jude and Alice. A fortunate accident at birth landed me with you people. It's been the making of me.

Acknowledgements

Thanks to all the girls: Amy Schumacher, Kate Ferraro, Ann Bleakley, Nan Dixon, Neroli Lacey and Greta MacEachern

And two boys: Jim Kuether and Joel Skelton

Prologue

New York City, 1:00 a.m.

ꙮ

These humans will be the death of me.

Caleb's pounding footsteps kept time with the helicopter blades above him. No doubt remained. The humans were herding him, just as they did the poor cattle in their slaughterhouses. They forced him west toward some unknown trap. To test this theory, he pivoted and sprinted north. A moment later, a tranquilizer dart whizzed past his head, missing him by inches. Left with no choice, he turned back west and increased his pace, trying to outdistance his attackers before they could close the circle.

The helicopter gunned its engine and swerved to avoid a chimney. For an instant, the circle of light that had been his constant companion lost him. He took advantage of the momentary respite and changed course, retracing his path over the rooftop. As he put on a burst of speed, he dug deep into his fading power reserve and channeled energy to his weakened body. The muscles in his legs tingled with power as he approached the end of the roof.

Fifty feet of air separated his roof from the next. Caleb silently thanked the Balance that New York was a typical, modern human city, everything packed together with no thought given to nature or future consequences. When they'd run out of room on the ground, forcing out or penning up every animal in their path, humans had done the only thing their small minds could envision. They'd built up.

He reached for the power and as he had done fifty times since the chase began, mentally placed himself on the other side of the gap, willing his physical body to follow. As soon as he cleared the roof, a gust of wind took him and he used it to surf the air current between the buildings. Even this high above the ground, the pollution in the air spoiled what would otherwise be a pleasant experience. He shut down his sense of smell and blocked the worst of it but the corruption still seeped into his pores, further depleting his energy.

A bone in his ankle snapped when he landed, forcing him into a controlled roll. Behind him, light swept the area he would have been in had he not changed course. Humans—so predictable, and yet so ruthless.

Unable to stand, he scuttled on all fours until he found the rooftop access. He forced open the door and threw himself into the stairwell a second before the accursed light flashed over it. The pain in his ankle finally registered and he used the last of his power reserve to knit the bone, sighing with relief as the pain faded.

The change of course had bought him one, maybe two minutes before they found him again. Time enough to form some sort of plan or at least review his options. If only Daniel were with him. Daniel, his human partner for over two hundred years, would have offered his life force to replenish Caleb's power. He could have drawn just enough of Daniel's precious essence for the strength he needed to get them both out of this impossible situation.

But the humans had killed Daniel. They'd snuffed out his life force with no more remorse than swatting a mosquito. Daniel, who had stood strong and tall beside Caleb, defending human kind against their worst enemy—themselves. Honorable, intelligent, steadfast Daniel. A man worth a hundred of those who pursued Caleb. His constant companion and friend though the centuries—gone.

Caleb pushed aside thoughts of Daniel and the bone-deep grief he knew would follow. There was no time for grief. The humans had robbed him of even that small comfort. With the net closing around him, he knew what must be done.

The same problem had plagued his race for eons—too many humans. The sheer number of them boggled the mind. They multiplied the same way they built their cities, with no thought given to what their increased numbers would do to the planet. A planet they shared, if unknowingly, with his race, the Dyads.

Loud thumps on the roof above him heralded the hunters' approach. Caleb used the wall to gain his feet, tested the ankle and frowned at the twinge of pain. Not his best work, but with no reserve left, it would have to do. As he ran down the stairs, he sent his senses out to search the building, hoping for a solution.

One thing was clear, he could not be caught. The prime directive of the Dyad race, what had kept them alive for so long, was absolute secrecy. The men chasing him only suspected the truth. If they got their hands on his body, he would become their lab animal, poked and prodded until all his secrets were theirs. Once knowledge of his race and what they could do became public, the true nightmare would begin.

His people would be hunted down, separated and imprisoned. The humans would fare no better. Wars would break out, nation against nation, to gain control of the Dyad power. It would be the end of them all and they would exterminate every living thing on the planet in their wake.

A dart whizzed past Caleb's face.

"Here," an excited voice above him shouted. "He's in the stairwell."

Caleb flew down the stairs, the soles of his boots barely skimming the concrete. Men poured into the opening above him, the sound of their footsteps thundering off the cement walls. He sent out his senses to encompass the entire building. Twenty-five floors of apartments sprawled beneath him, reminding Caleb of an organized anthill. In the small rooms people slept, ate, fought, and in a few lucky cases, made love.

Far below, in the basement, he sensed what he needed.

Pain shot through his upper body. He reached up and pulled a dart out of his shoulder. The drug spread quickly, numbing his entire torso before he stopped it. When he tried to reverse the effect, he found an empty void where his power usually lived. In this state, he was no better than the mortals who followed.

In the lobby beneath him, more men flooded in. They separated into three groups, one group to each of the two elevators, and the last headed up the stairs, cutting off his escape. The net was tightening.

Looking up, Caleb realized he'd managed to put some distance between himself and his pursuers. As quietly as possible, he slowed his pace and ducked through a door labeled twelfth floor. As he ran down the hall to the other side of the building, smells assaulted him. Each apartment sent out a flavor of the lives within. Cigarette smoke, garlic, body odor and sweet perfume washed over him as he ran.

At the far end of the hall, Caleb stopped and pulled open the garbage chute. With no other option available, he wiggled his upper body into the small opening and kicked his legs into the air. Gravity took over. He plummeted down twelve stories, his shoes and shoulders banging against the aluminum walls, sending echoes of sound up the chute, announcing his position. He braced for impact and the pain he knew would follow. There was just enough time after he cleared the chute to rotate his body before he hit. Instead of head first, he landed on his left side on a pile of plastic garbage bags that burst beneath him. He heard his collarbone snap but felt no pain. The drug in the dart had been a blessing after all.

As he struggled to stand, only the right side of his body responded. The left leg wouldn't take his weight. A hiss escaped him when he looked at his left forearm, broken so badly the bone protruded through his shirt sleeve. Still no pain. Was he in shock?

What would the other Dyads say if they could see him now, his body broken and covered in human garbage? Proud

Caleb brought low by a pack of primates. Cut off from all help, unable to reach for the Balance to channel power. Even though he knew it was impossible, Caleb centered himself and reached for the Balance. He sent his senses beneath the building, into the earth, searching for the life force of the planet, the foundation of the Dyad civilization, the Holy Balance. But without his brother Connor the Balance eluded him. After all, what was a Dyad but a group of two?

Like all Dyad pairs, he and Connor were one being born in two separate bodies. They could link telepathically, share each other's thoughts. They also shared physicality. Caleb looked at the bone sticking out of his shirt sleeve and knew that Connor's arm was broken in the same place. It took both of them together to reach the Balance and channel it into power. Alone, they were incomplete and could only draw power from their human partners. But the power from the humans paled beside the pure energy of the Balance.

For the hundredth time, Caleb cursed himself for separating from Connor. To separate when they knew the humans were hunting them seemed suicidal now, but he had thought it increased their chances of escape. He had counted on their human partners to replenish their power. Never, for one moment, had he thought the humans would kill Daniel. Once again, Caleb had underestimated the human lust for killing.

Caleb hopped to the center of the room and took in his surroundings. A gigantic boiler took up half the room. It reminded him of a metal spider lying on its back, its long legs reaching to the ceiling and going off in every direction, sending life-giving heat to the rooms above. Remarkable, when he thought about it. Humans had gone from huddling around fires to this complicated spider in a relatively short time span.

Pain shot down his arm, and when he looked at it, hope increased his heart rate. As he watched, some unseen power drew the bone in from the hole in his shirt. Once the bone had cleared the hole, Caleb pushed his shirt sleeve up for a better look. Like a puppet manipulated by an invisible puppeteer, the bone wiggled back and forth, adjusting itself until it lined up as if it had never been broken. The ragged tears in his skin started to close. In moments the arm looked good as new.

Caleb smiled. This could mean only one thing. Connor had escaped and reached a group of Dyads. The Dyads were using their collective power to heal Connor and as Connor healed, so did Caleb. He reached up and ran his fingers over his collarbone. Not a trace of the break remained.

Maybe he would live through this night after all.

Inhaling deeply, he focused and sent his mind down the mental channel reserved for his brother. From far away, Caleb sensed a flicker of Connor but was unable to reach him. Too much distance with too much pollution separated them. Human pollution always got in the way.

Caleb felt the moment when the men above him realized where he was. Soon after, both elevators were headed down loaded with rifle-toting soldiers, already anticipating his capture. In the stairwell, another group descended. Outside the building, all exits were covered.

The hope he had felt a moment ago drained away. Caleb had run out of options.

He went to the door and shot home the bolt. The sturdy lock would buy him some time. Forcing himself to the calm he needed, he sent a silent farewell off into the night for anyone who might hear it. He had a fleeting moment of fear and panic, but he pushed it away, walked to the center of the room and began the Dyad prayer of ending.

"We stand together before you, my brother and I.

In the sight of all who have journeyed on before us."

Behind Caleb, someone pounded on the door. He ignored them and continued on.

"We ask to be accepted into your company.

We offer all the knowledge we have acquired.

We offer all the love we have known.

We offer everything we have been and hoped to be.

In the name of the Balance, let us journey on with you."

With the banging door thundering behind him, Caleb went to the boiler and drew open the metal door. The heat generated by the one-inch gas jets washed over him. He reached over and turned the heat gauge to full. The jets tripled in size and the resulting heat seared his skin. Unfazed, he turned, walked to the center of the room and lined himself up with the boiler door.

One last time he tried to reach his brother, but failed. "Forgive me, Connor."

His biggest regret was not being with his brother at the end. It was unnatural for a Dyad to die apart. He hoped the priests were right and he would find his brother on the other side.

Caleb threw his hands above his head. Instead of the industrial ceiling above him, he envisioned a spring sky, full of hope and promise. "For the Dyad race. Long may it continue in the Balance."

With a running start, he headed straight to the boiler and dove in.

Twenty-five miles away, surrounded by Dyads, Caleb's brother, Connor, threw his head back and screamed in agony. He had only a moment to watch his skin melting before he whispered, "Caleb, no, not apart," and followed the other half of his Dyad into death.

Chapter One

Dyad Safe House
Upper Peninsula of Michigan
Ten minutes ago

ꟸ

Damien Stewart strode into the room like sin on a stick, causing the newly awakened nerves in Emma Langworthy's legs to go weak. Damien didn't enter a room, he conquered it. Emma had seen him in public a few times when she'd still been confined to Mildred, her wheelchair. Her unique view from the height of people's backsides always made his entrance an event. Buns tightened, hips cocked at fetching angles and in some cases, knees parted. It was as if the entire room came to attention, ready for anything, or did a full-body sigh, longing for something out of their reach. Women, men, young, old, it didn't matter. Everyone reacted to his inhuman beauty and aura of raw sex and now that Emma could feel what happened beneath her waist, she was no different.

"Emma, I did not expect to find you up so late. How is the categorizing going?" His voice floated toward her, and even though they were on opposite ends of the vast library, it sounded as if he were standing next to her. How did he do that, she wondered?

Refusing to appear as just another fawning female, Emma took a deep breath and tried to quiet her racing heart. She realized suddenly this was the first time she'd ever been alone with Damien. In the past, he'd always been in the company of his brother David or his human partner Jacob. "Oh. Hi." Even to her own ears her tone sounded forced. "Couldn't sleep. And since you have more books than most public libraries, I'm not even a quarter of the way through." She picked up a dusty volume. "Why exactly do you need five copies of *Moby Dick*?"

He closed the distance between them, moving with the fluid grace of his kind. It always reminded Emma of professional surfers. Those few who made it look as if the waves did their bidding, not the other way around. When he stopped next to her and took the book from her hand, Emma struggled to hold on to her casual air. Parts of her body started to ping and tingle. Other, more intimate parts, melted into a slow, throbbing heat.

For the thousandth time, Emma wondered if Damien could somehow sense what happened to her every time he was near. The embarrassment potential was too great to contemplate, so she told herself once again it was impossible. *Yup,* she thought. *Impossible. That's my story and I'm sticking to it.*

Damien opened the book with long, tapered fingers and fanned the pages, creating a gentle breeze that ruffled his shoulder-length blue-black hair. He inhaled deeply, licked his lips and let out a deep sigh. "Each copy is a treasure to me. Not only for the epoch between its pages, but also for the story of the book itself." He snapped the book shut and ran his index finger down the cover. "This one belonged to many people. My favorite was a German immigrant who settled in central Minnesota. Whenever he could spare the time away from his crops and animals, he would tuck himself in a corner and read by candlelight. In his youth, he had dreamed of a life at sea and for those few moments spent within these pages, he was young again with his life before him."

Emma took a step away from him. "Can you tell the entire history of everything you touch? I mean, public restrooms must be a challenge for you. It gives a whole new meaning to the soap dispenser."

The expression on Damien's face changed from confusion to surprise and then he threw back his head and laughed. Emma loved being one of the few people who could make

Damien laugh. He was always so serious and contained, never letting on what happened behind those dark blue eyes. She knew the Dyads had a great solemn duty to perform, saving the world, but a person ought to be able to have a little fun now and then.

Damien wiped at his eyes. "Soap dispenser. I will have to tell David. In answer to your question, no, we cannot pull history from all objects. Only those that have been in close, continuous contact with a human. The person leaves a fraction of his or her self and experiences behind for those of us who choose to read it."

"So, I can stop worrying about my dinner fork telling my life story to you guys?"

His face sobered. "David and I would never invade your privacy in such a manner. It is not our way. Reading the faint memory on a book from long ago is harmless history. Toying with the living is quite another matter."

Now she'd done it. When would she stop bumping up against the almighty Dyad integrity? Reading human minds was a piece of cake for them but one of their big rules was they couldn't do it without permission. It was a matter of honor to them. With her thoughtless remark, she'd just labeled him pond scum.

"I'm sorry, Damien. I know you and David would never invade my mind." She searched the room. "Where is David by the way? This is the first time I've seen one of you without the other."

"He and Aiden went to the Diarchy to visit Jude. Aiden has been too long without her and our quartet feels his…need."

Emma was still trying to figure out the quartet thing. A Dyad was a group of two. They each had a human partner, so two Dyads with their human partners functioned as a quartet. As long as a human partner stayed with his Dyad, he didn't age. Some of these quartets had been together for centuries.

Damien's partner Jacob was a Civil War veteran and David's partner Aiden had grown up in Henry VIII's England. After so long together, the humans could feel the emotions of the others unless they shielded their minds. From what she'd already learned, unless you shielded, you could quickly lose track of which emotions were your own.

"I didn't think you ever separated."

Damien put down the copy of *Moby Dick*. "Usually not. When apart, David and I are…unbalanced. We are experimenting with prolonged separation to strengthen our long-distance connections. With our human partners to draw strength from, the time apart is becoming easier." He leaned his perfect backside against the table and studied her. "What of you, Emma? It has been months since you came here. Do you find your life with us to your liking?"

What could she say? No matter how many times she'd tried to put into words her gratitude for what the Dyads had done for her, she couldn't seem to express what was in her heart. After a lifetime in Mildred, they'd given her the ability to walk. She didn't have to look at the world from waist high anymore. How do you thank someone for that?

"Emma." Damien touched her shoulder. "You do not have to stay with us much longer."

She tried to turn away but his hand on her shoulder stopped her. "Have we made you unhappy, Little Emma? Keeping you away from your family and friends?"

She let the "Little Emma" comment pass. "No, Damien. I've understood from the beginning why I needed to be here. How could I explain what happened? The tabloids would have been all over me. 'Lifetime paraplegic stands up and walks.' I'd have been on the same page as the monkey-boy and the latest abduction by nymphomaniac aliens. I get that. It's just…"

"Just what?" He took her chin in his hand.

The feel of Damien's cool fingertips on her skin sent a tingle all the way to her center. She wanted to tell him so many things but fear got in the way. She wanted to tell him what his nearness did to her. How she spent the day hoping she'd run into him. The conversations she planned in advance to show him how intelligent and witty she was. The endless hours she'd spent in the gym, getting her wobbly legs into condition, so she wouldn't seem as clumsy and awkward as she felt. And perhaps most importantly, how she alone out of everyone could tell him apart from his brother.

Unless you were one of the human partners, it was supposed to be impossible to distinguish between Dyad brothers, but she always knew when Damien hit her radar. Although he and his brother were exactly the same physically, down to the last strand of hair, Damien evoked feelings in Emma that David didn't. It had to mean something, didn't it? She also knew he didn't feel the same way about her and that's where her fear came from. If she told him what was in her heart what would she see on his face? Embarrassment, surprise, or worst of all, pity. She'd had enough pity thrown her way to last a lifetime.

His finger stroked across her chin. "Emma, what is it?"

She dug deep and tried to put something, anything into words. "I don't want to leave," she choked out. "Not ever."

"Why do you say that? You have a life waiting for you."

She pulled her chin out of his grasp. "I don't know. Everyone I know is going to freak. And my job? I was an effective counselor to the newly paralyzed because I was in the same boat with them. They saw me as an example of what life could be like, even if they were stuck in a chair. Now, I'll be just another non-disabled jerk who has no idea what they're going through."

Damien shook his head. "I have no doubt you will still be able to help them, but even if you find you cannot, there are more choices available to you now. Why would you continue to stay among, what did you call us, dual downers?"

"I was kidding about the downers thing. But you got to admit, you and David can be pretty grim at times."

"All the more reason to leave when you can."

Leave. One small word but the implications caused a knot to form in her stomach. "How can you expect me to go back to the normal human world? This—you—are the most amazing thing that's ever happened to me. I mean, you're fighting the bad guys. You and the others saved the world from global devastation just a few months ago, and in my own little way I've felt a part of it all. How can I go back to my little life in Minneapolis after all this?"

Damien let go of her shoulder. "Now is not the time for innocents among us. We are hunted."

"What do you mean, hunted? What's happened?" The knot in her stomach tightened.

"Nothing yet. But Dyads from all over the world are reporting suspicious events. We have the feeling of being watched. Something is building against us. You must be gone before anything happens."

"Why? Wouldn't I be safer here surrounded by all of you? How many Dyad pairs are here now? Six? Seven? What could stand against all of you?"

He smiled sadly and shook his head. "We are so few. Only one thousand of us. One thousand against billions of humans. The math is not in our favor."

Here was another Dyad rule Emma didn't fully understand. There could only be five hundred Dyad pairs or one thousand individuals alive at one time. Their females became fertile only when a Dyad died and needed to be replaced. Talk about Planned Parenthood.

She wasn't going to let him send her away without a fight. "All the more reason to gather as many supporters as possible," she argued. "We're not all power-hungry maniacs you know. There must be something I can do to help."

Damien pulled a chair out from the table and made her sit. He set another in front of her and took a seat, his knees touching hers. "There is no question of you staying. You must go, and soon." He raised a hand at her groan of protest. "It is useless to argue. I will not have you used as a pawn in the war that is coming. If you were ever taken by our enemies they would use your knowledge of our world against us."

"I would never—"

"You would have no choice. They would do…things to you, Emma. Terrible things. I will not allow that to happen."

Emma took in the resolution on his face. How long had he and David been planning this talk? The "goodbye, Emma, have a nice life" talk. You'd think with all his telepathic abilities, Damien would know what leaving him would cost her. Why didn't he just rip out her heart and start juggling it along with her self-esteem and confidence?

Anger rippled through her. When had she become this weak, needy excuse of a woman? She'd had more control over her life sitting in a wheelchair than sitting here next to her heart's desire. The fairy tales never said what to do if your handsome prince didn't want you.

Life in Mildred had hardened her. Childhood taunts from playground bullies—"Come on four wheels, get up and run,"—to overheard adolescent rejections—"What's the point of banging Emma? She can't feel it,"—to adult prejudice—"I'm afraid you're just not right for the position,"—had thickened her skin to rawhide.

A finely tuned sense of humor made sure people laughed with her, not at her. Her life had been hers to control. Why now, when she'd been given the one thing she wanted, had she lost the one thing she'd had?

All right, she thought. They wanted her to leave, fine. But she'd be damned if she slinked away without telling Damien how she felt about him. The old Emma would have gathered her courage and blurted it out. Looking into his eyes as she searched for the right words, the new Emma was so terrified she could feel her heartbeat pulse in her earlobes.

"Will you miss me, Damien?"

"Yes, David and I will feel your loss."

If he thought he was getting off that easy, he was nuts. "That's not what I asked. What about you, Damien? Just you."

His brows lifted. "There is no just me. Surely you know by now David and I…"

Damien sat bolt upright and gasped, "No."

Emma watched the color drain from his face. His eyes got the faraway look all Dyads did when they communicated without speech. His grip on her hand tightened to the point of pain.

"What is it? What's the matter?" she asked.

He let go of her and doubled over. Emma sprang out of the chair, alarmed. Hesitantly, she touched his shoulder. "Damien…"

With a scream, he leapt up. "Caleb, no. Connor, no. Not alone." Damien's body arched backward, his spine curving at an impossible angle. His hands tightened into fists at his sides, his eyes squeezed shut. A thunderous scream tore from his throat so full of agony and loss that Emma jumped away from him.

Unable to bear his pain, she put her hands over her ears and tried to understand what was happening. Ashamed of herself for turning away when he needed her, she pulled him upright and shook him. The scream abruptly cut off but echoes of it danced around the library. When he opened his eyes and looked at her, the bottom fell out of Emma's stomach. The beautiful blue eyes had gone completely black. He lowered his chin and stared up at her from under dark brows, like a lion marking its prey. Somewhere deep in his chest a snarl started.

She shook him again. "Damien. Stop."

For a moment, hesitation flooded his eyes and then his fists came up and pushed her away. "Run," he snarled at her.

Emma had no intention of leaving him in this condition. "Please, let me help you." Despite his actions, this was Damien. He would never hurt her.

He spun away and grasped the back of a chair, struggling for control. "Run, Emma. Get away from me. Without David or Jacob I cannot control…cannot channel…"

"I'm not going anywhere." She started toward him.

"You do not understand. A Dyad has died. We are all in flux…unbalanced. I am without the other half of my Dyad or my human partner."

"I do understand. You need to draw power to counteract whatever is happening to you."

Emma hesitated, remembering what it had felt like when Damien and David had repaired her spine. The power had flowed through her body bringing with it a pain so intense she'd almost passed out. It'd burned its way through her nervous system shooting fire up and down her legs and back until she didn't care if she ever walked, she just wanted the pain to stop. She had no wish to repeat the experience.

In front of her Damien panted and sweat dotted his brow. He clung to the back of the chair as if it was the only thing grounding him.

Despite her fear, Emma knew she must help him. She couldn't bear to see Damien like this. Pain was a small price to pay. "I've watched you draw power from Jacob. I know I can do it. Here." She offered her hand to him.

"No." The wooden chair split into pieces beneath his hands. He stared at the pieces for a moment as if he didn't believe what he had done. "Stay back. You are female—human. The Dyads are incomplete…we must increase our number…we must." He fell against the table, toppling the towers of books.

What had he said? A Dyad is dead. She searched her limited knowledge of Dyads for anything that might help. Once, she'd asked Jacob about female Dyads. Actually, she'd been trying to find out if Damien had a wife or girlfriend. He'd told her about the one-thousand rule, how the females became fertile only when a Dyad died and needed to be replaced.

She felt herself blush as realization of what Damien needed hit her. A Dyad was dead. The females were fertile. Damien needed…a female. She was a female.

The past few months, surrounded by magnetic Dyads and their Adonis-like partners, had been a never-ending cycle of lust and cold showers for Emma. The most frightening and yet wonderful thing about her new-found health was what happened to her body around men. She'd been attracted to the opposite sex before but it had always been a visual stimulus.

But now, when everywhere she looked she saw a hot-bodied, testosterone-overloaded feast for the eyes, her entire body hummed and sparked. It ran at a constant low idle, ready to rev up at the slightest provocation. It was as if she'd been saving up her sexual energy for twenty-six years and was ready to pop.

She'd thought about cornering a partner and asking him to put her out of her misery, but something always stopped her. She wanted her first time to be with someone she loved. All the books said it was better that way.

Well, she loved Damien. So what if he didn't feel the same way about her? So what if she left tomorrow and never saw him again? At least she'd have this one time with him. Her first time.

Before she could talk herself out of it, she went to him and took his face in her hands. "Please let me—"

Damien cut her off with a half-snarl, half-gasp. A gasp she echoed as power flowed into her. Energy shot up her arms and lodged itself around her rapidly beating heart. A presence brushed against her mind. It radiated lust and a need so great she pulled back, afraid of where it would lead. It prowled around her mind, searching for a way past her mental barriers.

Vertigo struck, spinning her consciousness like a top. She staggered in Damien's arms and then blinked as his grip tightened. She could see his face—his beautiful face, fierce with desire—but she could see her face too. Blue eyes large, lips parted in astonishment and fear.

Fear of Damien—yes. She shut her eyes.

Big mistake.

As soon as her eyes closed, every mental barrier she possessed melted away. The presence saw its chance and invaded her mind. Suddenly, Damien was all around her. His scent, his touch, his very being, cocooned the two of them in their own private world. They were linked somehow—one.

Panic engulfed her. She couldn't tell where Emma stopped and Damien began.

From far away she felt Damien's hands cover hers. The energy swirling around her heart intensified, gathering strength from deep within her and then it exploded out, shooting into Damien.

They both cried out. Every nerve ending in their combined bodies came alive with power. "Damien," she screamed. "I can't do this. Stop. We have to..."

No. There can be no stopping now.

Thoughts appeared in her mind. But they weren't her thoughts. She was Emma. Beautiful Emma. Witty, caring Emma. His Emma. He needed her. Wanted her so badly. Ached for her.

Emma.

He hadn't spoken, she'd heard him in her mind. For a moment she marveled at the wonder of it all, the wonder of him, and then a wave of desire crashed over her. Was it his desire or hers? It didn't matter. Lips closed over hers, drawing her deeper into him, into them. There was no Emma anymore. There was only desire. She gave in and let the wave take her.

You are mine.

* * * * *

What had he done? Damien looked down at the sleeping woman in his arms and felt a tug on his heart. Like all Dyads, he was drawn to goodness of spirit and this petite beauty had an abundance of it. All Emma had to do was enter a room and both his and David's hearts lifted. She approached life with a sense of fun and excitement, taking everyone around her along for the ride. This wondrous creature had given him her trust and he'd betrayed her.

How would he ever atone for his thoughtless taking of her innocence? For she had been innocent. Innocent, pure and perfect. She'd offered herself to him with a selflessness that humbled him and he'd repaid her by taking her on a library table like the animal he was.

As gently as possible, he disentangled himself and sat up. He straightened his own clothes and then dressed Emma. She stirred at his touch but didn't wake. *Thank the Balance,* he thought. He needed time to compose himself.

Standing, he focused and sent his mind down the mental channel he shared with his brother. But his world was too out of Balance to link with David. So much had happened. First the deaths of Caleb and Connor had shaken the entire Dyad race to its foundation. They'd all felt the moment when Caleb and Connor had traveled on, lost to them forever. The impact threw the Diarchy out of Balance temporarily. In the five hundred years since his birth, only a handful of Dyads had traveled on. In each case, Damien had been with his brother and was able to link with David and reach for the Balance deep within the earth. At those moments of great loss, each Dyad used the power of the Balance to collectively bring their race back into alignment.

Without David, Damien had been alone, at the mercy of the shifting energy around him. Before he could recover from the first shock, the Dyad females had gone into heat as the need to replace their loss overwhelmed them. Another instinct took over in him. The need to procreate—reproduce at any cost. If he had been with David this instinct was easily subdued. Without him, it had taken Damien over and Emma had paid the price.

The door banged open at the far end of the library, breaking through his deep contemplation. Jacob rushed in, followed closely by his wife, Eleanor. Both were dressed in riding leathers, Jacob's well broken in, Eleanor's shiny new. His human partner was just over six feet, his blond hair long enough to brush his collar. Eleanor was just the right height to tuck under his arm. Her long strawberry-blonde hair lay matted against her head.

Just the sight of Jacob brought some equilibrium back. The swirling currents of energy surrounding Damien calmed and he was able to focus on the tall man, standing battle-ready next to the woman he loved.

Jacob's steel-gray eyes darted around the room taking in Emma unconscious on the table, the chair in pieces on the floor and books scattered everywhere. "What the hell happened? Damn it, Damien. Why did you close our link? How can I help if I can't feel you? I almost killed the two of us getting back here."

Eleanor went to him and took his hand. At her touch, Jacob whipped to face her. Something in her eyes seemed to calm him. His shoulders relaxed a fraction.

She touched his cheek. "We're fine, love. Outside of a bad case of helmet hair and some bugs in my teeth, that is." She turned to Damien. "What's happened to Emma?" She started toward the prone woman.

Damien stepped in front of her and raised his hands. "Emma's fine. I…we," he stammered. As he looked at the two of them, their love an almost physical presence, shame overwhelmed him. This couple was an example of what love and commitment should be. Whenever he linked with Jacob, Damien could feel his partner's love for Eleanor. Not only feel it, but share in it. They'd each found in the other a perfect Balance. The other half of their souls. How could he stand before this purity and tell them what he had done?

"Damien," Jacob said. "What is it? I felt your scream and then nothing."

"We have been attacked. A Dyad has traveled on."

"No," they said together.

Eleanor took a step toward him. "Who? Someone here?"

Damien shook his head. "The Fitzgerald Dyad, Caleb and Connor. They were stationed in the safe house outside New York City. They were old when I was made." He swayed and leaned against the table.

Jacob dropped his wife's hand and went to Damien. Eleanor went around the men to Emma.

"Here," Jacob held out his hand. "Replenish yourself."

Damien recoiled. "I do not think it wise. I am…not right. I do not know what it will do to you."

"Don't be an ass." Jacob grasped his hand. "Take what you need."

Damien gave in and forced himself to the calm needed to link. He reached for Jacob's mind and felt the link sink home. The familiar essence of Jacob washed over him. Strong, loyal and honest, everything a Dyad needed in a partner. Unlike other times, he closed off a part of his mind, hiding what he had done with Emma. He couldn't face the other man knowing, not yet.

Damien focused and drew a fraction of Jacob's life force into his own body. The power snaked through him, strengthening, easing and bringing a semblance of Balance back to him. He took a deep, calming breath, opened his eyes and saw Jacob's stricken expression.

"You shielded part of your mind. What are you hiding?" Jacob asked.

Before he could answer, Eleanor came up to them. "Emma's out cold. I can't wake her. Did she get caught in a power surge or something?"

"You could say that," Damien said. Now that he could think clearer, he wasn't sure Emma would like the others to know about what had happened between them. He thought it best to ask her before he spoke about it.

"Will she be all right?" Jacob asked.

"She should be fine in a few hours. Her body's natural resilience will stabilize her. She just needs rest." Damien was almost positive he was correct about this. On the other hand, he had no idea how much of Emma's life force he'd stolen. He needed to get her away, have her all to himself again.

Jacob started for Emma. "I'll take her to her room."

"No, do not touch her," Damien shouted, surprising everyone, including himself. He couldn't bear the thought of anyone, even his partner, touching Emma. The need to protect her at all costs shot through him. When he looked at Jacob a part of him wanted to rip the big man's head off. What was happening to him?

"You wait for the others. I will take her," he said. He went to Emma and gathered her up in his arms. The lovely scents of Emma encircled him, lilac shampoo, rain hand lotion, peppermint breath mints, and underneath it all, the smell of what they had done together. Another reason no one else could touch her, he'd left his scent all over her.

"Stay here," he said to Jacob and Eleanor. "I will settle her and come right back."

As he climbed the stairs, he couldn't help drawing Emma closer. He nuzzled her neck and nibbled his way to her ear. She stirred at his touch, put her arms around his neck and settled her head on his shoulder.

They fit like two puzzle pieces. Why had he never noticed before?

In her room, he put her down on the bed. He thought about undressing her, but didn't trust himself. He took off her shoes and tucked her under the covers.

He stood and looked around the room. She'd only been with them a few months but she'd put her stamp on her surroundings. Bright colors dominated, from the red and orange bedspread to the rainbow of fingernail polishes lined up on the dresser. Posters of her favorite movies, *Casablanca, Young Frankenstein, Lord of the Rings,* were taped over the more traditional paintings on the walls. Her purse, one of the largest Damien had ever seen, lay open on a small table.

He looked back at the bed and marveled at how small she looked, just a bump really. Her brown hair streamed over her pillow. Her elfin features, usually so animated, were at rest.

What would she say to him when she woke up? He wouldn't blame her if she spat in his face. After what he'd done, he deserved no better. How would he ever make it right between them? What would he say to the others—to David?

Damien froze. For the first time in his long life he almost dreaded seeing his brother. The feeling was—odd. They were Dyads. At one with each other. Always together, never apart, two parts of the same whole. There had never been a need for explanations or excuses between them.

He sat on the bed and put a hand on Emma's forehead. Concentrating, he sent his senses into her body to assess the damage he'd caused. To his surprise, Emma was fine. More than fine. A vibrant energy bubbled through her, making it a pleasure just to touch her. If he'd taken any of her life force he must have given it back. Why couldn't he remember?

He bent and kissed her forehead. "Sleep and renew, little one. We will sort this out when you wake." A part of him didn't want to leave her. Another part wanted to run away screaming.

He used the time it took getting back to the library to pull himself together. Nothing worked the way it usually did. Even without David, he should have been able to reach an inner calm, quiet the churning emotions but peace eluded him. Was it the deaths of Connor and Caleb, the Dyads being in heat, what happened with Emma, or a combination of all three? Whatever the cause, Damien was off Balance, not one with the world around him.

Back at the library, the Goddard quartet had joined Jacob and Eleanor. As soon as Damien entered he could tell the Dyad brothers and their human partners were off Balance. Maybe not as bad off as he, but still, not right.

Sebastian and Samuel Goddard stood framed by their human partners, Luke and Emil. The humans were white-faced, shifting nervously, not at all their normal competent selves. To Damien, the Dyads seemed worse off. Sebastian and Samuel stood well over six feet with shoulder-length white-blond hair, strong chins and the slim athletic build all Dyads possessed. No human could tell by looking at them, but Damien could feel their inner turmoil. Even together, drawing directly from the Balance, the brothers struggled to keep their emotions in check.

Luke stood close to his Dyad partner, Sebastian. Usually easy going with a smile that devastated the female population, his countenance now was grim. Tension bled off him. Next to him, Emil, the newest of the human partners, looked from face to face, trying to gauge the collective mood.

"Brother, a great loss has come to us," Samuel said.

Both Goddards came toward him, arms outstretched, offering comfort.

Damien stepped back. "No. Do not touch me."

The brothers paused, waiting for an explanation, with dual looks of puzzlement on their faces.

"David is not here," Damien explained. "We were apart when the Fitzgeralds traveled on."

"Was Jacob with you?" Sebastian asked.

"No. I was without my Dyad brother or human partner."

The Goddards shared a dark look. "Alone? You were alone?" Samuel said. "Gods. How did you fare?"

Here was the perfect moment to tell them and yet he found he could not. "Not well," he managed. "I am still not in Balance. I must get to David as soon as possible."

"Just so," Sebastian said. "We are all summoned home to the Diarchy. The Elders have called for council and those of us with female alliances must nest. We must replace the Fitzgeralds. We are incomplete. We must procreate. We must—" He broke off, unable to continue. Damien could sense his struggle for control.

Samuel went to Sebastian and touched his arm. They looked at each other for a moment and then Sebastian relaxed. Damien was instantly jealous of the two of them. This was how a Dyad usually worked, each drawing strength from the other.

Jacob and the other humans joined them.

"Who killed the Fitzgeralds?" Jacob asked.

"Caleb committed suicide and brought Connor with him," Samuel said.

Eleanor gasped. "What? I didn't think Dyads ever took a life. Even their own."

Sebastian nodded sadly. "The human soldiers left him little choice. They had him surrounded, his capture moments away. Rather than exposure, Caleb chose to protect our race. He and Connor made the ultimate sacrifice to save us all. Long may they continue in the Balance."

"In the Balance," the Dyads echoed.

"You said soldiers. What soldiers?" Jacob asked.

"Before he died, Connor warned of a highly organized military group after them," Sebastian continued. "We are trying to get more information from Connor's human partner but he has lost his quartet. It is all the others can do to keep him sane."

"Poor man," Eleanor said and touched Jacob for support.

"Where are the other Dyads staying here?" Luke asked.

"They have answered the Elders' call and left for the Diarchy. We only stayed to collect Damien and David."

"What about Mike?" Jacob asked. "Should we take him out of school?"

"Lord, no," Luke said. "We just got him to agree to stay. We even hint that Damien and the other Dyads are in danger and he'll never go back to college."

Damien had completely forgotten about his human ward, Michael Murray. A few years ago, Jacob had stumbled upon Michael getting beat up by a gang in Chicago. Jacob had intervened and brought the boy home. Damien was grooming him to become a human partner. Would he be safe tucked away at the campus in Duluth? Probably. And he had his linking coin with him. He could use it to call for help. But Luke was right, if Michael knew about what happened to the Fitzgeralds, he'd be on a bus home in a heartbeat.

Damien turned to Luke. "Please call Michael and tell him we will be at the Diarchy for an extended visit. Tell him to stay put. We will get in touch when we return."

Jacob moved to leave. "I'll get our things."

Eleanor stopped him. "Aren't we all forgetting something?" She turned to Damien and raised a sardonic eyebrow. "What do we do about Emma?"

Chapter Two

༄

"Make a hole."

The command echoed down the stairwell crowded with soldiers. When they looked up and saw Alexander Ward's face, every single one of them hugged the wall. No, not hugged it—melted into it. Alex grunted. They better get out of his way. The incompetent idiots. The overpriced, steroid-stimulated, worthless fools. He started down the human cave, careful to avoid touching any of them.

At the bottom Major Powers, the leader of these mercenary monkeys, stood ready to accept the ball busting coming his way. Alex stopped next to him, close enough to invade Powers' personal space but far enough away not to subject himself to the man's constant halitosis. At six feet, Alex towered over the smaller man dressed in his pretend uniform with its pretend bars on the shoulders. The only thing real was the gun on his hip.

Alex pitched his voice in the quiet, deadly tone he reserved for occasions such as these. "What was the one thing I asked you to do…Major?"

Powers came to attention, his eyes focused front. "Take the subject alive, Sir," he barked out.

"And tell me, Powers." He moved to meet the man's eyes. "Did you achieve your objective?"

The major held his stare, the only sign of emotion a tightening of his jaw. "No, Sir. The subject is dead."

"So you, with all your troops and munitions and helicopters and black ops, failed?" Alex asked.

The major exhaled and Alex got a blast of some biblically bad stink.

"Yes, Sir," Powers said.

"No, Major. Don't 'yes sir' me. I want you to say it. Say it in front of your men." Alex saw a flash of anger in Powers' eyes.

"Well, Major?"

The man's jaw clamped down hard enough to break a tooth. "We failed, Sir," he managed.

Alex circled behind the major for two reasons. First, he wanted to unsettle Powers, who had to stay at attention facing front. And second, and more importantly, to get out of the stink path. "Louder," Alex hissed in his ear. "The men at the top of the stairs didn't hear."

Powers realigned his stance, braced himself and took a deep breath. "We failed," he shouted.

Alex waited for the man's humiliation to sink in good and deep before turning to the others. "Who's second here?" he asked. No one answered or met his eyes. He allowed a fraction of the rage he'd been suppressing out. "Second. Now," he bellowed.

"Here, Sir." A mountain of a man stepped forward. The giant was equal to Alex in height but outweighed him by at least fifty pounds of hard muscle, with a neck so thick his head looked small in comparison. *Good,* Alex thought. He'd tried smart with Powers. Now he needed big and stupid.

"Name?" he asked the mountain.

"Cronk, Lieutenant." He had a high-pitched feminine voice.

No wonder he's so big, Alex thought. *With a voice like that he's been fighting all his life.*

"Cronk," Alex said. "You are now in charge of this operation. Your first order is to get this worthless piece of shit out of my sight." He jerked his head in Powers' direction.

Cronk's eyes darted to Powers. He opened his mouth to answer but the major beat him to it.

"You have no authority to do that," Powers spat out. "I don't report to you and neither do my men."

A mumble of agreement rustled through the troops.

Alex smiled. Time to remind these robots who he was. "Listen carefully, Major Powers. This is the last time I will address you. The last time anyone will address Major Powers. I'm funding this operation. Your superiors, who work for me, were in full agreement when I spoke to them. It seems they don't accept failure any more than I do. They're waiting for you at the command center. You're in for quite a party."

The major paled. "But…but," he sputtered.

Alex turned, dismissing him. "Cronk."

After one more hesitant look at Powers, Cronk cut his losses and came to attention. "Yes, Sir," he shouted.

"Follow your orders," Alex said.

"You two." Cronk pointed at two men. "Disarm the prisoner and escort him to the command center."

No mumbling now. The two moved to flank Powers, who stared at them in disbelief. The closest took the gun from Powers' holster. The other motioned to the stairs. "Let's go," he said.

After a final look around the room where he found no support, Powers walked stiffly to the stairs and started up.

Alex watched his exit and then turned to Cronk. "Where is he?" he asked.

"This way, Sir." Cronk pointed to a hallway on the left.

When he looked at the exit indicated, the men surrounding it faded back in a manner that reminded him of synchronized swimmers. Hiding a smile, Alex strode to the hallway and almost halted when the sickening smell of burnt flesh washed over him. He knew better than to show any weakness in front of these goons, so he kept his feet moving.

Steeling himself against the odor, he opened his mouth a crack and sucked in air through his teeth.

At the end of the hall a wide, metal door stood propped open by a rifle, business end pointing down. In the center of the door a thick, metal bar twisted back on itself. For some reason it reminded Alex of a canned ham. Taking another deep breath through his mouth, he went in the doorway and was immediately assaulted by the heat and despite all his efforts to block it, the smell.

One end of the room was taken up by an enormous furnace. The old-fashioned kind with pressure gauges and gas jets. On the far end, storage rooms for the tenants labeled with their apartment numbers lined the wall. On his way in, Alex had noticed other rooms with the same labeling. Evidently these were the unlucky tenants' storage areas. Who'd want to come down to this god awful place to get the Christmas ornaments?

To the left, garbage bags were piled high, some torn open, adding to the already putrid aroma of the place.

Directly in the center, positioned on a table as if lying in state, the body rested. Alex spent a few shaky moments fighting his gag reflex. Wisps of dark smoke rose from the lifeless, blackened lump. No hair or clothes were visible. The burned skin peeled back in some areas revealing a deep red mass underneath. And the face, what was left of it, was set in an expression of agony, the mouth gaping wide, the eye sockets—empty holes. The creature had been beautiful once. No, more than beautiful, majestic. Alex had seen the photos. Now it lay here reduced to charred meat. Useless to him.

"How the hell long was he in there?" Alex shouted, pointing at the furnace.

Cronk stepped forward. "It took us just under six minutes to get through the door. Our objective was to take him alive so no explosives could be used."

When Alex thought about the secrets this being held, the power, everything he could have used, now lost; a blind rage came over him. He fought the urge to grab a rifle and shoot every last motherfucking one of them.

Alphonse Lambert chose that moment to make his appearance. He stumbled into the room holding a bandana with the words Scientists Rock embossed on it against his oversized nose.

"Christ, the smell," he gagged out. He started for the table with the body, tripped over some garbage and fell across the corpse. "Ahhh," he screamed and quicker than Alex thought the old man could move, pushed off the table and staggered back.

Why did he need this old pile of bones? For the thousandth time Alex thought about cutting this pompous windbag loose, but as much as he wanted to, he couldn't. The bastard knew about them. About the Dyads. He was too valuable to get rid of, but God, he was sick of this nincompoop. The man was like a gadfly, always buzzing around your head.

Hiding his revulsion, Alex turned to Lambert. "Do you know this one?" he asked.

Lambert tiptoed to the table and leaned over the charred face. "Impossible to tell. Too much damage. Are you sure it's dead?" He poked the body's shoulder with a bandana-wrapped finger.

Alex crossed to him. "Of course it's dead. It was in the furnace for over six minutes. You want to take a lie down in there and see how you do?"

Lambert's face got its condescending look. The look that made Alex yearn to roast him over hot coals. He shook his head. "I don't think that's very constructive, Alex. I was only saying. It's best not to underestimate these creatures."

Alex turned to Cronk. "What about the other one?" he asked the big man. "Did we manage to capture him?"

"No, Sir," Cronk answered, his high, girlie voice making a mockery of the situation. "He and the man with him evaded capture. They got away clean."

"I wouldn't say that." Lambert straightened and turned to them. "Remember, what happens to one twin happens to the other. Right now, wherever he is, his brother looks just like this."

Alex shook his head. "Both dead. Perfect."

Lambert simpered next to him. "It's not a complete loss," he said. "We have enough of the body left to study. Just think what his DNA will tell us. That is, if he even has DNA." He rubbed his hands together. "I can't wait to get him to the lab."

A soldier stepped forward. "Sir, command says to vacate the premises. One of the tenants just got a call through to 9-1-1. NYPD will be here soon."

"Another slip-up?" Alex asked Cronk. "I thought your team had all forms of communication to and from the building blocked."

Cronk ignored him and addressed the men. "You heard the man, we're out of here—stat. Mr. Ward, if you and the professor will lead the way, we'll bag the body and be right behind you."

Lambert bolted. Alex followed at a more dignified pace. He had as much to lose as Lambert if they were detained by the police but he'd be damned if he gave in to panic.

When he reached the street Alex heard sirens in the distance. He noted which vehicle Lambert had dived into and picked the next in line for his escape. As soon as he slammed the door, the driver pulled away and headed straight for the sirens. Adrenaline shot through him. The thought of getting caught, of actually spending a night in jail didn't bother him. His lawyers would have him out before his butt warmed in the chair. No, the police didn't concern him. He could control them.

Alex knew his enemy. The enemy he had no control over. The enemy who laughed at him whenever he slowed down.

Time.

Chapter Three

ꟹ

Emma dreamed of cool lips gliding over her skin. Of equally cool hands tracing the lines of her body, investigating each curve and indent, lingering at her breasts, the backs of her knees, her inner thighs. As Aladdin did with his lamp, the hands rubbed over her body, releasing the genie deep inside. No three wishes for her though. Instead, her genie's gift was desire. It shot through her, awakening pleasure points she hadn't known existed. Each place the hands touched created an epicenter of an earthquake, sending waves of pleasure in every direction. A sensation overload so sweet, so full of longing and expectation, Emma moaned on the razor's edge of pleasure and pain.

Out of the dream mist, a face took form above her. Damien's face. She recognized the dark blue eyes, so full of need, his Roman nose with nostrils flaring, full red lips parted in concentration and the fall of black hair just long enough to brush against her face as he moved over her.

You are mine.

Emma's eyes flew open and for a few moments she couldn't place where she was. Humphrey Bogart's familiar profile on the *Casablanca* poster brought reality rushing back. She was in bed in her room at the Dyad safe house. But…how had she gotten here? Why wasn't she still in the library cataloging books? Five copies of *Moby Dick*. Five copies…

Memories crashed in on her.

"Oh. My. God."

Had it all been a dream born of her body's need? Could it be possible after months of imagining making love with Damien, she'd somehow triggered a psychotic episode in which what she'd wished for had overpowered her reason and transported her to *Fantasy Island*?

She stretched and knew at once it had all been real. Parts of her body she'd never felt before were deliciously sore. When she moved her legs, the muscles in her inner thighs reacted like hot rubber bands. Her lower back throbbed, her abs ached, every inch of her body screamed in protest. In short—she felt wonderful.

A line from an old western, "Rode hard and put away wet," sprang into her mind. She half laughed, half groaned. Only she could take a moment like this that should have been full of the wonder of discovery, and reduce it to its most common aspects. Well, she was nothing if not practical and practically speaking, she needed a shower. Certain parts of her anatomy were sticky.

She threw the covers off and froze. Damien's scent had been hiding beneath the covers. Unable to help herself, she inhaled deeply. Memories of their time on the library table flashed through her mind. An erotic slideshow of clothes pushed aside, body parts melding together, his taste in her mouth, his hands holding her down, his body buried deep inside her own.

Emma gasped and sat up. It was too much. The suddenness of it. The changes to both her physical and mental state. And, try as she might, she couldn't remember how it had ended between them. She remembered intense desire. How her mind had linked with Damien's until she couldn't distinguish which thoughts were her own. She'd never forget the power flowing back and forth, a seemingly endless cycle of shifting energy that fed the heat between them, always growing, sending them higher and higher, until she thought they would both explode. And then—nothing.

Had she passed out? Fainted? Had she honestly spent one of the most important moments of her life unconscious? What must Damien think? Embarrassment hit her and she groaned. What if she'd been drooling? Or worse, snoring?

"No!" She sprang out of bed, ignoring the scream of stiff muscles. "Don't go there. Don't borrow trouble." Her Grandmother Langworthy's favorite saying didn't offer the usual comfort. But then, this wasn't her usual mess of unpaid parking tickets, overdue library books and late oil changes.

"No," she said again. "One thing at a time." Another of grandmother's sayings. Shower first and obsess about what a nerd she was later.

In the bathroom she hesitated, unwilling to wash Damien's scent off. She was sure this would be the only time she and Damien would be together and she wanted to savor the aftereffects. If only she could wrap up the experience in a bubble and relive it over and over until it seemed commonplace. Like that would ever happen.

In the end she compromised. She set the sweater she'd been wearing aside to wrap up. If Damien sent her away at least she'd have this little part of him to treasure. His scent on her sweater. How pathetic was that? *Seriously, Emma.* A part of her thought she was straying into stalker territory. But another part knew she would wrap that sweater in plastic and take it with her wherever she went.

She showered quickly, trying to keep her mind off what was washing away. Wrapping up in a towel, she went to the bathroom mirror to brush her teeth and slap on a little makeup.

When she looked in the mirror, she froze. She blinked a few times trying to sharpen her vision, took another look and waited for what she saw to click into place.

Nothing clicked.

After a few moments she raised her hands to her face and started exploring. Every blemish was gone. Even the pimple—one of the really bad undergrounders—that had appeared two days ago and should've stayed at least a week, had vanished. High on her left cheek the two small marks from a bout with chicken pox—disappeared. The skin on her face was flawless, every imperfection caused by normal living, gone.

A giggle escaped Emma. The woman in the mirror giggled with her. The woman looked like Emma, only better. The best Emma possible. Her lips were fuller, her cheeks rosy. Even her eyes sparkled back at her with a new brilliance.

No wonder the partners looked so drop-dead gorgeous all the time. The power shared with the Dyads kept them at their best. It constantly set them back to their perfect state. Why then was she so stiff? Shouldn't the magic mojo have taken care of her aches and pains as well?

Her fingers explored every inch of her face. "Amazing." Not since she'd babysat her newborn niece had she felt anything so soft. "Wow."

She reached for the foundation she used, but stopped. She didn't need it anymore. There was nothing to cover up, nothing that could be improved upon. It felt wrong somehow, not putting foundation on. From the day she'd turned sixteen and her parents' makeup ban had lifted, she'd never appeared in public without her face on. She'd feel naked without it. Finally, she settled on just mascara. At least it was something.

On her way out of the bathroom she grabbed the sweater. Until she could find a plastic container, she put it in her dresser underneath her socks.

As she searched for something to wear a feeling grew inside. She wanted, no needed, to see Damien. He would have the answers to all the questions popping up. How had this happened? How long would it last? What else had he done to her? Did he know how much she loved him? She'd keep the last one to herself.

Emma knew, as soon as she saw Damien's face, one of her questions would be answered. Did he regret what they had shared? If he looked embarrassed, or worse, ashamed, she didn't think she'd be able to bear it.

Whatever the outcome, she had to see him. The need inside her grew, making her hurry through getting dressed and brushing her hair. By the time she left the room it had gotten out of control. Her feet flew down the hall.

Find Damien.

She took the stairs two at a time.

Find Damien. Damien needed her.

Running full out, she headed for the library, sure somehow he was waiting for her.

The sound of her name on Damien's lips stopped her.

"Emma must go. Now."

She couldn't breathe. He wanted her to go, she'd known that, but so soon? *He's ashamed. Ashamed to admit he's been with me.*

A voice answered him, Eleanor's voice. "It's only been a few months. We need more time for a plausible cover story. Her parents, her friends, everyone thinks Emma is at a clinic in Europe undergoing experimental treatment. We send her back now, when these men are after us, and she'll stick out like a sore thumb. You might as well wave a red flag and say come and get her."

"I did not say send her home. I said away, to a safe place."

Emma felt another stab of pain. Her worst fear was realized. Damien wanted her as far away from him as possible. All the blood left her head and she leaned against the wall for support.

"Damien, why don't we just bring her to the Diarchy with us? There is no safer place," Jacob said.

"Why not ask Emma?" She recognized one of the Goddard's voices. "Emma, please join us."

Emma stared at the carved mahogany door. Great. The Goddards were here and they'd used their power to sense her hiding in the hall. That meant the whole Goddard quartet must have joined the party. She was going to have quite an audience when she faced Damien. Wonderful.

The last thing in the world she wanted to do was enter that room. How could she face him? How could she look into Damien's blue eyes and see the revulsion he felt for her? He'd answered her question. He wanted her anywhere but with him. The ache surrounding her heart grew until she gasped for breath. She'd known it was going to be hard, leaving him, but she'd underestimated the pain.

"Emma, you out there?" Eleanor called.

With her mind screaming at her to run, Emma walked into the library. She avoided eye contact with Damien, looking instead at the others, grouped in front of the fireplace. The Goddards, with Luke and Emil, turned her way. Emma had always liked Luke. His friendly teasing had gotten her through many a lonely day. He'd become her closest friend and confidant here among this strange group of men. The older brother she'd never had.

The look of surprise on Luke's face made her look down at her body, afraid she'd left the zipper on her jeans open.

"What?" she asked. "Did I forget something?"

Eleanor came toward her. "Em, wow. You look beautiful." She turned to Damien. "What did you say happened? Did Emma get too close to a power exchange?"

"No," Samuel said. "This is something else." He went to Emma and reached to touch her.

Suddenly, Damien stood between Emma and Samuel. One second he was across the room and the next—bam—he was in between them.

"Stay away from her," Damien shouted.

Sebastian joined his brother in front of Damien. They raised their hands and closed their eyes. A power flowed over Emma. It felt like goose bumps, only deeper, under the skin instead of on top. It started at the top of her head and wound its way down her body exploring, probing. No part of her was left untouched.

Damien snarled and raised his hands. "Get out of her," he screamed.

At the same moment the Dyad brothers flew back against the table, pushed hard by some invisible force. Luke and Emil rushed to stand between their partners and Damien's attack.

The power gripping Emma let go and she gasped in relief. Damien whirled to face her, his eyes blazing with fury. He placed her firmly behind him, turned to Luke and Emil and raised his hands for another attack.

"Peace, Damien," Sebastian said. He and Samuel pushed their partners out of the way and stood in front of Damien. They looked first at Emma and then at Damien.

Samuel's eyes narrowed. "What have you done?"

Shame coursed through Damien like a double shot of whiskey. A part of him marveled at this new emotion. How it affected him physically. His skin burned, his blood flowed in irregular patterns, his heart sped up, and his mouth lost its moisture. Amazing.

When he looked into Samuel's accusing eyes any wonder left him. How had he thought for one moment the other Dyads would not know what he had done? One look at Emma's perfect face had told the Goddards everything. But he could not share his experience with them until he had spoken to Emma. She deserved that much from him at least.

"I must speak with Emma," he said. Ignoring the surprised look on Jacob's and the other humans' faces, he took Emma's arm and got them the hell out of there.

Damien guided Emma down the long door-lined hallway, moving so fast conversation was impossible. He had no idea where he was taking her. His only thought had been to get Emma away from the others. Now that he had her all to himself half of him wanted to take her back to her room and force her to sleep. Avoid the confrontation completely. The more familiar half, the rational, fully balanced half, knew he must face this situation head-on. He owed it to Emma to ease her through any unsettling emotions she was having. To rectify and undo the damage he had caused.

Resolved, he picked the next door, opened it and pulled Emma in behind him. Turning, he let go of her and closed the door. He stood facing away for a moment, gathering his courage. Cursing himself ten kinds of coward, he turned to face her.

She wasn't where he'd left her. Rattled, he took a quick look around. Unconsciously, he'd brought them to Emma's favorite room; a glassed-in porch with an unobstructed view of Lake Superior. He and David had often found her here, listening to music and staring at the water, lost in that wonderful mind of hers.

Emma had put as much distance as possible between them. She stood with her back to him on the far side of the room. Damien took advantage of this momentary respite to pull his thoughts together. He searched for the right words to open the conversation. Nothing came to him.

Finally, he took a few steps toward her. "Emma, I would like to start by—"

"I don't know why everyone's making such a big deal out of this." She turned to face him.

Damien took in her put-on expression of nonchalance. She was a good actress, he'd give her that, but she couldn't hide the pain in her eyes. A pain he had put there.

"I am so sorr—"

"Save it, Damien." She shot him a dark look. "You don't have to tell me how sorry you are or how it never should have happened. Believe me, I get the picture."

"Picture? I do not understand."

"Well, this is a red letter day. I finally found something you don't understand. Strike up the band and blow the horns.

What? Doesn't my reaction fit into your perfectly balanced world? Too human for you?"

"No. I do not..." Damien didn't want to admit she was right. She had surprised him with her response. "Picture, you said. What picture?"

She snorted. "The picture you've been painting since I came into the library. First, I heard you say you wanted me gone. 'Send Emma away,' I think were your exact words."

"For your protection and..." he trailed off, unable to finish his thought without hurting her.

"And? And what?" She advanced on him, her eyes bright with anger. "How about I finish that thought for you. And you want me as far away from you as possible. Why? Is the great Dyad feeling some morning-after regret?"

"Of course I regret what happened. How could I not?"

Tears welled in Emma's eyes. She turned her back to him. Why was everything he said making things worse, not better?

He put his hand on her shoulder and tried to turn her but she was granite under his hand. A shameful urge to invade her mind came over him. If he could just sense what she was feeling he would know what to do, the right words to say.

As if reading his mind, Emma pulled out of his grasp. "Don't touch me. I don't need your pity. It's insulting." She moved and put a sofa between them.

Damien was at a loss. He'd expected recriminations on her part, even disgust. But anger? He'd never encountered this emotion in Emma. It was so unlike her. He would try reasoning with her. He came toward her, his hands out, palms up in the universal sign of surrender. If he'd had a white cloth, he would've waved it.

"Please," he said. "Could we start this conversation over? I seem to have said all the wrong things." His shins bumped against the sofa. "Truly, Emma. I do not wish to cause you further pain."

Instead of the calm he was hoping for, his words seemed to have the opposite effect. Emma's eyes flared wide and she hit the sofa with a fist. "Pain? You think what happened between us was painful? For you maybe, but I had a wonderful time."

He tried to interrupt but she held up a hand. "No, not wonderful. Mind-blowing. My first time at bat and I think I knocked it out of the park." She looked at him and snorted again. "Don't look so horror-struck. I know I was a virgin. So did you. But I also knew what I was getting into." She looked down at the floor. "Eleanor told me when Dyads link with humans they know what the human thinks and feels. Is that true?"

Damien could only nod.

She looked up at him. "Is it?"

He nodded again.

Emma paced behind the sofa. "Great. That's just great. Perfect." She ran a hand through her hair. "So, when you linked with me you found out how I feel about you. Didn't you?"

The accusation in her eyes silenced any response. Once again, he could only nod.

"What? Am I having a one-sided conversation? Are you so ashamed you made love to me you can't even speak? Where's the famous Dyad strength?" All the anger seemed to melt out of her. Her shoulders slumped. "Come on, Damien. Jump in any time. Don't make me do this all alone."

More than anything else, the tears in her voice made him speak. "Yes. I know what you feel for me."

She stopped pacing in front of him and gripped the back of the sofa. "And what do I feel?" she whispered.

"You think yourself in love with me."

"I didn't ask you what I thought. Don't evade the question. What do I feel for you, Damien?" Tears threatened to spill over.

"Love. You feel love for me."

"There you go. Was that so hard to get out?" She shrugged. "So, I'm in love with you. Have been since I first saw you. Can't help it. I knew you didn't feel the same. I knew the chances of us being together were almost nonexistent, so when I saw my chance, I took it. But," she paused, pointing a shaking finger at him, "you needed me, Damien. I watched you fall apart in front of me. You needed what I could give you. I wanted what you could give me. We used each other. No loss. No foul. Game over." Her tears reached their limit and spilled down her cheeks.

He was around the sofa before she could react. Blocking her escape with his body, he cupped her cheek. "Why are you trying to make this easier for me? It should be me easing the way for you."

Emma rubbed her cheek slowly back and forth across his palm. "I don't think you should be touching me."

He looked at her perfect face and missed the old Emma. The freckles on her nose, the scars on her left cheek—all the little flaws that had made up his lovely Emma.

"Is it such a tragedy?" he asked. "Your love for me."

"It is when you're the only one at the party."

In spite of the high drama surrounding them, he laughed. She always made him laugh. In over five hundred years he'd never met another being like her, who could at once see the sad and humorous side of things. Unpredictable. Even goofy sometimes. Delightful. Yes. That was the word for her. Delightful.

"I love making you laugh."

The love in her eyes humbled him. Against all reason, he enfolded her in his arms. "I am at the party, little one. Maybe on the sidelines, but definitely at the party. And one day soon I will have to watch some lucky man take my place. It is a necessary course of events, but it will cause me pain I think. Much more than you realize."

"Damien, I think you're going to be a tough act to follow. The man's going to have to be Albert Einstein, Gandhi and Brad Pitt all rolled into one."

The time had come to go but he continued to hold her close. *Why?* he thought. *Why let her go?* She loved him. Love couldn't, no shouldn't be discarded lightly. How many times had he encountered love? Not the lust he saw in women's and men's eyes, or even the imagined love he felt from women after he'd had them. Or the love he felt for Eleanor when he was linked with Jacob. How many times? Once before. Only once so long ago…

He blocked the memories. He would not go down that path. He would never go down that path.

"Damien." Emma stirred in his arms.

He kissed the top of her head. "Yes, little one?"

She leaned back and looked up at him. "Okay, first stop with the 'little one' stuff."

"All right."

"I know this ends our…whatever. I want one more thing from you."

"I am afraid to ask what that could be."

"Kiss me goodbye. And not a peck on the cheek. Kiss me goodbye and mean it."

The fear of rejection he saw in her eyes was understandable. The other emotions, desire flavored with a healthy dose of outright lust, surprised him. Intense male satisfaction shot through him. He had awakened this in Emma. No one had been with her before him. She belonged to him in a way she wouldn't belong to any other male. If he had to let her go, at least he could treasure the knowledge he had been her first.

Who would be second? Of all the partners, she seemed to favor Luke's company. The thought of Luke kissing Emma, of Luke stroking her body to life sent a stab of jealousy into his gut.

"You don't have to look like I asked you to eat meat. Forget the kiss." Emma tried to push out of his arms.

Damn. He'd done it again, hurt her without meaning to. He'd let his mind wander to what was important to him instead of helping her.

He pulled her back into his arms. "Emma, listen—"

She fought him. "No, Damien. Enough. I can't take any more. Let me go gather my shattered ego in peace."

"Emma, please." He cupped her cheek. "If I were not Dyad but human, I would never let you go. But I am Dyad. There is no future for us."

She put her hands on his chest and shoved away. "I understand. Really, I do. Let me go now."

"No. Not like this." He didn't want the last time he touched her to be this way. Emma was in pain, struggling to get away. "I believe you asked for a kiss." He closed the distance and put his lips on hers.

At first she continued to struggle but her human strength was no match for his and she soon quieted. Her lips were tense so he made a game of teasing the corners of her mouth with his teeth and tongue until she relaxed. He deepened the kiss, slipping his tongue past her lips to taste her again. Gods, she was sweet. Sweet and soft and perfect. Arms circled his neck, drawing him deeper into the kiss, into her. She made a small, sexy sound, almost a purr as her body melted against his.

The desire he'd felt for her in the library roared to life. He must have her again. She was his female to take. This time he would not allow her to succumb to the power and pass out. She must be with him at the end. They needed to climb higher before the wave took them.

He pushed her back against the sofa and felt her legs wrap around his waist.

Strong arms snatched her away from him. Damien snarled and attacked the beings that dared separate them. Two sets of arms imprisoned him in a vise grip. He searched the room. Why had they all come? Jacob and Eleanor hugged the doorway. Emil stood to their left. Their shocked faces insulted him.

"Damien, join your mind with us."

The words made no sense. Ten feet away Luke held a struggling Emma. How dare he touch her? How dare he put his filthy Scottish hands on her? The man must die. Breaking away, he threw himself at the human, aiming for his exposed throat.

Again the arms pulled him back. "Damien. Balance yourself."

More useless words. The Goddards held him back from his prey. He looked at Emma locked in Luke's arms, her eyes full of passion. Passion for him alone. They must not be interrupted. They must complete what they had started. Power. He needed more power. Where was Jacob? He used their special mental channel and summoned his human partner. *Jacob, I need you.*

"No, Jacob. Stay back," Samuel said. "You cannot help him now."

Damien felt a blast of power hit him. Furious, he struggled against it but was too weak to fight the combined force of the Goddards. Unable to resist, he let the brothers enter his mind. The power of the Balance was in them. He could no more turn away from the Balance then he could stop breathing. The holy Balance washed over him, bringing a calm that quieted his need for Emma.

Once again his eyes sought out Emma. When he found her still in Luke's embrace the rage threatened to build again.

"Luke," Sebastian said. "Let Emma go."

Luke passed a struggling Emma to Eleanor. "What the hell is this?" he asked. "The room is so full of broadcasted lust my John Henry is whistling Dixie. Unless we want an orgy on our hands everybody needs to raise shields, now. In the meantime, nobody touch me."

A white-faced Jacob came to Damien. "What is it? I've never felt you like this."

Samuel held up a warning hand. "Come no closer, Jacob. No male must get between Damien and Emma."

"Why?" Eleanor asked.

Damien was afraid he knew the answer but didn't want to believe it. How was this possible?

"Damien has put his mark on Emma," Samuel said.

Eleanor's head whipped back and forth between Emma and Samuel. "Mark? What does that mean?"

"He has chosen Emma as his mate."

Chapter Four

ꟾ

Mate? Emma didn't think she'd heard Samuel right. How could she be Damien's mate? How could she be anybody's mate? Humans didn't mate. They dated for a period of time and then got married. No one, except maybe Tarzan, mated anymore. Well, not since caveman times where all the guy had to do was grab the female, bonk her on the head and drag her back to his fire.

Mate?

Emma tried to focus but her mind was in a haze. Her body screamed with need. Damien's kiss had transported her back to the library table. The power had grown and flowed between them, bringing with it an intense desire. Now, she was cut off from his touch while every nerve ending in her body cried out for Damien.

She fought Eleanor's grip. Who did these people think they were, keeping her from Damien? Couldn't they see how he needed her? No one else could help him. It had to be her, Emma, who eased his pain. They were jealous, that's what it was. None of them could stand it that she and Damien had found each other. Why were they doing this? It was cruel to keep them apart.

"Let me go." She pushed Eleanor away and started for Damien.

Samuel stepped between them. "Emma, you are in thrall."

"Get out of my way," she snarled. Part of her mind marveled at the brutality in her voice. It was so unlike her. But she must get to Damien. He needed her.

Samuel made a grab for her as she sidestepped him. Emma beat back his hands and elbowed him in the stomach.

The whoosh sound he made filled her with deep satisfaction. Taking advantage of Samuel's incapacitated state, she shoved him into Eleanor and watched them stagger and then fall.

Another set of rock-hard arms encircled her waist. It smelled like—Luke. How dare he touch her? How dare he put his filthy Scottish hands on her? She would kill him for this. She kicked back at his knee but he managed to evade the hit. He captured her wrists, pinned her arms against her body and tucked her tight against him. Emma struggled but it was no use. Luke was too strong.

Samuel stood up. "Emma, you must listen to me. You are deeply in thrall to Damien."

With Emma struggling against him, Luke answered. "Sam, it never works to explain to the person in thrall that they are in thrall. The whole point of being in thrall is that the person doesn't realize it. Get it? Emma is human, not Dyad. Can't you feel her? The poor little thing is aching with need. She doesn't know how to shield. If you and Sebastian don't control this situation soon she's going to melt into a sticky puddle of 'somebody take me' right in front of us."

"No," Damien screamed. "Let her go, Luke. Let her come to me."

Sebastian moved forward and faced Damien. "I do not think that is wise. Let Samuel and me Balance Emma."

Emma had had enough. None of what these people said made any sense. "What are you talking about? Why don't you all go away and leave us alone?" She thrashed in Luke's arms, unable to break his iron grip. "Let me go." Tears of rage ran down her face. She needed Damien so much and no one would listen to her. Why was she so weak? If she were stronger, no one would keep them apart. Why wasn't Damien coming for her?

Samuel and Sebastian stood in front of her, blocking her view of Damien. They looked at each other for a moment and

Emma felt power crackling through the air. They raised their left hands and reached for her.

Fearing the worst, she shrank back in Luke's arms. "No." She didn't know why the twins touching her would be a bad thing but she knew she didn't want them to. What if they took away her love for Damien? She would have nothing left. Without him she was—nothing.

Fingertips glided over her temples and settled above her ears, massaging. Power flowed along her nerves like electricity. With it came the presence of the combined minds of Samuel and Sebastian. All her pent-up frustration washed away. Her body relaxed in Luke's arms as a feeling of peace crept through her. It was as if her body was a glass that slowly filled up with calm.

Come back to us, Emma, the twins whispered in her mind.

When they pulled out and stepped away, Emma was able to think clearly. She turned in Luke's arms to face him. "You can let me go now. I'm fine."

Luke released her and Emma looked around the room. The Goddard Dyad stood with their partners, Luke and Emil. Jacob held Eleanor against him. She was nursing her wrist. Hesitantly, she looked at Damien standing apart from the others. His face was blank—void of all emotion. Had it only been a few minutes ago when his eyes were filled with desire for her? And what of her? Had she been the one who injured Eleanor's wrist? Had she hit Samuel? It didn't seem possible.

"I…I'm sorry I behaved so badly. I don't know what came over me." She turned to Eleanor and Jacob. "Did I do that? Did I hurt you, Ellie?"

"It's nothing, Em. I'm okay."

As she looked over each of their faces, full of concern and pity, fear quickened her heartbeat. "What's happening to me?" she asked the room in general.

Damien came to her, his face still unreadable. "I have done this to us, Emma."

"Might I suggest everyone except Damien and Emma leave us," Sebastian said. "We will explain the situation to her."

Luke shrugged. "Great. Once you're done explaining things to Emma you can enlighten the rest of us. Come on, Emil." He slapped his friend on the shoulder. "I don't know about you but I could use a beer and a cold shower—maybe not in that order."

Luke winked at Emma and he and Emil left the room.

Eleanor took Emma's hands. "Don't worry. It will all work out fine, Emma. Take my word for it. No matter how bad things seem now the Dyads always manage to make things right."

Jacob gave her an awkward pat on the shoulder and led his wife out.

Emma turned to the Goddards. She felt like a condemned prisoner awaiting her sentence. How bad was this going to be?

Damien started for her but Sebastian stopped him. "No, Damien. The two of you must not touch. It will only awaken the drive again."

Damien stared blankly at Sebastian for a moment and then nodded. "Yes, you are quite right. If the two of you could answer Emma's questions I will…stay back."

One of the twins motioned to the couch. "Please, Emma. Will you sit?"

After another glance at Damien's expressionless face, Emma sat down. One of the twins sat next to her and the other took the armchair. Damien stood out of sight behind her.

During the struggle the twins had taken off their sweaters and Emma felt at a disadvantage. She'd used the sweaters to tell them apart. The red sweater had been Sebastian and the green Samuel. Now, both were dressed in identical black T-shirts and jeans.

"Before you start," she said, "I've lost track." She turned to the twin sitting next to her on the couch. "Who are you?"

The twin glanced at his brother and then looked back at her and smiled. "I am Sebastian," he said.

Emma nodded. "Okay, good." She pointed to the twin in the armchair. "That makes you Samuel. Sorry, but I like to know."

Samuel nodded. "We understand. Here, this will help." He dug in his jean pocket and pulled out a rubber band. In a moment, he had his shoulder length white-blond hair fastened behind him. "Better?" he asked.

"Yeah. Thanks." Emma looked over her shoulder, trying to catch a glimpse of Damien. No luck.

"I am here."

She turned and glanced over her other shoulder. He stood leaning against the wall, his hands in his jean pockets. How come he got to be so nonchalant about this?

"Emma," Sebastian said. "We need to explain a few things about what is happening to you."

"All right." She turned away from Damien and faced the twins.

Sebastian looked down at his hands for a long moment. He turned first to his brother and then to Damien.

Emma recognized the look in his eyes. "This stops right now or I leave."

Looking around, she saw three pairs of raised eyebrows. Standing, she turned so she could see all three of them at once. "Don't give me the surprised looks. Or the 'whatever do you mean' crap. The three of you are speaking telepathically. Probably trying to decide how best to handle me and I won't have it, understand? I get to be a part of the entire conversation, or I'm out of here."

Samuel grinned and shook his head. "You have been paying attention during your stay with us. How could you tell?"

Emma snorted. Sometimes these guys tipped the pompous scale in a bad way. "I'm right in front of you. I'd have to be deaf, blind and dumb not to know something is happening between you. You're not as subtle as you think you are."

The twins looked at each other and burst out laughing. Damien's lips twitched.

For once, Emma didn't see the humor. "I'm glad you find this so funny, but I don't. I've completely lost control of my life. You'll forgive me if I can't work up a chuckle."

The room sobered. "Forgive us, Emma," Sebastian said. "Please, sit."

"And you won't leave me out of any part of the conversation?" she asked.

"You have our word," Samuel said. "Would you like a spit bargain?" He spat into his hand and offered it to her.

"No. I'm not coming in contact with any Dyads until I know what's going on. I'll take your word for it." She sat on the couch.

Everyone resumed their place. "Damien, don't hide behind me. It makes me uncomfortable."

Damien moved around the couch and went to stand in front of the windows, his back to the room.

Sebastian smiled kindly at her. "To begin, I must explain a little of Dyad biology to you. Our reproductive cycles and procedures."

Emma was suddenly embarrassed. Here she was sitting alone in a room with three males and they were going to tell her about the birds and the bees just like her mother had done when she was eleven. She thought it best to cut to the chase.

"How about I tell you what I know and you fill in the gaps. It will save time, don't you think?"

Sebastian shrugged. "As you wish. What can you tell us about…us?"

Emma leaned forward on the couch and looked down. How much did she really know about them? Only what she'd overheard or been told by Jacob. What if she'd gotten it all wrong?

She looked at the twins. "Okay, here we go. Dyad males seem to be able to have sex whenever they want, just like humans. I mean, you and the partners are always talking about the women you've been with." She could feel a blush color her cheeks but she forged on. "Everyone staying here seems to be pretty…active that way."

She glanced at Damien and saw his shoulders tense. "But," she continued, "something happens to all of you when a Dyad dies. Your females become fertile for one thing. And the males, you all seem pretty edgy to say the least. And before… Damien, he lost control… He…" She trailed off, unable to continue. Some things were just too personal to share.

After a moment she shrugged. "Well, do I have it right?"

Sebastian nodded. "More or less. It is true, our females become fertile when a Dyad dies and our race is not Balanced at one thousand. The need to reproduce and replace our loss can be overpowering. Those of us with mates meet at once to nest. In all of us, the sexual drive is at its peak.

"We control ourselves with the help of the Balance. We use the power to dampen our urges and wait for a mated Dyad to conceive. Once conception has occurred, our race is in Balance again and everything goes back to normal."

Emma nodded. "That's pretty much what I thought. But that's not what happened to Damien. Is it?"

Sebastian glanced at Damien's back as if waiting for him to answer. When Damien remained immobile, Sebastian turned to Emma and sighed. "When the Dyad traveled on, Damien was not with his Dyad brother and could not reach for the Balance. He was alone, at the mercy of his urges and emotions. If you had not been with him, he might have been lost to the madness within. We are all very grateful to you for saving him."

"Why do I feel an enormous 'but' coming?" she asked.

The twins shared a glance and Sebastian continued. "Yes, Emma. There is a but. When Damien made love to you in his heightened state, he lost control and put his mark on you. You continued to make love to him thereby accepting his mark. With these actions the two of you performed the Dyad ritual of mating."

Why had her life turned into one big embarrassment after another? Once more she looked at Damien's back, now stiff as a board. No help there. She turned back to the twins and cleared her throat. "All right, Damien marked me as his mate. So what? Can't he just unmark me?"

The twins smiled sadly at her. "No," Samuel said. "Dyads mate for life. No Dyad has ever been unmated. I do not know if it is possible."

"But, don't Dyads always mate with another Dyad—you know, two males with two females?"

"Yes, it has always been so."

Emma stood. "Well then, Damien and I can't be mated because David wasn't here and I'm not a part of a Dyad. I'm human. The special marking mojo couldn't work—right?"

The twins rose. Samuel raised his hands in a calming gesture. "That is the problem, Emma. Against everything we know to be possible, it did work. We can feel Damien's mark on you. I can assure you, the two of you are mated."

"This is ridiculous." She marched over to Damien and pulled him around to face her. "You just undo what you did."

He stared at her hand on his forearm for a moment, transfixed. Slowly, he put his hand over hers. Desire leapt into his eyes. A desire suddenly echoed in her blood. Why wasn't he kissing her? The instant she thought it, Damien's eyes moved to her lips. His head lowered.

The twins pulled them apart. "You see," Samuel said. "Mated. During this time of nesting, even a touch can raise your need for each other."

"What are we going to do?" she asked, looking into Damien's troubled eyes.

"We must go to the Diarchy," Damien said. "To David. Maybe he and I together can reverse this."

"And if not?" Emma asked. "If you can't reverse this?"

Dark glances ping-ponged between the Dyads. Emma's dread increased with each look. Finally, Damien turned to her. "Let us cross that bridge when we come to it. For now, you must prepare yourself to meet the Dyad race in their home city."

* * * * *

Kathunk-Kathunk-Kathunk.

The SUV sped down the highway hitting cracks in the pavement every three seconds. Damien made up a jingle to match the sound. *Mated – you – stupid – selfish – un – principled – moronic – bastard.* Over and over in his mind, a litany of his actions since the Dyad had traveled on.

He had mated a human. Something so profoundly un-Dyad the Elders hadn't even made a rule against it—yet. That would change as soon as he and Emma reached the Diarchy.

Emma, his mate. He couldn't stop thinking of her. Right now she was in the vehicle following, sandwiched in the backseat between Eleanor and Samuel. The only two he trusted near her. They had separated him from his mate. His mind knew it was necessary but his hot blood sang another tune. It took every bit of his power reserve and Sebastian's and Jacob's continued presence next to him in the backseat to dampen his need for her. Even so, he was on edge, in a constant state of unease.

It didn't help that every time he thought of his brother a sinking feeling settled in his stomach. If he had truly mated

Emma, where did that leave David? Dyads chose mates in pairs. It was instinctual, primal. A male Dyad mated with a female Dyad. In most cases they did not switch partners, each having a natural attraction to a particular female. But all four minds were involved in a true mating. In some way he had joined David to Emma. But instead of four, there were three in this mating. Three.

There was no Balance in three.

"We're almost there," Luke said from the driver's seat. The others in the car started gathering their things. Damien hadn't needed to pack. The Diarchy was home. The rooms he and David had shared since they had left the children's dormitory were waiting for him. Everything he needed was there.

On the other hand, the human partners packed for a long ordeal. Extra thermal underwear and warm outer clothing. The Dyad race favored colder temperatures. Video games, iPods, DVD players and a supply of batteries. No electricity at the Diarchy. And pounds and pounds of dried meat. Dyads were vegetarians. The partners found all of this constrictive, hence the full packs.

Luke took a sharp right and steered the SUV across a clover field. Damien looked out the back window and saw Emma's blue SUV following. Behind them, the clover crushed by their wheels righted itself. Samuel and Sebastian's work. No trace of their passage must be visible. Strict secrecy rules were adhered to when traveling to a Diarchy portal. Their group was breaking one of the rules bringing Emma without permission. Another action Damien would be held accountable for by the Elders. But what choice did he have? Leaving Emma behind wasn't an option.

Jacob stirred beside him. "Are we in as much trouble with the Elders as I think we are?" he asked.

Damien should have known Jacob would pick up on his unease. "There is no we in this. I will take responsibility for my actions."

"The Elders will understand," Sebastian said. "This has never happened before. We had to act accordingly."

Jacob ran a hand through his hair. "The Elders might but what about the Brown Dyad and their group? They've been waiting for something like this to happen. Anything to promote their separatist, antihuman agenda. They will use this against us."

Luke pounded the steering wheel. "You're right. The Browns won't be happy until the Dyad race retreats completely from the modern world. If they have their way, the human partners would all be kicked out, but only after they'd wiped our memories. Bastards."

Sebastian leaned forward and put his hand on Luke's shoulder. "Peace, Luke. The Browns are our Dyad brothers. It is true they do not share our belief that infiltration into the modern human world is a necessity, but they are a part of our collective whole. Their opinions have worth and must be heard."

Jacob bristled. "If it were just their opinions voiced in an open manner, I would agree with you. But every time we return to the Diarchy we learn of a new plot or subterfuge they've hatched to force all Dyads to stay at the Diarchy. They honestly believe the human race is contaminating them. Remember how angry they were when Eleanor was granted immortality? Or when David and Aiden brought Jude to live at the Diarchy?"

Damien listened to the conversation with dread. He had forgotten about the Brown Dyad and how they would react to his mating with Emma. The Browns and their sympathizers had wanted no contact with the human race. Five hundred years ago, when the Elders sent small study teams out among humans, the Browns had warned it would be the death of the pure Dyad race. He and David had felt the opposite was true and volunteered to be one of the first Dyads to infiltrate.

For hundreds of years the study teams brought back information about humans. The human partners were founded and allowed entry into the Diarchy. And through it all, the Browns and their supporters had argued against it.

The policy of observe and report back had changed when the Americans dropped the atomic bomb on Japan during one of their wars. The Elders realized then that the Dyads must not just observe. Humans needed help through this difficult time in their history. With the future of the planet at stake, the Dyads could not afford to sit back and watch. They decided to act.

Even then, the Browns wanted to withdraw and build stronger shields between the Diarchy and the outside world. As if any shield could withstand a nuclear blast.

"We're here," Luke said and pulled into a small clearing. He maneuvered the SUV into a row of trees.

Everyone exited and gathered around the back. Luke popped the hatch and the humans picked up their packs. Damien turned and watched Emma's vehicle pull in. When Emma got out she locked eyes with him for just a moment. He couldn't interpret the look on her pale face but he thought she must be nervous. What would she think of the Diarchy? Each human reacted differently. It was one of the things he loved about their race. Their unpredictability. So refreshing.

Sebastian touched his shoulder. "Come, we must hurry. They are waiting for us."

Damien sensed his friend's excitement. Going home after a long absence was always a happy event. Each of them would finally be able to let their guard down and relax.

Sebastian and Samuel stood in front of the two SUVs nestled in the trees. Power crackled in the air as they linked minds and reached for the Balance. As one, they raised their hands and pointed to the trees. One sweet note filled the air. The brothers hummed softly, calling the trees to attention. Creaks and cracks sounded as the tree branches realigned to cover the SUVs. Underneath the vehicles the grass grew until it was over two feet tall. In a matter of moments, the vehicles were completely hidden.

"My God," Emma said from behind him.

Abruptly, the power shut off and the Goddards turned to the group. "Lead the way, Luke," Sebastian said and gestured to the left.

Luke started down a path through the forest and they all fell in behind him. First Luke, followed closely by Emil and the Goddards, then Emma between Eleanor and Jacob. Damien brought up the rear.

They traveled in silence for a quarter of an hour. Sometimes the forest grew so dense Damien lost track of everyone except Jacob, directly in front of him.

Sooner than he expected the group reached the clearing that hid the cave opening. It was the perfect place to hide a portal. The odds of a human stumbling upon this cave, deep in the forest, were miniscule. Damien searched the area. Even though he knew the cave was there, it took a full minute before he located the entrance, completely obscured by vines.

"Here," Samuel said as he lifted his hand. The vines parted to reveal the entrance just large enough for the women to walk through. The rest of them would have to squeeze their way in.

A feeling of unease washed over Damien. Not from within. He sent his senses searching and located the source. It was coming from Emma.

As Damien studied her, Emma shifted back and forth on her feet. "Nobody said anything about a cave." She took a few steps back. "A portal, you said. I thought, you know, like *Stargate*. Something out in the open that you step through. Not a small, dark hole full of who knows how many snakes and spiders."

Eleanor went to her. "I'm sorry, sweetie. I forgot." She put her arm around Emma. "It will be fine. It's a lot bigger than it looks from the outside."

Emma eyed the cave opening and swallowed visibly. "How big? Pup tent big? Shower stall big? What?"

Her frightened mind reached out to Damien's and he was unable to block her thoughts. *The opening is so small and dark. Anything could be inside. Something bad is going to happen if we go in there. What about a cave-in? We'll all be trapped, unable to see in the dark. I'll get separated from them, I know I will and then I'll be alone in the black just like before. Can't do it. Is it too late to change my mind? What will they all think if I turn back now? Oh God, I can't do this.*

Damien concentrated and blocked her thoughts. It wasn't right to eavesdrop like this. Before he could move to comfort her, Luke stepped in.

"No, lass," Luke said, exaggerating his Scottish brogue. "Nothing as tiny as that. Think cathedral big or shopping mall big." He waved his arms in broad arcs through the air.

"Mall of America big," Eleanor chimed in and gave her friend a squeeze.

Emma looked back and forth between the two of them. Damien felt her panic recede a little. Her eyes settled on Luke and she smiled nervously. "The size of your ego big?" she asked.

"Ouch," Luke cried. He made a big show of presenting his back to Emil. "Pull the knife out will you?"

The women giggled.

Luke is an ass, Damien thought. He fancied himself a wit. More like a buffoon. Always some practical joke or prank, always making the ladies laugh. He couldn't stand the man. Thank the Balance that idiot was not of his quartet. Sebastian was welcome to him. The dolt. The imbecile.

Emma took Luke's hand. "Thanks," she said.

The dead man. Damien growled softly. Growling was good. Why had he never known that?

A hand clamped down on his shoulder. "We need to get you home," Samuel whispered to him. "Before your baser instincts take over and you deprive my quartet of one of its members."

All Damien could manage was a grunt.

"You okay to go?" Eleanor asked Emma.

After one more wary look at the cave, Emma nodded. "Let's get it over with."

One by one, they went into the cave. Again, Damien brought up the rear. Luke and Eleanor hadn't lied. The cave was massive. In its dark interior the ceiling and walls were out of sight.

The partners clicked on their flashlights and led the way to an archway. Sebastian and Samuel moved in front of the group and faced the opening. Damien felt the brothers link and reach for the Balance. Luke and Emil moved behind their partners and put a hand on their Dyad's shoulder, bringing the full power of the quartet to bear.

"Open," the brothers said and pointed to the archway.

A blue light appeared in the exact center of the opening. It spread in a circular pattern until it encompassed the entire archway. From out of the light a gentle breeze blew causing Damien's hair to fan out behind him. He inhaled deeply and sighed.

"Home."

Emma stared into the blue light, unable to look away. In a few moments each of them would walk into that burning light. The thought paralyzed her with fear. This must be what divers felt like when poised on the highest of the high diving boards, contemplating the fall. The problem was she had no idea what awaited her when she hit. Would she slice through the water in a perfect arch and break the surface or be sucked down into a dark abyss, lost forever?

An arm went around her shoulders and she jumped.

"Easy now," Eleanor said. "I know how scary this looks. My first time through a portal Jacob had to carry me while I squeezed my eyes shut. I thought my atoms would be scrambled and I'd come out the other side with body parts in different spots. You know, my eyes where my ears should be, my nose on my forehead."

The mental picture did nothing to calm Emma's fear. "Oh. Great. I hadn't thought of that."

Eleanor squeezed her in for a hug. "Sorry. Not the best choice of stories. But really, there's nothing to it. You just go through. One second you're here and the next you're at the Diarchy."

"Does it hurt?" Emma asked.

"No, not a bit. No trauma, no molecule scrambling. You know the feeling you get when they're using power?"

"You mean the ripple across your skin like electricity?"

"That's the one. That effect is heightened as you go through and when I keep my eyes open, I get dizzy for a minute. Really, it's no big deal."

Emma stepped out of her arms and faced Eleanor. "No big deal?" she whispered. "We're standing in front of a portal, El. A portal. Right out of the Sci-Fi channel. And yeah, I know I have to go through, but come on. Doesn't it still weird you out a little?"

"After everything I've seen since I met Jacob and the Dyads this seems…normal. Besides, to be with Jacob I'd walk through a hell of a lot worse."

Eleanor's eyes found Jacob, standing a few feet away. The look of naked love on her friend's face made Emma uncomfortable, as if she were invading Eleanor's privacy. When Jacob glanced back at his wife with the same emotion, jealousy replaced Emma's unease. What would it be like for a man to look at her like that?

A familiar bittersweet yearning settled over her and she turned to Damien, standing apart from the others. As if sensing her, his gaze left the portal and found her. When their eyes met everything fell away, the cave, the portal, the Dyads and their partners, even Eleanor next to her. All gone. It was as if two spotlights shone down from the ceiling and bathed them in warm, amber light. There was only the two of them, Damien and Emma. But instead of the emotion she longed to see, Damien's face was expressionless. No, not expressionless, cold, hard around his mouth. If she had to sum up, she'd call it grim determination. For a few heartbreaking seconds he held her gaze and then he looked first at the floor and then back to the portal. Without so much as an encouraging smile, he'd dismissed her. Dismissed them.

Her surroundings crashed back in on her. Pain gnawed at her breastbone. Something large lodged in her throat. Everything was as she'd left it. The Goddard Dyad stood at the portal with Luke and Emil. Jacob and Eleanor stood beside her and Damien apart from the others—apart from her. Emma swallowed hard, trying to ease the choking feeling, but it did no good. The realization that whatever Damien felt for her had been forced on him—unwelcome—left her cold and alone.

A deep bass voice came from blue light. "Who calls the portal?"

Emma realized it wasn't one voice but two. Each saying the same words at exactly the same moment. Two as one.

In the same manner, Sebastian and Samuel answered. "We are Dyad. We ask entry into our home."

"Are you worthy?"

Emma turned to Eleanor. "What's going on? Aren't they going to let us in?"

"No," Eleanor whispered. "It's the same every time. Kind of a ritual."

"Never worthy," the Goddards chanted. "Always striving."

"In whose name do you ask entry?"

"We ask in the name of the Balance."

An image flashed into Emma's mind. A lion, a tin man, a scarecrow and a little girl and her dog standing before a stage with a giant head floating above it. She had to quell the urge to shout, "Who is the man behind the curtain." She suppressed a nervous giggle. There. That felt more like the old Emma. *Try to find the humor, try to find the humor,* she chanted. Her shoulders relaxed a fraction and she stood taller.

Simon and Sebastian raised their hands to shoulder height. "We ask admittance to the brotherhood. We stand before the Balance in humble supplication."

The slight breeze coming from the portal changed to a strong wind. Emma smelled sun-baked earth, sweet clover and a perfume that reminded her of patchouli. With the wind came power. It buzzed over her skin making her shudder. The light within the portal changed from blue to red-orange.

"Welcome home, Goddard Dyad. You and all with you may enter and commune with us. Enter and become one with the Balance."

Jacob turned to Eleanor. "Time to go," he said and took her arm.

Eleanor linked her free arm through Emma's. "Ready?" she asked.

"Absolutely not," Emma answered but she let Eleanor lead her closer to the portal.

Everyone gathered behind the Goddards, who had joined hands. They offered their free hands to their partners. One by one, everyone joined hands until the circle closed.

They all turned to the portal. After a moment when no one advanced, Emma started to ask a question but stopped. Instead of walking through the portal, the portal was coming to them. Every hair on Emma's body stood up as a current washed over her.

"Remember to shut your eyes," Eleanor said.

Too scared to answer, Emma hastened to follow her friend's advice. She squeezed her eyes closed and held her breath. Another current of power flashed over her and she heard a loud pop crackle sound, something like a power cable run rampant over tar, and then silence.

The temperature changed. Instead of the damp cold of the cave, arid warmth wrapped around her. The smell of earth and plant life intensified. Beneath it all, the sickly, sweet smell of manure.

"Open up, Alice," Luke whispered in her ear. "We made it through the looking glass."

Emma opened her eyes.

Instead of the outdoor farm landscape she expected, they were in a domed room. As the others dropped hands and shifted packs, Emma took a look around. The green walls moved. The effect made her dizzy. She walked to the closest wall and studied it. The structure was made up of an intricate weaving of tree branches and vines that shifted ever so slightly. She searched for the root and found it a few feet away. A single tree trunk sent its branches every which way to form the room. Above her, holes in the pattern let in warm sunlight that streamed down casting leaf patterns on the earthen floor. On the far wall an arch made a break. A door of sorts leading out to a hallway made up of the same material.

On either side of the door two men stood with their arms spread wide in welcome. Emma's mouth dropped open. This wasn't the Dyad she'd known so far. To begin with, they were the first redheads. But simply labeling them redheads wouldn't do. Every shade of the color, from blood to bright orange caught the light and glistened. It reminded Emma of fireworks when they burst, sending myriad colors streaking through the sky. Their hair cascaded down the tall bodies and stopped just below their slim waists.

With all that hair the effect should have been feminine but one look at their strong bodies and masculine faces put that idea to rest. Emma noted other differences from her friends. These Dyads had larger eyes with equally huge pupils. A thin orange circle rimmed the pupils. Their cheekbones were high and defined. Square chins dominated the lower half of the faces. Like all Dyad pairs, their faces were exactly the same.

On each right temple an orange circle stood out against their pale skin.

The overall effect was less human. Until now, Emma had secretly viewed Dyads as humans plus. You only had to look at them to realize that somewhere in history Humans and Dyads had a common ancestor. Now she wasn't so sure.

"You have been too long away, Goddard, Stewart," the Dyad on the left said.

"We felt the distance acutely since the death," the right Dyad said.

The Goddards stepped into the open arms of this new Dyad. Emma watched with a kind of wonder. She'd seen this display before. An outpouring of raw love, with no regard given to how it looked. Human males never touched in public with this open abandon. Too many social mores got in the way. This connection was visible. No back-slapping, macho crap here. They pressed their bodies together from neck to knee, their foreheads touching, their hands threaded deep into each other's hair. A pure note filled the air as first the redheads hummed and then the Goddards joined them. The beauty of that one note brought a lump to Emma's throat.

She glanced at the others to see what effect it had. Each person had a gentle smile on their face as if somehow taking part in the tender reunion.

A moment later they broke the embrace and the redheads turned to Damien with their arms open. Damien hesitated.

"Come, Stewart," the Dyad closest to him said. "We would reconnect."

When Damien remained immobile the Dyad started toward him. The two held out their arms beckoning Damien in. But Damien backed away.

"No, brothers," he said in a quiet voice. "I cannot accept communion with you."

The Dyad dropped their arms, a dual look of puzzlement on their faces. They gave Damien a once-over, finally settling on his blank face. As one, they raised their hands and felt the air around him. Once more Emma felt power against her skin. When the power cut off they lowered their arms and slowly turned to focus on her.

The look on their faces would have been funny if the situation were different. But nobody, not even Luke, found any humor in their quiet amazement.

Keeping their gaze firmly fixed on her, the two spoke. "How is this possible?"

Damn, Emma thought. If this was the reaction she and Damien were going to get from every Dyad, the situation was even worse than she anticipated. She might as well wear a bright red T-shirt with *Freak* written on it.

"Later," Damien said. "I will explain all. Now I must get to David."

"Yes, we feel your need." They turned to include the rest of the group. "You are the last to enter. All Dyads are within. The human partners are in attendance as well. The mated quartets are nesting. We expect conception at any moment. Once our numbers are complete, we will meet at conclave."

The closer of the two faced Damien. "That gives you time to Balance, Stewart."

"I must get to David," Damien repeated and left the room.

Emma tried not to show any emotion. Without so much as a see you later, he'd left her to fend for herself. A part of her left the room with him. She couldn't explain it but it was true.

Chapter Five

ꟽ

Time was running out. A vision of the hourglass from the soap opera his mother had always watched popped into Alex's head. He could almost feel each grain of sand slide through the small opening and crash against the bottom. Each grain that hit took him farther away from his objective. Everything depended on his finding and harnessing the Dyad power. Without it, all his wealth, all his power, accounted for nothing. He could not fail. The alternative was too horrific to contemplate.

Alex sucked in air through his mouth. It seemed this day was destined to be a never-ending battle against stink. He promised himself a long, hot bath and a walk in his flower garden when this was over. But for now, he swallowed hard and popped another breath mint in an effort to keep his gag reflex in check.

"What's taking so long?" he demanded.

Lambert and the surgically garbed, masked doctors surrounding him broke the huddle they'd been in for almost a half an hour and turned to Alex.

"We're deciding how best to proceed," Lambert said, the mask muffling his words. "We're only going to have one shot at opening him up." He pointed to the body laid out on the lab table. "We need to make sure everything is where it should be before we start."

"For the love of God," Alex said as he walked over to the group, pushed his way in and pointed at the screens they'd been studying. "Even I can tell what's what. Here." He pointed to a dark mass on the main screen. "That's the heart. And here, the kidneys. This is the stomach. Here's the liver and the lungs and these are intestines. What more do you need to know?"

Lambert let out a condescending chuckle. "Thank you for the anatomy lesson, Alex. We've been concentrating on this little object here." His latex-encased finger pointed to a half-moon shape nestled next to the heart. "We've labeled it heart two. It's something we've never seen before."

"Well, whoop de fucking doo, Alphonse. Call Guinness and get it in the book later. But now, are you going to stand around and talk about it until we all need a shave or are you going to crack him open and hold it in your bony scientist hands?"

"I don't like to rush," Lambert bristled.

"I don't like to wait," Alex answered.

The old man's eyes narrowed. Alex wished he could see his entire face. He was at a disadvantage with all these masked people surrounding him. He could read most people's faces easily but he needed to see all of it, not just the eyes.

After a sigh that made his mask puff out, Lambert moved to the table. "Very well. We will proceed."

The others jumped into action. Rolling tables with sharp instruments were positioned around the body. The tubes that were siphoning off the creature's blood were pulled out and the blood packed in coolers filled with ice. The catheter was removed and its contents joined the blood in the coolers. In under a minute, one of the doctors stood with a scalpel ready to begin.

"Someone turn on the camera please," Lambert said.

The only woman in the group obliged.

Lambert cleared his throat. "This is the autopsy of Dyad specimen A. Dr. Virgil Kunkle presiding with Dr. Alphonse Lambert assisting." He looked up and caught Alex's eye. "I'm not a medical doctor. I thought it best—"

"Yes, yes," Alex said. "Just get on with it."

"You might want to go and get some rest. This will take hours," Lambert suggested.

"I'm not going anywhere."

Lambert shrugged. "Very well. Please proceed, Virgil."

For over an hour Alex paced. Fifteen steps right, fifteen steps left. Steps six, seven and eight brought him closest to the worst odors. Added to the smell from the body, which Alex was almost used to now, was the acerbic alcohol, the latex gloves, the bleach from the surgical scrubs and after the first half hour, sweat from the team. This just kept getting better and better.

The hospital aromas brought back memories of his parents' deaths. The big C had claimed them both. First, his mother from breast cancer and only a year later, his father from pancreatic. Each of them had fought to the bitter end, sure in the knowledge that their wealth would save them. But the great leveler had taken them both. It didn't care that his parents belonged to the best clubs, lived in the best homes or even gave to the best charities. It certainly didn't care that it left Alex an orphan at the tender age of sixteen. No, the big C had laughed at all that and killed them anyway.

Alex looked at the doctors cutting open the creature on the table.

How long ago had he started down this morally shaky path? It seemed both an eternity and a mere heartbeat since Lambert had come to him with fantastic tales of superhuman creatures. Once Alex decided the answer to his special problem involved capturing a Dyad pair, he'd turned to a group of men only whispered about in his wealthy circle. Men who sat in a dark room so he couldn't see their faces. Men who could make anything happen for a price. They'd listened to what he wanted and hooked him up with his own private army.

The group around the table gasped in unison pulling Alex out of his maudlin trip down memory lane. He rushed to the table and peered over the shoulder of the shortest doctor. "What?" he asked.

"Put on a mask," Lambert chided.

"What the hell for? He's dead. We don't have to worry about infection."

Lambert's eyes above the mask rolled. "I wasn't thinking of him. I was referring to you. But, have it your way, Alex. You always do."

Alex ignored him and looked at Dr. Kunkle. "What have you found?" he asked, standing on tiptoe for a better view of the body cavity.

"One moment please," Kunkle replied. His hands were deep inside the body. He wiggled them back and forth for a moment and then, with great care, lifted out a bright gold mass.

"My God," Lambert gasped and reached for it. "Look at it." He took the object from Kunkle and brought it to eye level. "Here it is, Alex."

Alex couldn't take his eyes off it. Roughly the size and shape of a human kidney, but the color of a newly minted gold coin. He didn't know if it was a trick of the light, some optical illusion, but the thing seemed to pulse in Lambert's hands. Not unlike a beating heart.

"I don't understand," Alex said, his eyes still fixed on heart two. "What is it?"

Lambert moved his hands, cradling the thing, closer to Alex. "Haven't you guessed? This little piece of tissue is the source of the Dyad power."

"Are you sure? What makes you say that?"

"It's the only thing it can be. It's the only thing not remotely human we've found. It has to be related to what they can do."

Beside him, Kunkle spoke up. "Maybe not the source itself but a conductor of sorts?" he asked.

Alex allowed himself a moment of triumph. At last the sand was moving in the other direction. Closer, he could feel he was closer.

Maybe closer, but not there yet. "Well, don't stand there like idiots. Hop to. Do what I'm paying you for. Chop it up and get it under a microscope. Find out how it works."

All eyes turned to him. Alex didn't need to see their faces to interpret. They thought he was nuts.

"Now, Alex," Lambert started in a tone used to modify a petulant child's behavior. "We must take our time and confer on how best to proceed." He moved the gold blob from one hand to the other. "This is too important a find to blindly start chopping. We must..." He hissed and quick as he could, passed the object to Kunkle. "Take it. Something's happening to it."

Kunkle started the same back and forth, between the hands as Lambert had done. "It's getting hot, really—shit," he screamed and tossed it to the doctor next to him and the game of hot potato had begun. Each person tried to hold on, failed and tossed it to the next in line.

Alex looked over the tables where the used surgical instruments lay and found what he needed. He picked up a metal tray and stuck it under the hand of the doctor currently juggling heart two.

"Here," he said. "Put it in here."

Hissing against the pain, the doctor dropped it on the tray. Everyone relaxed a fraction and started to pull off their half-melted gloves. On the tray, the object pulsed in earnest now and the golden color changed to warm orange.

The female doctor stepped back from the table. "The whole body is getting hot," she said in a frightened voice.

A feeling of unease settled in Alex's gut. He didn't like where this was going. Carefully, he touched the body's shoulder and immediately pulled back, almost dropping the tray in his other hand. Even with the quick response, his fingers started a crescendo of pain. In a matter of seconds, blisters appeared. He went to the closest cooler and grabbed a handful of ice.

The others followed his example and dived for a cooler.

"You see," Lambert said pulling his mask down. "This is why we needed more time. Look at this." He held his hands up. Alex took a sick satisfaction at the size of his blisters.

"Look at the body," someone shouted and all heads whipped back to the table.

The sight reminded Alex of a campfire, except no flames were visible. White ash appeared on the surface while the cavity glowed red.

"No," Alex shouted. "Do something."

"There's nothing we can do." Lambert turned in a frantic circle, searching the room. "Don't you see? They're burning the other twin."

The meaning of Lambert's works sank in and Alex looked down at the object on the tray still clutched in his uninjured hand. It had changed color again. Besides the warm orange on the rim, the center glowed with a pure white light. This couldn't be happening.

Alex set the tray down and went to a cooler. "Throw ice over the body, all of you," he shouted at them. When he reached a cooler, he paused and looked around the room. Steam rose from every cooler. He looked into the closest one and saw blood bubbling, melting the ice that surrounded it. The coolers themselves started losing their shapes as they in turn melted.

The sprinkler system overhead chose that moment to erupt with water.

Coughing started as the room filled with steam.

"We have to get out of here," Lambert shouted. "Now. Everybody, get out."

"No. Goddamn it." Alex blocked the only way out. "Nobody's leaving."

Heedless of the burns on his hands, Lambert gripped Alex's shirt. "The heat—the steam. It will kill us, you fool." He pulled Alex's face down to his height. "If you die what will happen to them?"

Alex looked over Lambert's head to the tray with heart two. He had to squint against the light.

The others pushed him out of the way and he allowed it. The woman grabbed his arm as she went by and dragged him along. He allowed that too.

The last one out shut the door and they all hurried to the observation room. Alex elbowed everyone out of the way and stood in front of the wide window that overlooked the lab. Steam obscured most of the room, allowing only brief glimpses of what was happening to the body. For three agonizing minutes Alex tried to make out the condition of the body and heart two. Suddenly, a blinding light had everyone covering their eyes. When it receded Alex looked at the lab and gasped.

Ash. All that was left of the body was a pile of ash on the lab table. He searched for heart two and located the metal tray, melted into a bizarre shape lying on the floor. Gone. It was all gone.

The sands had shifted again, starting the seemingly inevitable downward spiral. His enemy had won again. He might just have run out of time.

Chapter Six

ꟷ

Damien rushed through the tree corridors, suppressing the urge to sprint. Now within the Diarchy, he could sense David's presence. The need to get to him, to finally be able to link minds with his twin, was physical. Their connection had been weakened when he put his mark on Emma. Now it strengthened with every step.

He passed no one. The nesting Dyads were understandably busy. The others were in deep meditation, using the Balance to send power to the nesting quartets. In this manner, the entire race contributed to the conception.

Even without being linked to David, Damien could feel the pure power of the Balance all around him. Despite the temptation, he didn't try to draw on it. The collective had to focus its energy on the new lives being created.

Damien turned a sharp corner and stopped. The Brown Dyad blocked his path. Perfect. Just what he needed to make this day even better.

Even by Dyad standards, the Browns were tall. They topped Damien by four inches and never missed an opportunity to look down at him. Everything about them conformed to the traditional Dyad teachings. Their hair had never been cut. It was past their waists, deep brown in color, pulled back from their faces and held in place by clasps made of sea shells. The robes they wore, floor length in earth tones with a simple belt and understated embroidery, had been their standard dress for over five hundred years.

As he glanced up, four huge brown eyes looked down at him without a hint of surprise. They'd been waiting for him. Lurking was more like it.

"Stewart," they said together. The Browns followed the old way of communication, choosing to speak as one. Only on rare occasions would they opt to speak individually. Not once had they called him Damien. Always Stewart, never Damien or David. Individuality was not valued by the Brown.

"Brown." Damien followed their example and did not use the plural. To these two, putting an S on their name was an insult. They were one. Like Dyads in ancient times, the Brown had not chosen first names. They looked down on the current fashion and kept to the old ways.

Damien nodded a greeting and tried to pass.

They moved to block him. "As always you are last in when the Elders call. Why is that?" they sneered. "What could have been more important than a nesting?"

Damien bit back a stinging remark and took a calming breath. "As you say, I am late. I must go."

The Browns inhaled loudly. "You stink of human." Their top lips curled in a snarl. "How can you stand the smell?"

Damien didn't have the time or the energy to spar with these two. It wearied him just to look at their disdainful faces. There had never been any arguing with the Browns. They never budged an inch in their narrow views.

They took a step away from him. "We have just come from the Fitzgerald burning ceremony. Only one of them to burn. No Balance. It was a sad thing and need not have happened. If only the Fitzgerald would have followed our advice and stayed safe within the Diarchy."

Rage boiled up in Damien. "The Fitzgerald gave their lives to protect our race. You should not demean their sacrifice in such a manner."

"We demean? Fine words from such as you. Your every action demeans our race."

"Stop," Damien demanded. "We are in the time of nesting. All our energy should be focused on creation." He pushed past them and although they called out, eager to continue the fight, Damien never slowed.

When he turned and started the climb to the rooms he shared with David, the mental channel reserved for his brother sputtered like a human radio. Two words made it through.

Damien, hurry.

Like a healing balm, David's essence shot through his body, quieting his taut nerves, easing the feeling of unbalance. He held on to David's presence a moment, reveling in the rightness of it, but the connection sputtered out.

"Ahh," Damien groaned. To have David so close and then ripped away almost undid him. He stumbled and caught himself, clutching the stone wall with its carpet of leaves for support. He forced his shaking legs to propel him up the long flight of stone stairs cut into the cliff. After the first ten steps, his legs strengthened, the need to get to his twin somehow fueling his energy. Fifty-eight steps higher, he turned a corner and froze. The sight before him trumped every emotion coursing through his body.

Above him, reaching to the sky, stood the heart of the Dyad homeland. The Haven.

Eons ago, when the Dyads had found this mountain with its multitude of caves, they'd searched for some sign of the beings that had once inhabited them but found nothing. Not a scrap of cloth, a shard of pottery, a rusty tool, or even a single bone was left to give a hint of the former tenants. Damien's ancestors knew whoever or whatever these beings were, they were advanced enough to carve the cave warren out of solid rock. Not with chisels or drills, but with tools that left smooth, rounded walls. Each cave had been located with great care, some with up to ten rooms, but never an odd number, always divisible by two. The long-ago Dyads had marveled at the symmetrical architecture. Even the placement of the caves on the mountain, facing east to catch the first rays of each new day, delighted them. It was as if this mountain had been waiting for them, left by their unknown benefactors as a gift. They'd moved in at once.

Within the mountain, all the caves were connected by a series of tunnels. In some places, the tunnels widened, creating large common rooms. Each room, no matter how deep within the mountain, had natural light made possible by a smaller series of tunnels that allowed sunlight in.

Of course, the Dyads had put their unique stamp on their new home. They'd planted immediately, bringing in rich soil from the valley below. The different species of trees, shrubs and vines soon took over the cliff face. And everywhere, flowers.

Damien tried to count the species in bloom but soon gave up and just drank them in. The blue morning glories, yellow daffodils, white lilies of the valley, and his favorite, the deep red roses, covered the mountain in a celebration of life. A gentle breeze brought the mingled scents and he breathed deep. He groaned again, this time with pleasure. It was almost worth leaving the Diarchy for this moment of rediscovery.

With renewed determination, he started the climb to the sixth level up and eighth cave to the right. His and David's home.

As he ascended, he tried to block out what was happening within the individual cave dwellings. But try as he might, the activities of the inhabitants invaded his mind. He and David had never been directly involved in a nesting, but he'd always wondered what it would be like. Now, just a cave wall away from the busy quartets, the sexual energy seeped into his psyche. His body reacted with a swiftness that left him gasping. Walking became difficult.

Emma's warm, silky-smooth body flashed into his head and he could swear he smelled her. For a moment, he thought about turning back and finding her. Of bringing her to his rooms so they could join in the coupling ritual. He needed to be inside her again. They were mated after all. Why shouldn't they take part?

"No." He cried out in an effort to rein in his lust. He pushed all thought of the nesting Dyads and Emma out of his mind and focused on David. David needed him. He must get to David. But every step away from Emma proved more difficult than the last. Would this climb ever end?

Finally, he stood in front of the Stewart cave. The familiar weave of the vines that served as a door seemed to welcome him home. He raised a hand, asking the vines to part and allow him access. The vines flowed back creating an entry just large enough for him to fit through. Taking a deep breath, Damien squeezed in.

"David!" Damien shouted and searched the living area. Nothing had changed in the months he'd been gone. The large room was still cluttered with centuries of treasures he and David had collected during their travels in the human world. An early printing press from Elizabethan England stood against one wall. A spinning wheel sat in another corner. A collection of model cars, from a Model T to a Sting Ray, sat atop a player piano.

"Here," a muffled voice from the sleeping chamber cried.

Damien sprinted toward the voice, desperate to reach his brother. In the sleeping chamber, David lay sprawled across the bed. His human partner, Aiden, paced beside it. His brother looked at him and Damien suppressed a gasp. Deep lines etched David's pale face. His chest rose and fell as if he'd been running a race.

"Thank God," Aiden said, crossing to him.

Damien took in the deep lines around Aiden's mouth, the dark circles rimming his eyes. His usually neatly groomed mane of dark brown hair stood up in tangled peaks. The clothes he wore were wrinkled and stained with sweat.

"Where the fuck have you been?" Aiden demanded.

The big man's question filled Damien with shame.

Aiden's butterscotch eyes searched behind Damien. "Where's Jacob? Why didn't he come with you? We need him to fully link the quartet."

Damien sank down on the bed and placed one hand on David's chest. Everything about this was wrong. He should be in the same shape as David. It had always been so. What happened to one twin happened to the other.

"How long has he been like this?" Damien asked, acutely conscious of his own good health.

Aiden towered over him. "Look at me, Damien."

Aiden's lethal tone allowed no other option. Damien looked up into eyes filled with fury.

After a long look at his face, Aiden took a step back. "What the hell's going on? David's been struggling to maintain consciousness for hours and you waltz in here as if you haven't a care in the world. And you don't bring Jacob with you. How are we supposed to fix this without him? We need our full strength. Why aren't you in the same shape as David?" He kicked the side of the bed. "What the hell is going on?"

"Peace, Aiden," David called from the bed, his voice barely a whisper. His eyes left his partner and focused on Damien. "It is good to feel you close again. The waiting has proved…difficult."

"Difficult my ass." Aiden put his hand on Damien's shoulder and jerked him around. "He damn near died waiting for you. You must have been able to feel what was happening to him. How could you take a chance with his life, with both your lives? What was worth the agony he went through?"

Damien placed his hand over Aiden's. He tried to send calming energy but Aiden wrenched his hand away.

"Don't try that calming shit on me. I want some answers. I want—"

"Enough, Aiden." David sat up, weaving slightly. "You forget who you are speaking to. We are Dyad. The emotion aimed at one of us encompasses the other. Do not weaken me further with this display of human anger."

The anger melted out of Aiden. He collapsed into a chair. "Forgive me, Damien. I've been unable to help him. I..." He put his head in his hands. "Forgive me."

Damien patted the big man's knee. "There is no need to ask forgiveness from me." He turned to David. "What has happened to you?"

"When the Dyad traveled on," David began, his voice hoarse, "I could not Balance. The pain, the loss, overtook me and I lost myself in the abyss." He turned to Aiden. "But then, as always, Aiden came and offered his strength. He pulled me back but I still was not right." David's hand trembled as he wiped his face. "And then the mating drive took me. I reached for you but could not link. I...I almost killed Aiden. I took so much. I..."

Aiden sighed. "I'm fine." He reached over and squeezed David's shoulder then turned to Damien. "Other Dyads came and tried to link with us but it didn't work. We unbalanced them and they had to pull back. I passed out and it broke my link with David. The others grabbed me and gave me back my Balance." He stood and towered over both of them. "Tell him, Damien. Tell him to take from me what he needs. He won't let me link. He won't let me touch him." Aiden reached for David.

"No." David pulled back. "You must not, Aiden." He turned to Damien. "Send him away."

Damien thought back to what it had been like for him in the library after the Dyad had died. If Emma hadn't been with him, if she hadn't given herself to him and brought him his release, the same thing that happened to David and Aiden would have happened to him and Jacob. All the while he'd dallied with Emma, while he'd taken his time deciding what to do, David and Aiden had been in this state. What had he allowed to happen?

Damien stood and faced Aiden. "You must go."

"No." Aiden rounded on him. "I am his partner. My place is here beside him."

"Leave us," Damien said. "You cannot help him and your continued presence upsets him. Leave him to me."

"Go, Aiden," David gasped. "Please, go."

Something in David's pained face seemed to convince Aiden. "I will be just outside the door."

"No," Damien said. "Jacob and the others are in the partners' quarters. Wait with them. Find Jude and bring her with you. Heal yourself, Aiden. Grow strong. He needs you strong now."

"Bloody hell," Aiden cursed. "This is all wrong." His finger rammed into Damien's chest. "You fix this, Damien. Whatever this is, you fix it."

He walked Aiden to the door. "We will get through this as we always have. Together, as one."

After one more worried look at David, Aiden left.

Gathering his strength, Damien went back to the bed. "What have I done to us?"

"We knew the dangers when we separated but I fear we have grown overconfident." A small smile eased the creases on David's face. "The Balance has smacked us back to reality. Our main flaw has always been hubris, has it not?"

Damien held out his arms. "Come, let us link. Can you stand? Let us see where this has taken us."

David clasped his hand and struggled to pull himself upright. Seeing his twin so weak sent another surge of shame through Damien.

"No," Damien said. He eased David down on the pillows. "There is no need to stand." He settled beside him on the bed. "Remember when we were boys and shared the same bed?"

"I remember you snoring. I used to make up songs to go along with your rhythm."

"And then you would sing them to the others at morning meal. How could I forget 'Damien, The King of the Snorting Hedgehogs'?"

"One of my best. They sang it for years."

Their eyes locked. "We are stalling," David said. "I am afraid to link. And even more afraid we will not be able to."

Damien smiled at him. "The mighty king and vanquisher of hedgehogs afraid? The young hero who wrestled the great snoring beast for two hours and plugged his nose with moss to quiet him—afraid? Impossible."

David held out his arms. "It is time, brother. Link with me." Damien eased into David's open arms, resting his forehead against him. Physically, it was as if two puzzle pieces came together, a perfect fit. They sighed in unison at the rightness of it. This was how it had always been between them. From the time they first formed a coherent thought, there had always been the two of them. One thought—two minds, only fully complete when together.

After taking a shaky breath, David started to hum their linking note. It was not his usual sweet tone. His hoarse voice couldn't seem to sustain the pitch. Damien took a deep breath and sent his own note out to meet it. He struggled for a few moments, manipulating his vocal cords to match David's perfectly. And then he had it. Their two voices came together as one. The pure note sent calming ripples up and down Damien's spine. David relaxed in his arms and he saw his brother's relieved smile. He beamed back at him. The first part of the link was a success. So far, so good.

Damien focused on the note they'd created. He closed his eyes, pressed his forehead against David's and sent his mind into the note. Within the beautiful tone, David's mind waited for him, welcomed him. He eased past his brother's mental barriers and merged their minds.

In a moment, their melded mind started to work. Their individual heartbeats pulsed in unison. Their breathing matched in pace. Their combined energy, which had been so lopsided, evened out between them. David grew stronger as Damien weakened slightly until the scale of power was balanced between them. This was good. This was right.

Now that the link was complete, images of their separate experiences flashed before them: Damien going into the library to meet Emma—David arriving at the Diarchy—Damien trying to convince Emma the time had come to leave the safe house—David sharing in Aiden's joy at being reunited with Jude—the horrible moment when each of them had felt Caleb and Connor travel on—Damien taking Emma on the library table—David drawing so much power from Aiden he'd almost killed him—Damien's connection to Emma—David's long wait for his brother to come to him, to make him whole again.

Each separate memory shared and experienced anew, only this time as one, made part of the whole.

The images finally stopped. They broke apart and moved to opposite sides of the bed. For a long moment they stared at each other and then David lifted an eyebrow. "Emma? You are mated to Little Emma?"

Damien lowered his eyes to the bedspread, shame flowing hotly through his veins.

David's voice changed. It grew darker, deeper. "Damien? We are mated to Little Emma?"

* * * * *

"Emma mated to Damien?" Wulfgar whispered. But the Viking's whisper, like everything else about him, was bigger than life. It carried across the crowded common area as if he'd shouted. The human partners had gathered in the large open room to meet old friends and trade stories as they waited for the outcome of the Dyad mating ceremony. At his words, every head turned to Wulfgar.

"Holy hell," Wulfgar continued. "Isn't that like a lion mating with a lamb? He'll have her for supper and then what?

Lamb chops?" The group of partners surrounding Wulfgar roared with laughter.

Across the room, Emma tried to disappear into her chair. She could feel the blush on her face. Even the partners thought she and Damien were doomed. At least Wulfgar hadn't called her Little Emma. That was something. She looked down at the teacup in her hand, feeling all eyes on her, determined not to let on she'd heard him. Sitting at the table next to her, she sensed Jacob and Eleanor stiffen.

"And where does that leave David?" Wulfgar rattled on. "Odd man out or will he go along for the ride? There's a picture for you."

Emma wanted to die. Out loud, in front of all the partners, most of whom were strangers to her, Wulfgar was joking about her sex life. She'd thought the hard part would be the Dyads' reaction, not the other partners'. Eleanor's arm went around her shoulder. Jacob gathered himself to stand but before he could, Luke came to her rescue.

"Wulfgar, you stupid git." He sauntered over to the Viking. "How many times do I have to tell you? It's called a whisper, usually meant for just one person. If you can hear your voice bouncing around the room, you're not doing it right." He leaned in and demonstrated the perfect whisper in Wulfgar's ear.

Emma watched a few emotions flash across Wulfgar's face. Puzzlement first, then surprise and finally, after he looked up and caught her eye, embarrassment.

He cleared his throat. "Emma, I didn't know you…" He looked to Luke for help.

Luke shook his head. "You dug this hole, Viking. Get out on your own."

Wulfgar shot him a murderous look and crossed the room to stand in front of her. The closer he got, the more Emma had to strain her neck to look up at him. Wulfgar, the tallest of the human partners, stood almost as tall as a Dyad and his shoulders seemed as wide as he was tall. Emma had always marveled at the sheer size of him. His hand was the size of her head. Back at the safe house, she'd seen him throw other partners around on the training mat as if they were feathers. But now, he stood looking down at her, shifting uneasily from foot to foot, picking at the outside seams of his jeans, his mouth working soundlessly.

Emma couldn't stay mad at him. Not when he looked like a big cuddly bear who had lost his best friend. She stood and once again felt all eyes on her. "It's okay, Wulfgar." She touched his rock-hard forearm. "It was a surprise to everyone, even Damien and me. And it's probably only temporary." She took a quick look around the room to gauge everyone's reaction.

The human partners were a mixed bunch. Every race on Earth was represented. Black, White, Hispanic, Asian, in all shapes and sizes. But they had two things in common, all were in the prime of life, and they were all looking at her with varying expressions of disbelief. She knew what they were thinking. How could someone like her be mated to Damien?

Wulfgar's hand engulfed hers. "Don't let me off that easy, Emma. My comments were thoughtless and caused you harm. I wasn't thinking."

Luke slapped him on the back. "Not thinking. Now there's the Wulfgar we all know and tolerate."

His comment broke the tension in the room. Emma heard male laughter all around her.

Wulfgar, finding himself the butt of yet another in a long line of Luke's jokes, took offense. He dropped Emma's hand and stood toe to toe with Luke.

"Scottish ass," he said with quiet menace.

Undaunted by his size, Luke looked up. "Viking dunce."

Wulfgar's eyes narrowed. "Why don't you go play that useless Scottish game with the thin sticks and small balls? Now that's a fine pursuit for a man. Prancing around an over-mowed lawn, swinging at a white ball, and all to do what?" He lowered his face to Luke's. "Why, to get that little sissy ball into a little sissy hole. Why don't you take up knitting instead? At least you'd have a scarf to show for it."

A few of the partners chuckled and moved to form a loose circle around Luke and Wulfgar.

Luke's index finger rammed into Wulfgar's chest. "Golf is the sport of kings. It requires something you lack, you great lumbering bull. Finesse. Oh, sorry. I forgot who I was speaking to. Finnnessse." He elongated the word. "Big words aren't your forte, are they?"

Cat-calls egged the battle on.

"Keep it up, little man." Wulfgar patted Luke on the head. "You'll get another lesson in humility soon."

Luke stepped back and assumed a fighting stance. "The day you teach me anything is the day pigs fly."

Wulfgar brought his beefy hands up and fisted them. "Look for pork on the rooftops come morning."

They circled each other, looking for an opening.

"Dunderhead," Luke quipped.

"Pipsqueak," Wulfgar shot back and feinted right with a speed Emma found surprising in such a big man. He turned left and caught Luke in a choke hold.

All the partners rose and joined the circle around the battling pair. Shouts of, "Take him, Luke," and "About time that wiseass was taken down a peg," were heard over the general calls of encouragement. Bets were placed on both who would win and how long it would take.

Lightning fast, Luke kicked his legs out and walked up the nearest man's body until he was able to propel himself over the Viking's head and land on his back. He wrapped his arms around Wulfgar's neck, his legs around his waist and held on for dear life.

Wulfgar roared and lumbered from side to side, trying to buck Luke off but the smaller man held firm. It reminded Emma of the bull rider event in a rodeo.

Suddenly, Jacob came from the left and, with a sweeping kick, knocked Wulfgar's legs out from under him. The two tumbled to the floor, arms flailing, and ended in a twisting heap.

"Enough," Jacob bellowed. He towered over the downed fighters, his hands opening and closing into fists. "Aren't we in enough trouble?" His eyes swept the room, meeting each man's gaze, and settled back on the pair beneath him. "Half of the Diarchy thinks we're one step up from Neanderthals and the two of you can't wait to prove them right. You know how they feel about fighting of any kind. Why don't you just piss on the floor in front of them while you're at it?"

Luke staggered upright, looking contrite. "Sorry, Jacob. Couldn't resist." He held a hand out to Wulfgar. "Need a hand up?"

"Sure," Wulfgar said and grasped Luke's hand. Luke went down as Wulfgar rose until their positions were reversed. He smiled down at Luke. "Need a hand up?" he mimicked.

"You know where you can stick that hand." Luke rose and backed away. The crowd broke up amid mutters about all bets being off.

"Spoiled children," Jacob muttered as he sat down next to Eleanor.

Eleanor rubbed his back. "We're all on edge, Jacob. Can't you feel it?"

Relieved that the focus of the room wasn't on her anymore, Emma thought about what Eleanor had said. It was true. Ever since she'd come through the portal she'd felt an energy all around her, bumping up against her body. She leaned forward and whispered, "Yes, what is that? I feel restless and...powerful. Kind of like my skin doesn't fit anymore. Is this how it usually is here?"

Jacob shook his head. "No. There is always heightened power here but never this unease and..." He glanced at Eleanor. "Need."

"Yes," Eleanor agreed. "It is need, isn't it? The need to—" She blushed.

The layers of embarrassment just keep piling on, Emma thought. She swallowed and voiced what they were all thinking. "To reproduce. We're all feeling the Dyads' need to reproduce, with everything that goes along with it."

Jacob scanned the room. "No wonder we're all so jumpy. None of us have been at the Diarchy during a nesting before. We have no frame of reference. Look at them all."

Emma scanned the crowded common room. Hardly any of the fifty or more partners were sitting. Most were on their feet, pacing. The few seated were all engaged in an activity. The activity of choice seemed to be cleaning various weapons. All of them held tension in their bodies, poised to spring at the slightest provocation. They reminded her of caged animals.

"We have to control this before something happens," Jacob said and stood. "Brothers," he addressed the room. "The energy the Dyads are creating for their nesting is affecting us."

"No shit," someone called out.

Nervous laughter rippled across the room.

Luke walked to the center. "And here I thought you all were just happy to see me." He was forced to duck and weave to avoid all the projectiles thrown at him.

Jacob ignored him. "We must channel this energy before it gets out of control." He moved to stand next to Luke. "I suggest those of you with Dyad lovers retire to—"

A few men bolted out of the room.

"Lucky sods," Wulfgar said. "What about the rest of us?"

"To the gym. Training drills. Work it off," Jacob said.

"Ha," Luke choked out. "Drills. I like the sound of that. Last one to the gym gets the Viking for a partner." He sprinted for the nearest exit.

"I'll show you a drill you won't soon forget." Wulfgar started after him. "Fore." He grabbed a cup and hurled it after Luke, missing him by inches. It stuck in the vine wall at an awkward angle. Wulfgar turned to the partners. "Want to watch me kill him?" he asked with an evil grin.

The room quickly emptied except for Jacob, Eleanor and Emma.

Emma glanced at the couple. She could feel the sexual tension sizzling between them. They were being very careful not to look at each other.

"Listen, you two," Emma began. "You don't have to babysit me. Why don't you follow your own advice?" She felt her face heat up again. "You know…ah." She couldn't voice the next part. What was she supposed to say? Go to your room and make like bunnies?

Eleanor turned to her. "You sure you'll be okay alone? It's your first time here and we've only just arrived really. You haven't been shown around. We haven't even assigned you a room."

"We can do the tour later and to tell the truth, I could use some alone time. I'm fine. Go," Emma insisted.

Eleanor locked eyes with Jacob. "Well, I am a little tired." She licked her lips.

Emma couldn't resist sneaking a peek at Jacob. As he stared at his wife, the heat in his gray eyes made her almost fear for her friend. Well, fear mixed with a heavy dose of envy. Why so much envy lately?

"Come, wife." Jacob's rich bass voice held a promise in it.

"See you later, Emma," Eleanor said absently as she let her husband lead her out of the room.

Now what? Emma thought.

After the crush of people over the past hour, the huge room with all its wooden tables and chairs seemed doubly empty now. When they'd arrived, she'd been surprised at how normal the common room was. With the exception of the walls, which were made of the same combination of trees and vines as the portal room, the common room could have fit in any urban habitat. With one important exception—no electricity. And nothing that needed electricity to run. How would she dry her hair? How would she listen to music? Unlike the partners, Emma hadn't thought to bring a stock of batteries. She looked up at the light streaming though openings in the ceiling. What did the Dyads do for light after the sun went down? Did everybody just give up and go to bed?

The quiet fueled her feeling of isolation. It suddenly struck her that if she wanted to go home, she couldn't. She had no idea where on the planet she was. Even worse, she didn't think she could find her way back to the portal room. There'd been so many twists and turns through the vine-lined corridors, she'd lost track. All she knew of the Diarchy so far was the portal area and this common room.

What had she gotten herself into? What would the Dyads do when they found out about her connection to Damien? True, they never killed. It was one of their big rules. But they could do other things.

Emma's heart sped up and the room was suddenly hot. What if they decided to modify her memory and wipe all knowledge of Damien and the others from her mind? What if they took away her ability to walk? Put her back in Mildred. She wiped at her face with shaky hands. The worst part was, she'd never know. Or would she? It seemed impossible that any power could alter the way she felt about Damien.

No. No one would take Damien away from her. Emma started to pace. Just let them try. She'd…

Emma took a deep breath and grasped the chair in front of her. What was she thinking? Did she think she could take on the entire Diarchy? Little Emma going up against the Dyads on their home turf. Right. It wasn't even a David-and-Goliath scenario. It was the ant on the ground next to the David-and-Goliath scenario. Any way you looked at it, the ant wasn't going to come out ahead. The Dyads could take away her feelings for Damien with a wave of their hands. Make her forget she'd ever met him, ever loved him.

She bumped a table with her hip. A teacup fell and shattered on the earthen floor. Emma ignored the mess and bolted for the nearest door. She had to get out. Run away. If she couldn't find the portal room, she'd just find any opening and beat feet for the nearest town. After all, she was still on Earth. Wasn't she?

Once out of the room however, her feet seemed to have a mind of their own. Instead of taking the corridor back toward the portal, she turned the other way and started to climb. Something, she wasn't sure what, guided her, urged her on, always upward. She passed many rooms but didn't bother to slow or even glance in. The need she'd been feeling since entering the Diarchy intensified until her skin burned.

Soon she was climbing steps cut into a cliff wall, heedless of the fall that awaited her if she stepped wrong.

After a sharp turn, a gasp escaped her and she stopped running. A mountain loomed before her. So close, how had she not seen it before? It was covered in vines and flowers. Heartbreakingly beautiful. Something about it pulled her in and brought tears to her eyes. So calm, and at the same time, so full of life.

Unerringly, her eyes found the sixth level up and eighth opening to the right. That was where she needed to be. She would find all her answers there.

It seemed to take hours to cover the distance but Emma finally stood at the entrance with vines blocking her way. As soon as she touched them, the vines parted and she squeezed in. Immediately, she smelled Damien.

She flew across the entrance room looking for the source of that wonderful smell. With a feeling akin to crossing a finish line, she stumbled into an inviting bedroom. On the bed, Damien and David stretched out, all long lines and silky, dark hair. They looked at her, startled, and Emma knew at once which one of the twins was Damien.

The only problem was, now that she'd found him, she had no idea what to do.

Chapter Seven

ℌ

Beep…Beep…Beep…

Such a little noise but it meant so much. Alex took comfort in the sound. As long as the beeping continued, he had hope. But if it ever stopped… He pushed the thought away and, as he had done for months, buried his fear deep in his gut. No time could be wasted on a future that would never happen. A future he refused to allow.

Determined, he looked down at the hospital bed and focused on the only thing in his fucked-up life that had ever made sense. Had ever given him any peace. Ever made him feel special. His wife. His Jenny.

It seemed as if they hooked her up to a new machine with a new tube every day. In the beginning, Alex had counted them but when he'd reached ten he didn't have the heart to continue. Digging into his pocket, he pulled out a bottle of the perfume Jenny favored. As he'd watched her do countless times, he sprayed once and carefully moved her wrist into the resulting mist. If you sprayed directly at the wrist the scent would overpower the wearer. This way, the scent became a part of the woman. Or so she'd always said.

"Mr. Ward?"

Alex jumped. He hated being caught off guard. Anger rose in him as he turned, ready to curse at the person who dared interrupt him. The look on Dr. Walji's face froze the words on his tongue. He knew what was coming. Bile rose in his throat.

The doctor had on his bad-news look. The careful, put upon, caring-but-not-too-involved look most doctors were able to enact with ease. To Alex, the look told him just how fucked he was.

Steeling himself, he took a deep breath and slowly let it out. "What's wrong now?" he asked.

Dr. Walji motioned to the chairs in the corner of the crowded room. "Will you sit?" he asked and took Alex's arm.

All the blood left Alex's head. The doctor had never touched him before. This couldn't be good. He let himself be led to the chair and made his knees bend so he could sit.

Walji settled in the other chair and took a moment to gather his thoughts. "Bad news I'm afraid." He fingered the stethoscope around his neck. "We've reached the end of what we can do for Jenny."

Alex put up a hand to silence him. "I've heard that before. In every hospital and clinic I've taken her to." He looked into Walji's sympathetic eyes and suppressed the urge to throttle the good doctor. "If I'd believed it every time I'd heard it, my wife would have died last year."

A hint of a smile played across Walji's lips. "If strength of will could keep your wife alive, I have no doubt you could do it. You've found every treatment that modern medicine can offer someone in her condition. Taken every chance there was to take." He leaned forward and steepled his fingers. "But the human body can take only so much, Mr. Ward. Jenny has put up the best fight possible." He turned to look at the bed and its occupant. "Her strength of will is a match for your own. I've never seen this in a patient before. It's as if she's refusing to let go. I wish I had known her before…" he trailed off.

Despite the circumstances, Alex smiled. This type of thing had been going on since he'd met Jenny. There she lay, half dead, in a coma, after months of wasting away, and still she worked her magic. The doctor was smitten. Without so much as a word, Jenny had made another conquest.

In the past, it had made him so jealous, caused horrible fights ending with him fuming and Jenny crying. Until he realized his wife had no idea of the effect she had on the opposite sex. Nor did she encourage or return the poor man's feelings. This ability was just another part of the wonder he held for her. She could have had any man she wanted and she'd chosen him. Even after all their years together, he couldn't understand why.

Alex might be sure of his wife's fidelity but the look on Dr. Walji's face, of admiration and respect, bothered him. "Doctor," he said. A bit too loudly.

The doctor's head whipped back to face him. He looked down at his hands, color rising on his neck. "Sorry, Mr. Ward."

"Tell me what's happened with my wife," Alex demanded.

Walji sighed. When he raised his head, the bad news look was back. "As you know, the new kidney responded well. We were able to discontinue dialysis and she no longer needs the Lasix medication to get fluids off."

"So you said." Alex waved his hand in a hurry-up gesture. "What's the problem then?"

"Besides the condition of her brain?"

Alex jumped to his feet. "I told you never to bring that up again." If Walji dared say "brain dead" to him one more time, Alex would knock his over-white teeth down his throat.

The doctor's hands went up in surrender. "Besides that, it's her heart. As with many type-one diabetics, your wife's heart is enlarged. The added stress from her condition and the kidney operation has weakened it further."

In his mind's eye, Alex saw the hourglass again. More sand on the bottom than the top now. "How bad is it?" he asked.

"It's only a matter of time, Mr. Ward."

Time again—always the enemy. "How much time?"

"At this point, it's impossible to tell. Her heart could give out at any moment, or continue to function in its weakened state for a few days, a week, maybe even two weeks."

A familiar out-of-body feeling washed over Alex. Each time the long parade of doctors had told him Jenny was dying, his soul, his essence, would leave his body and hide behind the nearest piece of furniture. He'd been doing this mental duck and cover since he was a teenager. It was as if he had to distance himself from the horrible words in order to continue. To retreat to safe ground and recoup his strength for the coming battle. A battle he would not lose. This time his mind chose to hide under the bed.

"Did you hear me, Alex?" Walji touched his hand.

At the doctor's touch, Alex was sucked back into his body. Damn. He wasn't ready to face this yet.

"Alex," the doctor repeated.

Alex started to pace. "Yes, I heard you," was all he could manage to choke out. A thought struck him. "What about a new heart?"

Walji shook his head. "Your wife is not a good candidate. In her condition I doubt we could get her on the donor list."

"That's what you said about the kidney." He stopped in front of the doctor and leaned to eye level. "If she needs a heart I'll get her one. You just say when."

The doctor waved his hands in a warding-off gesture. "No, no. This can't happen again. As I said before, I don't want to know where that kidney came from—ever. And before you make any calls about a heart, I have to tell you that a new heart would make no difference. Jenny would never survive the operation."

"That's your opinion."

"It's not opinion, it's a fact." He pointed to the vacant chair beside him. "Please, sit down. We have more to discuss."

Ignoring him, Alex continued to pace. "What more is there to discuss? You've told me you can't do any more for her. That means it's time for me to find another clinic, another doctor." The panic in his voice frightened him.

Walji stood and crossed to him. "You can of course take Jenny to another clinic. That is your right." He took Alex by the shoulders. "But you must examine all of your options before you do. As Jenny's heart weakens, so does her ability to pump blood through her body. Every moment that passes, you are risking—"

"No." Alex broke out of Walji's hold and flew to the bed. Had it finally come to this? His eyes went to Jenny. She looked so much better than before the kidney operation. All the puffiness was gone from her face. Her fingers were back to their graceful slimness, not the sausages they had become. The idiot was wrong about her heart. He had to be.

He felt the doctor come up behind him. "Don't say it," Alex said. He didn't recognize his voice. The man who'd just uttered those words was pleading, begging. It couldn't possibly be him.

"Mr. Ward, Alex," Walji said softly. "You have run out of time. If we perform a Caesarian now, your son has every chance at survival. If we wait, or if Jenny's heart should stop, I can't guarantee the shock wouldn't kill him as well."

"It's only been five months."

"I have seen younger survive."

"Everyone told me the longer she can carry him, the better his chances."

"And they were correct. We have constantly monitored your son. From all indications, he's a healthy twenty-two-week fetus. But that could change at any moment. If her blood flow gets any weaker, if her heart should stop, your son could die, Mr. Ward."

"What would a Caesarian do to Jenny?"

Walji put a hand on his shoulder and turned him around.

Here it comes, Alex thought.

"Her heart is not strong enough. If we perform a Caesarian, Jenny will surely die."

Back under the bed Alex went. How could any man make such a choice? Your child or your wife? Not accepting either option, he decided to gamble on more time.

If he could find the Dyads he was sure he could barter some kind of deal for his son's and Jenny's life. He would gladly give all his wealth to see her smiling up at him again. And while they were at it, they could take away her diabetes as well. Why shouldn't he get his money's worth?

The Dyads had the power to heal Jenny. Lambert had assured him it was so. All he had to do was locate them and make a deal. It should have been easy. If only those fools had managed to capture one of the twins, Jenny might be out of that sick bed now, puttering around the nursery, arranging myriad stuffed animals, trying out the rocking chair, listening to lullaby after lullaby, and all the while speculating on the color of the baby's eyes. She'd so wanted the baby to have Alex's eyes.

Anger rose in him again. But this time, instead of being aimed at the doctor, it was directed at Jenny. He'd told her and told her and told her—no children. Every doctor they'd spoken to had advised against it. Jenny's system wasn't stable enough to bear the extra strain of carrying a child. Besides, he didn't need children, she was enough for him. Somewhere deep inside, Alex was heartbroken that he hadn't been enough for her.

For the first decade of their marriage she'd seemed to accept her childless state. The few times she'd brought children up, Alex had argued for adoption or a surrogate. With the techniques available now it could be their biological child. His sperm and Jenny's egg. But each time Jenny would get a faraway look in her eyes.

"I want to do it," she'd say. "I have to know what it feels like."

The fights that accompanied these discussions were the worst in their life together.

He should have known something was up. The last year, Jenny hadn't mentioned children once. He'd thought, hoped, she'd finally found her peace with the situation. Looking back, he could follow her thought process. At thirty-seven, her biological clock was winding down. She'd started attending church regularly and had private meetings with that prick priest, Father Harrington.

If Alex ever got his hands on that scripture-spouting hypocrite, he'd send him to his God all right. The same God Harrington had promised Jenny would make everything all right. The priest and Jenny had prayed on it and decided, without any input from Alex, to stop using birth control and let God take it from there.

Once she was pregnant, there was no talking sense to her. Jenny thought abortion was murder, pure and simple. No gray area for her. She'd been so happy that first month. Bubbling with the knowledge of the life growing inside her. Assuring him over and over that everything would be fine. And then it had all turned to shit.

"Alex?"

Walji shook him. The action brought Alex up from under the bed and hurled him into the present.

"Are you all right, Alex?" Walji asked.

Realizing he'd been staring into space while in the doctor's arms, Alex felt heat rush to his face. Worse, tears streamed down his cheeks. He broke away and went to the door.

"Get out," he demanded.

"But," Walji said and started toward him.

"Go," Alex repeated and held the door wide.

The doctor hesitated a moment and then shook his head. "As you like, Mr. Ward." After one more look at the bed, he left.

Alex took a deep breath and centered himself. He went to the bed and noticed a few strands of hair in Jenny's mouth. She'd always hated when the wind blew hair into her mouth. With great care, Alex brushed the strands back into place. He leaned down and kissed her dry lips.

Straightening up, he put his hand over the swell beneath her waist. Shouldn't a five month fetus be bigger? Something kicked his hand and he gasped. He smiled, splayed his fingers wide searching and was rewarded with another, stronger kick.

Dear God, his son was really in there. It wasn't just a collection of tissue, bone and blood. It was his little boy. His and Jenny's.

"What do you say, Jr.? You want to gamble and give Mom a little more time?" As if answering, he felt another kick against his palm. The strongest one yet. Alex grinned widely. "Okay, Tiger. A few more days. You give me a few more days and I'll give you your mother back. It's a deal."

He wouldn't lose him. He wouldn't lose them.

The Dyads were their only chance.

Chapter Eight

ꙮ

The sight of his mate at the door to the sleeping chamber caused every nerve ending in Damien's body to come alive. Emma was out of breath, her breasts testing the seams of the blue sweater she wore. Its color matched her shocked eyes. Her warm brown hair looked just-out-of-bed tousled and infinitely touchable. Damien remembered the feel of it sliding through his fingers, gliding over his naked shoulders, tickling the insides of his thighs as she'd kissed her way down his body. And those lips—full and moist and so very soft—were set now in an O of surprise as she studied him. He could change that look with a touch. He could have her gasping with desire in a few heartbeats.

Holding her gaze, he rose from the bed and started toward her.

"Damien." David's voice broke the spell.

But spell or no spell, it took every ounce of willpower for Damien to stop, and even though his feet obeyed, his arms reached for her, beckoning her to him.

The look on Emma's face changed to desire as the current between them met and fueled their need. All the blood in his body rushed to his groin. Damien forgot David in the bed behind him. All the logical reasons keeping him and Emma apart melted away to nothing. She was his. He had but to reach out and claim her. For the first time in his long life, he could join in the mating ritual. The two of them could tap into the collective power of the Balance and truly mate.

With a little cry, Emma flew toward him, her arms outstretched. Before she reached him, David stepped into her path, blocking their reunion. Without thinking, Damien's body crouched to attack. A man stood between him and his mate. He must be eliminated.

"Stop," David shouted. He turned sideways, stretched out his arms and put one hand on Emma's shoulder and the other on Damien's chest. The instant physical contact was established, their minds merged. All the jealousy drained out of him. He and David were Dyad. What belonged to one, belonged to the other. He might as well be jealous of himself.

Before his eyes, the mating drive that Damien had worked so hard to suppress took David. Through their link he felt his brother try to shield but knew it was useless. They were deep within the Diarchy with nesters all around them. The Dyad collective even now drew on the pure power of the Balance and sent it to the quartets to fuel their mating. No mental shield could hold up against such an onslaught.

A low growl emanated from David as he turned and faced Emma. Wonder flooded through their linked mind. How beautiful she was. Why had they never noticed before? Why had they thought it necessary to sever the mating mark? The mark was a gift from the Balance. She was perfect for them in every way, and down to her last cell—theirs.

Damien held his physical body back and let David take the lead. He reinforced their link and centered his mind in David's body. In this manner, they would share each smell, each touch, each emotion.

David's arm shot out and wrapped around Emma's waist. In a heartbeat that seemed like an eon, he pulled her to him. The feel of her body tight against them had both brothers groaning. They allowed themselves a moment to look into her eyes, savoring the anticipation, and then they took her mouth.

The dual experience of Damien once again falling into her and David tasting her for the first time, almost undid them. This first kiss made all former couplings pale in comparison.

It was time for the next step in the mating ritual. They reached for her mind to link it with theirs and found—panic.

Emma twisted her face away and struggled in their arms.

"Do not be afraid," David whispered against her hair. "We are here in this body, Damien and David. Two as one. Your mate."

They tried again to link her mind but instead her panic bled into them, cooling their blood. When she pushed against David's chest, they dropped their arms and let go.

Emma put a shaking hand to her bruised lips. "No," she gasped and stumbled backward. After a quick look around the room, she darted behind an overstuffed chair, using it as a shield. "I don't understand what's happening," she began. "But I can see where this is headed and it stops now. I'm not going to sleep with both of you. I'm just not wired that way." She turned to David. "No offense David, but I don't love you, at least not the way I love Damien. So, you know," she said, making a shooing gesture, "thanks but no thanks." She let out a deep sigh and drooped against the chair back. "Is it really hot in here?"

What does she mean? David thought to him. *What has wiring to do with this? I can feel her need for us and yet she pulls back. How can she love you and not me? We are one.*

I do not understand either, Damien thought back to him. *We are mated. It is the time of nesting.*

Our link is frightening her. Let us sever the link. Maybe we will seem less threatening.

Once fully back in his body, Damien went to the chair she cowered behind. "We do not understand, Emma. There is no difference between David and me. How can you feel differently about him than you do about me? We are one. We are Dyad."

"Dyad, Schmyad," she snorted. "However you dress this up, you're still talking about a threesome—two men and one woman. Don't you understand? I'm uncomfortable just saying it out loud. Where I come from, the way I was raised, this kind of behavior is only talked about in shocked whispers."

David joined Damien in front of the chair. "Love shared is never wrong, Emma," he said. "It is a gift from the Balance. The best gift the universe gives us. Search your heart. What do your feelings tell you?"

"I know what I feel and right now I feel like my blood is boiling. It started when we got to the Diarchy and it's getting worse by the minute." She rubbed her arms. "I know I said I'd come here, but is there any way I can take it back? I think it's time for me to leave."

Even though he'd argued for it at one time, the thought of Emma leaving him left Damien cold, empty. Before he could answer, David spoke up.

"I am sorry, Emma. But I still do not understand your feelings for us. What am I lacking in your eyes that Damien has? We are genetically identical, down to the last cell on our fingernails."

Emma wiped at her face and shook her head. "Look. Maybe I should have said something before now but at first I didn't realize what a big deal it was. I mean, it's not as if you guys ever told me anything about Dyads and how you work. I had to find out secondhand and by observation."

"Find out what?" Damien asked.

Emma went on as if she hadn't heard him. "And then when I realized what a big deal it was and how nobody else could do it, I was already in love and too embarrassed to bring it up."

"Emma, please. Bring what up?" the brothers said together.

She looked back and forth between them and settled on Damien. "I can tell you apart." She shook her head. "No, that's not exactly it. I can tell who Damien is. I can feel when it's you. So, when I see one of you and don't get that feeling, I know it's you." She pointed at David. "Is there a shower here? I could really use a shower, preferably a cold one." She went back to rubbing her arms.

Watching her, the need rose in Damien. Before he knew it, he mirrored Emma's actions and rubbed his own arms. She was correct. The room felt hot.

"What you say is impossible," David said. "The only humans who can tell one Dyad brother from another are the partners and it takes most of them a decade to master the ability."

Emma put her arms around her middle and rocked slightly. "Sure, I know that now. I puzzled it out about a month ago. I thought it was because of the way I felt, about Damien I mean." She looked at the floor, embarrassment coloring her face. "I thought because I loved him, I could tell you apart," she whispered.

The brothers looked at each other, dumbfounded. Never in their history with humans had they encountered this. Human women were always falling in love with them. At least, what they thought was love, but the feeling had been interchangeable. The women could make no distinction between them and therefore didn't know or care if it was David or Damien in their bed.

How could Emma tell them apart? Even the word, apart, felt foreign to them. The human concept of oneness—to be apart from—had taken Dyads decades to comprehend.

I am at a loss, Damien thought to David. *How is this possible?*

Maybe the same ability Emma has to tell us apart made our mating possible, David thought back to him. *Your mating,* David corrected.

Our mating. You are as much a part of this as I am.

"Stop talking about me as if I'm not here," Emma shouted.

"You heard us?" David asked.

"Yes, in my mind somehow. Just Damien's side of the conversation, but I got the gist." She whimpered and rubbed at her face. "Seriously, I need a shower please. Where's the bathroom?" She came out from behind the chair and searched the room.

"We prefer baths," David replied.

"Of course you do." Emma laughed, hysteria creeping into her usual light tone. She started pacing before them, all the while rubbing her thighs.

"Emma, stop." David grabbed her wrist as she rushed by. He gasped and quickly let it go. "She is burning with power, Damien. Did you feel that? We must get her away from the nesters before it is too late. The energy of the Balance is fueling her need."

Another first, Damien thought. No mere human should be reacting as Emma was. The partners would feel the power, their mates as well. As impossible as it seemed, Emma, who had no training on how to detect and channel the Balance, was absorbing the energy swirling around the room. The trouble was she had no idea what was happening to her. She didn't even know how to shield.

"Damien." David gripped his arm. "We must get her away," he repeated.

"And take her where? The entire Diarchy is alive with power and we cannot leave. The Elders have called us home."

"Then call one of the unattached partners to ease her. Luke perhaps?"

White blinding rage rose in Damien. Never. Luke would never touch her. "No partner will come near her. How can you suggest such a thing?" He gripped David's hand, linked their minds and shot his rage through.

Ahhh, Gods, David cried. *Calm, brother. We cannot let emotion overtake us. Especially now. Center with me.*

They drew on the Balance and used the power to suppress the rage that threatened to overwhelm them. When they had reached a somewhat shaky but calmer state, David turned to Damien. *We have never felt that before. It was...exhilarating. Strong emotions can be disturbing but at the same time, wondrous.* He shook his head. *Why do I suddenly dislike Luke?*

Because he is an ass.

Yes, David agreed. *An ass. And those stupid jokes of his. People only laugh to be polite. How can Sebastian stand to be partnered with him?*

Better him than us. Damien severed their link. Emma whimpered again and he realized they had gotten off point.

David watched Emma pace and shook his head. "If she will not have us and we will not let a partner service her, what is to be done? I ache for her."

"What have I done to her?" Damien said. He remembered Emma when he'd first met her. Even in a wheelchair, she had a happy energy about her. Always making him laugh. Always making sure everyone around her was included in the fun. The life of the party. And now look at her. Half out of her mind with sexual energy. Thinking herself in love with him. She'd have been better off if she'd never met him.

David pulled him aside. "She will not have us but she will have you," he whispered.

"What do you mean?"

"We remain unlinked. I will leave the two of you alone and you will—"

"Stop talking about me. I'm right in front of you," Emma shouted.

Could he do this to Emma again? Take her without her true consent, when she didn't have any real choice in the matter? Some part of him could excuse what had happened at the safe house. He had been out of his mind, dying. But this?

His brother had followed his thoughts. "This time it is not your need but hers," David said. "Look at her, brother." He motioned to Emma who stood in the corner, her eyes squeezed shut, her arms wrapped tightly around her middle.

"She loves you and in our own way, we love her. We do you know. You have not realized it yet but I have. My thoughts are not as clouded as yours at the moment. I'm not even sure how that is possible, me thinking differently than you, but I do know what I feel. Love."

"But what of you?" The thought of David left alone, loving but not having the emotion returned, sickened Damien.

David shrugged. "Emma has refused me. I do not wish to go where I am not welcome."

"But, David," Damien said. "If Emma and I share love again, we may cement the mark so strongly, you and I may never be able to break it."

"For centuries you and I have prayed for a true mating. Why are you so eager to give her up?"

"You know why. There is no Balance in three."

David went to the door. "Do what you will, but do it soon. She is in agony." After one last look at Emma, he left.

Damien turned to his mate.

Burning.

All she could feel was the burning. A part of Emma knew what was going on around her. Damien and David were having an argument over who was stuck sleeping with her. If she had an iota of energy to spare, she might be mortified. But she needed all of her strength to manage the need growing inside her, the need to run across the room and throw herself into Damien's arms.

She fought the urge to close her eyes. Every time she did, her body screamed at her. Her breasts were heavy and thrummed with an energy that centered on her nipples. When she moved, the slight rub of her sweater sent a jolt of fire from her breasts to her center. She felt a constant onslaught of hot energy assaulting her body. It was in the air she breathed, in the ground beneath her feet, seeping into her pores. It grew inside her with no hope of release. Her blood bubbled with power. Soon she would explode. A part of her wished for it, needed it. Anything would be better than this burning.

"Emma, let me ease your need."

Cool fingertips brushed her cheek. The fire subsided just a fraction and she focused on Damien's face, so close to hers. She noted pain in his eyes, and longing.

"Yes. Look at me. Link with me and share your fire."

Once again, Emma felt a presence in her mind, circling around her mental barriers. But this time instead of barging in, the presence hesitated, as if asking permission.

"David has gone. We are alone," Damien whispered. "Let me in."

Emma put her hands on Damien's face. The temperature difference between her hot fingers and his cool cheeks felt wonderful. She ripped open his shirt and ran her hands down his neck, over his chest. Wanting more of the blessed relief, she pressed her face into him and rubbed back and forth, reveling in the easing coolness of him. Here was what she needed. The answer to what her body shouted for.

Damien raised her head and cupped her face. "Close your eyes. Be one with me. Only when we are one can we ease each other's need."

A warning bell went off in Emma's mind. Somewhere in her heat-crazed brain, she knew if she closed her eyes and linked with Damien, there would be no turning back. Not just from what they were about to do but from Damien himself. If she took this next step, she would be his, body and soul, forever. The thought should have frightened her, but it didn't. Instead, she felt joy. A joy so great it filled her heart with wonder. If she was his, didn't that make Damien hers? And even if it didn't, even if she spent the rest of her life longing for a love he couldn't return, she would still choose him. She would still choose this.

After one more look at his beautiful face, Emma closed her eyes, accepting what was to come. The presence gently pierced her barriers and merged with her. The familiar feel of Damien engulfed her and their collective mind sighed with relief. Immediately the burning power evened out between them. Emma felt the energy shoot into his body and then back into hers like a crazed ping pong ball, each time the space between bounces getting shorter and shorter until it was a constant banging echoed in her heartbeat.

"Now, Emma. Now we fly."

Lips closed over hers and she tasted Damien. The earthy, exotic taste she never could quite identify. Also, in the background was her taste as Damien experienced it. Her tongue hot, his cool. A delicious sensation as they relearned each other's mouths.

Search our thoughts. Even as he kissed her, Emma heard Damien's voice in her mind. *Do you feel how much I want you?* The voice continued.

Emma concentrated on the Damien essence she somehow shared and found he burned as hot as she. He ached to be inside her, pleasuring her.

He broke contact long enough to lift her sweater over her head and toss it aside. Soon his mouth was back on hers, more insistent than before. She pushed his shirt off his shoulders and their torsos met, causing both of them to gasp as bare skin met bare skin. His ice, hers fire.

Damien kissed and licked his way down her neck, pushing her bra strap from her shoulder as he went. He unclasped her bra and cupped her breast, peeling away the cloth just in time for his tongue to graze her nipple.

Emma moaned his name, "Damien." The pull of his mouth sent lightning down her body. Her hands sank into that glorious mane of dark hair and she pressed him tighter against her.

Big hands cupped her bottom and drew her to him. She rubbed herself up and down his erection, marveling at the size of him. A mental shiver went through her as she realized his hard shaft would soon be inside her.

"No, no fear," Damien gasped out. "Not between you and me. I would never hurt you, love. There will be no pain, only pleasure."

As if to prove his point, he unbuttoned her jeans and slid his hand underneath her panties. His fingers worked the cloth open until he found her most sensitive spot. Her head fell back and she moaned against his mouth. Some primitive instinct took over and her hips moved in a rhythm as old as Eve. As his fingers worked their magic, he once again trailed kisses down her throat, tracing a path of liquid fire to her breast. When he drew her hardened nipple into his mouth, an orgasm started to build.

Yes, Emma, come for me. Come for us.

His voice in her mind sent her over the edge. Both of them cried out at the force of it. Emma held on to Damien as wave after wave of aftershock swept through her body. When she could think clearly, she realized that the need, although momentarily satisfied, was even now building again. This time the burn centered on Damien. Just as he did before, he shot power into her body and drew it back out again, sharing his need between them.

Slowly, he lowered her to the bed. He slipped her shoes off, then her socks and finally, her jeans. His eyes traveled down her body. "You are beautiful, Emma. So beautiful."

At that moment, with his eyes seeming to eat her up, for the first time in her life, Emma felt beautiful.

Damien unzipped his own jeans and let them slide down his thighs. His erection sprang free. Emma couldn't look away. His penis was long and thick and seemed to throb with an energy all its own. Another thrill of excitement and fright shot through her.

He kicked the jeans aside and moved to the bed. Holding her gaze, his hands started at her feet and blazed a trail up her calves, then her thighs, until they reached her panties. He hooked the elastic and drew them over her hips and down her legs. Fully naked with a man standing over her, Emma waited for shyness to overtake her, but it didn't. Under Damien's gaze, she felt only the rightness of this.

Damien parted her legs, crawled up the bed and settled himself against her. He drew her hands above her head and had her grasp the headboard. "Hold on to this."

"But I want to touch you," she gasped out.

Damien smiled and shook his head. "I have been shielding us somewhat from the power of the collective. I wanted to give you time to ready yourself." As he spoke, his erection brushed against her, making her almost weep with need. "But I can no longer hold my shields. I must drop them and when I do, you and I will be swept up in the power around us." He brushed her cheek. "Do not be afraid. It will be beautiful. Stay with me. I will not let you fall."

He kissed her, gently, sweetly, and then he raised his head and looked at her. "Are you ready?" he asked.

He positioned himself between her legs and the answering wetness was the only encouragement she could manage.

Slowly, he pushed inside, filling her. Emma closed her eyes and concentrated on the parts of their bodies that were so perfectly joined. The feel of him, hard and thick, sliding in and out of her was an intimacy she'd never shared before. Hesitantly, she used their link to experience what Damien felt, thrusting into her, asking her body to accept his. It was as if with each stroke, he forged a closer bond between them. After one more thrust, Damien lowered his shields and the bottom fell out of her world.

Underneath Damien, Emma's body went rigid. An earth-shattering scream tore from her throat. It took him a moment to register his own scream joining hers. The raw power of the

Balance ricocheted through their bodies, leaving a path of heightened sensitivity in its wake.

Damien latched on to the power coursing through them. Slowly, with infinite care, he exerted his will and brought the great force to heel. He used a fraction of the energy to reinforce his link with Emma and the rest he sent to the physical parts of their bodies involved in their mating. Once he was sure of his control, he thrust back into Emma. Two voices cried out. Damien's ultra-sensitized penis felt every inch of her channel squeeze against it. From the Emma mind, he felt himself, long and rock-hard, slam into her.

"Damien," Emma screamed. "What's happening? I…oh God."

He reached for her mind, already so closely linked with his. The panic was back. Fear of the unknown threatened to take her over. Using their link, he sent reassurance to her. She was his Emma, perfect for him in every way. Nothing she could ever say or do would be wrong in his eyes. *I am here with you. Take from me the strength you need.*

Her panic receded and she opened her eyes. When their gazes met, he felt her love for him and knew he didn't deserve it.

You are Damien, Emma thought. *How could anyone not love you? You're always thinking of others, never yourself. Searching for a way our two races can exist in harmony. Dark, dangerous, powerful, mysterious, and sexy as hell. You are everything I've ever wanted in a man and more.*

For a moment, Damien let her love wash over him. He'd forgotten how it could transform a person, to both feel and receive love. Since she met him, everything Emma did had been colored by the wonder of this new emotion.

Damien wrapped her love around them, cocooning the two of them in its power. It swirled with the Balance creating a stronger link between them. They were joined now as closely as a Dyad pair. She was Damien. He was Emma. Two bodies, one mind.

When he thrust into her again, it was a perfect union of mind, body and soul. He drove them hard up one wave of pleasure and down the next, each time reaching higher, each time getting closer to the ecstasy of release. He lost track of time and space. There was no bed beneath them, no room around them. Everything dropped away, unimportant, except the waves they rode.

Now, Emma.

They rode the final wave, higher and higher, until they reached its crest. With a cry of triumph, Damien released the power he held so tightly in check and their orgasm burst inside. Damien felt his seed shoot into Emma and lived a moment of absolute perfection.

Chapter Nine

ꟾ

Emma woke to the delicious feeling of being safe and warm in Damien's arms. His body pressed up against hers, spoon fashion. Her shorter curves fit naturally into his longer ones. Smooth muscular arms, at rest now, wrapped around her, cocooning her in his strength. She felt the gentle rise and fall of his chest against her back. With every exhale, a cool breeze tickled the side of her neck and the scent of Damien permeated the air. She breathed him in, rolling his exotic taste over her tongue. She'd never felt closer to another person in her life.

Here it is, she thought. *My moment.* In movies, books and plays, people always talked about freezing a moment in time. A moment so perfect, you wanted it to go on forever. She smiled. When she'd thought about what such a moment would be for her, never once did it include a non-human male at his home in a cave-riddled mountain, surrounded by a race of super-beings in heat.

No, her moment had been simple, like her. She'd wanted a man to love who loved her right back. Someone who could accept her handicap and then forget about it because it didn't matter. A man who could see past the wheelchair and everything it meant to the woman sitting in it. In the past, she'd feared she'd never find him.

She'd dated many men both able-bodied and handicapped but something had always been missing. In most cases, when the relationship ended, she'd stayed friends with the guy. It was easy to stay friends when love wasn't involved. Besides, Emma didn't believe in casting people aside because they couldn't give you exactly what you needed. She collected people and kept them close. You could never have too many friends.

It hadn't been easy, watching everyone around her pair up and fall in love. "It's your turn next, Emma," they would always say. "Your guy is out there just waiting for you." And then they'd set her up with their husband's brother or their coworker's son and cross their fingers for a spark. Nothing much ever came from their matchmaking. No spark for Emma. She'd liked the men just fine but there was never a pulse-stopping, heart-flipping attraction. Not until she'd laid eyes on Damien.

That was another moment she'd like to freeze in time, her first sight of Damien.

She'd been helping with the wedding arrangements of her best friend Alice Hennen, Eleanor's sister. Emma had met Alice in kindergarten. When all the other children had shied away from Emma, or worse, made fun of her, Alice had come right up and asked if she could sit next to her. She was the first person outside of her family who treated Emma just like a normal person. Even then Alice was a beauty, with her long golden hair, startlingly green eyes and a natural gentleness that drew people to her. As Alice's best friend, Emma was included in everything she did. Emma had learned about true friendship from Alice. She would do anything for her. Even wear the apple-green bridesmaid dress Alice had picked out.

Emma, Alice and Eleanor had been working on the wedding centerpieces at the Hennens' kitchen table. With the last name of Hennen, the sisters had kept up their dead mother's tradition of collecting hens. The hen-on-a-nest centerpieces were fun to look at, but hell to put together. Emma was having a hard time getting her hen to sit upright when she felt a current rush through the room. Alice and Eleanor stopped talking and they both looked over Emma's shoulder at the back door.

"They came," Alice gasped. "I can't believe it." Both sisters jumped out of their chairs and stood at attention waiting for the door to open.

Emma, wondering what was going on, wheeled back from the table and angled her chair for a better look at the newcomers.

When they came in, Emma couldn't believe her eyes. Two tall men, identical in every respect. Perfection and its mirror image. It had to be some kind of trick. They couldn't be real…could they?

Behind her, Alice and Eleanor rounded the table and threw themselves into the men's arms. Shouts of, "Damien, David," from Eleanor and, "How good of you to come," from Alice registered on Emma's hearing but were ignored. She'd heard about people being thunderstruck but had never experienced it for herself. Until now. She'd never seen anything like these two. As they'd smiled and hugged each Hennen sister their presence took over the room, filling it with an excitement that caught hold of Emma.

One of the twins looked over at her, smiled and turned back to the sisters who were happily chatting about the wedding and how perfect it would be now that they were here.

The other twin had his back to Emma. She watched as his body filled with tension and he took a step back from the trio in front of him. Slowly he turned, his eyes sweeping the room, searching, until they settled on Emma in her chair.

Emma took in his shoulder-length, blue-black hair, Roman nose and strong chin. An involuntary gasp escaped her. His face came together in a symmetrical beauty that made her think of statues of the stoic Greek Gods. He was tall, well over six feet, with broad shoulders that tapered down to a slim waist and hips. The clothes he wore, jeans and a royal blue T-shirt, seemed out of place on his regal body. Even in casual attire, the man evoked an aura of power.

When their gazes met, Emma froze. His eyes were dark blue and had a brightness to them she'd never encountered before. There was something not quite right about his eyes but they were so magnetic. Emma fell into them. All the blood left her head, her heart sped up and she fought the urge to back her chair up and bolt out of the room.

With cat-like grace, he lowered himself to one knee beside her. How had he known to do that? She hated when people bent at the waist to talk to her. It made her feel inferior, like a little child a person had to bend down to speak to. She preferred people to pull up a chair and sit or, as this man had done, kneel so their heights were equal.

His action should have made her more comfortable but she had the opposite reaction. Just being this close to him, looking at his perfect profile, feeling the electricity in the air surrounding him, almost overwhelmed her. At the same time she would have liked to sit like this all day, with his aura rushing over her as she anticipated his first words.

He had a puzzled look on his face, almost comical. He raised a hand and felt the air around her head as if it was physical. An energy rippled across her cheeks, not unpleasant but disquieting nonetheless. When he looked back at her, surprise changed his features and then he smiled.

"You are Emma," he said. His low masculine voice seemed to enter her body and vibrate along her already taut nerves. All she could manage was a small nod. Her vocal cords refused to obey.

"I am called Damien," he continued. "Alice has told us of you. You are a true friend to her. You possess a great inner strength and have a giving heart. You were paralyzed at the age of five when you fell through a hole in the ground. It took the searchers almost a day to find you. It was dark in the cave and the experience left a mark on you. Dark, enclosed places frighten you. But you have managed to rise above what happened to you, helping others in your situation. A remarkable feat for one so young."

His impossible knowledge of her shocked Emma out of her stupor and her personality kicked back in.

"You gonna guess my weight now?" she asked.

Damien's eyes widened in surprise and then he threw his head back and laughed. The musical sound made Emma smile, proud that she had evoked this reaction in him. Not such a stoic god after all.

His laugh drew the attention of the others. Alice and Eleanor had identical guilty looks. Their faces told Emma they'd forgotten all about her.

Alice moved first. "Emma, sorry. These are Jacob's friends." She gestured to the twin standing next to her. "This is David and—"

"I have shared my name with Emma," Damien said, wiping his eyes. "My brother and I are the Stewarts."

"The Stewarts?" Emma said. "What are you, a musical group? Like the Jonas Brothers or the Jackson Five?"

This time both brothers laughed.

Eleanor came toward her, a worried look on her face. "No, Emma, they are…" she trailed off and looked at Alice who looked back at her, equally troubled.

Damien stood and turned to the sisters. "If you two will allow, David and I will acquaint Emma with our…situation."

Alice and Eleanor smiled, relieved. "That's wonderful," Alice said. "Perfect. Thank you, Damien, for including her."

Eleanor put a hand on his forearm. "You're not going to, you know, do anything to her? Right?"

Damien went behind Emma's chair and started to wheel her to the living room. "Always the fierce protector, Eleanor."

David moved to join him. "Be at peace." He put a hand on Eleanor's shoulder as he passed. "We will not do anything to Emma that she does not approve."

"Wait," Emma said and put on the brake. "Hands off Mildred. I get along on my own power thank you very much."

"Who is Mildred?" Damien asked.

Alice went to Damien and carefully removed his hands from the chair. "Um," she started. "Emma doesn't like anyone pushing Mildred, her chair. She likes to do it herself."

"You wouldn't push me around if I could walk," Emma bristled. Damien's actions had triggered her pet peeve. She whirled Mildred to face Alice. "How about you let me in on what's going on? As pretty as they are, I don't know Romulus and Remus here. Why do I get the feeling the rug is about to be pulled out from under me?"

"No, no," Alice said. "It's nothing bad. Damien and David are… Well, you see they…" she trailed off again.

The other twin, David, put an arm around Alice's shoulder. "It is not Alice's story to tell. It must come from us or not at all." He raised an eyebrow as if daring Emma to hear their story.

"Fine." Emma sighed. She turned Mildred and propelled her to the living room. "But if all this is some kind of a hoax and you two turn out to be the strippers for Alice's stag night, somebody owes me a Cosmopolitan."

Emma heard some rushed whispers behind her but ignored them. She entered the living room and turned to watch the brothers come in. She took a moment to study them. They were dressed the same. Each had on a royal-blue T-shirt and jeans. But even identical as they were, she could pick out Damien. When she looked at him she felt something in her body click into place. Her pulse sped up and warmth washed over her. Moving her eyes to the other twin, she waited for what would happen and felt—nothing. How weird was that?

"May we sit?" David asked. "This might take some time."

"Sure." Emma shrugged. "Why should I be the only one who's comfortable?"

The brothers took their places on the couch facing her. For the next half hour Emma vacillated between outright disbelief and wonder. In the end, they'd had to demonstrate their powers to make her believe. It wasn't until they made every knick-knack float around the room that she was won over.

It was then, when she finally believed, that they'd made her an offer she couldn't refuse.

They wanted to give Alice a wedding present that was worthy of her and Emma, up and walking, was their idea of worthy. At the time, a part of Emma resented being reduced to a gift but then the reality of what they were offering trumped everything.

Even now, wrapped in Damien's arms, a part of Emma still didn't believe what they had done. She kept expecting to wake up in her bedroom with Mildred next to the bed waiting for her. Maybe that was why the situation with Damien frightened her so much. If the other Dyads decided that their mating was not a true one, she could end up back in her chair. Only now it would be worse than before because she had had these few months of walking. Was she risking everything by staying with Damien? Should she cut her losses and insist on leaving him? Her heart hurt at the idea.

"No," Damien whispered. "You must not think that way."

She turned in his arms to face him. His eyes had a sleepy quality and his hair was messed up in a sexy pile. It was the first time she'd seen him with so much as a strand out of place. She liked this new, mussed-up Damien. He felt more—human.

"No Dyad would take away your ability to walk," he said.

"I wish I was as sure about that. You saw the way the Dyad at the portal reacted to me…to us being mated. Don't tell me this isn't going to cause problems for you because I won't believe it."

He ran a fingertip over her cheek, a look of tenderness on his face. "You always think of me first. Why are you worried about causing me problems? It is I who has changed your world."

"You can say that again three times." Emma snuggled in tighter against him.

His arms squeezed her in. "I recognize that saying but can't place it."

"My grandmother always says it. It's one of her favorites. She has a saying for everything." Emma yawned. "It's so quiet now. My skin feels almost normal. What happened to all the power swirling around?"

"The nesters are taking a break. The power will build again soon. It will continue in this cycle until the Balance gives us a Dyad to replace the Fitzgeralds." He rose to one elbow and gazed down at her. "Emma, if you could go back to your life and still be able to walk, would you?"

"You mean let them wipe my memory of you?"

He nodded. "Yes. Or if you prefer, leave your memory intact. You could return to your life unencumbered by Dyads and all the problems we have brought you."

Emma felt tears fill her eyes. "Is it so easy for you? After what we just shared you could walk out of my life like nothing happened?"

"The logical part of my brain tells me this would be best for you."

"What does the illogical part tell you?"

He touched his forehead to hers. "It tells me to keep you close no matter the price."

"Even if you don't return my love?"

Rising slowly, he looked into her eyes. "But I do, Emma. Did you not feel my love for you?"

Emma shook her head. "I couldn't tell what I was feeling. I don't know if it was my emotions or yours. With all the mind-linking and power swirling around how do you separate the two?"

"Ah, Emma. Now you start to understand." He brushed a stray hair off her cheek and tucked it behind her ear. "To be linked, to be Dyad means it is our emotions you are feeling. Not yours, not mine, but ours."

"But, Damien, if that's true how I will ever know what you feel for me? How will I ever know that it's not my love for you that I…or we're feeling?"

"What is the difference? Love is love. The love I felt when we were linked was pure and true, wondrous in its power." He bent and trailed kisses from one eyelid to the other.

"What about now?" She gently lifted his face so she could look into his steamy eyes. "We're not linked now, right? How do you feel about me?" Emma wasn't sure she wanted to know the answer. She held her breath, knowing the next words out of his mouth meant everything.

Damien gasped a second before a loud bell shook the cave. It was a deep tone, rich in texture. At the sound, Damien's body tensed and his eyes widened. The sound rang out again, this time so loud Emma wanted to cover her ears. Damien shot out of bed.

"What is it?" Emma shouted.

"It has happened." Damien laughed and dug through their scattered clothing. "We," he paused for another booming bell. "We have done it. Conception, Emma. A new Dyad is among us." He tossed her sweater at the bed. "Hurry and dress. We must go to the welcome ceremony." Quick as lightning, Damien dove into his clothes.

Emma struggled with the sweater, all thumbs. Damien laughed again and took the sweater out of her hands. "No time for that now." Rushing to a dresser in the corner, he brought out a blue robe. "You can wear this." He came back to her and slipped it over her head.

The robe was more of a caftan with holes for her head and arms. It fell against her skin, velvet soft, but was at least six inches too long.

Unable to contain his excitement, Damien grabbed her hand and pulled her out of the bedroom into the main room of the apartment. David was waiting for them, excitement coloring his every movement.

"We must hurry," David said and bolted for the door.

Emma gathered the robe in one hand and pulled it up so she could run beside Damien. The corridors were full of Dyads rushing everywhere. Every thirty seconds someone shouted, "Praise the Balance," and everyone would answer, "The Balance be praised." The energy in the air was electric.

Emma lost track of the twists and turns, all her concentration centered on keeping up with Damien and David, who seemed almost drunk with happiness.

After one more sharp turn, they headed down a steep corridor with open doors every few feet. Dyads paired off and went through the openings.

"Here," said Damien. "This is ours."

He pulled her through an opening in the rock into a smaller tunnel. Claustrophobia quickened her heartbeat. Before the familiar panic took hold, the tunnel opened and Emma found herself in a large amphitheater. Shaped in a semi-circle, the gigantic room had a gradual slope with stairs separating the many rows. The rows were divided by boxed-in areas, each of which had two chairs in it. To Emma, they looked like box seats at the theater. High above, vines wove in an intricate pattern forming a ceiling that seemed to float in space. She couldn't see where it was attached to the rock walls.

Damien led her to a box about halfway up in the center. David took one of the chairs and Damien motioned for her to take the other. Emma obliged and Damien stood behind her chair.

Emma looked around. Beneath them on the main floor, a dais stood with eight wooden chairs upon it. No one was on the dais yet.

All around them Dyads were arriving from the different entry tunnels and taking their seats. Some stopped to hug others, some merely waved their greetings but all of them were smiling and laughing. Jubilant.

Emma's eyes were drawn to a flash of color to her left and she got her first look at a female Dyad. They were tall and slim like their male counterparts. And like the males, the females possessed an otherworldly beauty. This particular pair had hair the color of fine burgundy wine. It spilled in soft curls over their shoulders and down their backs to end at the waist. Even from this distance, Emma could tell the hair was silky soft. It seemed to shine and move with a life of its own.

They wore long robes the color of a fall afternoon, reds and browns flowing together in an explosion of color. The robes were cinched in by bone-colored corsets that set off their tiny waists and full breasts. And the way they moved. Emma had seen this type of movement in one other place—the ballet. When a ballet dancer moved her arm in an arc so perfect, so full of grace that it almost breaks your heart. That was what these women moved like, but unlike the ballet dancer who took years to master the technique, it seemed second nature to these female Dyads.

One of them moved a hand to brush hair out of her eyes. A simple thing really. She must make the same movement hundreds of times every day. But that one gesture, so full of grace and style, made Emma feel hopelessly inadequate.

How could Damien be attracted to clumsy, wobbly-legged Emma when there were women at home like this for him to choose from? No wonder the partners had thought their mating odd. She didn't even want to stand next to these beauties. Not that Emma thought of herself as unattractive. Realistically, Emma would give herself "pretty". Pretty, perky, comic-relief-sidekick. That was her. Never the romantic lead. She was the character who ended up with the hero's best friend, not the hero. The problem was in her little life-movie, Damien was the hero and she didn't measure up.

The bell rang again, this time so loud the fillings in Emma's teeth ached. Every seat in the amphitheater was full now. As she looked around, Emma marveled at the Dyad race. Beautiful, powerful, elegant, everything a human strove to be and yet it seemed bred into these creatures. Effortless.

After another sweep around the room, Emma noticed she was the only human present and an uneasy feeling settled in the pit of her stomach. She felt so out of place, sitting here with these perfect beings in nothing but a flimsy robe. Why hadn't she taken the time to wash and comb her hair? Or at least put some underwear on. Could everyone tell she didn't have any underwear on? They could tell just about everything else about a person, why not that?

The bell sounded again, interrupting her paranoid rambling. The assembled Dyads quieted, their attention drawn to the small opening behind the dais.

"What's happening?" Emma asked quietly.

Behind her, Damien bent down to whisper in her ear. "We await the Elders. They will introduce the new Dyad to the collective."

"How do they do that? Didn't you just find out that a Dyad is pregnant?"

"Our biology is not human, Emma. The new Dyad is already aware inside their mothers."

Emma turned to him. "You mean they know what's going on around them?"

"It is hard to explain. They are not fully conscious but the essence of who they are, who they will be, has taken form. We will be able to sense them and they, us."

Emma shook her head. "Do you remember being in your mother's womb?"

Damien got a faraway, wistful look. "Oh, yes. I was loved. From the moment I became aware, I knew love."

Emma shook her head again. It was so much to take in. What would it be like to be aware inside your mother? What would you do for nine months? Wouldn't it get boring? That is, if Dyads took nine months to cook, like humans. For all she knew, a Dyad could pop out at any minute, fully grown.

She turned back to Damien with a question. The look on his face stopped her. His attention was riveted to the floor of the amphitheater. Emma swiveled in her chair to catch the action. From behind the dais Dyad pairs started to file in. She counted four pairs or eight individuals, six males and two females. Blonds, brunettes, redheads, all tall and statuesque and all wearing elaborate ceremonial robes. These were the Dyad Elders. The leaders of the race. Emma looked for anything that would set them apart from the others but couldn't spot a difference. She wondered how one became an Elder. Were they the oldest, the most powerful?

Her eyes kept going back to the female Elders. Their hair was the color blonde that women everywhere spent a fortune trying to attain. It was golden yellow with highlights that caught the light and shimmered with a vitality right out of a Disney cartoon. They had high cheekbones, straight delicate noses and cornflower-blue eyes that sparkled with excitement as they looked over the crowd.

"Who are they?" Emma asked and pointed.

He smiled. "They are the Orchid Dyad. The oldest of the Elders."

"They're breathtaking."

Damien leaned in close and whispered, "Do not let their beauty fool you. The Orchids are shrewd, masters at political intrigue. They have been on the Elders' council for over a thousand years."

The Elders took their places in front of the tall wooden chairs on top of the dais. The bell sounded again. When the last tones faded away, leaving a ringing in Emma's ears, one of the male Dyad pairs stepped forward.

"Brothers and Sisters," the two Dyad brothers said in perfect unison. "We are complete again. Our Balance is restored. The eighth Fitzgerald Dyad has arrived among us.

We grieve the seventh and pray they have found their place in the Balance. They gave their lives for our race and will be entered into the Book as heroes."

Around the hall murmurs of agreement and head nodding distracted Emma for a moment. Applause started in the center and quickly spread. Soon it thundered as loudly as the bell.

The Elder Dyad raised their hands for silence. "We will feast the seventh at evening meal. Now, center yourselves and prepare to meet our new life."

All the Dyads lowered their heads and joined hands. Damien moved to the other side of Emma and took David's outstretched hand. The hall grew quiet as each Dyad looked into their brother's or sister's eyes. Power crackled all around Emma. It brushed against her skin in waves of electric current. Just when she thought she couldn't bear any more, it lessened and all the Dyads turned back to the dais.

The Elders on the dais parted in the center and turned to face the small entry cave in the rear. A male Dyad appeared in the opening. Each of them carried a tall wooden staff with a carved form on the top. Emma squinted, trying to make out what the carving represented, but she was too far away.

Something about this new Dyad felt different. As she watched the males approach, they seemed to float above the ground rather than walk upon it. They were the first Dyads she'd seen with short hair, almost a military buzz cut. Their robes were plain compared to the others, flat gray with no ornamentation. But even without the hair or fancy robes, there was a weight to these two. Even as far away as Emma was, she could feel their power. Who were they?

As if sensing her question, Damien leaned down and whispered in her ear, "They are of the Chaldean, our priest caste."

When they reached center stage they paused. The anticipation in the room revved to high. At the same moment, each of the priests raised his staff and struck the floor of the wooden dais. Instead of the loud bang she expected, a quiet, pure note emanated from the staffs. They struck again and the note increased in volume.

Emma had it now. The staffs were something like tuning forks set to middle C.

The staffs hit the floor for a third time. The note rang out almost as loud as the bell. The priests slowly lowered their staffs, pointing them out at the crowd, one to the left and the other to the right. Emma looked to the left where the staff pointed. The Dyads in that area reached their arms toward the staff and started to hum, matching the note.

"What—" Emma began but again Damien anticipated her.

"This is how the collective links. Each Dyad meets the note and joins in, until we are all one."

As the priests moved their staffs toward the center, more Dyads joined in. When the staffs pointed at their area, power hit Emma. The strongest yet. But instead of knocking her flat, it flowed into her, filling her with warmth and an energy that made every hair on her body stand at attention.

Beside her, Damien and David found the note and joined in. When the staffs reached the exact center and every Dyad was humming, Emma started to cry. The beauty of the note, the absolute community of the Dyad race humbled her. Each of them was in perfect union with the collective. What would it be like to belong to this race?

Unable to help herself, she found the note and hummed along. Both priests' heads whipped in her direction and she met the eyes of the one on the left. The note strangled in her throat. The only betrayal of emotion on the priest's face was a raised eyebrow. Emma wanted to hide under the chair. Had she spoiled everything by joining in?

After holding her gaze for a moment, the priest moved on, surveying the room.

They raised their staffs upright and the note faded away but the power held. In unison, every Dyad stood and, after a moment's hesitation, Emma followed suit.

"The power of the Balance is in you," the priests chanted.

"The power of the Balance is in us," the crowd replied.

"Do you accept this power and agree to live by its dictates?" the priests asked.

"We do," the Dyads answered.

"Will you welcome into our community your new brothers?"

"We will."

"Do you promise to nurture them and make them whole in the Balance?"

"We promise."

"Praise the Balance."

"Praise the Balance."

With this last, the prayers seemed to come to an end. Damien and David relaxed as did the rest of the assembly.

On the dais, the priests smiled and spoke. "Brothers and Sisters, welcome among us the eighth Fitzgerald Dyad." The priests parted and gestured to the opening behind the dais.

A female Dyad appeared followed closely by a set of males. All four of them had beatific smiles beaming out at the crowd. The females walked almost shyly to meet the priests who took their hands.

Each priest placed a hand on a female Dyad's abdomen. "Welcome Fitzgerald," they said.

The remaining tension in the room eased and all but the first row of Dyads sat down. The standing Dyads started to file down the stairs and line up at the bottom of the platform. One Dyad at a time climbed the stairs and went to the pregnant females. In the same manner as the priests, they placed their hands over the babies and welcomed them.

Conversations broke out all around Emma.

"Is it okay to talk now?" she asked.

"Yes," Damien replied, smiling down at her. "I bet you have many questions."

"Only a few hundred or so." She smiled back at him. "That was beautiful. Is it always like that when you come together?"

"Usually, especially for a welcome ceremony. It is a special event."

Emma turned back to the dais and watched the procession. "Your priests are kind of scary. They don't look or dress like the rest of you and they feel…heavier."

Damien sat on the chair arm. "To become Chaldean you must put aside all distractions. They devote themselves to the study of the Balance. There is no room in their lives for anything else. It is a noble undertaking."

"Are they more powerful than the rest of you?"

"Oh, yes. It takes centuries you understand to become Chaldean. And the older ones insist they are still novices of the Balance. They channel the power on another plane than the rest of us. They live apart from us on the other side of the mountain. Most of us have never been invited in."

"Reminds me of cloistered nuns or monks."

"Yes. They are something like that."

"Are there female Chaldean?" Emma asked.

All emotion left Damien's face. He seemed to shut down right in front of her. "Yes," he finally said. "Chaldean are both male and female."

Emma knew she had missed something but didn't want to pry. Besides, it was their turn to start for the dais.

"I'll wait here," she said.

Damien and David looked at each other for a moment and she knew they were mind-talking again.

"That's very rude, you know," she complained.

They turned to her. "Sorry, Emma," David said. "Force of habit."

Damien rose and reached for her hand. "You will come with us and welcome the Fitzgerald."

"Are you sure I'm welcome?" Emma didn't really want to join in the ritual. It was one thing to sit in the audience and watch. It was quite another to be center stage in the middle of it all. What if the Dyads rejected her? She didn't think she was ready for this.

"You are my mate and as such, must take part in the welcome." Damien offered her a hand up.

"I hope you know what you're doing," she said and accepted the offered hand.

All the way down the stairs Emma felt eyes watching her. She wasn't sure if it was her imagination or not but it didn't matter. Real or imaginary, her nerves couldn't take much more of this.

Her legs shook as she climbed the dais stairs and she made every effort not to look at the crowd. At the top, Damien placed her firmly between him and David and as a unit they walked to the pregnant females.

As the group immediately in front of them took their turn, Emma sneaked a look at the priests. It was as she'd feared. Both of them were staring at her. Her eyes darted left and right and took in all the Elders focused on her.

When their turn came both Damien and David put a hand around her waist and moved forward.

A look of puzzlement crossed over the pregnant female's faces. *It must be strange to see three instead of two approaching,* Emma thought.

A second before they reached the females a voice cried out from behind them.

"Stop."

Damien and David froze.

"There is a human among us. Do we welcome them now to our most sacred rituals?" the voice sneered.

Emma couldn't move, couldn't speak. It was her greatest fear come to life. The Dyads would never accept her. They would wipe her memory soon, she was sure of it.

"Peace," the priests said.

Not even a murmur from the crowd.

"Stewarts." The male Elder who had opened the ceremony moved in front of them. "You pick an odd time to test this with us. This welcome is not about you and your," they said, glancing at Emma, "circumstance. Why do you risk disrupting the flow at this joyous event?"

"We seek merely to join in the Welcome," David said.

"With a human? We have not allowed the human partners to attend. Why would you think this human is an exception?"

"Emma is my mate," Damien said.

"Exactly. Your mate." He put a heavy emphasis on the "your" and looked at David.

The crowd murmured. Emma couldn't tell if they were for them or against.

"Enough." The priests moved in front of them. "You will come with us, Stewart, and bring Little Emma." Without waiting for an answer, they led the way down the dais and out the back opening.

Still holding Emma tightly between them, Damien and David followed.

Emma didn't feel the ground beneath her feet or the two men who held her so close. She seemed to be having an out-of-body experience. All of her attention focused on the Dyad in front of them. Did they hold her fate in their scary hands? If they told Damien and David to wipe her memory would they have no choice but to obey? At this moment, she would have given anything to know the answer.

Once outside the theater, the Dyad turned left and led the way into a small but cozy waiting room. Emma suppressed a nervous giggle. Every theater had a green room. A quiet place the actors could prepare before their performance. Why shouldn't this place have one?

Before the priests could speak, Damien cut to the chase. "She is my mate. We took part in the mating ritual. Our joining is a true one."

"We know this is unusual," David added. "But I have felt Damien's mark on Emma. They are one in the Balance."

The priest on the right raised his hand for silence. "Again, Stewarts, you bring to the collective a dilemma. Perhaps it is inevitable when you spend so much of your time away from us. You have been cautioned before about acting first and then when the act is done, asking for acceptance."

"This was not Damien's fault," David argued. "None of us could have known the Fitzgerald would travel on. We were apart. He was alone."

"Listen to your words." The other half of the priest Dyad spoke up. "Damien's fault? It is the Stewart you speak of. Not Damien, not David, but Stewart. Your very words are foreign in nature to us."

"The human is frightened. What does she fear from us?" the other priest asked.

"Her name is Emma and she is my mate," Damien insisted.

The priest Dyad came together and faced them. "The situation is not what you believe it to be. Whether or not Emma is your mate is not solely the issue. Neither is the unbalance within your Dyad."

Damien and David shared a dark look. "What other situation could there be?" Damien asked.

Both priests advanced on Emma. When Damien tried to get between them, they merely waved him away. They reached her and she suppressed the need to run. After a moment, each of them placed a hand on her abdomen.

"Emma is pregnant. She carries a Dyad within her."

Chapter Ten

ꝏ

"I am not impressed."

Alex swept a hard gaze over the two goons standing at attention on the other side of the makeshift desk. Lieutenant Cronk, his feminine voice blessedly silent, stared over Alex's shoulder. The resigned look on the large man's face told Alex he was used to getting his balls busted. The other man, General Reisdorph, leader of this band of merry men, didn't share Cronk's acceptance of the situation. Sure, he knew how to stand and take it, but he couldn't hide the eye twitch that happened whenever Alex got in a really good zinger about their monumental incompetence.

Reisdorph was the picture of every war movie commander Alex remembered from his youth. Almost as tall as the giant Cronk, with a granite jaw, gray buzz-cut hair, and not an ounce of fat on him. Alex put his age somewhere on the bad side of fifty. Clearly he was fighting the ageing process with countless pushups and fight routines. The man even had a scar running from his right ear to his chin. As he looked into the implacable face, Alex wondered exactly what kind of career path had landed Reisdorph here. Had he been forced to retire from the standard Armed Forces? Had he been so addicted to command that he couldn't give it up? Or was it simply the money that motivated him? When his contact had put Alex in touch with Reisdorph's group, one of the many conditions had been there be no questions about where these men came from or who they reported to. Alex had accepted all conditions. Desperation made for strange bedfellows.

Alex put his fingertips on the desk and stood, leaning toward the men for effect. "You haven't been able to complete even the simplest assignment. When I hired you, the timeline you gave me for—what did you call it?—oh yes, mission end, was two weeks. Two weeks to locate a Dyad and capture it." He pounded the desk with his fist. "Two weeks," he screamed.

The pain in his hand shot up Alex's arm and his temper threatened to rob him of all reason. It scared him. He knew what happened when he lost it. Sometimes during one of these ranting sessions he couldn't remember later what he'd said. All he could remember was the red-hot fury. He couldn't afford to lose control now. Not with Jenny lying in a hospital bed with Alex Jr. struggling to stay alive inside her.

He breathed in, pulling the cool air deep into his overheated body. When he was confident he could speak in a reasonable tone, he came out from behind the desk and stood between the two men.

"Two weeks," he said again, impressed with his calm façade. "Refresh my memory, General. How long has it been since 'mission onset'?" Alex enjoyed throwing another of their inane military terms at them.

General Reisdorph's eye twitched again and he swallowed so loudly Alex could follow the spit down his throat. "Two months," the general finally eked out.

Alex smiled, feeling every muscle in his face protest. "Not exactly two months, General. My calculation, civilian though it may be, puts it at nine weeks and three days. I thought the military were more exact in their reporting."

"Mr. Ward, we have done everything—"

Alex cut him off. "Maybe I don't understand how for-hire military squads work. I was under the impression that I pay you forty million dollars, tell you what I need done, and you." He sent his index finger into Reisdorph's chest. "Get…it…done." With each word, he drilled his finger harder into the general.

Reisdorph broke attention and blocked Alex's next jab. "If you had briefed us on the extent of the hostile's powers, we would have been better equipped to confine and capture,"

Reisdorph said. Using a strength fine-tuned by years of Spartan military training, he forced Alex's hand away from his chest.

Alex knew he'd never win a knock-down-drag-out with this guy. He fell back on the number one rule of all transactions such as these. The man with the money ran the show.

"I told you everything Lambert told me," Alex said.

"Maybe that's true." The general moved around the desk and sat in the only chair in the room. Alex decided not to object. It was his desk after all. After he sat, he began placing all of the items on his desk that Alex had disturbed back in their correct places.

"If we had known the true extent of their power, we would have approached the mission differently." He slid a pen back into its holder and angled it for easy reach. "That thing knew our every move. When we had it cornered in that basement, it knew we had it. It did the only thing it could do to avoid capture. Self termination."

"You sound like you admire it," Alex said.

The general snorted, picked up a thick stack of reports and tapped them into alignment. "Admire, no," he began. "But respect?" He nodded. "I can respect what that creature did. It followed a code, a discipline. Faced with no other option, it took the soldier's way out."

Alex leaned over the desk and put his hand on the reports, undoing the general's careful straightening. "And as a soldier it never occurred to you the Dyad would be so honor bound?"

"I can assure you, Mr. Ward, we will not underestimate these beings again." He pulled the reports out from under Alex's hand and tapped them into place again. This time, he put them in a drawer, out of reach.

"I thought the trail had run dry. How will you locate another Dyad pair? Even with all this." Alex went to the window and gestured. "You haven't been able to find where they live." He looked out at all the mobile vehicles outside arranged in a complicated pattern to create the illusion of a group of RV enthusiasts on vacation in a campground eighty miles inland from Manhattan. From the outside each RV looked harmless. Just a bunch of senior citizens, a few of whom were placed in lawn chairs or who stood grilling their four o'clock dinners, scattered around the camp. But inside was another world entirely.

Two of the recreational vehicles housed every weapon known to man, carefully tucked away behind false walls. Five more came together to form the command center with state of the art computers that could hack into any country's software. From the Department of Motor Vehicles to the Department of Defense, these guys had access to it all. And at a moment's notice, they could pack up everything and be on the run. A frickin' military circus.

But even with all this they still hadn't found the Dyad home city.

"We'll find them, Mr. Ward. It's only a matter of time."

"How the hell much time?" Alex wanted to scream at the idiot but managed to control his voice. The only person here who knew about Jenny and Alex Jr. was Dr. Lambert and that old fool knew if he breathed a word about them, it would be his last.

As if on cue, Lambert burst in waving papers in each hand. "I knew it," he cried. "I knew we'd find the trail in Michigan. Didn't I tell you so, Alex? Didn't I?" The old man shook with excitement, his face a mixture of condescension and justification.

For his part, Alex didn't care who found the trail even if it meant Lambert lording it over him. He needed the Dyads found and soon.

Lambert elbowed his way in between Cronk and Alex and slapped a page on the desk. "I knew they had to be staying somewhere in the upper peninsula of Michigan. They couldn't appear out of nowhere. They had to have a hidey-hole close to Meir Industries."

Lambert referred to his former employer, Meir Industries, headquartered on the shore of Lake Superior. He'd tangled with the Dyads months ago over unsafe practices at the chemical manufacturer. The only reason Lambert was walking around free was because the Dyads had wiped all memory of them from his mind. But the old man had tricked them. Seeing what was coming, Lambert had left detailed diaries about his run-in with the Dyads in several safe deposit boxes. He'd also set up a delayed delivery, which sent his clueless self to the boxes after the memory wipe. Not bad for a befuddled old has-been.

It was important because it proved one thing to Alex. The creatures were not infallible.

The Dyads had cost Lambert his reputation, not to mention almost a billion in profits from a fertilizer he'd developed. It hadn't mattered to Lambert that his fertilizer would eventually poison the land, rendering it useless for crops. No, Lambert had figured by the time that happened he'd be on a tropical island, sipping an umbrella drink, with big-breasted women at his beck and call.

The Dyads had intervened, spoiling Lambert's plans and now all the old fart could think of was revenge. Well, revenge and harnessing the Dyad power so he could live forever.

Alex didn't care what Lambert's motivation was. He still needed him. Hadn't Lambert just proved it by finding the trail?

"What do you have, Alphonse?" Alex asked.

General Reisdorph picked up the single sheet of paper and scanned it. "A property tax statement?"

Lambert laughed smugly. "Yes, gentlemen. It seems even the Dyads must pay their taxes." He snatched the paper out of

Reisdorph's grip and thrust it at Alex. "Look who's listed on the bill."

"Aiden Rawlings. Holy Christ. This is it," Alex said as his heart sped up.

"I knew it," Lambert said again. "They think because they wipe the memory of everyone they run into that they don't even bother to use a false identity." He turned to the general. "Aiden Rawlings is the leader of the humans who work with them. He brought those things into Meir Industries and destroyed all my plans. He blindly follows them, doing whatever they ask, siding against his own kind. They all thought they got away clean. But I'll show them. I'll—"

Alex had heard this particular rant from Lambert too many times. He cut him off. "We know, Alphonse. We know. You're preaching to the choir." He turned to Reisdorph. "How do we use this information?"

The general nodded and grabbed the paper. "What else have you got, Doctor?"

Lambert jumped and looked at the paper held tightly in his left hand. He'd been so wrapped up in his tirade, he must have forgotten it. "It's the real estate listing on that address. It has all the information about the estate. It's an eighty-room mansion built on a secluded cove. No neighbors in sight. Perfect for a large group of people who want to hide, don't you think? Close enough to populated areas to slip in and out quickly but far enough away not to draw attention."

Energy ripped through the room. *At last,* Alex thought. They had something to work with. It seemed the Dyads, just like these military men, needed a command post to run things from and the old doctor had found it.

An aura of authority came over the general. He stood taller, his eyes bright with excitement. "Cronk," he barked.

Cronk, who had been standing at attention this whole time like a mindless robot, came alive. "Yes, Sir," he barked back. Cronk's bark sounded like a little girl scolding her dolls.

"Take this to ops. Have them run the address through every possible avenue of discovery. I want satellite pictures in under an hour."

"Will do, Sir." Cronk took the paper and started for the door.

"And, Cronk." The general stopped him. "I'm ordering a bug out. We are on the road in under fifteen. Mobile plan B."

"End coordinates?" Cronk asked.

The general shook his head and looked down at the desk, searching for patience. "The address on the paper you are holding, Lieutenant," he said quietly.

"Yes, Sir," Cronk replied and left the room.

"Not a big thinker, your Lieutenant Cronk," Alex quipped. He couldn't help needling the general one more time. After all, what did Alex have to show for his forty million so far? A pile of ash, that's what.

"He'll follow orders," Reisdorph said. "They all will. The whole party is moving to Michigan. You two coming along for the ride?"

"Absolutely," Lambert almost purred.

Alex thought of the hospital room again. He went to the window. Outside everyone had sprung into action. The general's orders about bugging out must have reached them. The fake senior citizens were moving with a surprising agility, packing up chairs and grills and rolling up the shade awnings.

These guys were good. Alex would give them that. They would be on the road headed west in a quarter of an hour, all trace of them gone.

"Are you in, Mr. Ward?" the general asked.

Alex turned and looked at the two men. Excitement bled off them. He should go with them. He knew that. But Jenny?

"I have to make a call," he finally said.

Reisdorph came out from behind the desk. "You can use this office. I want to check with ops." As he passed Lambert, he grabbed his arm. "Come with me, Doctor. I want to hear everything you know about this Aiden Rawlings."

"Of course. Of course." Lambert allowed Reisdorph to pull him to the door. "Alex," he said in a voice so full of pity Alex flinched. "If you need anything. If there's anything I can do."

"Get out," Alex snapped. He didn't want the doctor's pity. He didn't need it.

Once they were gone, he pulled out his cell phone and dialed the hospital. It took a few minutes for the operator to locate Dr. Walji but he finally came on the line.

"This is Dr. Walji, Mr. Ward. How can I help you?"

"How's Jenny? Any change?"

"At the moment Jenny is resting comfortably. Her condition has not altered since you saw her."

"Good. That's good," Alex said.

"If that's all, Mr. Ward. I'm in the middle of rounds."

"No, wait. I have to leave town."

The phone was quiet for a long moment. "I don't think that's advisable at this time," Walji said in a careful tone.

"It can't be helped," Alex replied.

Walji sighed into the phone. "Let me be clear, Mr. Ward. Your wife's condition could deteriorate at any moment. If you leave town, there might not be time for you to get back before…" He trailed off.

"Before she dies," Alex finished for him.

"Yes. I'm afraid so."

Alex weighed his options. The Dyads were still Jenny's only chance. Modern medicine had failed her just as it had done his parents. If he went with Reisdorph and the others, he could hurry things along. Make spot decisions. Protect his interests. He had to go.

"It can't be helped," Alex said. "I have to go."

"Alex," the doctor whispered. "You're not going to come back with a new heart? Because if that's what you're planning, I have to tell you, no one at the hospital will be involved."

"No. Damn it, Walji. That's not the plan. I'll be in Michigan. A short plane ride away. Let me know the instant anything changes."

"Wait, don't hang up," Walji pleaded.

"Look, Doctor. I've said I'm not after a heart. You don't have to worry."

"It's not that, Mr. Ward."

"Then what?"

Another sigh. "In the event that Jenny's condition worsens quickly and it is impossible for you to be here, I need to know what you want done."

A lump rose in Alex's throat. He knew what the doctor was asking. The time had come for him to make a choice. The choice. Did he tell the doctor to kill Jenny to save Alex Jr. or let Alex Jr. die along with Jenny? He knew what Jenny would say: "Have you lost your mind, Alex? For the love of God, save our child. I've had almost forty years of life, the happiest of which were spent with you. For me, Alex. Save him for me."

A switch clicked in Alex's brain and all emotion drained out of him. Reason took over. One thing became crystal clear. If he chose Jenny over Alex Jr. and by some miracle, either from the Dyads or God himself, she lived; she would never forgive him for killing their child. It was as simple as that.

Alex gripped the phone tighter. He knew what he had to tell the doctor.

"Save the child."

Chapter Eleven

ꟃ

"Emma is pregnant. She carries a Dyad within her."

Damien stared at the priests standing so calmly with their hands on Emma's abdomen. It was as if they had just told him the weather would be fine today or what would be served at evening meal. So calm they were, so matter of fact. Didn't they know those few words had changed everything?

Instinctively, Damien's mind reached for his brother's. He linked with David and felt his other half's astonishment. But underneath David's surprise, in a place he fought to shield from Damien, he found—envy, with a heavy dose of resentment. David endeavoring to shield his emotions from their collective mind was a thing so foreign, Damien didn't know how to react. Even though they were linked, Damien felt apart from his brother, alone. Not wanting the priests to notice anything amiss between them, he severed the link.

A small cry from Emma brought his attention to her white face and wide, frightened eyes. He cursed himself. He'd done it again. Left her alone, unconnected, in a situation she could not possibly comprehend. When would he start putting her needs before his own?

Damien crossed to her and gently pulled her out of the priest's grasp. She clung to him with a desperation that intensified his shame at his neglect.

"They're wrong, right?" she whispered. "I'm human. Luke told me it's impossible for Dyads and humans to have a baby." She fisted his shirt and pulled his face to her level. "So, the priests are wrong, right?"

So many emotions broadcast off Emma, Damien had trouble separating one from another. He sensed fear first, followed by shock and then, just as David had done, she tried to shield a feeling of—hope. He remembered then that the human doctors had told Emma she could never conceive a child. Dear God. What had he done?

"Whatever happens, I am with you." He kissed her forehead and then turned to the priests. He knew better than to doubt their pronouncement. They were never wrong in matters such as these. If the Chaldean priests said Emma had a child within her—his child—it was so.

From behind him, David spoke. "How is this possible? Only the Balance can choose where a Dyad life will grow. Only the purest are chosen for the honor. It has always been so."

Almost imperceptibly, the priests nodded. "You are correct," the priest on the right said. "The holy Balance knows where life should begin and bestows the blessing to the worthy. Sometimes we wonder at the choice, but we do not question, we do not presume to understand."

David came to stand next to Damien. "But how?" he asked again. He looked at Emma, put a calming hand on her shoulder and gave her a reassuring squeeze. He turned back to the priests. "When we were first allowed to go out among humans, you addressed this question. You told us it could never happen. You allowed us to couple with human women to fully study them."

Identical ironic smiles lit up the priests' faces. "It is not possible," they said together. The brother on the right continued alone. "Or has not been. The Chaldean are but novices in the ways of the Balance. We study the past and the present. We cannot study the future, and there." He motioned to Emma still holding on to Damien. "There is the future."

Within his arms, a shudder ran through Emma. She took a deep breath, pushed out of his embrace and went to stand in front of the priests.

"Look, Sir…err…Sirs," she began. "I mean no disrespect to your…priest knowledge but just exactly how many pregnant human women have you been around?"

"None."

Some of the tension left her body. She put a hand on her waist and cocked a hip. "So you have no experience with human reproduction?"

"None," he said again.

"Ever read about it or seen an informative documentary maybe?"

"Some of the Chaldean have but my brother and I have not chosen that field of study."

"So, you admit. You don't have the knowledge to make this assumption." Emma let out a relieved sigh. "In other words, you don't know what you're talking about."

"Emma," Damien warned. No one spoke to the Chaldean in this manner. No Dyad ever questioned their knowledge. It simply wasn't done.

Without turning, Emma raised a hand and made a be-quiet gesture in his direction. At a loss what to do, he shared an astonished look with David.

"Little Emma—" the priest began.

"Don't call me that," Emma cut him off. "I don't particularly like it and anyway, you don't know me well enough to use it."

Confusion colored the priests' faces. They looked first at Damien and David and then back to Emma. "Little Emma. That is not your name?"

She turned her gaze to Damien. "Are they yanking me?" she asked.

Despite the situation, Damien smiled. He loved a good culture clash. "No, Emma. They are not."

"Why would we yank at you at such a time?" The priests seemed genuinely upset.

Emma raised her hands. "We've gotten off the subject. Just call me Emma. That'll do."

"Emma," the priest said carefully. "We admit we have no firsthand knowledge of the human reproductive process. However—"

"Stop," she cut him off again and Damien cringed. She was playing with fire and didn't know it.

"Well, let me educate you," she said. "It's impossible to tell if I'm pregnant. Damien and I only..." She blushed furiously and shot him a scathing glance. "Damien and I only made me being pregnant a possibility a little over twenty-four hours ago. And despite what the nuns told me in Catholic school, sometimes you can make love without it resulting in a pregnancy. And from what I know about my body and its cycle." She paused.

Damien hadn't thought it possible but Emma's blush colored to a deeper hue. She was not having an easy time of this. It was too personal, too intimate.

"It's highly unlikely I would have conceived," she continued. "Not impossible, but highly unlikely." She gave a dismissive shrug. "So, you're wrong."

Damien thought it best to jump in. "Emma means no disrespect. She is merely stating what she believes to be the truth. Moreover, she is correct in her assessment. It would be impossible for a human woman to know of a pregnancy so soon. We shared love for the first time yesterday at the Dyad safe house and then again today, we joined in the ritual."

The priests nodded and turned to Emma. "We understand now. We will allow you are correct, Emma. A mere human would not have knowledge of a pregnancy so soon. However, what you now carry within you is not human. It is part Dyad and it is that part we claim knowledge of. As Chaldean, we can sense new life."

The priests went to Emma and put their hands on her abdomen again. After a moment, they smiled. "There is new life here. You carry the first Dyad-Human coupling."

"Abomination," someone shouted from the door.

Damien turned and his heart sank. The Brown Dyad filled the doorway. The look of disgust on their faces heralded their stand on the pregnancy. Perfect, just what they needed to make the situation worse.

"As always, Stewart," the Brown on the left spat the words out, "you act without permission from the Elders and debase our race yet again. But we do not think even the Elders, with their progressive bent, will allow this." He motioned to Emma as if she were something he would scrape off his shoe. "This half ape thing to contaminate the purity of the Dyad collective."

Anger rose in Damien. Who were these two to question his actions? If it was left to the Browns and their ilk, the Dyads would hide behind their shields and cross their fingers that the world would go on. While humans made war and contaminated the planet with pollution, they would close their eyes to the suffering of the land and animals as if it didn't concern them. They looked on Emma, his Emma, as a sub-creature, below the lowest of all animal life. An abomination of nature because she could think and talk and reason.

Damien stepped between the Browns and Emma. David joined him. "What business is this of yours, Brown?" they said together.

One of the Browns held his hand up as if to shield himself. "We wish for no part in this. But just as you have done countless times in the past five hundred years, you make this our business. Studying the humans to learn how best to deal with them, that we saw a need for. How better to keep them away from us? But first to partner up with them. Sharing knowledge and Balance with them. That we never agreed with." They turned to the priests. "We warned of this. We warned if you and the Elders allowed the human partners among us, more liberties would follow." They turned back to Damien and David. "But this? We never imagined you would fall so far. Even you. How could you bring this among us?"

Damien tempered his rage. The last thing he needed was to show strong emotion in front of the Browns. It would only serve to prove their point. "I have chosen Emma as my mate. The Balance allowed us to become part of the mating ritual. Are you putting your opinions above the Balance?"

The Browns sneered at him. "How do we know the Balance let you in? Humans can produce their offspring in any rutting. For that matter, this human could have been pregnant before you ever touched her. They do not follow our ways. They lie at the slightest provocation."

Both he and David tensed. The Browns had no love for them. They had been on the opposite side of every question as long as Damien could remember, but no Dyad would so insult the mate of another. The Browns were spitting in their faces and neither he nor David could let this pass.

He saw it then and paused. The Browns were deliberately provoking them. They wanted this to go to the next step as soon as possible. All disputes were taken to the Elders. It was a trap. They'd probably been planning this for months. True, Emma's pregnancy was a situation they couldn't possibly predict, but they would use it as the impetus to advance their plan. They knew they would have the advantage. The Browns had had years to build alliances within the Diarchy. Damien and David had spent the better part of the last five hundred years away from the intrigue that came in an isolated community.

Quickly, he linked with David and shared his suspicions. David concurred. They needed some time before this question came before the Elders. Time to assess the temperature of the collective on Human—Dyad relations. Before they could think of a stalling tactic, the Browns spoke, confirming the plot.

"I think we should go immediately to the Elders—"

"Wait a minute," Emma broke in.

Damien could have kissed her.

"Not that it matters because I'm not pregnant, or that it's any of your business." She looked at the priests who still had their hands on her. "Let me go, fellas, will you?" They complied and Emma went to stand between Damien and David and the Browns.

"Up until yesterday, I was a virgin. So there's no way I could have been pregnant. Not that I am now."

"You see," the Browns scoffed. "Lies, always lies. Human women never reach your age as virgins."

Emma put her hands on her hips and drew herself up to her full height. "I may be a mere human but I know bad manners when I see them, and you two are just plain rude."

Astonished, the Browns looked around Emma to Damien. "Your human needs controlling," they said.

"That's it," Emma said and whirled to face the priests. "Do we need these two involved in our discussion? Didn't they follow us in here, uninvited, and start insulting me without the slightest provocation? You two are the peacekeepers, right? Well, do your job and get them away from me before I forget that I'm a lady and I tell them exactly where to go and how to get there."

The room froze. No Dyad had ever ordered a Chaldean so. Damien looked at the priests and couldn't tell from their expressions how much she'd offended them. He shot a quick glance at the Browns and their faces were an open book. They stared at Emma with a mixture of disgust and hate. He would have to be very careful never to leave Emma alone with them.

After the priests had weighed her words for a full minute, they came forward. "Emma is correct," they said to the Browns. "You were not invited into this discussion and yet you left the welcome ceremony. Why, Brown?"

The first sign of unease crossed the Browns' faces. "We came to find out what new problem the Stewarts have brought upon us."

The priests shook their heads. "This was more important to you than welcoming a new life among us?"

All emotion left the Browns. They knew they were walking on thin ice. "We think it of great importance that the Stewart not be allowed—"

The priests held up a hand, silencing them. "We suggest you go to your quarters and meditate, Brown. For a Dyad to behave so is not natural. The Stewarts, whatever they have done, are your brothers and should be treated as such. Also, for a Dyad who thinks so little of the human race, we find you are acting quite like them."

The Browns started to say something but again, the priests raised their hands for silence. "Take yourselves away and reflect on what we have said. You are Dyad. There is no room for hate within you."

Although they looked like they might explode with anger, the Browns turned and left.

"Am I mistaken, or did you just send them to their room for a time-out?" Emma asked the priests.

They smiled at her. "Yes, Emma. Even the best of us strays from the path now and then. The Brown, with all their faults, are still a part of the whole. Without them, we would be incomplete."

Damien breathed a sigh of relief. Emma, without realizing it, had bought them some much needed time. But they couldn't hurry away. The priests were not done with them.

Both priests turned to Emma, who moved closer to Damien as if she knew something bad was about to happen. "Now, Emma," the right priest said. "Would you allow us to prove to you that you are pregnant?"

Emma's hand reached for Damien and he took it. "How exactly will you do that? And I mean exactly," she asked.

"We will link our mind with yours, take you into your body and introduce you to the life within you."

The hand in his tightened, signaling her aversion to such an act.

"Emma is not used to linking. So far, she has only linked with me and only to ease her through the mating ritual. She has had no training."

All expression left the priests' faces. "Are you refusing our link?" they asked.

Emma sighed. "No, I guess not. But can Damien come with?" she asked.

The priests spread their arms wide, indicating the three of them. "All are welcome and we think it best since this involves David as well as Damien."

Damien searched for any way to make this easier for Emma. "Emma and I will link first and bring David in then you may join us. Is that acceptable?"

After the priests nodded, Damien turned to Emma.

She licked her lips nervously. "I still say they're wrong."

He smiled and took her face in his hands. "It is easier if you close your eyes."

"Whatever you say," she said and closed her eyes.

Damien sent his mind out to hers. Even without the power of the mating ritual swirling around, he found it as easy to link with Emma as it was with David. It should not be so. A part of him stowed that information away to study later and another part merged with Emma and evened out her overwrought emotions. When they had achieved a level of calm, Damien reached for David and found his brother waiting. He carefully introduced David's mind to Emma's, smiling at the sensation of his two favorite people sharing a link with him.

Are you ready to link with the priests? he asked both of them.

Now fully linked, Damien could control Emma's fear. He and David let reassurance flow through their link. They surrounded the Emma essence, making it very clear she was safe with them. Nothing bad could get through them to threaten her. They were one.

With the link under control, Damien raised a hand to signal the priests. Instantly, the priest mind was with them. Damien had always marveled at the ease with which the Chaldean were able to link with others. To them, it was as simple as breathing. He felt their elevated power and confidence and knew they were in good hands.

He allowed this feeling to flow to Emma, asking her to accept his knowledge of the situation. Her body trembled against him and he realized even linked, Emma was frightened.

The priest mind felt her fear as well. Their essence swept over them, sending calm through the link. It was impossible to resist their power. In a matter of moments, Emma's body quieted against him.

Come with us now, the priests thought to them. *We will introduce you to your offspring.*

Their power wrapped around the shared Damien, David, Emma link and they effortlessly pulled them into Emma's body. First to her beating heart, then the lungs and stomach and finally, her womb.

Out of nowhere another mind appeared. Innocence washed over them. Wonder overcame them. Here was an essence so new, so pure, their mind was afraid to touch it.

Welcome, little one, the priest mind said and sent love and reassurance to the new essence.

Tentatively, the infant mind reached out, testing this new ability. Too young to form words, the little one explored in the only way it could. It was like a sponge, soaking up emotions and knowledge from everyone it touched.

For the Damien link, it was love at first touch. A boy. A son. Their son. The Stewarts had always envied those who were chosen to parent. Emma had thought she would never be able to bear children. The same accident that had left her paralyzed had also left her barren. But now here they all were, parents to this perfect being.

They sent love to their son and just as parents of any newborn, played with him. They cooed and tried to make him laugh. They told him how wonderful he was, how perfect.

Wait, the priest thought. *Come out, little one. Have no fear.*

Peeking out from behind their son's essence hid another. A little girl.

Twins.

* * * * *

Pregnant?

Twins?

Emma reverently ran her hands over her abdomen for the hundredth time in as many minutes. After the mind-blowing session with the priests, she had asked for some much needed time alone to take it all in. There was no doubt left in her mind. How could there be when her mind had touched her children? Her perfect children. This mind-meld, trip-through-your-own-body deal took the ultrasound to a whole new level.

The love she felt for the little ones had been immediate and all encompassing. In an instant, her world had changed. One touch of those precious beings and Emma knew a clarity of purpose she'd never felt before. She would do anything to keep them safe. Anything.

She shook her head, trying to clear her racing brain. Looking around Damien's bedroom, she searched for one thing that would remind her of her life before all this. She needed grounding, to find Emma again. Not Damien's mate or the vessel of the first Human-Dyad cross, but plain old Emma.

Across the room on his dresser, she noticed foreign tools. A set of wooden fork-like objects that fit into each other and formed a circle. Glass balls set atop a metal base that balanced on another ball, defying gravity. A coiled fuzzy rope with a sponge on the end sat next to a comb thingy with a three-foot handle. It was impossible from their appearance to determine what they were used for.

The wall hangings had woven patterns Emma had never seen. The blanket underneath her was made from a cloth she'd never touched before. All was foreign—not human.

Her eyes settled on the table by the bed. Books stood stacked in precarious towers, ready to topple at the softest touch. Typical Damien. Never far from a book. She picked up the top one and smiled. Yet another copy of *Moby Dick.* Isn't that where all this had started? Five copies of *Moby Dick.* It seemed years ago that she had been in the library cataloging books for something to do. A part of her desperately wanted to go back to that time, before the mating, before the children.

God help her. Was she ready to be a mother? And not just any mother. No, she was the über-mother to a new race of beings.

The sunlight brought in by the smaller tunnels started to fade. Movement on the wall to her left startled Emma. The vines covering the rock walls were shifting.

Starting at the center of the wall, the vines drew back as if they were curtains pulled by an invisible cord. They moved first apart and then up until they were grouped in a tangled mass close to the ceiling.

Her eyes darted around the room and she saw the same bizarre movement from all the vines. Uneasy, she sat up straighter and pulled the covers to her chin. The vines had reminded her of sitting in a movie theater as the lights dimmed and the curtain went up. She always experienced a few shaky moments as her claustrophobia and fear of the dark kicked in.

As the sunlight faded her heart sped up. Soon the room would be completely dark. What if Dyads didn't need light? For all she knew, they could see in the dark. She had to get out while she could still see but her body wouldn't move.

Memories of her time in the cave when she was little crashed in on her. It had been so dark she hadn't been able to see anything. Like now, she hadn't been able to move. The only sense that worked was her hearing. Surrounding her in the black, she could hear little scuttling noises, always getting closer and closer. She still bore the scars on her feet and legs from where she'd been bitten. At least she had until her time sharing energy with Damien. She hadn't thought to check but just like her chicken pox scars, they had probably disappeared too. Too bad Damien couldn't cure the emotional scars as easily.

Panic almost had her. She opened her mouth to scream for help and then paused. The room was getting lighter. She looked around for the source and noticed a glow coming from the walls. The vines had hidden a moss-like plant. As her heart slowed, the glow from the walls intensified until the entire room was lit with warm, amber light.

Leave it to the Dyads to use nature in such a way. But where in nature did you find moss like this? The only glow-in-the-dark moss Emma had ever seen cast an eerie green light. This wall-hugging plant gave off a light softer than candlelight but twice as bright.

How had she not noticed this transformation last night? She remembered what she and Damien had been doing all last evening and felt a blush. She'd been too busy to notice.

The door swung wide and Luke sauntered in, followed somewhat hesitantly by Wulfgar.

Luke flopped across the bottom of the bed. Emma raised her knees to make room for him and sat with her back against the headboard.

"So, Fertile Myrtle, I hear you're knocked up," Luke said.

Wack! Wulfgar's beefy hand moved so fast, Emma missed it. But the effect was obvious. Luke lay flattened against the mattress.

Wulfgar loomed over him. "Watch your mouth, you Scottish ass. Show some respect."

Luke rose to one elbow, using the other hand to rub his chin. "That hurt, Wulf. Just like you to take a man unawares."

"Unaware is your constant state. A toddler could take you unaware."

"Can it, big guy. Don't you have something to say?" Using his head, he indicated Emma.

"Yes, yes I do." Wulfgar straightened to his full height and looked at his boots. "Emma," he began in a rehearsed tone. "What I said in the common room about you was unforgivable." His eyes came up and he seemed to search for something. Finally, he looked to Luke for help.

"And I wanted," Luke prompted.

The Viking nodded and turned back to Emma. "And I wanted to apologize again for the offense I have given you. I am ready to take any punishment you deem fit to make this right between us."

Emma smiled. She had a soft spot for Wulfgar. He could flatten most people with a wave of his hand, but she'd never met a more kindhearted person. Well, maybe Alice, but Wulfgar was a close second. "I told you before. It's okay. Really, Wulfgar." She put her hand on his. "Let it go."

"There, see, you big idiot," Luke said. "I told you Emma wasn't upset about what you said. You can stop fretting now."

Wulfgar took a deep breath and sent a murderous look at Luke. "I do not fret. Women fret." He turned back to Emma. "I must make amends in some way. If ever you have need of me, I will be there. You have my word-bond on it." He spit into his hand and held it out to her.

Knowing what was expected, Emma spit into her own hand and clasped Wulfgar's. "Done," she said.

"Done," echoed Wulfgar. A tension seemed to seep out of him.

Emma sighed. "I don't suppose you could dig me up a cheeseburger and fries?" she asked wistfully.

His face fell. "We only brought dried meat. But I could grind some of that up for you."

"I'm kidding, Wulfgar."

"So," Luke broke in. "A mom huh? Bet you didn't see that coming."

Emma laughed. It felt good to laugh. "No, I sure didn't."

"Well don't fret." He emphasized the last word and Wulfgar cringed. "We're just the advance guard. Eleanor and Jude should be here soon. Damien sent for them but they've been…busy with Jacob and Aiden. You can have a nice girl-talk gab session soon. You know, feelings and crap like that."

"Good, that'll be nice."

Luke stood and took her hand, suddenly serious. "Emma, whatever happens, we are with you. Not only Wulfgar and me, but all the human partners. We stand ready to protect you and the children. You are a part of us now."

Emma swallowed past a lump in her throat. "Thank you. I may need to take you up on that."

"Besides," Luke said with a twinkle in his eye. "Think of the clothes you get to wear. And none of this mommy-plus stuff. No, we are going designer all the way. I hear Armani is bringing out a new line any day. Remember, I'm the clothes expert in the group. You have to let me dress you."

Emma remembered Luke was the disguise expert of the human partners. He had a natural affinity for it. She'd never known a straight guy who loved clothes as much as Luke. She supposed it was part of what made him so good at his job.

"The last thing on Emma's mind is clothes," Wulfgar chimed in. "Why do you always reduce everything to what a person wears on their back?"

"Listen to him." Luke cocked his head in Wulfgar's direction. "He'd be perfectly happy in an animal skin that some poor woman had to chew on for a month." He shook his head. "Vikings. The first race to make the worst-dressed list."

Muffled voices from the next room rose in volume. Some type of argument was going on. Luke and Wulfgar shared a dark look.

"How's it going out there?" Emma asked.

Luke shrugged. "A lot of debate about Dyad politics and power struggles. What Damien and David's next move should be. All very intriguing and boring as hell."

"Who's all here?"

"The usual suspects. The Stewarts, the Goddards, the Matthias, the Dobervichs and a few more Dyad pairs you've never met. And all their partners. It's pretty crowded out there."

"Sounds ominous." Unable to help herself, Emma put her hands protectively over the children again. "How bad is this going to get, Luke?"

"You're not to worry about any of this," Luke insisted.

"That's right," Wulfgar added. "Leave it to our Dyads to work this out. They know what's best."

"Exactly." Luke slapped Wulfgar's back. "Well said, my friend. We should let you rest now. I'll send Eleanor and Jude in when they get here."

Once they were gone, Emma reflected on male-female roles. Did they really expect her to lie around like some animated incubator while her children's future was decided? If that was the case, they had greatly underestimated her. These were her children, hers and Damien's, and nobody, not the Elders or the Priests or the Browns, were going to tell her what to do about them. True, she had nothing figured out yet but she didn't doubt she'd come up with a brilliant plan.

It was time to stop hiding and let these guys know who was running the show. She got out of bed and went to her pack. Rummaging through it, she picked out a change of clothes and her toiletry bag. The adjoining bathroom had a tub and sink. No showers at the Diarchy, and God only knew how the water came in. After a quick bath, she dressed, fixed her hair and makeup and felt ready to face the music.

Halfway to the door, she stopped as Eleanor and Jude came in. Eleanor didn't hesitate. She rushed to Emma and drew her into a rib-crushing hug. When Emma groaned, Eleanor gasped and released her.

"How stupid of me. I didn't hurt you, did I?" she asked.

"No, I'm fine," Emma said and glanced at Jude who put a tray loaded with food and drinks on the table. When Jude turned, she stood back, seemingly unsure what to do. Emma had only seen Jude a couple of times back at the safe house. She was Aiden's—what? Girlfriend seemed too tame a word. Lifemate maybe?

Jude was one of those women who had no idea how beautiful she was. She had shoulder-length auburn hair with a natural curl women spent countless hours at a salon trying to get. A drop-dead curvy figure that earned her a second look from every man she passed. And delicate facial features that reminded Emma of the Disney cartoon princesses. She'd spent her childhood in orphanages and her adult life in the lab at Meir Industries. As a result, she had a social ineptness Emma found charming but others interpreted as cold and unfeeling. Emma knew they were wrong. If she'd won Aiden's love, unfeeling and cold couldn't apply.

Jude took a step forward, but didn't presume to touch Emma. "Aiden has filled me in on the situation. How do you feel? Any nausea yet? Are your breasts swelling? Do you notice increased sensitivity in your nipples? How about cravings for odd food groupings? Pickles and ice cream? Mashed potatoes with pineapples on top? Hot dogs dipped in—"

"Stop." Laughing, Eleanor looked at Jude and shook her head. "You're such a scientist."

Jude colored. "I'm sorry. I've never been around a pregnancy. From my limited research... I just wanted to establish the base level Emma is at so we can assess..." She trailed off. After a moment of deep thought, Jude made a decision, closed the distance between them and gave Emma a stilted hug. When an appropriate interval had passed, Jude released her and stepped back. "Congratulations on your pregnancy, Emma," she said.

Emma burst out laughing. Eleanor joined her, which only served to make Jude more uncomfortable.

"Thanks, Jude," Emma finally managed. "But I think it's a little early for all the physical side effects. At best, I'm under forty-eight hours pregnant. Although, I really do want a cheeseburger."

"I know what you mean," Eleanor said. "Why is it that I never crave meat until I come to the Diarchy where you can't get any?"

"I was about to join the party out there but I'm glad you're here, Jude. Let's sit for a minute." Emma motioned to the table with the tray of food and her stomach grumbled. She couldn't remember the last time she'd eaten. When they were all seated, Emma chose one of the largest oranges she'd ever seen and started to peel it.

Eleanor took a cover off an object on the table and Emma had to shield her eyes.

"What's that? More fluorescent moss?" she asked.

Eleanor smiled. "Yes. Isn't it something?" She realigned the cover to soften the light. "Think what the electric companies would do to get their hands on this?"

"Wouldn't do any good," Jude said. "It only glows at the Diarchy. Take it out of here and it's normal ground cover. When I asked, the Dyads told me the Balance is responsible for the glow." She sighed. "Like so many amazing things surrounding us, it will not translate to the human world."

Emma turned to Jude. "You've been living here a few months, right?"

"Yes. Aiden and David brought me here last fall." Her eyes lit up. "I'm working with their botanists on a project centering on crop production. You should see their crop fields. It's amazing to watch the process. Using their power, they are able to accelerate growth at an astounding rate. Starting with soy beans, I'm studying exactly what happens to an individual plant when—"

Emma broke in. "That's wonderful, Jude, and I want to hear all about it, but later. Right now I want to know what you've learned about the Dyads themselves."

"In what capacity?" Jude asked.

Emma put an orange wedge in her mouth and groaned. "This is the best orange I've ever tasted."

Jude actually grinned. It looked good on her. "I know. Isn't it delicious? Wait until you try the strawberries. They're my favorite. Aiden likes to eat them with…" she trailed off and colored a deep red. "Never mind. What were we talking about?"

Emma promised herself someday she'd get Jude to tell her just how Aiden liked his strawberries, but now she needed information. "How do you think the Dyads will react to my pregnancy?" she asked.

Jude nodded and thought for a moment. "Yes, I see what you're after."

"Well," Emma prompted.

"From what I know, and you have to understand that even though I've been living here, my knowledge of their social mores and economical structures is limited."

"I understand," Emma said impatiently.

Jude shrugged. "Their reaction will be mixed. One contingent, led by a Dyad called Brown, have you met them yet?"

"I've had the pleasure," Emma said, chewing on another orange wedge.

"They are what I'd call Isolationist. They strongly believe interaction with humans will be the downfall of the Dyad culture. At every possibility, they argue for a withdrawal, even to the point of disbanding the human partners and wiping their memories. They think that only by complete isolation can they keep their race pure."

"Small-minded idiots," Eleanor grumbled.

Jude shook her head. "No. They have a valid point. You only have to look at our history for examples. Look at what happened to the Mayans, or the Aztecs."

"But those were conquered people," Eleanor said. "I can't see the Dyads in that position, can you?"

"Well, then look at the present in New Guinea," Jude continued. "The indigenous tribes are experiencing a stripping away of their culture because of contact with the rest of the world."

Emma didn't want to hear any more about New Guinea. "You said the Isolationists are one contingent. What are the others?"

"On the other side are the Dyads who've volunteered to live with humans. I call them the Progressionists. Over the years, they have argued for more assimilation into the modern human world. We need them, you see, we humans. They want to help us stop pollution and wars and advance medicine and food production. They believe the only way the Dyads will safely continue is if the human race evolves into a peaceful, responsible society."

"With you so far on the two groups. What about the rest?" Emma asked.

"Well, everything in the spectrum. If you think of it in the same manner as the American political model, it's easier to understand. The Dyads have two parties, the Isolationists and the Progressionists, with an independent party that encompasses everyone in between. I don't think we can change the Isolationists' views. It's the independents we have to convince."

"So. What? Do they vote on things?" Emma asked.

Jude shook her head. "Don't think of it that way. Remember, the Dyads have the ability to link all their minds into one collective mind. It is the will of the collective, with the gentle guiding of both the Elders and the Chaldeans that decide matters."

"What's your gut feeling? How will they react to the babies?" Emma asked.

"My gut feeling?" Jude's brow furrowed.

"Just go with it." Eleanor chimed in. "Don't overanalyze. Say the first thing that pops into your head."

Jude shrugged. "I really don't know. If it were just the mating between you and Damien, that I think would have eventually been accepted. But the babies are another matter."

"Why?" Emma's mouth was suddenly dry and she lost her appetite. "What could these babies do to them?"

Very gently, Jude took Emma's hand in hers. "Emma, the babies change everything. Remember, the Dyad race, for whatever reason, is set at one thousand. You saw what happened when that number is altered. The Fitzgerald died and the whole race went half insane until they were replaced."

"Yeah, so. I don't see what—"

"You were allowed to attend the welcome ceremony. You met the pregnant Dyad."

Emma smiled, remembering. "Yes. It was wonderful right up until the time we were sneered off the stage."

"Well that pregnancy brought the Dyads back to the magic one thousand number. Or, as the Dyads like to say, they have achieved the perfect balance. Their world clicked back into place. Everyone went back to normal."

Emma looked to Eleanor and then back to Jude. "I got that but I still don't see how my babies fit in."

"Your babies make their number one thousand and two."

Eleanor threw down her empty grape stem. "Then why aren't they reacting to the upset? I've been watching and everybody seems okay to me."

Jude nodded. "For now. The children are only half Dyad. But what happens if their Dyad powers grow along with their bodies? What if they become Dyad enough to threaten the Balance? I bet the Chaldeans are busy on that puzzle. Two above one thousand is just as big an upset as two below. Anything more or less than one thousand and their world is plunged into chaos again."

Emma sighed. Her stomach was upset and she felt a little dizzy. "So, that's it? That's how you see this?"

"There is one more hiccup."

"Great," Emma snorted. "What?"

"It has to do with the babies themselves."

"What about them?" Emma looked down at her body, picturing the lives within.

"There has never been a male-female Dyad grouping before. You've seen the way it works. Two females, who make up a single Dyad, mate with a male Dyad and each of the females carries one half of the new Dyad. But the new Dyad is always the same sex. Either two males or two females."

"Oh, I guess I never made that connection. I just assumed…" Emma trailed off, realizing for the first time just what an enigma her babies were to the Dyads.

Jude poured a glass of water and took a drink. "It's new," she said. "And if there's one thing I've learned about this race, it's that they don't adapt to change well. I think it's one of their few faults."

Emma rubbed her forehead. "All right. I get it all now. I see all the possible problems the babies represent. But bottom line, what can the Dyads do about them? They don't kill, right?"

"That is correct, Emma. The babies' lives are not in danger," Jude assured her.

Something relaxed inside of Emma and she took a deep, cleansing breath. Somewhere in the back of her mind, she'd been afraid the Dyads would terminate the pregnancies. Now that she knew that wasn't a possibility, she could face anything they threw at her.

"So what's the worst that could happen?" Emma asked.

Jude shook her head. "I'm not positive but I can see two possibilities. The first is they ask you to leave. They may or may not wipe your memory but either way, they will sever all contact with you and the children."

"I can live with that," Emma said.

Beside her, Eleanor gasped.

"What?" Emma turned to Eleanor. "What do you see that I don't?"

Eleanor shook her head and the look of pity she gave Emma made her heart speed up.

Jude continued in a quiet voice. "I mean all contact will be cut off. Even Damien."

"They can't do that," Emma cried. "He's the babies' father. They can't ask a father to give up his children. It's inhuman."

"But they are not human, Emma. They are Dyad. They act for the good of the collective, not the individual. Neither you nor Damien will be given a choice in the matter."

"What's the second possibility?" Emma asked, almost positive she didn't want to know.

"The second is they accept the babies, in what capacity I'm not sure, into the Dyad race."

"I like the second one," Emma said. "Let's go with that one."

Jude and Eleanor were gravely silent. They shared a worried look.

Emma groaned. The dizziness she'd been fighting intensified. "Come on, guys. What don't I see this time?"

Jude took both her hands as if preparing Emma for some horrifically bad news. Emma braced herself. "Let me have it," she said.

"If they accept the babies fully, when they are born, they will take them away from you and wipe all memory of them from your mind."

"Oh," Emma said. The dizziness turned into a whirlwind. The room around her spun, Eleanor and Jude's faces flashed by and the floor somehow became the ceiling. "I think I'll just pass out now," she said and let the darkness take her.

Chapter Twelve

ꧠ

"Damien, come quick."

Damien heard Eleanor's words an instant after he sensed Emma's loss of consciousness. He was up and through the bedroom door in a heartbeat with David on his heels. He took in Emma's limp form. Eleanor and Jude were just now coming to her aid.

"Stand back," he ordered and ran to her. As gently as possible, he lifted Emma and carried her to the bed. David beat them there and rearranged the pillows and bedclothes for a perfect nest. Damien laid her down with her head elevated. He and David took their places on either side of the bed.

"What happened?" David asked the women.

Jude stepped forward. "We were discussing the situation as it pertains to Dyad political and social mores. Theorizing on the possible outcomes the pregnancies will have on the Dyad collective, when Emma lost consciousness."

"Eleanor, quickly, interpret," Damien asked while he checked Emma's physical condition.

Eleanor sighed. "Emma found out that her babies could be taken away from her when they are born and she passed out."

There was only one person in the room who would have told Emma about this possibility. He turned to Jude. "Why did you feel the need to tell her that?"

"Because she asked," Jude said.

"Leave us," Damien snapped. He'd wanted to acquaint Emma with that possibility himself. With him there, she wouldn't have been so upset. He sensed Eleanor and Jude leave the room and heard the door shut.

"She's fine," David said, taking his hand off Emma's forehead. "Merely a faint brought on by strong emotions."

"I know, but." Damien looked at his brother, guilt riding him. "Look what I have done to her."

David tucked an errant curl behind Emma's ear. "You have given her children to bear. It should be cause for rejoicing, not lamentation."

Damien shook his head. "Even if her children are ripped away from her?"

"Whoever raises them, it will not alter the fact that they exist," David said.

"You have been around human women long enough to know what taking her children away will do to Emma. She is not Dyad. Raising children is not a communal thing for her as it is with us. Bearing young is primal among humans. Her instinct to protect her offspring has already overtaken her."

David sighed. "Do not borrow trouble." He paused, thinking. "Who always said that?"

Damien smiled and looked down at his mate. "Emma's grandmother."

"Already her memories are ours. She is an amazingly strong personality."

"Strong and yet insecure at the same time. An interesting mix." Damien bent and kissed her forehead.

Emma's eyes fluttered open. Confused, she looked around the room and then fear filled her eyes. She shot to a sitting position. "I want to leave," she announced.

"Emma, we cannot leave yet," Damien began.

With a strength that surprised him, Emma pushed him off the bed. She swung her legs around and was going for her pack before Damien could stand.

"I don't care what you two say. I'm leaving. No one is going to stop me. Not the Elders or your Voodoo Priests or those assholes the Browns, or even you." She began stuffing things into her pack. "I don't care where on Earth this place is. I'll walk if I have to."

David came around the bed, his arms raised in a peacemaking gesture. "We are hundreds of miles from the nearest human village."

Emma turned on him, her eyes blazing. "You think I can't make it? Just watch me. I'd walk through hell itself to get out of here."

Damien sought to intervene. "Please, Emma. Be reasonable." As soon as the words left his mouth, he knew he'd said the wrong thing.

"Reasonable?" she shouted. "They're going to take my children." Her hands fisted at her sides and her voice took on a quiet, deadly tone. "If they so much as try, I swear I'll…" She pulled a long knife out of her pack. "I didn't take the partners' oath not to kill. If they make a single move toward me, I'll show them just what a barbaric human I am." She turned to Damien. "You get me out of here. Do you hear me, Damien? I want out." Hysteria crept into her voice.

Carefully, Damien took the knife away and passed it to David. He gently caressed her shoulders. "Leaving is not an option. Please trust me."

"No." She pushed him. He stumbled over a chair and went down.

David came up from behind and placed a hand on her head.

Sensing his intention, Damien cried out. "David, no."

But he was too late. Emma's eyes closed and she crumpled. David caught her on the way down and lifted her.

Furious, Damien shot to his feet. "You should not have done that."

Nonplussed, David laid Emma on the bed. "What other choice was there? Sleep seemed the best option."

"You have no right to take Emma's will away from her. She is my mate. You would never treat a Dyad in such a way."

An anger Damien had never seen before filled David's eyes. "*Your* mate. *Your* children. But it will be *our* downfall if this goes ill. You have left me with nothing to gain and everything to lose from your selfish actions."

"Emma is as much your mate as she is mine. The children are our children, David. Yours, mine and Emma's."

"I do not believe that is so." David gestured to the sleeping woman. "Emma will never agree. She sees you as her mate, not us. The children belong to the two of you, not the three of us. You know that this is so."

Desperate to solve this dilemma, Damien fell back on old habits. "Link with me. We need our Balance. We can solve this if we face it together."

David shook his head. "No. Our link has felt wrong since you first shared love with Emma. We are not in harmony. We may never be again. The priests were correct. We have become something other than pure Dyad. We are the embodiment of what the Browns fear."

Afraid he was right, Damien tried again. "No, David. Link with me." He reached for David. He was able to establish a link but only for a moment. For the first time, David pushed him out of his mind and raised his shields. But not before Damien caught a glimpse of his brother's troubled thoughts.

"You think of them," Damien said. "You think of the Rose."

David turned away. "I do not wish to speak of this." He went to the far side of the room and picked up a hairbrush from the dresser.

Damien moved to follow and then stopped. His brother's rigid posture and raised shields made him uncertain how to approach. "It has been hundreds of years since the Rose Dyad took up the Chaldean path. They made their choice and it did not include us." He crossed and put a hand on David's tense shoulder. "Elizabeta and Eleana rejected our love. They broke with us forever."

David shook off his hand. "You do not know that. Others have left the Chaldean. Others have returned to their lives."

"A handful only. Besides, can you believe the Rose Dyad, as we knew them, would ever doubt their chosen path?"

David threw the hairbrush across the room. It smashed against the bookcase, sending a few dusty volumes to the floor. "It does not matter anymore. You have changed all that."

"What do you mean?" Damien asked.

"If the Rose did leave the Chaldean for us what would they find? You mated and me…alone. Elizabeta would never agree to be my mate unless you were mated to Eleana."

"David, they will never leave the Chaldean. They will never come back to us."

"I love her still, Damien," David whispered.

The anguished look in David's eyes sent another stab of guilt into Damien's heart. As young men he and David had fallen in love with the Rose Dyad. David with Elizabeta and Damien with Eleana. They had never doubted their love was returned. Not until that horrible day when the Rose had told them of their choice.

David shook his head. "What about you, Damien. When linked I could feel your love for Eleana was still as strong as mine for Elizabeta. Where has your love gone?"

Damien searched his feelings. Up until a few days ago he knew what his answer would have been. He did still love Eleana. Time had not dimmed his need for her nor the pain of her rejection. He thought of her and waited for the familiar ache of longing.

Emma's face filled his mind. He could hear her teasing laugh, see her infectious smile and feel her smooth skin against his. Love welled up in him. A love so strong it left him breathless. He looked over at the bed and took in his mate. She was everything he needed, everything he'd ever dreamed of in a mate. But what about David?

He turned back to David. "You must link with me and share this new love. Let it replace the old as it has done with me." He reached for David.

"Stay away from me." Just as Emma had done, David pushed him away. But David was much stronger than Emma. Damien crashed into the table, breaking it.

The door flew open and their human partners rushed in. From his place on the floor, Damien saw Jacob and Aiden take in the scene. Him on the floor, bleeding from a cut on his hand, Emma passed out on the bed and David standing over him with his hands fisted. What had they come to?

"What's happened?" Jacob asked. "Is it the Browns?"

"Are you two fighting?" Aiden asked.

Jacob came to Damien and helped him stand. He took a white handkerchief out of his jeans and wrapped it around his partner's bleeding hand. "Do you want to heal this?" he asked.

Damien ignored him and looked at David. Aiden had reached him. The two were locked in an unspoken conversation. What was David telling him?

After a minute, Aiden shook his head and waved. "No. No, this is all wrong. We can't afford this now. With the Browns breathing down our necks, the last thing we need is the two of you out of Balance."

"I agree," Jacob added. "We have worked for centuries to move the Dyads closer to the modern world." He turned to David. "You risk everything we have accomplished."

"I risk?" David snorted. "I did not bring us to this point. Look to your Dyad, Jacob. It is his actions that have brought us to this. Not mine."

"What the hell is going on?" Jacob shouted. He took a deep breath and continued in a normal tone. "This is the first time you two have disagreed on anything. Up until now, I would have said it was impossible. You are angry at each other. Angry. How? Why?"

"Because David is correct," Damien said. "My actions have brought this on. I have cracked the Stewart Dyad in two. And in doing so, I have gained and David has lost. I gained a mate and children, making it impossible for David ever to have either. He will always be on the outside, watching, yearning for something he can never have. Because of me. Because of what I have done."

The room fell silent as each of them mulled over their circumstances. Did this fissure mean the end of their quartet?

Impossibly, Aiden laughed. "Well isn't this a fine kettle of fish? It finally happened. For centuries I've watched you two study humans, study us. But always from a distance, behind the Dyad wall of intellect and reservation. And now here you are, struggling with the most basic of human problems." He turned to David. "You, partner, are suffering from that old chestnut envy. You want what your brother has and can't have it. And you resent Damien for it. You are angry with him. And you," he turned to Damien and shook his head. "You are battling two of my favorites, guilt and regret. You know exactly what you've done to your brother and you feel terrible about it. You'd undo it all if you could, but you can't. Your happiness means David's unhappiness and it's eating you alive inside. At the same time you are angry with him for not accepting the situation and being happy for you."

Aiden took a step back to include both of them in his gaze. "Anger, guilt, envy, regret." He ticked them off on his fingers. "Strong human emotions directed at your Dyad brother."

Impatiently, Aiden grabbed David's wrist and pulled the shocked Dyad over to his brother. He lined them up and stood before them, hands on hips. "Well, suck it up gentlemen. You should know how to do this. You've watched Jacob and me battle similar problems and helped us overcome them. We're better men because of it. How many times have you urged us to find inner peace? To overcome hate with reason, anger with temperance? So, it's your turn now. Are you going to put your money where your mouth is or are you going to wuss out on us and let your emotions rule you?"

Damien's thoughts tumbled, one after the other. Aiden was correct in his assessment. Had he and David spent so much time among humans they were starting to think and feel like them? He was angry at David. He did feel shame and regret. In the past, he'd never realized just what he and the other Dyads asked of their human partners. He'd had no idea how difficult it was to curb these strong emotions. And alone, without a Dyad brother to help, it seemed insurmountable. His respect for Jacob and Aiden went up a few notches. But how would he and David, broken as they now were, overcome this?

Jacob appeared before him. His Jacob. Strong and forthright. Honest and brave. If Aiden was the heart of the human partners then Jacob was their rock. He'd taken the Dyad teachings and rebuilt himself from the ground up. He never let his emotions rule his actions. Always the rational choice, cool and calm. He stood as an example of what a human could become when hate was conquered. Now he looked at Damien with compassion in his eyes and offered his hand.

"When you found me all those years ago," Jacob began, "I was much worse off than you. I had nothing left. My family had all been murdered. I'd slaughtered the men who'd killed them and was left an empty shell. Only my hatred kept me alive. You brought me back from that, Damien. You showed me the way. Let me return the favor now. Accept the peace that I can give you."

Next to them, Aiden offered his hand to David. He cocked his head in Jacob's direction. "What he said. You man enough to give it a try?"

At the same moment, each Dyad took his partner's offered hand. Damien reached for Jacob's mind and felt the big man's strength flow into him. There was no judgment about

Damien's actions, no recrimination, only acceptance of him as a whole. Flawed and broken as he was, Jacob still respected him, loved him. And just as Damien had done for Jacob countless times over the last century and a half, his partner latched on to the raging emotions inside Damien and beat them back with his strength of will. Like a glass slowly filling, calm rose in Damien, easing his mind, bringing him back to normalcy. After the last two days of upset, it felt wonderful to shelter in his partner's strength.

Jacob took Aiden's hand and the shared minds merged, four individuals becoming one. To Damien, it was like coming home after a long absence. The bond between them, forged by decade after decade of loyalty and companionship, clicked into place and held. They were strong together. The four of them could overcome any unbalance and even if it could never be exactly the same between them, their quartet would endure. They would find a new Balance. The Dyads would rely on their humans to guide them through this.

Within the link, Damien sought out David and found his brother waiting for him. How could they have been angry at each other? Whatever the circumstances, they were one. They were Dyad.

It was time to sever the link and face the world again with all its problems. Damien, reluctant to leave this safe haven, wished they could savor the link a while longer. For the first time since the quartet was formed, the humans broke the link.

The four of them settled back into their individual minds and looked at each other.

Jacob smiled first, one of his rare, open smiles that reached his eyes. Aiden's face cracked next, his smile more chagrin than happiness. Damien looked at David and watched as his brother's eyebrows rose in wonder. He knew his face had exactly the same shocked expression.

Aiden slapped both of them on the back. "Well, boys. Welcome to the new world." He threw his head back and laughed.

Jacob put a hand of each of their shoulders and joined in the laughter.

Unable to resist, the Dyads joined in, relieved and somewhat hysterical laughter bubbling out of them.

After a moment, Aiden slapped them on the back again. "Gentleman," he announced. "The Stewart quartet is back in town and ready for business."

"That is good," a voice from the door said.

The quartet whirled and found the Goddard Dyad filling the doorway, their faces grave.

Samuel continued. "Because the Elders have called for you. They await you in the meeting room."

* * * * *

After arranging for Eleanor to sit with the still sound asleep Emma, the Stewart quartet set off for the meeting with the Elders. Damien was grateful the situation between David and him had come to a head. Gratitude for their partners' strength washed over him. What would have happened to the Stewarts if their partners had not intervened? Damien didn't want to think about it.

He was surprised the Elders had acted so quickly. Usually, they were slow moving to the point of inertia, often taking months or years to debate and ponder even the smallest of questions or disputes. It was a sign of just how dire the situation that they picked this moment to discover haste.

When they reached the Elders' meeting room, they were stopped by a Dyad pair who guarded the door. The Philostrate Dyad, Tiberius and Titus, had held this position since long before Damien and David were born. Luke called them the Elders' social secretaries. Nobody got into the meeting room without first being vetted by them.

To Damien's surprise, rather than detaining them with the formal questions about who they were and what their business was, the Philostrates reached behind them and opened the double doors.

"Enter, Stewart," they said. "The Elders await you."

Damien exchanged a shocked look with David. This did not bode well. He wished the Stewart quartet could take a moment to examine what this meant, but the Philostrates were gesturing them in.

"Courage," Jacob whispered. "Remember who we are."

With their human partners flanking them, they entered the large room. Damien felt as if he was Daniel in the lion's den, but he quickly pushed that picture from his mind and made every effort to present a strong, united front.

The room was in the exact center of the cave warren. On one side, rough wooden benches, large enough for a Dyad pair to sit comfortably, were arranged to form an audience area. On the other side, sitting in eight chairs on a slightly raised platform, the Elders waited for them to approach.

Surprised again, Damien noted no other Dyads were in attendance. The room was empty except for the Elders and the Stewart quartet. He'd expected the Browns to make an unwelcome appearance and felt sure at least one Chaldean pair would be here. The Elders must have closed the meeting to all but them.

Damien gazed at the eight seated figures, trying to gauge their mood but their shields were firmly up. Another bad sign. He thought of linking with David and suggesting they raise their mental shields but decided against it. After all, they had nothing to hide from this august group. If shields were raised, it could indicate the Stewarts weren't willing to cooperate. Not the best way to start this meeting.

The quartet reached the area before the chairs and spread out in a line, the humans even with the Dyads. In this subtle way, Damien hoped to set the right tone. He wanted the Elders to know how much the Stewarts valued their partners. Not as master and servant but as equals.

"The Stewarts have come in answer to your summons." Damien and David said the formal words together as any Dyad would. "We stand ready to answer—"

"Stop," the Salazar Dyad, spokesmen for the Elders, said. "Why have you brought the humans?"

Ready for this question, the Stewarts replied. "Since Dyad-Human relations are to be debated here, we thought it prudent that humans be in attendance."

The Salazars shook their heads. "You misunderstand, Stewart. There will be no debate here today, only censure and direction from the Elders to the Stewart Dyad."

"We are not to be allowed to state our case?" David asked.

"You have nothing to say that would change our decision. We know the series of events that have brought us here. We understand the Stewart did not intentionally bring about this dire situation. Your intent makes no difference. The effect on the collective remains the same. Danger, unrest." Their voices lowered to a harsh whisper. "Unbalance."

Here it is, the Stewart link thought. The one word that could invoke terror in any Dyad's heart. Unbalance.

They could not leave it like this. They must be allowed to speak. "Always in the past, we have been allowed—"

The Salazar cut them off again. "Silence, Stewart. If you are even Stewart. We sense your unbalance." They continued in a tone more sneer than questioning. "Should we address you as Damien and David?"

"We are Dyad," the Stewarts said.

"That point will be tested in time. Your conduct will be the proof."

Damien tried again. "May we not even link with you so you may experience our version of the last forty-eight hours? Is not firsthand knowledge better than relayed information?"

Quiet settled over the group on the platform as they linked and debated the question before them. The minutes ticked by and Damien fought to control his impatience. Finally, a consensus was reached among the Elders signaled by the Salazars turning back to the quartet and nodding.

"We accept the reason behind your words. Come forward, Stewart."

Relieved at being allowed at least this small request, Damien linked with David and the two of them went to stand in front of the Salazars. Each placed a hand on Damien and David's head.

"Accept our link," they began, "and show us what has brought about these events."

The Stewart link felt the combined mind of the Elders merge with them. Each time they had come back to the Diarchy, Damien and David had gone through a similar process. In this manner, they'd shared with the Elders everything they had learned about humans and their culture. But the Elder mind was different this time. Instead of the calm strength that usually defined them, the Elders were troubled and although they tried to hide it, divided in their opinions.

Knowing it best not to draw attention to the unrest among them, the Stewart mind relayed in great detail all that had happened to them since the death of the seventh Fitzgerald Dyad. They showed them what it had been like to be apart during the upheaval. Damien's first coupling with Emma. David's near-death experience with Aiden. The unbalance within their Dyad. They hid nothing, even their anger with each other. They laid themselves bare before the Elders.

But they also showed them Emma's courage when she offered herself to Damien. Aiden's willingness to share his Balance with David even though he knew it might possibly kill him. Damien's blossoming love for Emma and their acceptance into the mating ritual. And finally, they shared how their partners had helped them a few minutes before.

The Elder link soaked it up like a sponge, not allowing a hint of reaction to bleed to the Stewarts.

When they were finished, the Elders broke the link. The Salazars took their hands off Damien and David. "You may take your places by Jacob and Aiden," they said.

The Stewarts joined their partners back in line. The Salazars had called Jacob and Aiden by name, not "the humans". Damien took that as a good sign. Had their shared experiences helped the situation or made it worse? As the minutes dragged on, Damien and David linked their quartet. First, they brought their human partners up to date and then the four of them drew strength from each other. Whatever the Elders' decision, they would face it together.

Finally, the Salazars spoke. "First, there is the problem of Damien marking a human as his mate. The Chaldean ruled since the Balance allowed you to join in the mating ritual, your mating is a true one and should be treated as such."

Damien almost cried out with relief but there was more to come.

"However, Damien's mating creates a problem within your Dyad. As you have shared with us, Emma is not inclined to accept David into the mating." They focused on David. "You will never find a mate among the Dyad females. To do so would create yet more unbalance. You must open yourself to the possibility of finding your mate among humans. The Chaldean believe if the Balance allows this, it will go far to set the Stewart Dyad back to normal. Or, as normal as you can ever hope to be."

Before Damien could digest this news and everything it meant, the Elders continued.

"Now, we address the graver problem. The children you have created."

"Problem?" the Orchid Dyad said. "Children are never a problem. They are a blessing from the Balance." Their lovely blue eyes met Damien's and they smiled.

Damien was amazed. The other Elders never spoke during these sessions. They always left it to the Salazars to present their verdicts. All the Elders shifted in their chairs. A further sign of dissent among them. Damien would've loved to be a part of their link at that moment.

A full five minutes later, the Salazars turned back to them, not as unruffled as before. "However much a blessing, these children represent a great threat to the collective. Some would argue they are a greater threat than the human bombs or pollution for they endanger the Dyad race from within."

The Orchids spoke again. "Only the Balance can decide that."

The Salazars each raised a hand. "Agreed. End of discussion." They waited a few seconds and when the females didn't reply, they lowered their hands and continued. "The Chaldean say it is too early for them to tell if your children will upset our number and throw the collective into chaos. But we believe we should prepare for the possibility."

Here it comes.

"If the children are merely human and do not threaten us, we give you two choices. The first: you must take your mate, Emma, from the Diarchy and never return. You will raise your children in the human world as a human. You must never again draw upon the Balance. You must allow yourself to age as all humans do and when the time comes, you will travel on away from your race. In this manner, the children will have a true human father. You, David, must accept exile with your brother and make what life you can among the humans."

Absolutely unacceptable. Damien wanted to scream the words at the Elders. How could they ask this of David?

"What's the other choice?" Aiden asked.

"The other choice is simple. If you wish to remain among your people, we will wipe all knowledge of Dyads from Emma's mind and send her and the children back to her people. We will monitor the children from afar but you,

Stewart, will have no contact with either Emma or the children. You must break with them so they may build a life without you."

"How long do we have to make this choice?" David asked.

"You have until the Chaldean determine the nature of the children, Dyad or Human."

Damien glanced at David and all the emotions he'd worked so hard to suppress roared to life. Guilt, shame, regret pounded against his equilibrium until he grew dizzy. How could he ask his brother to give up being Dyad? Never to link, never to feel the warmth of each other's mind or the healing power of the Balance. Could such a thing even be done?

"What's the other scenario?" Aiden asked. "What if the children are Dyad?"

Just like Aiden, Damien thought. *Get the worst out into the open and deal with it.*

"If the children are Dyad they will be accepted into the Diarchy and raised by the collective. Emma's memory of them will be erased and she will be sent away. The children must not be influenced by human interaction."

"Emma will never allow this," Damien said.

"What Emma will or will not allow has no meaning to us. If Dyad, the children will be Dyad."

"And what of Damien and David?" Jacob spoke for the first time. "Will you still make them leave?"

All the Elders tensed in their chairs. "That is our question to the Stewart," the Salazars said. "If the children are true Dyads, they will cause chaos among the Diarchy. Our number will be one thousand and two. You, Stewart, have brought this upon your people. Do you see a solution?"

Damien saw at once where the Elders were headed and his blood froze. Quickly, he linked with David and found his brother had come to the same conclusion. He had never foreseen this. He'd thought things had gotten as bad as they could but he'd been wrong. How would he live with the guilt?

David's arms went around him. His brother pulled him close and whispered. "Always and forever."

With Damien still enfolded in his arms, David turned his head to face the Elders. "If the children are Dyad and as a result the Dyad race is threatened, the Stewarts will act accordingly."

The Elders relaxed.

"You are indeed Dyad," the Orchids said. "Thank you, Stewart."

"What did you just agree to?" Jacob asked, white-faced.

"Tell me that doesn't mean what I think it does," Aiden said.

Damien stepped out of David's arms and faced the Elders. "When the time comes, the Stewarts will bring our numbers back to one thousand." He turned to Jacob and Aiden. "To save our children and our race, we will travel on together. We will commit suicide."

Chapter Thirteen

ꟸ

"You cannot kill yourselves," Jacob said for the tenth time since the argument began. Emma had watched the drama unfold from an overstuffed chair in a corner of the Stewarts' living room. She hadn't joined in. The numbness that had settled over her since Damien had told her of their meeting with the Elders made speech impossible. Maybe she was in shock. Maybe their available options were so horrific, she refused to face them. For all she knew, Damien could be working his Dyad mojo on her, keeping her in a calm, numbed-up state. One thing was clear. She sure as hell couldn't do a thing about it.

Even on her worst day in Mildred, she'd never been completely helpless. There'd always been a way to overcome her problem and go on. But this? When every option Damien had outlined was worse than the last? When she had no power to change even the most minute detail of their situation? The Elders could wave their hands and take her children and her memory away. How did a mere human fight that?

For a terrible moment, Emma longed for the memory wipe. Let the Elders take it all. Let them have Damien and the children and give her oblivious peace. Why not? It would be so easy, just to give in. Give up.

At that second, with the argument still in full force around her, something clicked inside Emma. She remembered lying in a hospital bed, her parents standing gravely beside it while they broke the news to her that she would never walk again. Even though she'd only been five years old, she knew what it meant. She remembered what her first thought had been. This would not break her. She was still Emma, Mommy and Daddy's little girl, and this would not break her.

Where had that strong little girl gone? Was she still hiding inside somewhere? Damn right she was. If a five-year-old Emma could find a way to go on, well then so could she. There had to be an acceptable way out of this mess. She just had to find it.

The room rushed back in on her and she looked over all the occupants. Damien and David sat at the table looking resolute. Jacob and Aiden paced back and forth in front of them, arms waving wildly as they hammered away. The Goddard Dyad, Sebastian and Samuel with their partners Luke and Emil, stood back but interjected a word now and then to strengthen Jacob and Aiden's point. Eleanor sat in the far corner with Jude beside her, the former chewing on a fingernail, the latter zeroing in on each speaker, analyzing every word.

Emma took a deep breath and uncurled from the chair. She stood and moved to the center of the room. "Enough," she announced.

All heads turned to her. Damien stood. "Emma, are you feeling ill?"

If he had to ask, what must she look like? Awful, that's how she looked. "No, I'm fine but I've had enough for one day. I think we all have."

Aiden shook his head. "We need to work this through."

She went to him and put a hand on his forearm. "You can't change their minds." She indicated the Stewarts. "They are determined to play the martyr and nothing you do or say will make any difference."

"Bullshit," Aiden said. "I don't—"

"Put yourself in their place," Emma began. Although she addressed the room, she went to Damien and gazed into his soulful blue eyes. "If every human being's life was in danger and you were the cause? If it was your life or the lives of your children and everyone you knew and loved? What would you do? What would any of us do?"

A profound silence settled over the room as her words sank in. Damien and David, being who and what they were, couldn't entertain any other course of action. They would give up their lives so that others might live. It was as simple as that. She knew it and the rest of the room did as well. They just didn't want to accept it.

"I'd like some time alone with Damien. Would you all please leave?" she asked.

Maybe it was the tone of quiet desperation in her voice. Maybe it was the fact that she never took her eyes off of Damien, or he her. Whatever the reason, the room emptied of all but Emma, Damien and David.

Emma finally broke eye contact with Damien and turned to David. "You really got the short end of the stick in this, didn't you?"

He gave her a twisted grin. "As short as they come."

"I wish I could love you both. It would make everything easier." She took David's face in her hands and watched his eyes widen in surprise. Slowly, giving him every chance to object, she drew him down and put her mouth on his. His body tensed but she ignored it. His lips were cool and unyielding against hers.

Emma let her mind empty of everything but the man in her arms. She teased his lips open with her tongue and teeth. His breath tasted like Damien, and yet different. David made a strangled sound in the back of his throat and his arms wrapped around her, pulling her tight. His tongue invaded and she met him with a determination to please. He took his time, sparring with her as they learned each other's mouths, hers warm, his cool. She threaded her hands through his thick hair and examined her feelings. The kiss was pleasant, David knew what he was doing all right, but although she hoped for more, nothing happened.

David released her mouth and drew back, his eyes searching her face. After what seemed an eternity under his scrutiny, he smiled sadly and kissed her forehead.

"Well," he said in a choked voice. "My ego may never recover. I do not understand it, but the spark of love does not exist between us and cannot be forced. Remarkable."

"Sorry, David." Emma stepped away from him. "I'm so very sorry."

"Not your fault." He ran a hand through his hair and looked around the room. "Not your fault," he said again as if to prove he meant it. "I will leave you two alone. I will…" He paused. Emma got the feeling he didn't know where to go or what to do. This must be so strange for him. At least she and Damien had each other. For the first time in his long life, David was truly alone. On the outside, looking in. Her heart went out to him.

Finally, David shook himself. "I will just go," he said and slowly walked out.

Both she and Damien watched his exit. When they were alone, Emma turned to her mate. The look on his face, stern and dark, surprised her.

"I did not like you kissing him." Disgust colored his voice. "I did not like my Dyad brother kissing you. How can I be so selfish?"

Emma shook her head. "Sorry, but I had to try. For David, for you, even for me. I had to see if there was any way I could…" She trailed off.

Damien crossed to her and gripped her shoulders so hard it hurt. "You will not kiss him again, or any other. You are mine, Emma." His eyes bored into hers, full of anger and passion, scaring her a little.

He took her mouth and his kiss was everything David's was not. She matched his hunger, greedy for his touch. Her heart pounded. Shivers of pleasure coursed up and down her body. Damien was staking his claim. A part of Emma reveled in his dominance. She surrendered to him, marveling that this perfect being could want her so much.

After a few minutes, Damien tore his mouth from hers and struggled to gain control. "We have so much to discuss. We should—"

She put a finger over his lips, silencing him. "Not now. I don't want to waste this time together talking about what we can't change."

"But, love. We must plan."

"No, Damien. I want you to do something for me."

He stroked her cheek. "Anything."

She kissed his palm. "I want you to make love to me. But no mind links or power flows. Can we, just this once, make love the human way?"

"Yes." He kissed her eyelids. "Yes, we can do that."

"And afterward," she continued. "I want you to hold me until we fall asleep and then wake in the morning with your arms around me."

"That may be the easiest and most pleasant task anyone has set for me." Damien smiled tenderly. "Let us begin the human way." He picked her up, carried her to the bedroom and spent the next two hours granting her request.

He made love to her with a tenderness that both surprised and delighted Emma. Whenever he forgot himself and she felt his mind brush against hers, she firmly pushed him away. She wanted this time with him. She needed it. She planned on living on it the rest of her life.

More importantly, she couldn't link minds with Damien. A plan had started to form. A plan he couldn't know about until it was too late.

When Damien fell asleep, Emma rose from the bed and dressed. As quietly as possible, she gathered her things and put them in her pack. Before she left, she took one last look at Damien asleep on the bed. His long hair lay strewn across the white pillows. One arm was thrown out as if searching for her warmth. The other arm curled up over his head, its fingers threaded in his hair. A soft smile curved his full lips.

He looked so innocent and young it broke her heart to leave. Steeling herself, she turned and crept out. It was the only way. Her leaving was the only way to save him. The only way to save everyone.

Quietly, she slipped out of the Stewarts' rooms and went to find the one Dyad who could help her now.

The Browns.

Emma rushed along the vine-lined rock corridors, trying to be as inconspicuous as possible. Not an easy task. A human woman stuck out like a sore thumb around here, but she gave it a try anyway. Thankfully, the halls were almost deserted.

A Dyad approached her. She thought it best to meet their eyes. "Good evening," she said and put on a warm smile.

The males, another redheaded pair, glanced at her quizzically. "Good evening, Little Emma," they said. She continued walking, afraid they would stop to chat, but they didn't.

She had a cover story ready if she ran into any of the human partners. Something about needing some air and time alone. If that didn't work, she planned to fall back on the old female ploy of crying. Faced with her tears, she was betting the males would give in and let her go.

But how to find the Browns? It wasn't as if there was a map posted or mailboxes with the inhabitant's names on them. In the end, she stopped a female Dyad and asked. The women looked puzzled at first but good manners won out and they gave her detailed directions, somewhat slowly as if she'd have trouble understanding, to the Brown's apartments.

On the way, Emma rehearsed what she would say to the Browns. Her plan would be easier if the Browns were still stuck in their rooms meditating. She was counting on the meeting Damien and the others had with the Elders not being common knowledge yet.

All too soon she stood before what she hoped was the opening to the Browns' quarters. The vines forming the door were more tightly woven than the others. No surprise there. Of all the Dyads she'd met, the Browns seemed the most closed off to her. The tight weave on the door confirmed their character.

For a moment, she thought of turning back. It wasn't too late. If she ran, she could be next to Damien in bed in a matter of minutes. Once she entered the Browns' rooms, it would be too late. Was she doing the right thing? She thought of the options the Elders had given Damien. Damien and David exiled from the diarchy, forbidden to touch the Balance or even link minds. Her memory wiped and her children stolen. Or worst of all, Damien and David dead, lost forever. Faced with those gruesome futures, the sacrifice she was about to make seemed like a walk in the park.

Hesitantly, she placed a hand on the vines. "Hello? Can I come in?" she called.

Nothing happened.

"Hello, Browns," she called louder this time. "It's Emma, Damien's human. I need to speak to you." To her relief, the vines parted just enough for her to squeeze through. As it was, she almost lost her pack but managed to pull it in before the vines closed shut.

The dark room made it impossible for Emma to make out anything. The temperature was close to freezing. Panic threatened to overwhelm her as memories of the dark, cold cave she'd lain in all those years ago rushed in on her. She could almost feel the pain in her broken back and arm. Her pulse and breathing sped up and she fought the urge to scream. Alone. She was alone and no one was coming for her.

A small light flickered to life to her left, another to her right. She blinked, trying to focus as the light brightened.

Emma saw two tall men dressed in loose white robes, on opposite sides of the room, moving the vines apart. When they turned, there was enough light for Emma to recognize the Brown Dyad, looking grim and somewhat surprised.

"Thanks for seeing me," she managed.

"It will not work," the Brown to her right said.

Emma took in his proud, handsome face, set now with a look of distaste and wondered again if she'd done the right thing in coming here. "What won't work?" she asked.

"This ploy of the Stewarts. Did they think by sending you here we would change our minds? What have they asked you to do? Will you sit up? Roll over? Beg for food?"

"They don't know I'm here."

That got their attention. The brothers locked eyes for a moment, and then moved to stand before her. She tried to not let their height intimidate her but boy, they were big.

"You expect us to believe the Stewarts do not know you are here?" they said together.

Emma's temper got the better of her. "I don't give a rat's ass what you believe." She regretted the words as soon as they left her mouth. The Browns looked as if they'd just sucked a lemon.

"Sorry," she hastened to add. "This isn't the way I wanted to start."

"Undoubtedly," the Browns said. "Your human crassness is showing."

Emma took a deep breath and prayed for patience. These two took arrogance to a whole new level. Pompous pricks, both of them. But she needed these pompous pricks so she sucked it up. "I came here because I agree with what you said to the priests."

Four eyebrows shot up in front of her. "You agree what you carry inside your body is an abomination?" they asked.

Emma groaned. "Can you do me a favor and tone down the bigotry?" When they sucked lemons again, Emma waved dismissively. "Never mind. No. I don't think my baby is an abomination. But I don't think there's any place for either me or my child among the Dyads. I think you were right about that."

The Browns studied her. Emma tried to keep her face and thoughts neutral. Would the Browns sense a lie? What if they invaded her mind and read all her thoughts? If that happened, the jig was up. They'd find out about the meeting with the Elders and never help. Also, she didn't want them to know she carried twins. Twins might seem more Dyad to them.

"Let us speculate for a moment," the Browns said. "Let us say we believe you. What do you want of us?"

"I want you to help me get away and if possible, shield my whereabouts from the others."

The eyebrows hit the roof again. "We would be risking the anger of the Elders and the Chaldean. Why should we do this for you?"

Emma knew the Browns' biggest fear. It was the same as bigots everywhere. "Because the only way you are assured of getting what you want is if I leave. What if the others accept my baby and allow us to live here? Babies being what they are, all cute and helpless, everyone will fall in love with it. They won't be able to help themselves. Before you know it, more Dyads will take humans as mates and pretty soon there'll be half-human children running everywhere. Contaminating everything they touch. One day, maybe even allowed a seat on the Elders council. Tell me, how pure will your race be then?"

"The collective will never allow such a thing."

"You sure about that? From what I hear, you've lost every argument against Damien and David over human issues. What makes you think you'll win this one? Why gamble when I'm offering you a sure thing? Me gone. Problem solved."

The Browns' eyes lost focus and Emma knew they were linked and mulling over her offer. Uncomfortable, she swung her pack off her shoulders and let it slide to the floor. They hadn't offered her a seat but she was bone weary. She went to the closest chair and sank into it.

It took a full twenty minutes for the Browns to come to a decision. With every passing second, Emma's anxiety grew. How long would Damien stay asleep? What if the Elders called the Browns to a meeting? She had to get away, now, while there was still a chance.

The Browns finally broke their link. Emma stood to hear their decision.

"We want to know why you would do this. Most humans would give up everything they have to live among Dyads. To extend their life spans by hundreds of years. But you would turn your back on us. Why?"

Emma thought of lying. Giving the Browns a reason they could readily understand would be easier. But in the end, she told the truth. "I'm doing this for Damien and my child. And David too. I love Damien and want what's best for him. If I leave, he and David will be able to find a Dyad mate someday. They will live as they were meant to, with their people… And my child will not be a strange half-breed living among people like you. Who think he or she is beneath them."

Their bodies tensed. "So, our helping you will benefit the Stewart?"

Emma realized her mistake and tried to rectify it. "They won't see it that way. They'll be angry, at both you and me, for spoiling their plans. And think how weak they'll look to the others. I mean, they couldn't control their human. It could set back their agenda by decades."

"But is not the Stewart agenda your agenda? You are human. According to the Stewart, the human race will only survive with Dyad intervention. If you believe what they say, you are dooming your race to extinction."

"The life and well-being of my child is more important to me. I'm only one person. A pregnant person at that. I won't be held responsible for the future of both races. Damien, David and the rest of you will just have to continue the struggle without me. You can count me out."

The Browns shook their heads. "Typical human. Always putting the individual first. Never a thought to the collective good."

Emma had had enough. "Yeah, I'm a real selfish pig of a human. But that doesn't change the situation. Are you going to help me or not?" She held her breath. Now that she'd gotten this far, she had no idea what to do if they refused.

After another agonizing minute, the Browns nodded. "We will see you safely to the Dyad house in Michigan."

Alarmed, she shook her head. "No. Just get me to a portal and shove me through. I can take it from there." The last thing she wanted was these two as traveling companions.

"The Elders will link with us and see these events. It will temper their judgment of us if they know it was your decision to leave and we not only granted your request, but saw you to your destination."

Emma saw the logic. "All right, fine. But can we go now?"

"We will ready ourselves for the journey."

"How long will that take?"

"A few moments only."

Resigned to more anxious waiting, Emma nodded. "Please hurry."

The Browns sprang into action. One of them left the rooms and the other went into the sleeping chamber.

Left alone, Emma used the time to write two notes. One she addressed to Damien and the other to the Goddards. As she wrote, tears blurred her vision but she forged on, fighting back all emotion. She needed to make sure Damien knew she left of her own free will. Even though she didn't like the

Browns, they were doing her a favor and she didn't want them blamed for this. And maybe, just maybe, Damien would grant her request and not follow her.

While she wrote, one of the Browns rushed in from the corridor, his arms loaded with clothes. He ignored her and went to join his brother.

Emma finished her notes just as the Browns returned. Each had on jeans, a T-shirt, leather jacket and running shoes. As they stood before her, they picked at the clothes, rearranging them on their bodies. To Emma, they looked uncomfortable and she wondered if they'd ever worn anything except loose fitting robes.

"We are ready," they said and lifted heavy backpacks.

Emma tucked the notes into her pack and rose. "Let's go then."

The Browns raised a hand, stopping her. "Are you resolute in this decision?"

She realized what they were doing. When this scene played back to the Elders, the Browns wanted to appear as if they'd given her every chance to stay. Two could play at that game.

She spoke not to the Browns, but to the Elders. "I have asked the Browns to take me back to the human world."

They shook their heads. "Do not call us that."

"What do you mean?" Emma asked. "Aren't you the Browns?"

"We are Brown. Do not insult us by adding an S. We keep to the old ways. We are Brown."

"Okay, okay, sorry." She cleared her throat and began again. "I have asked the Brown to take me back to the human world. It is my decision to leave. I have not been coerced. It is my wish that the Dyads let me go to build a life for myself and my child in the human world. As mother to the first Dyad-Human cross, I renounce any rights or claim my child has among the Dyads. I ask you not to banish the Stewarts to the human world. I don't want them there. I don't need them." She stopped before her voice broke.

The Browns smiled, pleased with her words. "Come then." They gestured for her to precede them.

When she reached the door, the vines opened wide and she had no trouble getting through. The temperature in the corridor was considerably warmer. Her body relaxed into the warmth.

"Follow," the Browns said and hurried down the hall.

It didn't surprise Emma that the Browns made no allowance for her shorter stride. As they darted around rock corners and down low-lit hallways, Emma had to move at a trot to keep up. At least her mind was occupied with keeping up with them and not mulling over her decision, wondering if she was making the biggest mistake of her life.

Just as Emma reached her limit and was going to swallow her pride and ask the Browns to slow down, they took one more sharp turn and entered the portal room.

The same redheaded Dyad Emma met when she'd first entered the Diarchy stood facing them. When she saw their stern faces and rigid bodies, she feared her escape would be over before it started.

"This is highly irregular, Brown," the redheads said. "You ask us to call a portal without first consulting the Elders. Why?"

Disappointment and panic hit Emma. What could the Browns say to that? It's not as if they would make up a whopper of a lie to get them to cooperate. Dyads never lied. But the Browns were ready for this.

"This human has asked to leave. Both the Elders and Chaldeans are in conference and unavailable for link. Will you keep her against her wishes?"

The portal Dyad turned to Emma and studied her, puzzled. "You are mated to Damien. Why would you leave him?"

Maybe Dyads couldn't lie, but right now, Emma didn't have a problem with it. "I don't want to be Damien's mate. I was never given a choice. He forced this situation on me." Her voice faltered. She swallowed hard and continued. "You have no right to keep me here. Either open a portal and let me leave or I start walking. Either way, I'm out of here."

They shook their heads. "This does not feel right. A mate would never act so."

The Browns stepped forward. "We take full responsibility and will answer to the Elders and Chaldeans. Please, brothers. Open the portal and let us on our way."

After a few tense seconds during which the redheads stared at the Browns and Emma tried not to run screaming, they relented.

"Very well." They moved to the archway. "Stand back."

They linked and power swirled around Emma. They formed the portal. "Go in peace," they said and gestured for Emma and the Browns to go through.

Emma walked slowly to the portal and hesitated. She turned to the Browns who were frozen in place. She saw a hint of fear on their faces. Had they never been through a portal before?

"Is this your first time?" she asked. "Don't tell me you're portal virgins?"

Her words snapped the Browns out of their fright. "We will be back within the hour," they said. Without a backward glance, they strode to the portal and went through.

Emma turned to the tall redheads. "Thanks. Would you give these to Damien and the Goddards for me?" She handed over her notes.

The two looked down at her, concern and sadness coloring their features. "Little Emma, are you sure you want to leave him?"

Not trusting herself to answer, Emma turned and rushed through the portal.

Pitch black surrounded her. A dank cave smell filled her nostrils. An all too familiar pre-panic heart flutter distracted her. Were the Browns even with her? Had this been an elaborate trick? Could they have sent her to a different destination, deep within the earth?

A rasp of a sound came from the right and a blessed light, no bigger than a pea, lit up a small circle. The light ignited a candle. Emma breathed a sigh of relief as the Browns came into view. It was the same cave Damien and the others had brought her to. Thank God.

Emma remembered the flashlight in her pack and got it out. When she turned it on, her confidence grew. After all, now she had the bigger light. She swept the beam to get her bearings.

"The entrance is this way," she said and started out.

As she neared the cave opening, fresh, damp air hit her. It smelled of pine trees and moss after a hard rain. Familiar. It was good to be back in the human world where vines didn't form doors and power wasn't constantly assaulting a person. And you could drive though a fast food joint and get a cheeseburger whenever you wanted. Her mouth watered at the thought.

A dim glow guided her to the entrance, the Browns close on her heels. Through the vines cloaking the entrance she could see the setting sun. A new fear occurred to Emma. What if she couldn't find the way back to the vehicles? If she did manage to find them in this fading light, how would she start one? If she managed to start one, could she find the safe house?

One problem at a time. First, find the transportation. Looking around the clearing, she recognized a break in the trees. "It's this way," she said and started out.

To her relief, she spotted a trail of sorts as soon as she entered the woods. Trampled moss, broken lower branches and upended leaf piles pointed the way. Behind her, the Browns' breathing became at first audible and then labored.

When it became clear something was wrong, she stopped and turned to them. "You guys okay?" she asked.

The Browns stopped. Each of them leaned against a tree for support and took in great gulps of air. "The air is polluted," one of them wheezed out. "How can you stand it?"

The Browns had lived their entire lives in the Diarchy bubble where everything was as pure and perfect as it had been since before man's industrial age. If they thought this air was bad, what would they make of L.A. or China? "This is about as clean as our air gets," Emma told them. "Are you sure you have to take me all the way to the safe house? Couldn't you tell the Elders you saw me this far and had to turn back?"

They drew themselves upright, defiant. "If the Stewarts can live among this filth, so can we. Lead the way."

"It's your funeral." Without another thought for their welfare, Emma turned and trudged down the path. Because they'd mentioned Damien and David in a derogatory tone, Emma quickened her pace. The Browns huffed and puffed behind her. After a few minutes, she slowed. Her payback didn't give her any satisfaction and guilt settled in. They were helping her after all.

"It's not far now," she said encouragingly. "And then you can rest."

"We do not need comfort from you. Lead on," came the cold response.

Emma gave herself brownie points for not sprinting. She continued at a steady pace, stopping often to let the Browns catch up. Twice she lost the path and had to backtrack. When she reached the clearing where the SUVs were hidden, she felt proud of herself.

The Browns entered the clearing supporting each other. Emma almost felt sorry for them—almost.

"The cars are over there covered by trees. You'll have to ask the trees to uncover them."

The Browns simply nodded and started for the tree stand.

"If I were you, I'd draw some Balance and use it to help you breathe," Emma called after them.

The surprised look they gave her let Emma know they hadn't thought to do this.

The Browns linked and power crackled through the air. Their breathing eased. Each of them pointed a hand at the trees and branches rearranged to reveal the blue SUV Emma had arrived in.

She ran to it and tried the door. It opened with ease. Hopping in, she looked around for a good place to hide a key and was surprised to find them in the ignition.

"Get in," she called to the Browns.

"This is an automobile?" they asked, dubiously.

"Yes."

"We have read about them. Seen them in link with the collective. They are bigger than we imagined."

"This one is. Hop in."

"How do we hop and enter this conveyance at the same time?"

Emma sighed and got out. She opened the back door and motioned them in. When they were both settled, she reached around the nearest one and showed him how to buckle the seatbelt.

"Why are you confining me with a strap?"

"It's called a seatbelt and it protects you if we get in an accident."

"You are protecting me?"

Embarrassed, Emma blushed. "Sure. A good driver always makes sure her passengers are safe."

The Browns grunted.

Emma went around the car to the other Brown. When she reached for his belt, he stopped her. "I understand what to do, human," he grumbled.

She shrugged and went to the driver's seat and buckled her own belt. The engine roared to life and she put it in reverse. She swiveled in the seat to look out the back and had to suppress a smile. Each Brown had a death grip on the seat in front of him. Emma took pity on them and backed out slowly.

Once they were on the road, Emma forgot about her passengers and concentrated on the way back to the safe house. About fifteen minutes later, she looked in the rear view mirror and caught the Browns with wide grins on their faces. It changed their entire look.

The expressions of innocent joy took ten years off at least, not that Dyads ever looked old. They were enjoying their first car ride.

For the rest of the trip, Emma contemplated where she should go. Her family and friends in Minneapolis weren't an option. It was the first place Damien would look. Also, she didn't relish showing up at her parents' house after all these months pregnant with no father in sight. What could she tell them? She'd taken an oath not to reveal any information about the Dyads, even to her family. No matter what happened, Emma would honor her oath. And her parents and friends didn't know she could walk. They all thought she was in Europe taking part in an experimental treatment. The plan had been for her to eventually go home still in her wheelchair but much improved. Gradually, first with a walker then crutches and finally a cane, she would slowly gain her ability to walk in front of everyone. Even with the prolonged recovery, the possible media frenzy over a paraplegic who stood up and walked needed to be avoided at all costs.

Where then? Another problem occurred to her. Since being swept away by the Dyads she hadn't spent a single dollar. Everything had been provided for her. What would she live on? If she accessed her bank account or credit cards, the human partners could track her down in a matter of hours. Maybe she should have thought this flee-at-all-costs plan over more carefully.

Deep in thought, she almost missed the turn in to the safe house. Her foot slammed on the brake and she took a hard right. Behind her, the Browns let out dual startled gasps.

"Sorry," she cried. "Almost missed the turn in."

Emma followed the mile-long twisting drive. Now that her escape had reached an end, she was almost sorry to see the Browns leave. Once they were gone, all contact with Damien and the Dyads would be cut off. She would be on her own, solely responsible for the lives growing inside her. If things went as planned, she would never see Damien again. A sinking feeling settled in her stomach and she pushed that thought away. Later, when she was safely tucked away in some secluded spot, she would open that wound and let it rip her apart.

After a hairpin turn, the mansion came into view. She pulled the SUV as close to the front door as possible.

"Here we are," she announced to the Browns. "Are you coming in or..." She stopped as a thought occurred to her. "Hey, how are you getting back to the portal?"

The lemon-sucking expression reappeared on the Brown's faces. "That is not your concern. We will enter the house for a moment only." After fumbling at the door handles, the Browns managed to exit the SUV. Emma grabbed her pack and went after them.

The large wooden doors to the mansion were locked. She contemplated breaking a window but then remembered something Luke had told her. She turned to the Browns. "Can you use your power to open the door?' she asked.

Without a word, they moved past her and each put a hand on the door. After a sharp click, the doors swung wide and the Browns entered.

Emma followed them into the wide foyer. She fumbled along the wall until she found the many light switches and flicked them all on.

The Browns couldn't hide a look of astonished awe. A crystal chandelier, marble floors, deep red wood for accents and a glorious staircase leading up to darkened levels spread out before them.

"So, thanks again," Emma said. "I'm going to grab the few things I left here and head out."

"Wait. We have one more duty to perform." The Browns crossed to her and put their packs on the floor at her feet. "This is for you."

Curious, Emma bent over the packs. The first was stuffed to bursting with hundred dollar bills. The second contained a mountain of jewels. Brilliant green emeralds, sapphires, diamonds and pearls shined up at her. A fortune of immeasurable wealth was contained in the two packs.

"I can't take this," she said.

"You asked us to aid you in escaping and making a break with the Diarchy. From what we know of the human world, you will need this paper money. Once the paper is used up, you can turn the gems into paper. We will not have it said of us that we set you adrift, alone and destitute."

"Destitute? Gentlemen, there's millions of dollars here. I can't possibly accept it."

"That won't be a problem," a voice from the dark stair said.

Suddenly, men in military uniforms appeared all around Emma. Each had a deadly looking rifle pointed at them.

Emma and the Browns froze. Her heart sped up so fast, she felt ill. The Browns seemed merely annoyed.

"Don't worry about accepting the money." The voice from the stairs again. A tall, older man with a buzz cut and scar on his face came into view. "It's not as if you'll get the chance to spend it."

Chapter Fourteen

ഇ

Hidden in darkness at the top of the stairs, Alex surveyed the scene in the foyer below. The young brunette stood stiff and terrified, her wide eyes mesmerized by the guns pointing at her. She'd forgotten the fortune spread at her feet. No surprise there. A gun to the head trumped money every time. What had the payoff been for? He made a mental note to find out later and dismissed the woman. She wasn't important.

The creatures next to her, however, were worth their weight in gold. Alex took a moment to stare in awe. Lambert's notes hadn't done them justice. He wasn't short but these beings topped him by a good six inches. A basketball coach's wet dream. Their bodies were trim but had a quiet strength with wide shoulders tapering down to a slim waist and hips. They wore their hair long, reaching past their waists and it was a color he'd never seen on a human head. Primarily dark brown, like rich tilled soil ready for planting but with other hues mixed in. The hair looked alive, always moving slightly as if blown by an invisible wind. And their faces. Alex's eyes shot back and forth between the two, looking for any variation and found none. The two faces were exactly the same—remarkable.

The tall creatures seemed unaffected by this turn of events. As they gazed at Reisdorph and his men, they looked as if something smelled bad. Didn't they realize the danger they were in? Or were they so confident in their powers that twenty guns pointing at them were of little consequence?

"Humans and their guns," the Dyads sneered.

At first Alex thought the one on the right had spoken but then his mind caught up with what his ears had heard. Both of them had spoken at exactly the same instant with identical vocal inflection. He'd read about this in Lambert's notes. How a Dyad pair could link their two minds together as one, but to see it in action—fascinating.

Reisdorph stomped down the last few steps. "That's right, Dyads. Humans with guns. Half the guns are standard-issue with bullets that will rip through your bodies leaving holes the size of baseballs. The other half are tranquilizer guns loaded with enough drugs to bring down a bull elephant in less than ten seconds." He walked behind the circle of men until he faced the Dyads. "I feel one ripple of power from you two and we open fire."

Alex's heart thundered at the general's words. What did Reisdorph think he was playing at? He needed these creatures alive and whole. They were no good to him dead or so injured they couldn't use their powers. They couldn't screw this up again. Not when he was so close he could almost see Jenny smiling up at him.

Before he could bark an order to Reisdorph, two things happened simultaneously. Alex's skin broke out in goose bumps brought on by some invisible force and Reisdorph gave the command to fire tranquilizer guns.

As the guns fired, the brunette screamed and wrapped her arms around her middle.

In the seconds that followed, Alex let out an involuntary gasp at the sight below him. The two Dyads stood back to back with their arms outstretched. In between the Dyads and the soldiers, hanging in midair, the tranquilizer darts wobbled for a moment and then fell to the ground, harmless. It was a scene right out of a science fiction movie, only this was real. If this power could be harnessed and controlled, the person who pulled the strings could do anything, take anything.

"Again," Reisdorph barked and another round of darts flew and was stopped. But unlike the first volley, these didn't fall to the floor. Instead, the points turned and shot back. Cries of pain rang out as darts found their marks and two men hit the floor, unconscious.

Reisdorph stood with the brunette clutched in front of him as a shield. He spoke into a small radio attached to his arm. "Cronk, reinforcements, stat. Bring shields." He broke the connection and shouted. "Again, tranquilizers only. Fire at will."

Even though he was only thirty feet away, Alex had trouble following the action. Volley after volley of darts sped through the air and were stopped and propelled back at the soldiers, some of whom had taken cover behind tables or in doorways. In the center of the action, the Dyad pair stood, their faces a study in concentration, hardly moving a muscle. Not one dart had gotten close to them.

By the time reinforcements arrived, three more men were down. The new arrivals fanned out among the remaining troops and formed a tight circle around the Dyads. Every other man carried a see-through shield that they raised to protect the line. Loud thunk noises filled the air as the darts hit the shields.

Behind the men, Reisdorph shook the woman. "Tell them to surrender," he demanded.

She tried to pull out of his grasp. "Why? So you can dissect them? Better to die here."

"Cease fire," the general shouted. He pulled the woman to the circle of men directly in front of the Dyad pair. "Surrender or I'll kill the girl." He drew a wicked looking handgun and put it against the woman's temple.

Alex flinched. Was he going to stand by and watch Reisdorph kill that woman? Could he cross the line and condone murder? Before he could decide, the woman spoke up.

"Boy, did you pick the wrong bargaining chip," she said, her voice a mixture of terror and humor.

As if to prove her words, the Dyads spoke. "She is of no importance to us."

"I'll shoot her dead right in front of you," Reisdorph threatened.

"Humans are always killing each other. What is one more in your death toll?" The Dyads turned away, dismissing Reisdorph and his gun.

"See," the woman said. "No bargain to be made here."

The general's face turned scarlet. His fingers twitched on the gun.

Looking into the woman's frightened eyes, Alex made his decision. "General, I want her alive," he shouted.

An inner struggle went on in Reisdorph. Alex bet he was weighing killing the girl, which he thought was the right thing to do, against following the orders of the man with the money. In the end money won out.

"Take her," he said and shoved the almost fainting woman at Cronk.

"Tranquilizers only. Fire at will," he shouted.

Alex fought the urge to cover his ears at the thunderous volume from the guns. On and on it went. The darts flew back and forth between the Dyads and soldiers so fast he couldn't track them. How long could the Dyads keep this up? Was their power unending?

A flash of movement from Reisdorph caught Alex's eye. The general raised his arm and pointed the gun at the Dyad closest to him.

"No," Alex shouted but his voice was swallowed by the sound of the guns.

Reisdorph took careful aim and fired. Somehow, the lead bullet did what hundreds of tranquilizer darts could not. It found its mark. Both Dyads staggered and touched their left shoulders. It was just as Lambert had said. What happened to one twin happened to the other. Only one of the Dyads had been hit with the bullet, but both of them were injured.

"Cease fire," Reisdorph called out.

An eerie silence came over the room. After the prolonged period of booming gunfire, Alex's hearing buzzed and throbbed.

The Dyads drew their hands away from their wounded shoulders and stared at the blood, astonished. They collapsed against each other for support, barely keeping their feet as blood gushed down their torsos.

Reisdorph raised the gun and once again took aim.

The woman broke from Cronk and ran between Reisdorph and the Dyads. She raised her hands, palms up. "Don't hurt them anymore, please."

From behind her, the Dyads spoke. "We do not need help from a human." Their chests heaved with the effort to speak. "Especially one who led us into this trap."

She ignored the insult and faced the general. "Please. No more. They haven't harmed anyone. What do you want?"

"Absolute surrender," Reisdorph shouted. "Nothing less. Or we keep making holes."

The Dyads straightened to their full height and faced each other. They leaned in until their foreheads touched. More goose bumps erupted on Alex's skin. The creatures were drawing on some unseen power. Were they using it to heal their bodies? This was just what he needed them to do for Jenny. Alex leaned over the balcony for a better look.

"We stand together before you, my brother and I," they said in a singsong, almost reverent cadence.

The woman turned to them, puzzled.

"In sight of all who have journeyed on before us."

"What are they doing?" Reisdorph asked. "Who are they talking to?"

"We ask to be accepted into your company," the Dyads droned on.

"Oh my God," the woman cried.

It dawned on Alex what was happening and he sprinted for the stairs. "No," he screamed. "General, they're going to kill themselves. Stop them."

"We offer all the knowledge we have acquired."

"Tranquilizers. Now. Fire," the general called out.

In the answering volley, the woman went down, a dart sticking out of her chest. But the Dyads were able to stop the rest.

Alex had reached the floor and hesitated, uncertain what to do. Another volley of darts ended useless on the floor.

"We offer all the love we have known."

Alex grabbed two darts from a pack on the floor. With a dart in each hand, he ran at the Dyads in a crouch. An unseen force threw him to the floor. He lay panting for a moment, the breath knocked out of him. Only a few feet separated him from the nearest Dyad. As more shots rang out, he belly crawled until he was within reach. He gauged his moment between volleys, sprang and plunged both darts into the Dyad's thigh.

For a few seconds nothing happened. Almost imperceptibly, the leg in front of him started to shake. A groan escaped the Dyad pair as the drug flooded their systems.

More shots over Alex's head. Darts stuck out from the Dyad's arms and legs.

"Enough," Alex shouted. "You'll kill them."

"Cease fire," Reisdorph ordered.

Alex watched in fascination as the Dyads wobbled, looking at each other with a quiet desperation. When they fell, it reminded him of a majestic ancient tree. The loud crack when they hit the floor made him wince. For some reason, he felt sad to see them lying on the ground.

"Get the medics in here," Alex demanded. He went to the fallen pair and drew spent darts from their bodies. He felt for a pulse but was unsure exactly how to do it and besides, he didn't know what a Dyad heartbeat felt like.

The medics pushed him out of the way and got to work.

Reisdorph started barking orders again. "I want to be out and away in under ten. Keep these creatures separated at all costs. I don't want them in the same vehicle. I don't want them taking the same route to our destination point."

A flurry of activity went on around Alex. He went to the woman. "How is she?" he asked the medic attending her.

The medic shook his head. "She should be dead. That much tranquilizer in a body this small…her heart should have stopped. But…" Using a stethoscope, he listened to her heart. "It's weak but still beating."

"Is she human?" Alex asked. "Could she be one of their females?"

"Who knows? Seems human to me," the medic replied.

"We are out of here," Reisdorph yelled. "Cronk, get that woman to the med unit. Mr. Ward, we need you to head out. I want to get as much distance between us and this place as possible. Who knows if those two got off a message to their pals back home?"

Now that he had some idea of what they were up against, Alex had no wish to face a room full of the creatures. Especially if they were pissed off about two of their number being drugged and kidnapped.

"As soon as she wakes up, I want to talk to her," Alex told Cronk.

"If she wakes up," the medic mumbled.

Chapter Fifteen

Damien drew in a deep breath. Emma's scent entered his body and he savored the experience of waking up next to his mate. How many mornings would they have like this? Would this be the last? He pushed aside the possible scenarios and decided to live in the now. At least for the next hour or so. Last night, they'd shared love the human way. This morning, Damien intended to further Emma's education on Dyad coupling. When he took her, their minds would be deep in link. So deep, neither of them would be able to tell where one stopped and the other began. His body hardened in anticipation as he reached for her.

His questing fingers met empty space. Confused, Damien rose to his elbow and looked under the covers, sure her luscious body was but a reach away. The bedclothes were cold, her scent fading, indicating to his heightened senses she'd vacated the bed hours ago.

Cold settled deep in his gut. Sitting up, he searched the room. Emma's pack was gone. So were the scattered clothes they'd strewn about in their haste the night before. If not for her indent on the pillow, she might never have been with him. Hadn't her wish been to fall asleep in his arms and wake together?

He dampened the growing panic inside and sent his mind searching for her. First his rooms and when he couldn't feel her, he widened his search to include the entire cave warren. Nothing. Could she be blocking him? Impossible. Emma didn't know how to shield. Dear God. Had she made good on her threat and started walking?

Damien vaulted out of bed, his mind reaching for David and Jacob. He woke both their minds from a sound sleep and shared his fears. The three of them agreed to start a discreet search within the Diarchy. Damien would continue looking with his mind and David and Jacob would rouse the others and do a physical search. Discretion was the key. The last thing they needed was for the Elders to get wind of this. They must find Emma and quickly.

He dressed with no thought given to what he put on, went to the outer room and crumpled into a chair. After what they had shared last night, how could Emma leave him? Had it been her plan all along? Had she asked to make love the human way because she feared what her linked mind would reveal?

With a great effort, he cleared his mind and focused on the special mental channel reserved for his mate. As the minutes went by with no answering flicker, his panic grew. Either someone was intentionally shielding her or she had found a way out of the Diarchy. He feared both scenarios but hoped for the former. The thought of Emma out in the world on her own chilled him. Besides the danger to her, it meant she'd taken his children away from him. Would she do that to him? Did he mean so little to her that she would take both herself and his children away? Every instinct urged him to pursue Emma. They were mated. Apart they would be incomplete. He faced the prospect of being apart from the two most important people in his life. Emma and David.

He had separated his Dyad, risked his quartet, and accepted the anger of the Elders all because of his mating with Emma. After all that, had she simply walked away?

The thought of never seeing her again, never hearing her infectious laugh, never watching the way she moved trying to hide her slight wobble, her teasing eyes when she tried to make him laugh, or those same eyes glazed with passion as he took her, made something deep inside him tear apart.

Emma had asked him once what his feelings for her were. He'd never given her an answer. Not really. At the time he hadn't known if what he felt for her was due to their mating or not. Once a Dyad male marked his female, he was bound to her body and soul. Had he been in love with Emma before the mating drive took him? Did it matter? He loved her now. Needed her as much as the air he breathed or the food he ate. It seemed impossible he could feel this way about someone who would turn her back on him. Emma loved him. He had experienced her love firsthand while linked and yet she had run away.

David burst in followed by Aiden, Jacob, Eleanor and Jude.

"Have you reached her?" David asked.

"Where did she go?" Eleanor added.

The newcomers formed a semicircle around him. Their expectant faces made him want to shout at them to get out. He had no answers.

Damien stood and shook his head. "I am unable to find even a trace of her. Either someone very powerful is shielding her or she has gone beyond my reach."

David put a hand on his shoulder. "Emma knows no one here powerful enough to shield her from her mate. She must have left the Diarchy."

"What of your search?" Damien asked. "Did no one see her?"

"No, but everyone was exhausted after the upheaval of the mating ritual and welcome ceremony. Most Dyads were in their quarters recovering."

Aiden drew a hand through his hair. "I don't understand. Why would Emma leave? How could she leave? Eleanor, you know her best. What do you think?"

Eleanor shrugged. "Not sure. She was spooked yesterday. Who wouldn't be? Let's face it, the girl has had a lot thrown at her the last few days. A mate, the Diarchy, children. She's always been resilient but there's a limit. Poor Emma."

Jacob put an arm around her. "There's only two ways out of here. On foot or through a portal. She knows it's hundreds of miles on foot. Would she risk her life and the lives of the children to get away?"

"Wouldn't that depend on what she wanted to get away from?" Jude said.

"From me," Damien said. "She wanted to get away from me and everything I have done. Look what loving me could cost her. Her freedom to come and go, her memory, maybe even her children."

The Goddards appeared in the doorway with Luke and Emil. "We carry a message for Damien from Emma." Sebastian held up two envelopes. He offered one to Damien.

Damien stared at the little paper rectangle. For some reason, he feared that envelope. It was only paper with words written upon it but somehow he knew it contained an ending between him and Emma. Would the others understand if he refused to read it?

"Did you see her?" Eleanor asked the Goddards.

"No," Samuel said. "They were passed to us by the portals."

"Portals," David said. "Then Emma has indeed left the Diarchy and gone back to the human world. Why did the portals let her go?"

The Goddards had reached Damien with the dreaded envelope. "Perhaps Damien should read this now," Sebastian said.

The paper was dry in his hand. All eyes were on him, waiting for Emma's words. But Damien found he didn't want to read Emma's message with an audience. He preferred to face Emma's words alone. It might be the last thing he shared solely with his mate. A last treasured moment of intimacy.

"Forgive me," he said and turned his back on the group. He could still feel them behind him, their minds assaulting his fragile calm. He fled to his sleeping chamber.

Unable to put it off a moment longer, he sat down among the rumpled bedclothes and opened Emma's note.

Dear Damien,

First, know that I love you. Nothing will ever change that. I know your feelings for me are all tangled up in Dyad mating rituals and how you marked me but my love for you has been clear since the moment I saw you. So please believe that my leaving is in no way a reflection of diminished love or respect.

I understand you are bound to your race's needs. I've seen how each individual Dyad is a part of the larger collective, bound together in ways I can't fully comprehend.

You are unable to act with just yourself in mind. Each decision you make must take into consideration the needs of your people. Your wants and needs will be last on your list. I can see where this will lead. You will give up everything you are, everything you ever hoped for, even your life so the Dyad race can continue.

Well, that just doesn't fly with me.

I think it's funny that the only way I see out of this mess is to act the selfish human and put what I want at the top of the list. To me, the way out is simple. I want you and David as you were before this all began. I want our children safe and healthy.

The only way I get what I want is to take the decision out of your hands and make it mine.

So, I'm leaving. I'll find a way to raise the children by myself. I can do it. You know I can.

Tell the Elders if they try to interfere, I intend to fight and fight dirty. I'll use every resource available, including outing the Dyad race to the press. Paint them a picture of me standing up and walking in front of a room full of cameras as I explain how I was made whole. That ought to give them pause. Tell them this insignificant human will not allow the Elders to take her children. Nor will they steal my memories. No one gets to do that to me. Not even you, Damien.

Please, if you love me, trust me in this. Let me go. Let us go. It's the only way.

All my love,

Emma

Damien crumpled the page. How brave she was. What a noble being. To save their children, to save him, she'd thrown a gauntlet at the Elders' feet and dared them to pick it up. How could any Dyad, even the Browns, look down on a race capable of such a selfless act? And all alone. His Emma, out in the cold human world without friends or family. He knew her. She'd never go near her family. Not if it meant endangering them. She meant to make her way in the world by herself, without him.

Well, that didn't fly with him. Two could play the selfless game.

He hurried back into the main room where anxious faces turned to him. Instead of giving them Emma's words, he approached the Goddards.

"You were holding two envelopes before. What does the other contain? Who is it for?" he asked.

Samuel sighed and shook his head. "It is addressed to the Goddard Dyad."

After a pregnant pause, Luke slapped Sebastian's shoulder. "Do we have to pry it out of you? Come on, man. What did Emma write to you?"

Sebastian made a very un-Dyad shrug. "We do not know if we should share Emma's words at this—"

Luke cut him off with another, harder, shoulder slap. "Enough." Luke pointed first at the Goddards and then Damien. "You boys need to stop acting like teenage girls with a secret. We are up to our ears in Dyad political shit. Now is not the time to withhold information. Out with it. First you." His finger jabbed at the Goddards. "And then you." The finger found Damien.

Sebastian locked eyes with Samuel. After a moment, they both nodded. "Very well. We see your logic in this," Sebastian admitted. He held up Emma's note. "Emma has given Samuel and me a sacred task. She has left the Diarchy, never to return. If things do not go her way and the children are returned to the Diarchy and her memory of them is erased, and if." His gaze fell to the floor. "And if Damien and David are…unavailable. She has charged us to watch over the children. Keep them safe, protect them within the Diarchy. We would be…she called us their godfathers."

Unavailable? Damien knew Sebastian had softened Emma's words. The word was dead. If the children were indeed Dyads, he and David would fulfill their commitment. They would have traveled on beyond the veil and be unavailable to safeguard the children. It seemed Emma had thought of everything. She'd wrapped up all their problems in an Emma solution box, put a bow on it and handed it to him. There was nothing left for him to do except sit back and watch events unfold.

"Your turn," Luke said, pointing to Damien again. "Spill."

Damien's throat was suddenly dry. Would they think less of him after he shared Emma's words? What kind of Dyad male couldn't protect his mate? If Emma had foreseen his useless state, would she have provided yet another solution? Probably.

"Damien?" Jacob put a hand on his arm. "Whatever Emma wrote, we are here for you."

Humbled again by his partner's unfailing support, Damien cleared his dry throat and read Emma's words exactly as she had written them. When he finished, the room remained silent as each of them mulled over what his mate had done.

Typically, Luke voiced what they were all thinking. "Guess we can all just go to dinner now. The little mother hasn't left us anything to do."

"Don't be an ass, Luke," Aiden said. "We can't leave Emma out there all alone. What if whoever chased the

Fitzgeralds finds out about her? At the very least, we must protect Emma and the children."

"I agree," Jacob added. "As human partners, it is our duty to protect and defend all Dyads in the human world. Even if they aren't born yet."

Eleanor took his hand. "It would be hard enough raising twins on your own. But these children might have some of the Dyad's powers. How will Emma hide that from the world? Who could she trust? Of course we have to find her."

"Wait," David said and joined the circle around Damien. "I think we should at least entertain the idea that Emma is correct." When Eleanor started to object, David held up a hand, silencing her. "Hear me out." David focused on Damien. "Emma has provided us a possible solution. She has effectively tied the Elders' hands with her threat about the human press. You know how they feel about exposure of any kind. If the children remain human enough not to threaten our numbers, we may continue as we have always done. The Elders will have no reason to banish us. Emma has, in effect, set things back to the way they were before you marked her. The question remaining is, can you accept this? Will you be able to let your mate and children go?"

The small pain in his chest that had been bothering Damien since he woke to discover Emma gone, tore open. This was a trap of his own making and he was well and truly caught. He could not ask David to go after Emma and risk banishment simply because he wanted his mate with him. If Emma could bear separation from him, could he not do the same? But the price? Never to see Emma again. Never to see his children. Eternity stretched before him in a colorless wasteland, a loveless parade of days wishing for what might have been. *Holy Balance. Give me strength.*

"Damien," David said, his kind eyes moist with unshed tears. He knew what he asked of his brother. "I will follow your lead on this. Say the word and we will search for Emma."

Samuel cleared his throat, drawing everyone's attention. "Before matters are settled, there is one more thing you should know."

David went to Damien, put his arm around his waist and drew him close. Just the touch of his brother helped to quiet Damien's raging emotions. The pain in his chest lessened. Maybe with David's help, he could go on without Emma.

United, they faced the Goddards. David spoke for them. "Tell us."

Samuel waved Emma's note. "This was given to us by the portals. When she went to them, she was not alone."

The arm around his waist tightened. His own muscles tensed, preparing for the worst. The tone of Samuel's voice—they were not going to like this.

"The Browns," Samuel said. "Emma and the Browns entered the portal together."

Everyone spoke at once.

"Oh my God," Eleanor said.

"Holy Christ," Aiden said.

"I'll be dipped in shit," Luke said.

And from Jude, "Of course. Exactly."

Aiden looked at his mate, puzzled. "Why exactly, love?"

Jude shrugged. "It's what I would have done. Don't you see? The Browns are the one Dyad who wanted Emma and everything she represented gone. It would have been easy to convince them to help. With Emma out of the picture, they could argue what a close escape the Dyads have had. It would be the perfect opportunity to pull all Dyads into the Diarchy indefinitely while the Elders decide how to proceed. As we all know, that could take years. A very intelligent move on Emma's part. She gets away and at the same time, locks the rest of us inside the Diarchy, unable to follow."

"Little Emma," Luke sputtered. "How could she do that to me?"

"A mother's instinct to protect her young," Jude said and then looked at Damien. "A woman's need to save the man she loves. Powerful motivations and coupled with Emma's strength of will, formidable."

"Formidable, yes but she made the wrong choice of Dyad." Jacob spoke for the first time since the Goddard's revelation. "The Browns are not equipped for the human world. To my knowledge, they've never been out of the Diarchy. Think what that means. They will be weak, unable to even breathe properly."

Damien knew what Jacob meant. When he and David had first left the Diarchy bubble for the human world, Henry VIII had been King of England. Even in that long ago time, the difference between the pure, clean environment within the Diarchy and human civilization took some getting used to. In these days of mass pollution, a Dyad entering the human world for the first time needed weeks to acclimate. Even drawing on the Balance, a simple act within the Diarchy, took much more effort outside. It was as if you had to relearn even the simplest of tasks. The Browns would not know any of this and they would have no Dyad or human partner to advise them. As pompous as they were, they would never doubt their abilities until it was too late. Without any knowledge about the human world, they'd taken his Emma away and would be unable to keep her safe.

"Serves them right," Luke said. "I hope they choke. Might bring them down a peg or two."

"One more thing," Samuel said. "The portals told us the Browns planned on returning within the hour. They are now six hours overdue."

David stepped away from Damien. "That settles it. We must see that Emma is safe. And the Browns, whatever else they are, remain our Dyad brothers. Whether they want our help or not, they will get it." He moved toward the door but Damien grabbed him.

He wanted to tell his brother so many things. How much it meant to him that he would go after Emma, how selfless Damien thought he was, how noble to put aside everything he wanted, risk the Elders' disapproval for Emma. But when he looked into David's eyes, all he could manage was thank you.

Damien turned to the others. "Thank you all."

"Your thanks are premature," Sebastian said. "The portals are unwilling to let anyone else leave without consent. We will have to go on foot."

"It's the only way if we want to keep the Elders out of this," Aiden said.

"That will take too long," Damien said. "We have no choice. Jacob, ready a small party of Dyads and their partners. The Goddards and the Stewarts will go to the Elders."

"What if they don't let us leave?" Aiden asked.

David gripped Damien's shoulder, his fingers digging deep into muscle. "Then we will go anyway."

Chapter Sixteen

ꕥ

What the hell hit her?

Emma made the mistake of trying to move her head. The answering ice-pick-through-the-temple pain made her cry out. At least, try to cry out. Her tongue was twice its size, thick and paper-dry, and sandpaper had replaced her eyelids. Not since the morning after she'd foolishly taken part in a drinking contest at a fraternity house back in college had she felt this bad. No, she took that back. This was worse. At least after that night of stupidity, she could move. Now, her arms were leaden weights. Even her fingers refused to budge. And for the life of her, she couldn't remember where she was or how she'd gotten here.

"Try to get some of this down," a kind male voice said.

She tried to open her eyes but the feel of a glass against her lips and cool water rushing over her parched tongue distracted her. For a moment, there was only the feel of blessed moisture seeping into her starved body. Heaven itself come to call.

"Better not give you too much," the same voice said.

She groaned in protest when the glass was taken away. A cool wet cloth was laid over her face. The groan turned to sighs of pleasure. The water had given her some strength and she lifted her hands to her face to press the cloth tighter against her skin.

A sense of her body's position took shape. She lay on her back with the top part of her body semi-upright. A light material covered her from feet to chest. Alcohol and floor cleaner permeated the air. Hospital—had to be.

Unable to help herself, she sucked on the cloth, greedy for moisture. Funky taste.

"No, don't do that. I think they bleach them." That kind voice again. "Here, drink this. But slowly."

A glass was placed in her hand. She lost no time getting it to her lips. When it was gone, she looked around, blinking her eyes into focus. A man came into view, sitting in a chair next to the bed she lay on. The room around them only had enough space for the bed, the chair and a small table. She'd been in small hospital rooms, but this was ridiculous. If she stretched her arms wide, she might be able to touch both walls.

"Feel better?" He smiled at her.

Emma put him somewhere around forty-five. Tall, blond, with sharp facial features. And wearing a suit that cost more than her first car.

"Who are you?" she asked, only a little raspy now thanks to all the water.

The smile widened. "My name is Alexander Ward. You and your friends are my…guests."

"Your guests? My friends? My fri—" The memories hit, rushing in so fast and furious, she put her head in her hands and groaned. Holy shit. Was she in it. What had she been thinking? She hadn't even made it an hour out of the Diarchy before she'd been caught. Not only that, she'd managed to get the Browns captured as well. What had they hit her with? The babies. Were the babies all right after all the drugs in her system? She put her hands over her middle and rocked back and forth.

"I see your memory is back," Alexander Ward said. "I'm going to need you to answer some questions. You feel up to it?"

"What did they hit me with?"

"A powerful tranquilizer. The doctors tell me you should have died. But you didn't. Why is that? Have the creatures done something to you?"

Well, hadn't he just said a mouthful. They'd done something to her all right. Repaired her spine for starters. And the babies. The babies.

"Will there be any lasting effects?" she asked.

Ward shrugged. "They don't know. They say you're human. But are you?"

His voice sparked a memory. "You the guy from the balcony who wanted me kept alive?"

"Yes."

"Well, thanks for that anyway. Where are the others?"

"Safe for now. Separated of course. We're keeping them unconscious."

Emma shook her head. "You have no idea what you're dealing with, especially with those two."

"Which is why you need to answer my questions."

She had no intention of telling him anything. At least, not willingly. What if they tortured her? What about the babies? Should she tell him she was pregnant? Would it make any difference? Time, she needed time to think.

"Why do you want them?" she asked. "Are you going to hurt them?"

He flashed that brilliant smile again. "I can tell you truthfully, I have no intention of hurting either you or your amazing friends. Quite the contrary, I want their help with a very special problem."

"And if they refuse?"

All semblance of a smile left his face. "That is not an option. For them or for you."

Emma looked around the room for a weapon. Nothing. Unless the plastic pitcher on the table was a hell of a lot heavier than it looked, she had only her wits to get out of this. She wasn't even dressed. The one-size-fits-all hospital gown scratched her skin. And no underwear. How come she was always without underwear lately? Talk about vulnerable. It's hard to feel you can defend yourself when one wrong move and your bottom is out there for everyone to see.

She sighed and turned to Ward. "What special problem? You need to get richer, more powerful?"

His eyes narrowed. "And what about you? They spread a fortune at your feet. What was all that money and jewels for? Looked like a payoff to me."

Emma snorted. "If you were watching, you saw I wasn't going to take it. Well, not all of it anyway."

"What powers do they have? How do they work?" Ward asked.

Emma decided to lie and lie big. "They have the power to come in here and crush you like a bug."

"You're lying. We know they don't kill."

"I don't know where you're getting your information, but I can assure you, they kill."

"Then why didn't those two kill the soldiers?"

"Those two are youngsters. Their powers are not fully developed yet. When their big brothers get here, there's going to be hell to pay. They won't leave one of you alive. They can't afford to. How do you think they've kept secret so long? Every human who's found out about them ended up dead."

Ward grinned and raised an eyebrow. "Except you," he said.

Emma had always sucked at lying.

The bed suddenly lurched right and then left.

"What was that?" she asked. "Are we moving?"

Ward stood and took her empty glass. He turned to the small table and refilled it. Emma salivated at the sound. Lord, she was thirsty.

"You are in Mobile Med Unit One," he said. "Or two, I can't tell. All military vehicles look the same to me."

He handed her the glass and she upended it.

"We are en route to a base located between Des Moines and Omaha," he continued. "Did you know John Wayne was born in that area?"

"Who?"

He shook his head. "Youngsters."

The water was doing its job. Emma felt stronger, ready to act. She still had the mother of all headaches, but if she saw a chance, she'd be able to make a break for the door. Only, what was on the other side?

"Where did you say we are? Mobile what?"

"Mobile Med Unit." He swept an arm around the room. "A hospital on wheels. On the inside that is. The outside looks like a harmless mobile home."

"Are the others here?"

He shook his head. "No, we thought it best to keep you apart."

Great. Even if she could overpower this smiling, well-mannered goon, who outweighed her by ninety pounds easy, she'd never get off a moving vehicle. And what about the Browns? She'd gotten them into this mess. She couldn't abandon them.

"Look, Miss." The smile came back with just a hint of irritation. "What's your name?"

"Emma."

"Just, Emma?"

"That'll do for now."

He shrugged wide shoulders. "Have it your way, Emma. We need information from you about the Dyads. If it's a matter of money, name your price. It you don't want money, how about your freedom? Doesn't matter to me." He leaned in. "One way or the other, you will give me what I want."

Expensive cologne drifted toward her. This guy positively screamed money. Should she string him along? No, she was so far out of her element, it was best to stick with the truth. Look how lying had gone before.

She sat up straighter and patted the sheet smooth around her body. "Look, I probably don't know any more about them than you do."

Ward came to attention, already anticipating the answers he wanted. "I'll be the judge of that. Start at the beginning. When did you first encounter the Dyads?"

"I'm not telling you anything until you tell me what you want them for. What's this special problem?"

His face hardened with anger. Emma met his cold stare and didn't back down. After a moment, he dropped his eyes. A full minute went by. She'd never been good at the silence thing. It went against her nature. Shouldn't she be doing something? Forming a plan.

Think, Emma.

Alexander Ward shot to his feet and Emma jumped, wary of his sudden movement. Would he call in the military guys now? The ones who specialized in interrogation? How long would she be able to hold out? One hour, two, a minute? It looked as if she was going to find out what she was made of. She had a chilling thought. If it was just her life in danger, no problem. To keep Damien and the others safe, she'd endure anything. But what about the babies? She couldn't let anything happen to them.

In front of her, Ward seemed to fold in on himself. His broad shoulders slumped, his head lowered almost to his chest. He fumbled in his suit pocket. Was he going for a gun?

"Here," he said and thrust something at her. At first, Emma couldn't register the object in her hands. Her heart still thundered from the whole torture scenario.

"Stop looking so terrified," he snapped at her. "I told you, I don't want to hurt you. But I will if you give me no choice." He gestured to the object she held. "You wanted to know why

I need the Dyads. What my special problem is. Well, there it is. Look at it," he shouted.

"Okay, okay," Emma said and focused on her hands. She held a small picture frame, very heavy, probably solid gold. In it, a pretty woman with long, chestnut-brown hair and sparkling hazel eyes looked out at her as if they'd just shared a secret. There was mischief in those eyes, and laughter. She had the wrinkles of a woman who was used to smiling. Emma liked her at once. Unable to help herself, she smiled back at the picture.

"She does that to everybody. My Jenny," Ward said, his voice flavored with love.

"She's lovely." She handed the picture back. "How does she fit into all of this?"

He gazed at the picture for a moment and then put it back in his pocket. "Jenny is my wife. She...she's..." He broke off, unable to continue. "Here." He fumbled in another pocket, produced a phone and, after punching a few keys, held it out in front of her.

When she reached for it, he pulled it sharply away. "No phones for you. Just look at the picture."

Carefully, he held the phone in front of her. His fingers shook so badly, she couldn't make it out. Finally, she reached out and steadied his hand. It felt hot and dry within her cold fingers.

She recognized the woman from the picture immediately. She lay in a hospital bed with tubes going into every possible orifice. The once-shining hair had streaks of metal gray and it lay matted against her scalp. Her cheekbones stood out in an otherwise sunken face. What a tragedy this was. How had she gone from the smiling, playful woman in the picture, to this husk?

"What's wrong with her?" Emma asked in a hushed tone, afraid to cause more pain to her captor. Why was that? He'd kidnapped her and she was worried about causing him pain. If she was going to get out of this whole, she'd have to toughen up. Put the children first and foremost in her thought process.

"Diabetic coma," Ward choked out. "She's a type-one diabetic. Had it since she was thirteen. But she wanted a baby. She wouldn't listen to me. She wouldn't..." He stopped and swallowed hard. Despite her resolve, the pain in his eyes made Emma look away.

"The doctors say she's dying," he continued. "They want me to authorize killing her to save the baby. I'm almost out of...time."

The way he said the word time, with such hate, scared Emma. Reminded her he was the villain in this piece.

Ward put the phone away and straightened. "Well, that's my special problem. I have it on good authority the Dyads can heal Jenny. Is it true?"

The hope on his face almost undid her. Damn. Here she'd been all set to hate this man and he pulls this shit. How could she fault his motivations? Wasn't she doing the same thing? Weren't both of them willing to do anything to save the people they loved?

"Yes," she finally said. "I'm pretty sure they can help her."

Triumph lit his eyes and a wide grin spread across his face, making him look years younger. "I knew it." He jumped up.

"Wait a minute. What makes you think the Dyads will help you? You and your army aren't exactly their favorite people."

He shook his head. "There was no other way. I couldn't take the chance they would deny me. I had to come at them with a strong hand to play."

"But nothing's changed. If you're thinking of using me as a bargaining chip, forget it. Won't do you any good. And the two you've captured? Think they will be in the mood to help you? Remember, they're the guys you shot and kidnapped.

The same guys who were willing to die rather than be captured."

Ward waved a dismissive hand. "I have the deal all worked out. They can't refuse. Here's how it's going to work. They heal Jenny and then wipe our memories. They can do that. No one need know about their involvement. There'll be no lasting effects. When I get what I want, they simply walk away. No one the wiser."

"And if they refuse?"

All emotion left his face. Emma could almost feel cold coming off him. "If they don't help me, if Jenny dies, first I kill the three of you with my bare hands. Then every scrap of information I've gathered about them goes to CNN."

Again she felt a kinship with this man. Hadn't she used the same trump card on the Elders? Exposure.

"Let me get this straight," she began. "If the Dyads heal your wife, you'll let them wipe your memories and allow them to leave, unharmed?"

He nodded. "Yes, that's the deal."

"What about the others?"

"Who?"

She motioned to the door. "Those military guys. Their leader didn't look like the type of guy who would let something like the Dyads slip away. You remember him. He's the guy who put a gun to my head. I can't see him accepting a memory wipe."

"They work for me and will do what I tell them."

Emma snorted. "Sure they will. After a firsthand look at the Dyad healing powers, that commander will pat them on the back and say, 'Thanks, you can go now. Wipe my memory please.'"

Ward made a slashing gesture. "Look, Miss, Emma. The deal is on the table. My wife's life or the Dyads see their faces on television. And you're free to go with money in your pocket. Don't forget that incentive."

Emma held up her hands. "What do you think I can do?"

"You're going to broker the deal."

She groaned. "With the Browns? Are you nuts? It'll never work."

"The Browns. Is that their name?"

Emma flinched. She'd given something away. She'd have to be more careful. No need to give Ward extra information.

"Yeah, that's their name," she admitted. "And they hate me. Really hate me. What makes you think they'll listen to me?"

"Because you're not me. Besides, you're all I've got. Will you do it?"

Emma mulled over her options. Healing Jenny Ward seemed a small price to pay for keeping the Dyad secret. But the Browns? How would they view this? For all she knew, the healing would violate some ancient Dyad rule. Had the Browns gotten off a message before they passed out? Could help be on the way? Damien? The familiar ache of yearning came over her. She missed him so, needed him. If only she could see him one more time. Hold him, breathe in his smell, feel his arms around her.

No. She'd made her decision. How could she wish for Damien to walk into all this? No, she had to get the Browns and herself out of this mess. She—Emma—with no Dyad help.

"All right, I'll try," she said.

"Excellent." He turned to the door. "I'll make the arrangements. Be ready. As soon as we get to the base, you'll meet with the creatures and get me what I want." He almost sprinted out the door. Emma heard the click of a lock.

Why bother locking the door? Even if a magical escape road appeared, she wouldn't take it. Not with the future of the Dyad race in danger. She had to stay and get Alexander Ward what he wanted. Because one thing was clear. She didn't want to be around if he didn't.

* * * * *

As the Mobile Medical Unit sped south, Alex hurried down the narrow corridor, his arms outstretched, using the walls for support. His mind whirled with the plans he had to make. Logistics first. Jenny had to be moved from the hospital in New York to the secret base in Iowa, wherever that was. Two phone calls should do it. The first to Walji and the second to the pilot he kept on staff. Thank God he'd left his plane in New York. It would save time.

He smiled. Time, his old enemy, had lost some of its menace. He could defeat it, crush it under his foot just as he had every other foe. Jenny would soon be back in his arms, smiling up at him, as she held their son in her arms.

Take that, time. You fucker.

Laughter rumbled up from his belly and he let it loose. The knot around his heart, his constant companion for months, loosened. When was the last time he'd laughed? As the laughter continued, despair floated away and was replaced by hope. This impossible plan of his was going to work. He could feel it. All he had to do was get the players together and let them do their thing. Afterward he'd—

The laughter dried up as suddenly as it began. He'd lied to the woman. To Emma-what's-her-name. Damn, he wished he didn't like her. But she'd smiled at Jenny's picture. Alex wasn't at all sure he could fulfill his part of the deal. Lambert would never let the Dyad pair—the Browns—simply walk away. The old man wanted revenge and power. But even half-mad as he was, Alex could take care of Lambert. No, the old fart wasn't the problem. The true threat came from Reisdorph and his men. How much control did he have over them? When push came to shove, would they do what he told them? Allow the Dyads to wipe their memories and give up the military advantage the creatures in their ranks would give them.

Maybe if he offered a bonus. Double their fee. Another forty million.

Never mind all that now. He'd cross those bridges when he had to. First, Jenny and Alex Jr. Nothing could get in the way of his happy ending.

A part of his mind protested. A great many things had been said about Alexander Ward over the years. Ruthless businessman, brilliant strategist and son of a bitch asshole to name a few. But up until now, Alex had never broken a deal. Whenever he'd entered into an agreement, even with a simple handshake, he'd come through. A son of a bitch, true, but an honorable one. An asshole, yes, but this asshole kept his word.

Nothing could get in the way of the Dyads healing Jenny but if there was a way, Alex would keep his word. Problem was, if he had to lay odds, he'd give Reisdorph four-to-one.

Putting all that aside, Alex entered a room that was a mirror image of the one Emma was locked in. He sat on the bed, pulled out his phone and dialed the hospital.

When Walji came on he smiled. "Hello, Doctor. Feel like a plane ride?"

Chapter Seventeen

ꟈ

"You and everyone who goes with you without first gaining our approval risks permanent banishment," the Salazar Dyad said.

"Elders," the Goddard Dyad replied. "We have no wish to go against you in this. However, every minute we delay is another minute Emma and the Brown are in danger. You said yourself, even the combined mind of the Elders cannot connect to the Brown. Neither can the Chaldeans. You know what that means."

The Salazar bristled. "No, they have not traveled on. Our race would know at once."

"Will you wait until they have to act?"

Damien ran a hand over his heaving stomach. How long would this go on? He and the others had been arguing with the Elders for over an hour. It had been a mistake for him to speak first. In retrospect, telling the Elders they were leaving with or without their consent wasn't the best way to begin. He'd thought it would save time. Cut to the chase as Aiden would say. But instead, it had put their collective back up. Damien and David had remained silent after that, leaving it to the Goddards to plead their case.

"The Brown left the Diarchy without our consent," the Salazars ranted. "Worse, they intentionally ignored our wish for all to remain. They have brought this calamity upon us."

"Whatever they have done, they need our help," the Goddards pleaded. "You must let us take our partners and leave."

"Must? You do not dictate to the Elders, Goddard. Nor you, Stewart. And do not think we have forgotten the cause of all this." The Salazars pointed at Damien. "It was your human who took the Brown away."

Damien couldn't remain silent any longer. "The Brown were not taken anywhere. Especially by a human. You know this. Why do I have to state the obvious?"

David and the Goddards looked at him with a mixture of astonishment and anger. He'd ceased to care. Arguing with the Elders was a waste of precious time. They had to go.

The Salazar Dyad remained silent but their faces gave away the strong emotion coursing through them. Damien had spoken to them as if they were his equals. No one did that. Again, he didn't give a shit. He was a millisecond away from turning his back on them and walking out.

A beautiful sound came from the Orchid Dyad. Unaccountably, the females were laughing. The sweet sound seemed to suck the tension out of the room. Damien's stomach finally relaxed.

"He got you there, Salazar," they said. "The Brown would never follow a human. We all know this. And yet, you felt the need to voice the opposite. Interesting."

"Until we are able to link with the Brown and share their thoughts, we do not know what the human did to them." The Salazar on the right held up Emma's note to Damien. "The human has threatened us with exposure. We do not know what else it is capable of."

Fury shot through Damien. Before David or the others could stop him, he dashed to Salazar. "Emma is not an it. She is my mate. The mother of my children. How dare you speak of her in that manner?"

David pulled him back in line with the others. He struggled for a moment but then saw the uselessness of throttling the Salazar.

"Peace." The Orchids rose and moved between Damien and the Salazar. "We weary of this fight, Salazar. The Goddard is correct. We need to act quickly."

When the Salazar tried to interrupt, the Orchids held up a hand to silence him. "Salazar, once the Brown are safely back among the collective, we will have all the time you wish to debate the future. But now we must lift our ban on leaving and allow the Stewarts and the Goddards and whoever else they need, to do what they have trained to do. Deal with the humans, keep secret the Dyad race and bring the Brown back to us."

"The Salazar does not agree."

"Look behind you, my friends," the females ordered. "You have been outvoted."

When the Salazars whipped around to face the other Elders, the Orchids faced Damien. "A first," they said and winked at him.

"Thank you," the Goddards said.

Damien was so relieved, he couldn't find his voice. David seemed to be having the same problem.

The Salazars collapsed into their chairs, astonished. Damien wondered what this power shift on the council would mean in the future.

As if to answer this thought, the Orchids spoke again. "Make no mistake, Stewart. Our letting you come to the aid of the Brown does not change our earlier rulings. You have the same decisions to make. Your options remain unchanged."

"We understand," David said.

All the Elders except the Salazars stood. The Orchids continued to speak for them. "Go then. If we can be of aid, send to us." They smiled. "We are but a thought away."

They turned to leave.

"And Damien," the Orchids called after him.

Damn, he thought he'd gotten away clean. "Yes, Elder," he replied.

All the gentleness had left the female's faces replaced by blank but cold expressions. "Do not come back without Emma and the children."

* * * * *

Forty-five minutes after leaving the Elders, Damien stood in the entrance of the Michigan safe house. What he saw confirmed all their fears. Evidence of a battle was strewn everywhere. Tables overturned with darts sticking out of them. Bullets scattered across the floor. The chandelier hanging from two of its four supports. Scuff marks on what usually was a pristine marble floor. And most disturbing, in the center of the upset, two pools of blood.

Samuel straightened from bending over the blood. "The Brown, both of them."

Sebastian held up a dart. "Tranquilizer, very strong."

Damien couldn't think. Each foreign object drew his eye and he couldn't help wondering, had that dart struck Emma, had that bullet grazed her flawless cheek? What if the worst had already happened? What if Emma was lost to him forever?

Calm flooded through him a moment before he recognized Jacob's touch. "We will find them. Emma and the children will be with you soon. Don't worry."

"I wish I knew what happened here."

"If they didn't locate the surveillance cameras, Aiden should have that for you shortly."

Damien had forgotten about the partner's seemingly paranoid need for security, including the surveillance equipment. Thank God they were paranoid. If it showed them what had happened here, he'd never doubt them again.

Luke ran down the stairs. "Doesn't look like she made it to her room. None of the upper rooms have been disturbed."

Emil came out from under the staircase. "Lower rooms untouched," he reported.

Wulfgar entered from a door on the right. "Back garden door's been forced. It's our entry point."

Jacob turned in a circle. "Looks like most of the action happened right here."

"Damn," Luke said. "This was my favorite house. I hate giving it up."

"You know the rules, Luke," Jacob said. "The place has been compromised. It's done. We'll either sell it or donate it."

In his mind, Damien felt David. *Damien, come. Aiden has something for us to see.*

He started for the stairs to the lower level. "Come, everyone," he announced. Two words but everyone automatically followed. No questions, no arguments. It was good to be away from the Diarchy for a while. Here decisions could be made in the wink of an eye and when the situation warranted it, no one argued, they simply followed.

He led them to the room that held all the computer equipment. Aiden sat poised in front of a large screen, typing furiously with David standing next to him.

"They were either unable to hack the system or didn't have enough time. I think it's all here," Aiden began almost absently as his fingers flew over the keys. "I should have it in a second."

Damien wanted to shout at him to hurry. Every second of not knowing if Emma was dead or alive ate away at him. Where could she be? What was happening to her? He rubbed his stomach again.

"Here," Aiden said triumphantly. "Here's the playback from about nine hours ago. That fits our timeline."

On screen, the entry room was displayed before the carnage. The light was dim but Damien could make out the familiar room.

"I'll fast forward," Aiden said and hit a few keys.

Damien watched the clock on the screen speed forward. One minute, two, five. Couldn't Aiden make it go any faster?

Suddenly, lights came on and the Browns appeared, followed by Emma, whole and healthy. Aiden hit another few keys and rewound the playback to just before the lights came on.

The sight of Emma with the Browns brought her betrayal back to him. Anger at her warred with concern for her welfare. If, no, *when* he got her back, he wasn't sure if he would kiss her or shake her.

Aiden turned up the volume and they listened and watched the scene unfold.

When the Browns presented Emma with two backpacks, one loaded with money, the other with jewels, Luke whistled. "Those boys really wanted her gone for good."

"Quiet," Damien demanded.

Back on the screen, the military had arrived.

Damien managed to control himself until the commander put a gun to his mate's head. A choked sound escaped him. All the blood left his head. If Jacob and David hadn't supported him, he would have fallen.

"Aiden," Jacob pleaded. "Can't you fast forward so we can quickly see what happened? This is torture for Damien."

Aiden turned and took in the three of them. Damien hardly registered his concern. He was holding on to his sanity by his fingernails. Were they watching Emma's death scene? All those bullets flying through the air. That evil commander with his gun. The coward.

"I'll speed it up twice as fast," Aiden said.

Before he could hit the keys, a new voice came through the speakers. "General, I want her alive," it said. Whoever the blessed man was, the commander complied and thrust Emma into the hands of the giant next to him. Damien relaxed a fraction.

Blood exploded from the Brown's shoulders.

"Why were they not able to deflect the bullets?" Wulfgar asked.

Samuel snorted. "Typical Brown. Overconfident. They became used to the weight and feel of the tranquilizer darts and let their guard down."

Emma ran in front of the Brown. Once again, Damien thought her death was imminent. She went down with a dart in her chest and he cried out in anguish.

He hardly saw the rest of the battle. He couldn't take his eyes off Emma, lying unconscious or…not, in the middle of the action.

A few minutes later, David shook him out of his stupor. "She's alive, brother. Did you hear the medic? Emma is alive."

A part of Damien came back to life at that moment. There was no other way to describe what happened inside him. After he'd seen the entrance room, he'd doubted Emma had survived. How could she have? A mere human surrounded by guns firing. Whoever the tall blond man was who insisted she be kept alive, Damien owed him. He could breathe freely again, his heart slowed to its normal rhythm and his stomach—whatever had been happening to that lately—finally eased, the burning gone.

"Did the dialogue the men shared give any hint of where they went?" Sebastian asked the room.

Aiden shook his head. "None that I heard. Let's watch it again."

The second time through proved easier than the first. Even so, Damien flinched at the gun at Emma's temple, and when she went down, he had to look away.

When it was finished, Aiden whirled around to face them. "Not even an inkling of where they were going."

"At least we know what we're up against," Luke added. "I counted forty-two total. But that doesn't mean there aren't others. We need more men."

"Sebastian and I will link with the Elders and ask them to send twenty Dyad pairs and their partners," Samuel said.

"Twenty," Aiden said, surprised. "Don't you think that's excessive? Eighty more men?"

"No," Damien chimed in. "I am wondering if it is enough."

David put a hand on his shoulder. "We must find a way to track them. Emma had no linking coin with her. The Browns are still a blank to us."

"Are you thinking about a reverse link?" Samuel asked.

"Unless you have a better idea," David replied.

When no one answered, Damien started for the door. "Since I will be the focus of the link, I will go to Emma's room and pick out the linking object."

The more intimate, the better, David thought to him.

I know. Damien made his way to Emma's room. As soon as he entered, her smell tantalized him. He looked around expecting to see her and pushed back a stupid disappointment when she didn't appear.

Everything was as she'd left it. The bed neatly made. The fingernail polishes lined up like little colorful soldiers on the dresser. The posters on the wall. It all screamed "Emma lives here". Only she didn't. Not anymore. Even if they found her, Emma would never be back here. Damien found that thought very sad.

Shaking himself out of his melancholy, he looked around for a linking object. It must be something that either had prolonged contact with her or was of significant emotional value. A ring worked best. Or a necklace. He went to the dresser, looking for her jewelry.

His own scent from deep within the drawer stopped him. He dug through her belongings, pushing aside pair after pair of socks. His scent grew stronger. Finally he found the source. A sweater. When he picked it up another scent hit him and he remembered when he'd last seen it. Emma had been wearing it when they'd first shared love in the library. Their mingled scents were all over it.

Why had she buried it in a drawer otherwise housing socks? Curious.

Impulsively, he decided he'd found the linking object. To Damien, the sweater represented his and Emma's beginning. It might even have been the time when the children were conceived. So, at least in his head, his whole family was connected to this object.

Family. Would he and Emma end up as a family with the children? Now that he was alone, without even David in his head, Damien could indulge in a perfect moment of what if. If he could have any future he wanted, what would he choose?

Emma. He would choose a life with Emma and their children.

Impossible. He knew it was impossible. Not even a remote possibility. But it felt good to admit it, if only to himself.

Putting aside this fantasy, he folded the sweater and headed back down to join the others.

Ten minutes later, Damien stood in the middle of a circle made up of Dyads and their partners. He'd chosen the library for obvious reasons. What better place to start the search for Emma?

All the Dyads were linked and ready to begin. All that remained was for Damien to center himself. When he'd found the calm he needed, he reached for David's hand. At his brother's touch, the combined Dyad-Partner mind flowed into him. He took a minute to drink them in and then he put the sweater against his nose.

Emma appeared in his mind. He dug deeper, pulling memory after memory of her from his subconscious and sharing them with the collective mind. With every inhalation, a new memory took shape. Emma as he'd first seen her, sitting in Mildred staring up at him with wonder in her eyes. Emma taking her first, wobbly steps, elated. Catching her looking at him when she thought he wasn't watching. Emma sitting in the garden lost in music. Emma beneath him, riding waves of shared passion. Emma, Emma, Emma.

Now that he had her essence established in link, he sent his mind searching for any trace of her. He found a glimmer of her on the southern wind. When he tried to follow, the trace weakened. Power, he needed more power.

Almost before the thought was done, David and the others fed to him. They drew on the Balance deep within the earth, channeled it and pushed it to him. With this renewed strength, he was able to follow the Emma trace. South and west. Moving, always moving, never stopping. South—west.

Suddenly, Damien felt another mind and then another. Far away, mixed in with the Emma essence. Love shot back at him. Love and recognition. He knew these minds. Innocence, love. The children. The children were reaching out to him.

A collective gasp came from the group as they all shared a joining with these perfect beings. Damien had their essence now. More importantly, with their help, he'd be able to find them anywhere.

Chapter Eighteen

ꙮ

"He looks terrible." Emma surveyed the Dyad on the small bed. Funny, it was odd to see only one of the Browns. They'd become a single unit in her mind. Looking now at one twin, the picture was incomplete. He looked so alone, so vulnerable.

The Brown's skin was a sickly gray. His shoulder was bandaged but the gunshot wound still bled, seeping through the cloth. Puncture holes from the tranquilizer darts dotted his otherwise smooth chest. The proud Brown brought to this. Emma bit her lip. Her fault.

"What else did you do to him?" she asked.

"Nothing, nothing," Lambert replied defensively. "Merely kept him asleep, that's all."

"With what?" she demanded. "More elephant tranquilizer?"

"Hardly." The old man sounded offended. "We've designed a special sedative consisting of two parts—"

"Save it." Emma held up a hand. "I won't recognize the names." She turned to Alexander Ward. "Did you know this was happening?"

Ward nodded. "I knew they were being sedated, yes."

"He looks half dead," she complained.

Next to her, Lambert bristled. "I can assure you, Miss, every precaution for his safety has been taken. We have some of the best medical minds on this. Someone with your limited knowledge of these things should not make snap judgments."

Who was this asshole? Ten minutes in his company and she wanted to kill him. Or at least put a gag over his condescending mouth. His name rang a bell but she hadn't been able to place him yet. Ever since Ward had brought her here, Lambert had been hovering over her, moving like a crazed Mexican jumping bean. Always in her way, clucking his tongue. What a dick.

Ignoring Lambert, she turned to Ward. "Look, I don't know what you expect me to do with him in this condition. I think talking is out of the question. I guess I could sing him a lullaby if you wanted."

Ward raised an eyebrow and gave her a sardonic look. "Point taken," he said and turned to Lambert. "How soon will he be able to talk?"

Lambert shrugged. "We can have it awake in a matter of moments. I know what I'm doing, Alex."

"Look, Alphonse. I don't want you to take any unnecessary chances." He glanced at his Rolex. "We have some time yet. How long will it take to safely wake him up?"

Lambert sighed loudly. "I just told you. Tell me when you want him awake and I'll make it happen."

Ward fisted Lambert's lab coat and yanked him off his feet, lifting until they were eye to eye. The doctor cried in alarm but Ward ignored him.

He drew Lambert close. "Now you listen to me, you pompous shit. I am too close to have you screw this up because you think you know what you're doing. You and I both know you haven't a clue." Ward shook him. "Don't we, Alphonse?"

"You shouldn't treat me like this, Alex," Lambert whined. "Without me, you never would have known the Dyads existed. You owe me."

Slowly, Ward lowered the wiggling doctor to the floor. He pulled his hands away. "Listen closely, Doctor. If anything goes wrong, I'm holding you personally responsible. I will give you to Reisdorph for target practice."

Lambert flushed a deep red. Emma tried to keep her poker face. It must be hard for a guy as stuck on himself as Lambert to keep quiet. But in the end, good sense and self-preservation usually won out. Even with pompous pricks.

"No need to get upset, Alex," Lambert assured him. "Everything will go as planned."

"You haven't answered my question. When will he be able to talk?"

"Give me an hour. We'll bring him out of it slowly."

"Want some advice?" Emma asked.

"I don't think we need your—" Lambert began but Ward cut him off.

"What? Do you know something that will help?" Ward asked.

Emma thought about the knowledge this would give Ward, but she needed the Browns whole and healthy. And she wanted them in the same room. "You need to bring the two of them together," she said. "Touching each other, I mean. From what I know about them, they'll heal more quickly if they're touching."

"Impossible," Lambert said and waved his arms at Emma in a shooing motion. "Much too dangerous."

Ward nodded and turned to Lambert. "Don't make me go through this again with you, Doctor. Get the other one in here right now. Put the beds close enough so they can reach each other."

"But…the danger," the doctor stuttered.

"Use your head, man. Bring in armed guards. But get it done. Understood?"

Lambert's mouth pursed into a pucker that reminded Emma of a hen's hind end.

"It's against my better judgment but I'll see it's done," he said.

"Fine." Ward turned to Emma. "This way." He motioned her out of the room.

Once they had left Lambert behind, Emma let out a sigh. "Can't say I think much of the company you keep."

"Alphonse was a necessity who's quickly becoming a liability. I don't like him any better than you do."

She tripped and he caught her. "Do I have to wear these?" Emma pointed at her leg shackles.

"If you want to be anywhere but a cell."

"Fine." She shuffled forward. "Where are we going?"

"To eat. I haven't eaten today and I know you didn't. Did you think the food I had sent to you was drugged?"

Emma didn't answer. He'd hit the nail on the head but she didn't want to admit it.

"Thought so," Ward said, as if she'd spoken.

He led the way out of the converted barn and headed to the large farm house. This base of theirs was quite a place. Besides the house and barn, there were six other buildings housing God knew what. If Ward hadn't told her they were somewhere in Iowa, Emma would have no idea where she was. After countless hours locked in Mobile Med Unit One, they'd arrived here and transferred her by gunpoint to a room in the barn. She'd been locked in the small room long enough to warrant two services of food and three bathroom breaks. The inactivity and constant worry was driving her mad. At this point, she was willing to follow Ward anywhere, as long as it wasn't back to that room.

Emma halted at the stairs leading to the house's wrap-around porch. With the leg shackles, she couldn't lift her foot high enough to clear the stair. She thought about sitting down and going up backward, but that was just sad.

Ward scooped her up and managed the stairs. His expensive cologne made her stomach queasy. Once at the top, he gently set her down. "Don't ask. I'm not taking them off."

She thought of mumbling a slur about his mother's lack of marital state but the scent of fried chicken and mashed potatoes wiped the thought from her mind. Her stomach grumbled noisily. Ward laughed and led the way.

The large living room of the farm house had been converted into a mess hall. Six long wooden tables with benches underneath sat in perfectly straight rows, three on each side. Men were scattered about in small groups, some talking, others too busy eating for any conversation.

Emma checked to see the flimsy robe Ward had given her hadn't gaped open. With only a hospital gown and knee-length robe, she felt almost naked. What she wouldn't give for a pair of jeans and a T-shirt. And she would sell her soul for a pair of underwear.

Ward led the way to the chow line where great tins of fried chicken, mashed potatoes, gravy and warm rolls waited for them. Typical male pack mentality. Not a vegetable in sight. Emma didn't care. She loaded her tray. *Your eyes are too big for your stomach.* Another of her grandmother's favorite lines popped into her head. Emma smiled.

"If you get this happy over slop like this, Jenny and I will take you out to dinner in New York someday. You'll think you've died and gone to heaven," Ward said.

Emma didn't point out that they would never be going to dinner together. If Ward kept his word, he wouldn't remember Emma when this was over. If the deal fell through, Emma would be dead. Either way, there'd be no night on the town in New York for them. She kept silent and tucked in. Ward might think it was slop, but Emma found the food delicious. *Hunger is the best spice.* Why was she thinking about her grandmother so much?

When she came up for air, Ward was staring at her, an odd look on his face.

"What?" Emma said. "I was starving," she continued, defensively.

"It's not that, it's… I just realized how hungry you were." He frowned. "I'm not a bad man, Emma. I don't enjoy making you suffer. You seem like a good person."

Emma's stomach rebelled. "But you'll kill me anyway, won't you?"

A haunted look came over him. "Yes," he whispered. "God help me. I will."

Emma lost her appetite. What had she been thinking? This man with his dying wife and baby was nothing like her. There were limits to what she was willing to do. How could she have felt a kinship with this killer? Dear God, she was even starting to like him. She must never forget he would kill her without a moment's pause. Or more likely, order her killed because he wanted to keep his hands clean. Either way, she'd be dead.

"If you're expecting me to say something to make you feel better about killing me, forget it." She pushed her half-eaten plate away. "I want to go back to my room now."

Ward looked as if he was about to say something but stopped. After a tense stare-down session between the two of them, he shrugged. "What? No dessert?"

In any other world but this, Emma would have laughed. It was her favorite kind of witty comeback. But not here, not now. The stakes were too high.

She stood and started to shuffle her way to the end of the bench.

"Sit back down," Ward said with menace in his voice.

Emma turned and took in the cold expression on his face. *Here's the real Alexander Ward,* she thought. Cold, hard, a man used to having every order followed without question. This whole, "Let's get you fed" nice guy had been a ploy. He wanted something from this meeting and she was about to find out what.

She sat where she stood, about three feet down the bench from Ward.

He sighed and slipped down his side of the table to face her. "What were you doing with them? The Dyads." When she didn't answer, he continued. "I can't make it out. You don't seem the type. Did you fall in with them by accident? Were they paying you off to keep silent? Why didn't they simply wipe your memory?"

"You don't get to know that."

"What difference does it make if I know or not? My memory of all of this." He waved a hand at her. "Will be erased."

"Or I'll be dead," she shot back. "Don't forget that part. Only your memory of having me killed won't be conveniently wiped away. You'll have to live with it the rest of your guilty life. See my face in your dreams."

"Shut up," he demanded.

She ignored him. "I bet this will be your first kill. What are you going to do, Alexander? Will you stand there and watch them put a bullet in my head or give the order and run away?"

"Shut up," he shouted again.

"Because it doesn't matter who pulls the trigger. It will be on your head. You brought me here, you held me prisoner, you threatened me, frightened me, hurt me. And it's you who'll kill me."

"Shut the fuck up." He shot to his feet, eyes blazing with fury. His hands opened and closed into fists at his sides.

"What?" Emma let sarcasm seep into her voice. "You don't want any dessert either?"

"You," he pointed at a nearby soldier. "Take her back to her cell." After one more burning look at her, he stalked off.

The soldier, an evil-looking bald man with too many tattoos, threw down a drumstick. "Shit," he spat and got up. "Come on."

Unsatisfied with her pace, he grabbed her arm in a vise grip and hurried her along. With every step, the shackles dug painfully into her ankles. To annoy him she said ouch every time she felt pain, which ended up being every other second.

Halfway to the barn, he shook her. "Shut up," he ordered.

Emma wrenched her arm away. "It's only a chicken dinner. It'll be there when you get back."

He gave her a cruel smile. "Never have liked a smart-mouthed woman." He put his hand to the small of her back and heaved forward.

Pain screamed up her legs as the shackles snapped tight and she went down hard, scraping her knees and hands on the gravel.

He pulled her upright. "What? No smart-assed comeback? Now, move."

This shove didn't have as much force behind it and she was able to stay on her feet. Shuffling as fast as she could, she tried to stay ahead of Baldy.

"That's it. Bet you didn't know you could move so fast," he sneered. "You just need the right motivation. I want to get back before my CHICKEN DINNER," he screamed the words in her ear, "gets cold." He laughed.

The sound of his laughter brought home to Emma just how much trouble she was in. These men were monsters, used to pointing their guns at people and pulling the trigger. Taking lives for money was a way of life for them. Humanity at its worst. Maybe the Browns were right. The Dyad race might be better off completely isolated.

She felt ashamed to be grouped together with creatures such as this bald nightmare.

By the time they made it to her cell, she almost wept with pain. Baldy opened the door and, just because he could, shoved her in. Emma tried to keep her feet but failed. Pain exploded in her temple as she hit the corner of the metal bed frame. Behind her, she heard the lock sink home.

A little dizzy, she sat up and leaned against the bed for support. Something warm ran down her neck. She brushed it off and examined her hand. Blood. With shaking fingers, she searched for the wound and found a gash about two inches long above her left eyebrow. Probably needed stitches. Her head fell back against the bed and she closed her eyes. Pain ate at her from many areas. Both knees were scraped raw, her palms stung, her head throbbed, but the worst were her ankles. How could they hurt so much and not be broken?

A memory came out of nowhere. Waking up in her room at the safe house after her time with Damien in the library. She remembered the warm feeling of discovery, of wonder. All that hope. How long ago had that been? Damien. What she wouldn't give to be in his arms.

Emma sank to the floor, pulled her knees to her chest, and wept.

* * * * *

Alex's grip on the steering wheel made his hands ache. How dare that woman question his actions? How dare she make him doubt, for a single second, his course? He would have to stay away from her. Who was she anyway? Nobody. Just another tool he needed to accomplish his goal. Like Lambert or Reisdorph and his men. She was nothing to him.

"She's nothing," he yelled and beat at the steering wheel with a fist.

"Mr. Ward?" Dr. Kunkle said from the passenger seat. "Everything all right?"

Damn. He'd forgotten the man was there. He'd forgotten where he was. Kunkle had showed up a half hour ago with a fully equipped ambulance. They were on the way to meet the plane carrying Jenny. Alex had insisted on driving. He'd needed something, anything to do.

After his meeting with...the woman, he'd been off-balance. Unsure of himself. Could he order Reisdorph to kill the woman? Emma, damn it. Emma. If he couldn't even name her, how could he see her dead? She was just like Lambert and Reisdorph, expendable.

But she'd smiled at Jenny's picture.

"Mr. Ward," Kunkle said again.

"What?" Alex snapped. "I'm fine."

Kunkle nodded warily. "Good. We're almost there." He looked at the GPS device in his palm. "The turn for the airstrip is a half mile up on your right." He turned around and gave a get-ready look to the orderly in the back.

"Okay," Alex replied. He took a few deep breaths and tried to calm down. Focus on the now. On Jenny and Alex Jr. They were the important ones. Not some woman he'd known for five minutes.

"There," Kunkle cried, pointing at the turn.

"Got it." Alex made the turn and saw the plane approaching. Impatient, he increased their speed. As the plane landed, he emptied his mind of everything except its precious cargo.

The door finally opened and Walji appeared. He took in the nearly deserted air strip and shook his head. Alex got out of the ambulance with Kunkle following and met Walji at the bottom of the stairs.

"Where the hell are we?" Walji asked. "Are you it?" He gestured to include Kunkle.

Kunkle stepped forward. "We have a fully equipped medical facility not far from here. The patient will be well cared for."

Walji eyed him dubiously and then turned to Alex. "I hope so. She flat-lined on the way here."

Alex's heart froze.

Walji continued. "I was able to resuscitate her but we are nearing the end. It's a matter of hours now, not days."

"I only need a few hours," Alex said.

"For what?" Walji grabbed his arm. "What do you hope to accomplish? What miracle do you think you've found?"

"Your part in this is over, Doctor. Thank you for getting them here in time."

His grip tightened. "Mr. Ward, I must insist. I can't just hand over—"

"Walji, I'm paying you twice your yearly salary for this trip."

"It's not the money, Alex. It's about your wife's care and that of your son."

Alex relaxed. He couldn't fault the doctor because he cared for his patient. The doctor was a good man. Alex put his hand over Walji's, still clutching his arm. He looked deep into the other man's worried eyes and smiled. "You're going to have to trust me, Hussein." It was the only time he'd used the doctor's first name. "This is a chance at life for both Jenny and the baby. You have to let them go."

Behind Walji, medical personnel were easing Jenny down the stairs. Alex lost interest in the doctor. Jenny lay on a gurney. It took four men to hold all of the equipment attached to her. They made an odd tableau, coming down the stairs. It reminded Alex of a puppet show, all those tubes and machines held aloft, all attached to his Jenny. Only in this puppet show, the puppet pulled the strings.

When they reached the bottom, Alex ran to meet them. He slipped in between the men and took Jenny's dry hand as they moved toward the ambulance. She looked much the same as he'd last seen her. Paler, perhaps.

As they passed Walji and Kunkle, Alex ignored the instructions coming fast and furious from Walji. Let Kunkle take care of all that. All he wanted to do was stare at his wife. He put a hand on her swollen abdomen to say hello to Alex Jr. No answering kick this time. The little guy was probably asleep. Didn't airplane rides do that to babies?

He had to step away so they could settle Jenny in the ambulance. Once in, the orderly went to work checking all the machines.

"Why won't you let me come?" Walji said from behind him.

Alex turned and put a hand on Walji's shoulder. "Sorry, this is as far as you go." He held out a hand. "Thank you for taking such good care of them."

Walji looked as if he wanted to say more, but shrugged and took Alex's hand. "I leave them in your care. My best wishes go with you."

"Bye, Doc," Alex said and headed for the ambulance. "Okay if I sit next to her?" he asked Kunkle.

Kunkle smiled at him. "Sure, but if I need to get in, you have to move away fast."

"I understand."

"Let's go," Kunkle shouted to the orderly. The man started the engine and carefully eased the ambulance into motion.

Alex took Jenny's hand. She was so cold. He brought his other hand up and sandwiched her hand between his, trying to warm it. As he looked at her, all remaining doubt drifted away. His resolve reaffirmed itself. He would do anything to have her back. Anything.

"Hold on, love," he whispered. "Just a little while longer. We're almost home."

Chapter Nineteen

༻

Damien looked out at the airplane and tried not to panic. The terminal noise in the background added to his unease. Every time he had his panic in check, a melodious voice announced another flight reminding him of exactly where he was and what he was about to do. How could humans do this? Voluntarily walk onto a metal tube and let themselves be hurled through the air at impossible speeds, without any control over their bodies. And all the while trusting a pilot, a human, to keep them safe.

Could he do this? Could any of the Dyads? His race never flew. Never lost touch with the earth. To be cut off from the Balance, unable to reach for its warm embrace, was unthinkable, insane.

"Let's go over this one more time," Aiden said from behind Damien.

Damien turned and took in Aiden standing in a circle of forty human partners in the small gate area.

"Your Dyad will be completely out of his element," Aiden continued. "We will seat them in the middle of the plane, as far as possible from the windows, which will have the shades completely closed. Each Dyad pair will be next to each other with their human partners on the other side. Once the plane is in the air, never leave your Dyad. Offer your Balance to them often, whether they ask for it or not. Understood?"

The crowd around Aiden murmured in agreement.

"How bad is this going to get?" Luke asked.

Aiden shrugged. "I'm not sure. No Dyad has ever flown before. It has the potential to get ugly. All their senses will be affected. Without the feel of the Earth and its life force, they will be blind. Unable to function normally."

"Good thing it's a short flight," Luke said under his breath.

"Short for us maybe, but to your Dyad it will seem like an eternity," Jacob added.

Damien jumped and then recognized David's touch. "I'm trying to think of this as an adventure," David whispered. "Another in a long line of our human studies." He eyed the plane warily. "What do you think it will be like? Without the ground beneath our feet, will our hearts even continue to beat?"

Damien shuddered. "The Chaldean believe we can make the trip safely. With our partners to draw strength from, it should be no different than when we separated and could not reach for the Balance directly."

David ran a hand through his hair. "Excellent theory. I wish it had been tested."

"If only we had not wasted so much time, we could have driven or taken a train."

"Mobilizing and equipping forty Dyad pairs and their partners is quite an undertaking. We have never sent a group this large before." David squeezed his shoulder. "Do not think about the time wasted. Rather, think about the time we will save by taking this flight. Ten hours by car or ninety minutes by plane." He shook his head. "Remarkable, really."

Damien nodded. "I am amazed Aiden and Jacob were able to pull this off so quickly. Chartering a plane on such short notice? These partners of ours show their worth every day. How can the Elders question our continued relationship?"

"The Elders will do whatever the Elders will do. In the end, you and I may not have to worry about them."

A familiar punch of shame hit Damien's stomach. Would he be the cause of his brother's death? "David, brother, what have I done to you?"

His brother smiled warmly back at him. "Even if we travel on tomorrow, I would not change a thing." The smile widened. "Well, maybe your snoring. I could have done without that."

"I love you, David."

David put a hand over Damien's heart. "And I you. Together, forever."

Damien placed his hand over David's. "Forever," he agreed.

"Damn it." A hoarse whisper from the left broke the mood. "I told you, Betty. No man that pretty is not gay. Look around, must be a gay convention."

Damien glanced over and saw two middle-aged women, decked out in travel attire, peeking around a corner at them.

"Yeah," Betty whispered back. "But don't they look like twins to you? Maybe a gay twin convention?"

Damien suppressed a laugh. After all Luke's careful preparations to make the Dyad brothers look different from each other, Betty over there had seen through it. Luke would be devastated.

Damien looked around the gate area. Forty Dyad pairs out in public. Unprecedented. None of them were sitting. Like David and him, they were all too nervous to keep still. Love and admiration for each of these Dyad brothers overcame him. Most of them didn't care for the Browns. They were doing this for him. Him and Emma and the children she carried.

In the hours following his brush with the children's minds, Damien had to do the reverse link five more times. Each time, more Dyad pairs and their partners joined in to offer their power. He always started with the sweater to establish Emma's essence. Through her path, he found the children. After sharing in Damien's love for Emma, after touching the innocent child minds, each new person involved in the link fell a little in love. In love with both Emma and the twins. In a way, Damien felt guilty about it. His brothers and their partners never stood a chance. How could anyone not love his Emma? How could anyone not feel the need to protect the children? Like shooting fish in a barrel, Emma's grandmother would have said.

The Goddards came up to them, breaking Damien out of his deep contemplation.

Sebastian positively rippled with tension. "The Elders must order more portals. We should not have to do this." His eyebrows rose and he let out a deep sigh. "I am…frightened."

"As am I," Samuel agreed.

Damien nodded. "Any Dyad who says he is not has gained the ability to lie."

"Almost time," Jacob said, arriving with Aiden behind him. "Do you want to link and search one more time before we leave?"

Damien thought about it. The last two times he'd followed the path, Emma and the children had been stationary. He put them somewhere within sixty miles of Des Moines, Iowa. There were flying straight to Des Moines. He doubted they'd moved and even if they had, this trip would quickly get all of them in the area.

"No," he finally said. "I see no need."

Beside him, Sebastian laughed nervously. "Damn, I was hoping they would come back this way before we all had to get on that…thing." He pointed a shaking finger at the tarmac.

The rest of the group turned to look at the plane.

"I guess one more link would not hurt anything," Damien admitted.

Jacob tried to hide a smile but failed. "Come," he said. "I've arranged for a private room just in case we needed it."

Quickly, all the Dyads and their partners went to the room. Anticipation filled the air. Damien tried not to be jealous. Each of them wanted another taste of Emma.

He pulled the sweater out of his carryon and started the process. With so many Dyads feeding him, the path was easy to follow. He would have to disappoint Sebastian. It looked as if Emma and the children hadn't moved.

He paused. Something was wrong.

Pain filled his head. The room around him gasped in shock.

More power, give me more power, he broadcast to the others.

A wave of power crashed over him. He used it to push his senses to their limit. The pain intensified. He smelled blood. He had the children's minds then. In pain, frightened, full of despair. Damien tried to soothe them but he was unable to cut through the constant onslaught of pain.

Something shook him.

"Damien, come out of it. There's nothing you can do for them now," Jacob pleaded.

He blinked his eyes back into focus and saw Jacob before him. Grabbing the big man's T-shirt, he pulled him close.

"Get us on that plane. Now."

* * * * *

The door to her cell flew open. Emma flinched.

"It's time. They're waking up," Alexander Ward said. He stopped in his tracks. His jaw hardened at the sight of her. "Who did this to you?" he demanded.

Emma thought about how she must look. Blood crusted in her hair, more blood on her hands and neck, her eyes red from crying. Must be quite a picture to stop a man as ruthless as Ward.

"Get used to it," she croaked. "I hear gunshot wounds create a lot of blood. Especially a head shot. You also get brain matter with those."

"Enough of that. Stand up," he ordered.

"Might be a problem with that." Emma winced as she moved her legs forward. Her ankles were coloring up, dark blue mostly but some purple had shown up in the last half hour. They'd swelled double their size and were cascading over the shackles in great swollen blobs.

"Goddamn it," Ward swore. He reached in a pocket and drew out a key. As he knelt on the floor next to her he said, "Why didn't you call for help?"

"Who says I didn't?" Emma gasped as he released one ankle and then the other. Carefully, she stretched her legs out and took a look. The skin had rubbed away in some spots creating angry looking red patches. The biggest one looked like Australia, the smallest, Oklahoma, the…

"Emma, do you hear me?" Ward asked and gave her shoulder a shake.

"Huh? What?"

"Are you in shock?" He sat back on his heels. "I don't have time for this shit."

"Sorry to inconvenience you," Emma mumbled. "I'll try to bleed quietly."

"Oh, for Christ's sake," Ward swore again.

"My grandmother always says that. But only when she's really pissed."

"Are you delirious?" Ward asked.

"Odd question, don't you think," Emma answered. "I mean, what can I say? If I was delirious I wouldn't know, right? If I'm not and say I'm fine, how do you know I'm not really delirious and telling you I'm not?" She rubbed her forehead. "My head hurts."

Ward stared at her a moment and shook his head. "We have to get you cleaned up and put together. I can't take you to them like this. Come on, I'll help you stand."

Gently, he helped her rise. When she put weight on her feet, pain tore up her legs. "Don't think I can do this." She grabbed his shoulders for support, which made the cuts on her hands sting.

Ward set her on the bed. "For what it's worth, I apologize for this. Stay here. I'll be right back."

"As if I could go anywhere," Emma grumbled.

He wasn't gone long. When he returned, the thing he'd brought with him made her see red.

"I'm not getting in that," she stated.

"What? It's just a wheelchair." Ward navigated the chair to the bed.

"I know what it is and you can stick it where the sun don't shine."

Ward looked at her, puzzled. "Look, you can't walk. I have to get you to the bathroom to clean up and then to where the Browns are waiting."

Emma stared at the chair. Wasn't this what she'd been afraid of all along? Ending up back in a chair. And not even a good chair. This one was way too big for her.

Ward had run out of patience. "Emma, you either get in this chair or I will call Reisdorph's men in here. I'll have them strip you, clean you up and tie you to this chair." He wheeled the chair closer. "Which is it to be?"

Tears trickled down her face. "I hate your guts," she said. "You'll have to put me in it, I can't manage it alone."

In the process of moving to the chair, her ankle hit the bed frame and she hissed in pain.

"That won't work," Ward said. "Tears. Pain. I'm too close to give a shit. Come on, Emma. Buck up. You're almost done."

Once she was settled, he swiveled the chair to face the door. She put her hands on the wheels. "I got this," she said.

"You sure you know how to drive it?" he asked.

"Pretty sure," she replied. "Am I headed to my usual bathroom?"

"Yes. I'll wait outside while you clean up. Hurry. Jenny doesn't have much time."

"She's here?"

"Yes, in the room next to the Browns. Please, I know you hate me but think of my wife and child. The doctors say she could die any minute. I'm out of time. We have to hurry."

Her arms found the old familiar rhythm. Just like riding a bike. The muscles remembered.

In the bathroom she caught a glimpse of herself in the full-length mirror. Emma in her chair. No, not her chair. This wasn't Mildred. This wasn't permanent.

She took her best shot at cleaning up. Right now, she just wanted to get this over with. Either the Browns would agree to the deal or they wouldn't. She'd either get out of this alive or not. At least it would be done. For the babies' sake, she tried to muster up some gumption.

Ward pounded on the door. "Almost done?"

"Coming," she said.

Once out of the bathroom she paused. "Which way?" she asked.

"Follow me," Ward said and took off down the hall at a trot.

They didn't go far.

"In here." Ward opened the door wide and motioned her in.

Tentatively, she wheeled in. Two beds were placed close together, each occupied by a Brown. Five men in white lab coats, one of whom was Lambert, milled around looking busy. In each of the four corners a soldier stood with his rifle at the ready.

Wasting no time, Emma moved herself to the small area between the beds. The Browns were still asleep, their faces at once beautiful and stern.

"Everybody out," she announced. "I don't need an audience for this."

"That's out of the question," Lambert said.

Emma dismissed Lambert and turned to Ward. "You want this to work or not?"

He shot a look at the Browns, glanced at his watch and then turned to Lambert. "Everybody out," Ward said.

"Alex, that is not a good idea." Lambert pulled Ward aside. "Who knows what she will think to them."

"If she's thinking it to them, we won't be able to hear anyway. Out," Ward demanded.

The room emptied of everyone except Ward. "You, too." Emma waved him off.

"Not on your life," he replied.

"Have it your way," she said. Emma wished she could stand. It would be easier to see the Browns' faces when she spoke to them. But then again, Dyads didn't need to speak to communicate.

She took one of the Brown's hands in each of hers. She tried to remember what it had been like to link to Damien. How had he started the process? Calm, he'd said. Always begin with calm. She took a few deep breaths and cleared her mind. On impulse, she started humming what she hoped was middle C. That had been the note all the Dyads had used to link at the welcome ceremony. At the same time she formed words in her mind.

Brown. Brown, can you hear me?

Nothing.

She tried again. *Brown, please if you can hear me, answer. We are in big trouble.*

Nothing.

Brown, please, she screamed the words in her head. *Can you hear me, BROWN?*

Stop shouting, human. We heard you from the start. How is it you are able to link?

Relief flooded through Emma.

Stop pushing all that human emotion at us or we will break the link.

Are you awake? Emma asked.

We have been for over fifteen minutes. We thought it best to pretend otherwise until we could gather more information.

You need to share my memories fast. You can do that, right? It would take too long to explain everything.

Emma felt the Brown's disgust through the link. *We have no wish to share memories with a human, especially you.*

Do you want to make it back to the Diarchy?

We are ready to travel on rather than subject ourselves to you.

This isn't just about you and your hate for humans. The Dyad race is in danger of exposure, especially if you travel on. Now, you do what's best for your people. Hold your nose if you have to but read my memories right now, she pleaded.

What makes you think we need do anything with our noses to read you?

Never mind. Just do it.

Very well. Prepare yourself and think of what you wish us to see.

Emma slowly relaxed and sent her mind back to when she woke in Mobile Med Unit One. As quickly as possible, she took them through each meeting with Alexander Ward. She tried to hide some images but found it impossible. It was as if the Browns were sucking the memories out of her.

When it was over, the Browns pulled back a little.

What do you think? Emma asked. *Will you heal Mrs. Ward?*

Astonishment bled to her confusion. Before she fully understood what was happening, the Browns spoke in her mind. *We will break link with you now. We must commune.*

And then they were gone, out of her mind as if they had never been there.

She straightened and turned to Ward. "They're thinking it over."

"Did you tell them Jenny's out of time?" Ward demanded.

"Believe me, I told them everything."

Sooner then she'd expected, the Browns were back in her head. Their first thoughts surprised her.

You would not leave us. You might have been able to get away, yet you stayed to help us.

Well, sure.

Why?

Because that's what people do.

You acted as a Dyad would.

I'm not Dyad. I acted as a human. We don't leave our own behind if we can help it.

And yet you kill each other, often. With no remorse.

We are flawed, yes. We aren't able to link like Dyads can. The individual has to decide what's best. You have to stop grouping us together in one disgusting lump. We are individuals.

After a long pause, the Browns asked, *How do you bear the loneliness?*

We don't know any other way.

Their minds drew back again. Emma didn't want to waste this opportunity for showing the Browns humans weren't all killing monsters but there simply wasn't time.

Please, Mrs. Ward could die at any moment. If you're going to help her, you have to act now.

We do not trust the human behind you.

Neither do I, but I don't see any other way. If you heal his wife, he might do what he has promised. If you don't, he'll make good on his threats. He'll expose the Dyad race. After that, there'll be no turning back. The humans will find the Diarchy sooner or later. Life as you know it will be over.

We are weak. Drugs flow through our bodies. There are holes in our shoulders. In our current state, we may be unable to heal the human.

Use the Balance to heal yourselves first. Get the drugs out. Close the gunshot wounds. That's what the other Dyads do when they've been hurt. They draw on the Balance and heal their bodies. Please, will you try?

After what seemed like a lifetime, they replied. *Yes, Little Emma. For the good of our people, we will try.*

Emma turned to Ward, standing tense behind her. "They said yes," she told him.

Ward let out a relieved sigh and headed for the door.

"Wait, they have a few conditions," she added.

"Conditions?" Alex asked. "No conditions." There wasn't time for this. Jenny could die at any moment. So close. He was so close.

"Mr. Ward. I've gotten them to agree to this," Emma said. "Believe me, they're not happy about it. Nor are they stupid. They don't trust you. Neither do I. But there's one sure way to make this go smoother."

"There's no time. Tell them I'll give them whatever they want, agree to any condition, once Jenny is out of danger."

"It will only take a minute and they won't do it until you agree."

"What is it?"

"You have to let them into your mind. You have to..." She trailed off. Her eyes lost focus. Her hands, still clasped by the creatures, tightened.

"What is it? What's wrong?" Alex asked.

"Oh God," Emma gasped. She tried to pull her hands away but the Dyads held on tight.

"What's happening?" Alex stood by, helpless as she threw her head back and moaned.

"Burning, the burning. Stop, let me go. You don't need me for this," she screamed.

Electricity ran across his skin. He reached for the wheelchair, uncertain what to do. The woman was in pain. Had the creatures lied to her? Had Emma lied to him? Were they powering up to ready their escape? Frantically, he pulled at the chair. It came away but Emma stayed put. She fell to the floor. The sound of her knees hitting wood made him wince.

"What should I do?" He rolled the chair out of the way and reached for her.

"No, don't touch," she managed to cry. "Don't touch us."

"Why? What are they doing…" He understood then. As he watched in wonder, the dart wounds on the creature's chests closed up. The IVs in their hands dropped to the floor. Right before his eyes, they were healing. If he pulled the bandages away, would there be any sign of the gunshot wounds?

Their eyes opened suddenly and focused on him. Alex jumped back, afraid. Emma was still incapacitated. He faced the creatures alone.

They sat up. A move so graceful it looked as if they hadn't used any muscles. Each swung his legs to the center where Emma knelt, still clutched in their grip. They put their free hands on her head.

"Your pain distresses us," the Dyads said. "How could bald soldier treat you so cruelly? Was he unaware of the lives you carry? Why did you not tell us about the twins?"

Alex took another step back. If these creatures chose, they could incapacitate him in seconds; wipe all memory of Jenny dying in the next room. The thought horrified him. He reached for the small handgun hidden in his suit pocket but then thought better of it. If he pulled a gun, they'd never heal Jenny. Besides, their focus seemed to be on Emma. What had they said about a bald soldier? And lives she carried. Lives? Was Emma pregnant?

Dear God. If he ordered her killed now, he would not only be responsible for her death but for the lives of the twins she carried.

Before him, Emma sat down hard on her backside. Her legs unfolded so he could see her damaged ankles. The sight brought on another rush of shame he tried to suppress. No matter how he tried to justify this, he was responsible for what had been done to her. The cut on her forehead, the scrapes on her hands and knees, were his fault. She'd been hurt under his orders. If only he'd added a few words when he'd told the soldier to take her back to her room. *Don't hurt her* was all he'd had to say.

Goose bumps erupted on his skin. The sensation intensified as if small insects crawled all over him. As he fought the urge to run, the Dyads closed their eyes and started to hum. The clear, beautiful note shot calm into him. His taut muscles relaxed and his breathing eased. Even as he welcomed the changes in his body, a part of him rebelled. Was this how the mind wiping process started?

On the floor, Emma went rigid. A pitiful moan escaped her. Something was happening to the cut on her head. The skin around it blurred for a moment and then, as if pulled by an invisible zipper, the wound closed. The angry, red skin changed to a healthy pink. Soon, the only evidence left was the dried blood.

Against his better judgment, Alex moved closer for a better look. In the same manner as her forehead, the scrapes on her hands and knees faded. His gaze went to her ankles and he watched the colors change from purple, blue and yellow, to the same healthy pink.

Emma's body went limp. The two Dyads stopped humming, opened their eyes and maneuvered her to lay on one of the beds. Alex touched the skin on the ankle closest to him. A miracle. He'd just witnessed a miracle.

Lost in thought, he missed the Dyads turning their attention to him until it was too late. A hand clamped down on each of his wrists.

"Now, Alexander Ward," they said and moved closer. "Show us why we should heal your wife."

"You know why. If you don't I'll…I'll…" Alex stammered. Their eyes stopped his attempted threat. Their irises were huge, like owls. The look of them hammered home how foreign they were, how *other*. Staring into them, any threat he was about to make seemed useless. After what he'd just seen, who was he to demand anything of these proud, noble creatures?

"We know what you have threatened. We know what you have offered." They leaned in. One of them raised Alex's chin to look up at them. "Show us, human. Show us the why."

Trapped. He was trapped. The fingers surrounding his wrists were granite. Should he scream for Reisdorph's men?

No. Not even the general and all his men could force the Dyads to heal Jenny. He would have to let them invade his mind. But how?

"I-I don't know how," he finally managed.

Their free hands wove into his hair, strong and cold. "Calm," they chanted. "We must begin with calm."

Cold, hard terror shot into Alex. Control, he'd lived his life always being in control. Any time bad things happened, it was because he'd lost control of the situation. His parents' deaths, Jenny's condition, even her pregnancy had happened while he'd been helpless to change anything. He couldn't do this. He wouldn't let—

Oh, but you will.

"Who said that," Alex cried out.

We are with you.

Double vision overcame him. He could see the Dyads so close, their faces a few inches from his own. But he could also see himself, his eyes wide, his mouth gaping open, from their perspective. They were in his mind. God help him. They were in his mind.

Surrender your why. If you want us to heal your wife, give us the why of it.

Out of nowhere, a slide show of memories flashed. Little boy Alex, playing with his nanny Mary, the only person besides Jenny who truly loved him. Adolescent Alex, at boarding school, starting fight after fight because all he wanted to do was go home. Young adult Alex, going through woman after woman, searching for something other than the cold, money-driven relationships he seemed doomed to. Boardroom Alex, taking over one company after another, heedless of the lives he ruined. His mother's death. His father's death. The memories came quicker now as if sucked out of him. Meeting Jenny. Her laughing eyes. Her playful smile. She'd refused to go out with him at first. He'd had to win her over. Their life together. Their childless state. And finally, the pregnancy, Jenny's initial joy and final decline.

They stole it all from him, these creatures. He could hide nothing, keep nothing back for himself. His life, his thoughts, everything was laid bare before them. They sucked it all in like a couple of psychic vampires, gaining knowledge about him but giving nothing back in return.

Finally, they let him go, both mentally and physically. A cold emptiness settled around his heart. He wiped away tears he hadn't realized he'd shed. After seeing his life and every hurtful, wrong thing he'd done, they'd never heal Jenny.

The creatures went to stand on either side of Emma as she rested on the bed. Each of them placed a hand on her head. Without looking at him, they spoke.

"This human, with all her flaws, is worth a thousand of you, Ward. Her history is filled with helping others, always putting her needs last. Faced with great adversity, she has shown a strength of will we thought only Dyads achieved." They turned to him, their faces unreadable. "Your history is quite another matter. You embody what we know to be true of humans. Selfish, weak creatures. Never thinking of the greater good. A useless waste of space."

All Alex's hope disappeared. It was just as he'd feared. After seeing him for what he was, they wouldn't help. They would let Jenny and Alex Jr. die. Yes, he could kill them and Emma too. He could expose their race. But their deaths would not give Jenny back to him. It was over. He was done.

"Please," he begged. "Please save my wife. Save my boy. Please."

"Your love for your wife and child is the only pure thing in your heart. You have done many evil things to get us here. Because of you and your wife, two of our number are lost to us."

"I'm sorry. I didn't want them dead. I didn't know—"

The Dyads raised their hands and came toward him. "We accept your deal. Let Emma go, let us go, keep secret the Dyad race and we will heal your wife."

Alex was ill with relief. "Thank you," he choked out.

"Humans," they scoffed. "You back us into a corner, force us to do your will and then thank us." They frowned. "You are a backward people."

He didn't want to take the chance they would change their minds. "She's this way. In the next room."

"So are men with guns," they said.

"Don't worry. I'll take care of them."

"Remember, Ward. We know your thoughts on Reisdorph and his men. They must pull back far enough so we may get away after the healing."

"All right," Alex said. He would have promised them anything. He turned to make it happen.

"Alexander Ward," they called out, stopping him.

"Yes."

"You have never broken a deal in your life. Do not start with this one."

Chapter Twenty

ꝏ

For the hundredth time since he'd felt the children's pain, Damien fought back the need to kill. He wanted these soldiers dead. If he got the chance, he'd snuff the life out of them with his bare hands. Better yet, he'd suck out their energy and use it to fuel the slaughter. One after the other, he'd drain them dry. The evil commander with the scar on his face would be first. He'd dared put a gun to his mate's head.

What would it be like to watch the life leave the man's eyes as he killed him? It would be good. It would be right.

"Damien, stop." David shook him. "You are projecting. Everyone is picking up your killing fantasies. Look around you, brother."

Startled, Damien took in his brother's worried face. Beside him, Aiden and Jacob were equally tense. Turning, Damien counted twenty men in a loose circle around him. From his vantage point on the ridge he could see other groups of Dyads and their partners, all waiting for him to lead them. After the horrific plane ride, all eighty had made their way to this secluded spot, sixty miles west of Des Moines.

He could do it. He could release the partners from their vow and send them out to kill.

"Would you turn us all into killing machines?" David shouted.

Damien's teeth smashed together at the force of David's shake. A snarl tore from his throat. He shoved his brother away and watched him fall into Aiden's arms. Snarling again, he turned in a circle waiting for an attack, wanting a fight. He needed to hit something. Pound with his fists, beat someone bloody. Who would it be?

Luke's face came into view. *Perfect.* He'd flirted with Emma one too many times. The arrogant Scotsman never missed a chance to try his feeble charm out on Damien's mate. Always the witty barb, always the veiled sexual innuendo designed to make Emma look his way. It was long past time to put this weak human in his place. How would his legendary smile appear without any teeth?

Damien focused the killing rage and moved toward Luke. His hands itched to squeeze the smaller man's throat. Jacob stepped in his path.

"Here," Jacob said. "If you need to pound someone, it's going to be me."

"No, Jacob." Luke pushed him out of the way and sneered at Damien. "You've been itching to fight me ever since you put your mark on Emma. What's the matter, Damien? You afraid without your mark on her, Emma would have chosen me?"

"Luke, stop," Sebastian cried from the left. "You are only fueling him."

Luke ignored his Dyad and continued. "But you took away Emma's choices, didn't you? Deep down, you knew all I had to do was snap my fingers and Emma would be in my bed."

Red light blurred Damien's vision. In a heartbeat, he was on Luke, punching, kicking and trying to bite. He threw off the hands that tried to separate them. With each connecting jab, satisfaction flooded through him.

More hands on him. He couldn't break free. They pulled him away from his prey. "No," he screamed.

"Enough," Samuel shouted in his ear. "Damien, come back to us. What good are you to Emma and the children in this state?"

Emma? The children? Hurt and alone. Helpless. Surrounded by men who wished them harm. Emma. The children.

What was happening to him? Dear God. Would he never put Emma's needs before his own?

Samuel's mind linked with his and the rage ebbed and then drained away. Damien took stock of his situation. Samuel and Jacob, with two others, held him back. In front of him, Wulfgar held a limp Luke in his arms while Sebastian rushed to them. To the left, Aiden supported a shell-shocked David. In a circle around him, all the Dyads with their partners stood, their faces a mixture of pain and uncertainty.

He had done this to them. Damien lowered his eyes, too ashamed to look at any of them. Unworthy. His actions made him unworthy to stand with his comrades. Wouldn't they be better off if he left? Slinked back to the Diarchy where he could do no more harm?

A few minutes went by, the only sound the deep breathing of the many men surrounding him. Damien kept his eyes down. He felt drained and curiously light, as if he could float away.

Boots came into the small patch of ground he'd focused on. One of the boots started tapping impatiently. Damien followed the boots up jean clad legs, past a muscled T-shirt and settled on Luke's face.

Luke wiped blood from the side of his mouth. "Well, now that we've got that out of the way, can we save your mate?" He gave Damien a crooked smile and because he was Luke, winked.

Snorts and guffaws echoed around him. The hands holding Damien let go and he straightened.

"Luke, I..." Damien started but couldn't find the words to continue. Shame got in the way.

The Scotsman laughed and slapped him on the shoulder. "Think I can't tell when a man's lid is ready to blow? I just knew the quickest way to pop your top." He flung his arms wide to include the group. "We all needed to clear the air and a good Luke whopping was just the ticket. Now that Sebastian has healed the effects, we can get on with the business at hand."

"Luke, please let me..." Damien began but Luke cut him off.

"Save it, Damien. You're not the first man who's wanted to ruin my perfect smile." He sobered. "But, for the record. There's never been anyone for Emma except you. She was yours from the moment your eyes met." He slapped Damien's shoulder again. "The poor, misguided lass."

Another round of chuckles washed the last of the pent-up tension away. Shoulders straightened. Some of the men jumped in place. Others swung their arms back and forth. Everyone readied their bodies for the coming fight.

Sebastian went to the circle's center. "Come, Damien. Find Emma and the children one last time. When we have their exact location, we will plan our onslaught."

With David and Jacob flanking him, Damien went to Sebastian. He took Emma's sweater out of his pack and placed it against his nose. As he drew in her scent the others began to link with him. First David and Jacob, then Aiden followed quickly by the Goddard quartet. As each individual joined the link, the power surging through Damien grew. One after the other, eighty minds joined in. Damien drew on their power and pushed his senses out.

This close, it took only seconds to locate Emma and the children. Less than two miles separated them. Such a little distance but so much could happen in the time it would take to reach them.

It hit their combined link then—the pain, the fright. So close now, Damien was able to break through and send reassurance and love to the infant minds. Recognition and relief came from the children. Both of them latched on to Damien's consciousness with a strength that surprised and delighted him. What wonderful little people they were. They had been so brave. *Everything will be fine now,* he thought to them. *Father is on the way. Father will take care of Mother.*

But Mother is so frightened, so alone, his son thought back to him. They could not reach her mind as they could his. They could not help her, ease her aloneness.

Come quickly, Father. It hurts.

As quick as it had appeared, the pain was gone. From nowhere, two more minds invaded their link. Healing power crashed over them, forcing the Damien link out. He snapped back into his body with a force that left him reeling.

The combined link broke apart. Damien opened his eyes and found himself back in the circle of Dyads and their partners.

"What was that?" Jacob asked.

Damien turned to him. "The Browns have woken up."

* * * * *

"What you're asking is impossible." Reisdorph slapped one hand into the other for emphasis. "Impossible," he reiterated.

Emma bit at a nail and watched Ward plant himself in front of the general.

"Never could abide that word from a subordinate," Ward said in a quiet, controlled voice. "If I tell you to pull your men back, you give the order and pull them back. That's the way this works. I give you an order and you give your men orders. Following orders is what you do."

Reisdorph's face colored. "Not when the order puts our whole mission at risk."

"Your mission is to do whatever I tell you."

"Mr. Ward, if we leave you alone with these creatures," he said, gesturing toward the Browns standing on either side of the bed Mrs. Ward lay on. "What's to stop them from incapacitating you and escaping?"

"Their word," Ward said.

Reisdorph shook his head. Next to him, Lambert snorted.

"Their word." Reisdorph added his own snort. "Well, why didn't you say so? That changes everything." He waved his arms wildly about. "Let's pack up the troops and head out." He turned to Lambert. "Talk some sense into him."

Emma could see where this was headed. Reisdorph would never pull his men away from the Browns. In his place, she wouldn't. It would be stupid and Reisdorph wasn't a stupid man.

"Come now, Alex," Lambert placated. "Surely we can reach a compromise. What if the general agreed to pull out of the building?" He turned to Reisdorph. "You can agree to that, can't you?"

The general bristled. "I don't like it but it's doable."

"There, you see." Lambert all but danced. "Compromise. The men out of the building. Will that do, Alex?"

Ward looked to the Browns who, after a moment, nodded. Emma wished she were still linked with them and knew what they'd planned. As it was, she had to settle for speculation in this power play.

"Fine," Ward said. He went to Reisdorph and ushered him to the door. "Hurry. Everyone out of the building."

Reisdorph broke Ward's hold and turned to the Dyads. "We will be just outside these walls," he warned. "You try anything and we're back in seconds." He pointed a finger at them. "Remember, I beat you once and I can do it again. Only this time, I won't stop at wounding you. Maybe we'll see how many holes you can take." He turned and headed out. "We are out of here," he said. The six troops hugging the walls lowered their guns and followed.

After they left, Ward turned to Lambert and the three medics. "You too. Out," he ordered.

"Absolutely not." Lambert waved a dismissive hand. "If you think I'm going to miss this, you've lost your mind."

Before Ward could answer, the Dyads spoke. "The woman is dying. Her heart is stopping. The child starts to fail."

Emma gasped. Despite everything Ward had done, she couldn't bear it if he lost his wife and child. Besides, Mrs. Ward and the baby were innocent. They'd done nothing wrong. Would Ward and Lambert argue as their lives slipped away?

She needn't have worried.

A gun appeared in Ward's hand. He stuck it right in Lambert's face. "Move now or I'll shoot you dead."

Lambert seemed unable to take his eyes off the gun barrel. With it so close, the effect of his crossed eyes was comical. Emma suppressed the urge to let out a nervous giggle.

A metallic click made her jump. Ward had pulled the trigger back. The sound got Lambert moving. He backed toward the door with his hands up.

Ward waved the gun at the medical techs. "You too. Out."

The techs wasted no time following Lambert out.

Once they were gone, Ward rushed to the bed. "How is she?" he choked out.

"Almost gone," the Browns said. "Stand back. Do not touch us once the healing has begun. It would not go well for you."

"Please hurry," Ward begged and backed away.

"Emma." The Browns turned to her. "While in the healing trance, we will be unaware of what is going on around us. If anything goes wrong, you must leave us. Flee."

"I'm not going anywhere without you," Emma replied. "I got you into this, I'll get you out." When they looked at her with respect, she didn't know how to react. Respect from the Browns? Had the sky turned green? Did gravity still work? A lump formed in her throat. Why should their good opinion matter so much? "Get to work," she ordered.

The Dyads put their hands on Mrs. Ward and the now familiar buzz of power rushed across Emma's skin. Ward stood to the side, a hand over his mouth with tears running down his cheeks.

Pity overcame Emma. Pity and admiration. He'd done it. The whole world had told him his wife and child would die and he'd found a way to prove them wrong. Was it arrogance that drove this man? As she watched the tears fall, Emma bet on love.

She went to him. "It'll be okay," she said and stroked his arm.

Surprising her, he took her hand gently in his. "Do you think so?" he whispered. To Emma, he sounded like a frightened little boy.

"I know so," she assured him. "When I met the Dyads, I'd been in a wheelchair for over twenty years."

For the first time since the healing started, Ward took his eyes off his wife. Curiosity lit his face. "And they healed you?"

She smiled at him. "I'm walkin', ain't I?"

A relieved sigh escaped Ward and his focus went back to the bed. He patted her hand. "Yes, you're walkin'."

The Browns started to hum.

"Such a beautiful sound," Ward said. "It makes me feel clean and young."

Emma thought of the welcome ceremony. "If you think this is beautiful, you should hear the whole choir."

Time went by with Ward holding her hand as they listened to the Dyads. Emma thought about the child inside Mrs. Ward. What had he called her? Jenny, the child inside Jenny. The little one would have a father and a mother now. The whole family unit would be intact. Their main purpose in life, to love each other.

If only she could have that with Damien. A happy family unit with Dad coming home after a hard day's work. She allowed herself to picture it. Damien would kneel at the front door so the twins could rush into his arms. After he picked them up, he would stop to kiss her on the cheek as they flew by, twirling madly. A vegetarian dinner would be baking in the oven. Uncle David would be joining them tonight. A perfect little life.

The pain in her chest made her wince. Not for her, this scene of domestic bliss. If she and the Browns made it out of here, her choices remained the same and none of them included Damien.

How would she live without him?

* * * * *

A pitiful groan came from the bed. Alex knew that sound. He'd heard it countless times in the past when Jenny had been in pain and although it indicated her distress, he took heart at the sound. It was the first intelligent sound he'd heard her utter in months. Whatever the Dyads were doing, it was working.

He let go of Emma and moved closer to the bed.

"Remember," she warned. "Don't touch. It could kill you."

Heeding her warning, he put his hands behind his back and stopped at the foot of the bed. He examined Jenny's face. Her blue lips were back to their normal color. The sunken cheeks were filling out. And, dear God, the expressions crossing her face. After so long, after months of slack-jawed emptiness, there was intelligence there. She was in pain. She could feel it.

Another, louder moan escaped her and Alex reveled in the sound. "That's it, Jenny," he cried. "Come back to me."

Her mouth opened wide in a grimace and she screamed in agony. Her arms and legs went rigid as her torso bowed upward. The Browns held her down and continued humming.

Frightened, Alex turned to Emma. "What are they doing to her? Why is she in so much pain?"

Emma drew him away from the bed. "The healing process hurts."

"I can see that. Can't they mask the pain?" He ran a hand through his hair. "Look at her, she's in agony."

As if to prove his point, Jenny thrashed from side to side, her arms and legs locking into odd angles as if each of her joints were acting independently of the others. Another scream tore from her throat.

"Jenny," Alex screamed and lunged for the bed. This had to stop.

Emma beat him to the bedside and pushed him away. When he tried to go around her she pushed again.

"Listen." She grasped his arms. "It hurts worse than anything. It burns like a fire consuming you. When they did it to me, I thought I would lose my mind from the pain." She shook him. "But in the end it worked. As painful as this is to watch, you have to let them finish."

Another scream ripped through the air. Alex peered over Emma's shoulder and gasped. In her distress, Jenny had kicked the cover to the floor. The hospital gown had ridden up around her waist. Alex Jr. was on the move. It looked as if he were trying to pound his way out of his mother. Jenny's skin puckered and bowed, like a balloon being squeezed at one end and then the other.

He started to throw Emma to the side but stopped. The Dyads placed their hands over Alex Jr. Immediately the motion stopped. Jenny's taut body relaxed. The screaming ended.

Both he and Emma sighed with relief.

She eased her grip on his arms. "I don't know for sure but I think that should be the worst of it."

"Lord, I hope you're right. I don't know how much more of this I can take."

"Keep thinking about the endgame. Your wife and son healthy. Your whole lives before you." Her eyes teared up. "Think of that," she whispered.

Something about the longing in her voice made Alex think of what the Dyads had said about her. "Are you really pregnant with twins?"

Her face paled and she let go of him. "That's none of your business."

He nodded. "That's what the payoff was for. Did one of those creatures get you pregnant? Was it one of those two?" He motioned to the Browns.

Emma snorted. "God, no. We are not talking about this. Wait, who told you I was pregnant?"

"Before, in the other room. Those two said something about the lives you carry." He had a horrible thought. "What did they do to you, Emma? Are you some kind of experiment? Dear God, how many of them are growing inside you?"

"Interesting idea," Lambert's voice came from the door.

Alex whirled and took in the old man standing with Reisdorph beside him. The gun in Lambert's hand was steady, pointing at the center of Alex's chest.

Lambert's mouth twisted into a cruel grin. "I think we'll start with an ultrasound followed by exploratory surgery, don't you, General?"

Reisdorph drew his gun and pointed it at Emma. "Sounds like a plan to me, Doctor."

Chapter Twenty-One

ഇ

"We go in from four different directions." Aiden used a stick to point at the makeshift map he'd created in the dirt. "Emma and the Browns are here in the barn or what poses as a barn. The Rapacz Dyad and their group will come from the west." He tapped the dirt. "Concentrate your efforts on this group of buildings. Engage as many soldiers as possible."

"Understood," the Rapaczs replied.

"At the same time, the Dobervichs group will attack from the north, close to the farmhouse. The Matthias group will approach from the south, out of the cornfield here. Once the three groups have engaged as many enemies as possible, the Stewart and Goddard quartets will come out of the woods here and make for the barn. We will locate Emma and the Browns and get them away to a safe distance.

"By that time, the rest of you should have the soldiers under control and you can start wiping memories. Any questions?"

"You make it sound so easy, Aiden," Luke said. "What kind of firepower are we up against?"

"Wulfgar?" Aiden motioned to the Viking. "What did your scout party see in the way of weapons?"

"Each man carries a semi-automatic rifle. Some have tranquilizer guns, some grenades. But I think we can expect a few surprises. Shoulder missiles, maybe even chemical weapons. They seem a professional unit."

"Remember, brothers," Jacob said. "Honor the partner's oath. We do not kill. Trust your Dyad to stop the bullets and fight mostly hand-to-hand. If you must fire your weapon, aim for the shoulder of the gun hand and the opposing side leg. That usually incapacitates your opponent."

Murmurs of agreement came from the partners. Once again, Damien felt a swell of pride. These men humbled him. He had had a taste of what they battled, the killing lust. Each of the human partners had to conquer their instinct to kill the men who would kill them. They went into battle with the greatest handicap imaginable. They faced guns and knives with only their bare hands and their faith in their Dyad to see them through. And why? Because they'd given their word. Remarkable.

"Come," Sebastian said. "Dyads, prepare your partner for battle."

At the traditional words, each Dyad quartet gathered. David, Aiden and Jacob came to Damien and clasped forearms. Although the four of them had done this countless times in the past, this joining had a newness to it.

"Why do I suddenly feel like an adolescent at his first dance?" Aiden said and smiled nervously.

"My fault," Damien replied. "Again, my fault. You are picking up on my fear."

Jacob squeezed his hand. "We must put fear aside. Fear, jealousy, envy, all those demons have no place here within our circle."

"Calm," David began. "We must begin with calm."

Damien tried to empty his mind and follow David's command but putting aside his fear of what they might find in that barn proved impossible. Would they be too late to save Emma and the children? If they engaged the soldiers, would it trigger a chain of events they would all regret?

Brother, David whispered in this mind. *Link with us and find the strength you need to put aside your fear. We will get to your loved ones in time. Do not doubt. Do not fear.*

The combined link of his companions seeped into his consciousness, pushing aside all worry. Confidence welled up in him. After decades of their partnership, how could he think that now, when it mattered most, they would fail? Surely the Balance would not allow such a thing to happen.

"It is time," David announced.

Damien reached for the Balance deep within the Earth and touching it, knew they wouldn't fail. He drew the power deep within himself and then centered on his human partner. Jacob's strong essence opened to him and he pushed the power into him. It centered on his beating heart, gaining strength with each pulse. Damien concentrated on that part of Jacob that was truly unique, his soul, and matched the pulse of the power from the Balance to the tempo of Jacob's life force. The two power sources merged and found their own rhythm.

Again Damien concentrated, this time on the spark of combined power in Jacob's chest. He compressed it into a ball around his partner's heart. Tighter and tighter he squeezed. And then as if pulling back a slingshot, he let it fly. The power shot through Jacob making the big man gasp. The energy raced through his body changing every cell it touched. Jacob's senses sharpened, his arms and legs filled with power. He would be able to run faster, hit harder, and see farther.

In this manner, each Dyad in the clearing raised his human's Balance. As a result, the humans were almost equal to the Dyads in strength and endurance.

Damien drew back from first Jacob and then the link. He looked around at the groups of four, all breaking apart. The power surrounding them was almost visible. It hummed against his skin.

"We are ready," Samuel called out. "Safe travels."

"Safe travels," echoed everyone.

Groups started to break off and head in different directions. Luke gave their quartet a thumbs-up accompanied by a toothy smile. Others nodded their way. Still others slapped Damien on the back as they passed. Each look and every touch confirmed their purpose. They would not fail him.

"Our turn," David said. He led the way into the forest.

* * * * *

Emma couldn't take her eyes off Reisdorph's gun pointing at her forehead. She put her arms around her middle, the only thing she could do to protect the babies. Her biggest fear had come to life. Lambert and Reisdorph knew about the babies. They would never let her go.

Alexander Ward positioned himself between the gun and her body. Points for him.

"What the hell do you two think you're playing at? How dare you point a gun at me?" Alex sneered at them.

The gun in Lambert's hand started to shake. "The general and I have come to an understanding," he began. "We've been listening. We can't let your moral sensibilities get in the way anymore. But don't worry, Alex. You still get what you're paying for. We will allow the Dyads to heal your wife and child."

"You will *allow*?" Alex snorted. "You two seem to have forgotten who's in charge. How about you *allow* me to refresh your memories?" He pulled his cell phone out and held it up as if it were a gun. "One call to the men I met in that dark room in New York and you two are history."

Ward turned and pointed the cell phone at Reisdorph. "You remember them, don't you, General. The same guys who took Major Powers down when I was displeased with him. Whatever happened to Powers? We haven't seen him in a while, have we? Want to join him, General?"

Emma had no idea what Ward was talking about. This was the first she'd heard of the men in the dark room or Major Powers. But from the look on the general's face, he knew all right. Reisdorph paled and his Adam's apple bobbed up and down as he tried to swallow. His eyes darted to Lambert and then back to Ward. The moment drew on, the only sound the continued hum from the Dyads.

Emma used the time to search for options and came up empty. With two guns pointing at her all she could do was watch this power struggle play out and hope her side won.

Finally, Reisdorph squared his shoulders. "We're a long way from New York, Ward. Besides, once I confirm to my superiors the Dyad power, I'm sure they'll agree with me. The way I see it, I hand over the woman and Dyads to them, collect my reward and retire. Now," he said, waving the gun. "Get out of the way and let Lambert take the woman."

Again, Ward surprised Emma. Instead of turning her over to Lambert, Ward pushed her firmly behind him, shielding her with his body.

"I made a deal with the Dyads. They heal my wife and in exchange they get to wipe all our memories and go free."

Lambert gasped. "How could you, Alex? What about the deal you made with me? I help you find the Dyads and I get my revenge."

Ward rounded on him. "I never agreed to anything of the sort. I certainly didn't agree to let you harm helpless women. A pregnant, helpless woman at that."

"But-but," Lambert stuttered.

"You came to me," Alex shouted. "And I paid you well for your services. That's the only deal we made."

"Enough." The general's sharp command silenced them. "I don't give a shit what deals you made. I don't care about your wife or your baby or your money. That's all over with, Ward. Get it? Just be happy I'm letting you take your wife and leave. But make no mistake. The Dyads and the woman are coming with us."

Emma searched the room for a weapon. A surgical kit sat on a table to her left. A variety of sharp, gleaming scalpels shined up at her. She inched toward it, using Ward to shield her actions.

"And what if I say no?" Ward asked. "You going to murder me? How will you explain that? I've left instructions.

Anything happens to me and the word gets out that the men in the dark room can't be trusted. No more billionaires coming to them for help with special problems. The money will dry up. The party will be over. And it will all be laid at your door, General. I wonder? Will they kill you quick or slow? I'm betting on slow, one body part at a time."

Emma took another step toward the scalpels. Two more yards. Only two more yards.

Crack.

The sound of bone hitting bone shot through the room. Alex Ward crashed into her, sending her sprawling. She hit the table hard but managed to grab a scalpel before she let the momentum carry her to the floor. With her back to the men, she tried to conceal the small knife but with only a hospital gown for cover, she had to settle for cupping it in her hand with the handle going up her forearm.

"Get up, both of you," Reisdorph ordered as he nursed the fist that had sent Ward to the floor.

When neither she nor Ward rushed to obey, the general closed the distance. He grabbed her wrist and pulled her upright. Thank God he'd chosen the hand without the scalpel.

Emma put her arm against her middle, cradling the scalpel between her body and her arm. She tried to act as if she were injured.

"Here," Reisdorph said and pushed Emma at Lambert. "Take her and start your tests. But nothing too invasive until I speak to New York. Understand?"

Lambert grabbed her upper arm and squeezed. "I understand perfectly." He gave her a once-over, his excited eyes making her sick to her stomach. "She can't be too far along by the look of her. But we'll see. What about them?" He motioned to the Dyads.

"We let them finish what they're doing. After all, Mr. Ward has to get what he paid for. And then we sedate them and wait for orders from New York."

"But I get to oversee the experiments?" Lambert asked.

"Yes, yes," Reisdorph confirmed. He looked at Ward, still on the floor nursing his bleeding mouth. "After all, a deal's a deal. Isn't it, Ward?"

"You're making a bad career move, General." Ward's words were slurred.

"Not after the Dyads wipe your memory I'm not."

Emma watched the realization of the general's words hit Ward. He turned to her, a look of horror in his eyes. She knew as well as he did, once the Dyads wiped his memory, all knowledge of the general's actions would disappear. Ward wouldn't remember Emma or the Dyads. He'd be with his wife, happily awaiting the birth of his son.

Could Reisdorph force the Browns to wipe Ward's memory? She doubted it but Ward didn't know that. Besides, this was his chance to get away clean. No guilt, no remorse, just happily-ever-after time. Meanwhile, her future looked grim. God only knew what the half-mad Lambert had planned for her.

"Alphonse, you can't do this." Ward scrambled to his feet. "Take the Dyads if you must but not Emma. She has no part in this."

"I am so sick of you telling me what to do. I'll do whatever I want to her." Lambert shook her.

Emma had had enough. First it had been the Dyad Elders expecting her to let them wipe her memory and take her children. Then Damien, thinking she'd just stand by and watch as he and David killed themselves. Next Alexander Ward blackmailed her into getting the Browns to go along with his deal. And now Lambert and Reisdorph, thinking she'd quietly accept whatever tests Lambert cooked up.

She was so done playing the victim.

She fingered the scalpel, moving it to a better position for a strike. If she gauged it right, she could wound Lambert, grab his gun and shoot Reisdorph before any of the men could react. Her body tensed as she waited for an opening.

Two things happened at once. The sound of distant gunshots filled the air and Reisdorph's radio came to life.

"Report," the general shouted.

The high, feminine voice of Cronk came through the radio. "Those things. They came out of nowhere. They're everywhere. Fire. All units, fire all weapons."

"Damn it," Reisdorph swore. "I have to get out there. Doctor, you stay here and cover them. I'll be back when I have the situation under control." He rushed out of the room.

Lambert pushed Emma at Ward and pointed the gun at them.

Emma couldn't help smiling. She turned to Ward. "Told you they'd come."

Well this just kept getting better and better, Alex thought. He stole one look at Jenny and the Dyads. In the last few moments their humming had changed in tone and volume. The serene expression on Jenny's face, her relaxed body and easy breathing comforted him. The healing was nearly over. The Dyads had kept their part of the bargain. Now he'd keep his.

He turned back to Lambert and the gun. "Get behind me, Emma," he ordered. For once she did what he'd asked, no arguments. Keeping his eyes on the doctor, Alex maneuvered until Lambert's back was to the Dyads.

"Stop moving," Lambert demanded.

Alex obeyed. He had what he wanted. All Lambert's attention was focused on him. Jenny and the Dyads were as safe as he could manage.

Screams and rapid-fire gunshots came closer. Lambert's eyes widened.

"I think you picked the wrong side in this fight," Alex said. He inched his hand toward the gun hidden in his lapel pocket.

Lambert chewed on his lower lip. His eyes darted left and right. "The general can take care of them," he said, the panic in his voice at odds with the statement.

"Doesn't sound like it. Listen." More screams rang out, closer than ever. "They're losing, Alphonse. If I were you, I'd make a run for it while you still have the time."

"No," Lambert spat. "I will have my revenge. Those things took everything I had. Everything I was. I'd be a billionaire now if it wasn't for them."

Alex cocked a hip and in a gesture that he hoped looked harmless, folded his arms across his chest. He slid his hand inside his suit and touched the gun. "What good is revenge? What good is money if the Dyads get their hands on you again?" He pulled the gun free of the pocket, masking the movement behind the suit lapel. "This time they won't settle for a simple memory wipe. What do you think will be left of your mind when they get done with it? They'll turn you into one of those drooling vegetables who shits in his diaper."

Something big crashed against the outside wall. Lambert jumped. "You shut up." He clutched the gun with both hands and steadied his aim on Alex's chest.

The window behind him shattered. Alex ducked as something whizzed past his head. He used the motion to pull the gun free. Straightening, he pointed the gun at Lambert. Beside him, Emma gasped.

"Put the gun down, Alex," Lambert shouted.

"I don't think so. We have a standoff, Doctor. You shoot me and I'll shoot you. Or we can wait for the Dyads to get here. Either way, you're done."

Too late, Alex realized his mistake. In this position if he missed Lambert, the shot could hit Jenny. No way could he fire his weapon. It was a bluff then. Fine. He'd always been a master at the bluff.

"Stop this, you two," Emma said. "Put the guns down before somebody gets hurt." She shouted to get over the constant noise of the battle raging all around the building.

"You heard the lady," Alex began. "What do you say we both lose the guns and you make a run for it?"

Lambert's eyes snaked to the door behind Emma.

"Better hurry," Alex goaded. "Come on, you know you want to get out of here."

A sneer curled Lambert's lip. "So you get exactly what you want and I get nothing. Again, I'm left with nothing. No money, no social standing. All my old colleagues laughing at me or worse, pitying me." His shaking hands quieted. The half-mad look was back in his eyes. "Not this time. The general and I have a plan."

An explosion rocked the room. Lambert screamed and his gun went off.

For a moment, no one moved. Alex tried to point his gun at Lambert but his arms didn't respond. The colors in the room were suddenly sharper. All the blood left his head and he had that behind-the-ears tingle he got just before throwing up.

Next to him, Emma gasped. "Oh my God," she cried.

Her voice sounded as if it came from the next room. So far away and yet she was right above him. How had he gotten to the floor?

Her hands pushed his suit jacket off his shoulders. Why was she doing this? He wasn't hot. The room was freezing. As soon as he had the thought, his teeth started to chatter.

He looked down at her fingers fumbling with his buttons. His shirt had turned red. Hadn't he worn a white shirt today?

"I-I didn't mean to do it," Lambert cried. "That explosion—it startled me. I didn't…" He trailed off.

"You shot him in the chest," Emma screamed. "If you're a real doctor get over here. If not, go get help."

Pain hit Alex. His chest was on fire. That colossal moron Lambert had shot him. Wait until he got his hands on the old fool. He'd— Where had all the air gone? Why couldn't he get any air? Something large and hot blocked his windpipe.

Emma was shouting. "He's dying. Get some help."

"No," Lambert whimpered. "I have to go and you're coming with me. Leave him."

Dying? Had Emma said he was dying? Abruptly, the fog that clouded his mind lifted. He looked at his hands. They were covered in blood. Emma's terrified face swam before him. Dear Christ, she was right.

"Browns," Emma screamed. "Help, please. He's bleeding to death."

Alex clutched Emma's hand and tried to form words. "Promise," he managed. The liquid sound of that one word confirmed what was happening. This was it for him. His number was up. After everything he'd been through to save Jenny, he would be the one leaving. But not before he knew Jenny and Alex Jr. were safe.

"Promise me," he said with more force.

Lambert stuck his gun against Emma's temple. "Get up now," he shouted.

Emma rose but her tear-filled eyes never left his. "I promise," she said. "I'll make sure your wife and child are safe."

Alex tried to thank her but could not get the air to form words. He watched silently as Lambert dragged Emma out of the room.

With a great effort, he rolled his head until he could see Jenny and the Dyads still locked in their healing tableau.

Jenny was smiling. She looked as if she dreamed about something wonderful. One hand moved back and forth over her swollen abdomen, caressing.

A feeling of peace overcame Alex. He'd done it. Given Jenny and Alex Jr. back their lives. If the price was his life in return was that so great a price to pay?

Love you, Jenny.

Alexander Ward focused on his wife's face and let the darkness take him.

Chapter Twenty-Two

ജ

The world around them had gone mad.

Damien concentrated and stopped the bullet mere inches from Jacob's head. His partner shot him a look of thanks and ducked a blow from the left. They hadn't made it ten feet out of the forest before the attack hit. The barn housing Emma and the children stood tantalizingly close, less than one-hundred yards away. In between, soldiers huddled in groups behind clear shields firing round after round at his small party.

In the distance Damien caught glimpses of the other Dyads. The Rapacz group had formed a large circle out in the open in front of the main house. Soldiers swarmed around them. As he watched, one of the brothers levitated a grenade forty feet in the air. It exploded, the spent pieces falling harmless to the ground. Other objects floated above the squad. Rifles, knives, even a few men levitated high above, where they could do no harm.

The constant noise beat against his taut nerves. Loud booms from grenades, the sharp *rat-a-tat* of the rifles, men everywhere shouting orders or screaming in pain all threatened to break his concentration.

"Damien."

Jacob's warning shout brought his focus back just in time to duck a beefy fist. He came up in a fighting stance. The bald soldier outweighed him by at least fifty pounds. Tattoos stood out on his neck and arms. He shot Damien a look of disdain.

"Come on, you freak. Afraid to face me one on one?" He bobbed and weaved, looking for an opening.

The half-mad look of hate in the soldier's eyes startled Damien. He recognized the look. Killing lust. This man wanted to beat, to pound, to rip him apart. Hadn't he wanted the same? Here was his chance. Complete with a willing victim.

No, he didn't have time to indulge his base cravings. Emma and the children were in danger. He must get to them.

Damien dropped his arms and straightened. The soldier did what Damien knew he'd do. He attacked. Or tried to. The huge fist stopped inches from Damien's chin, blocked by the shield he'd formed. With another burst of power, Damien levitated the man feet first into the air. He caught a look of shocked eyes and flailing arms as he flew by. He linked with the Rapacz brothers and passed the floating soldier to them. Damien couldn't afford to waste energy on keeping him aloft. He would need all his power to get Emma and the children safely away.

"Jacob," he called. "We must get inside the barn."

Jacob nodded. "Form up," he shouted to the others.

Instantly, their group of eight formed an arrow. The partners at the point with the Dyads in the rear. In this formation, they started for the barn.

Guns sounded and Damien reached for the bullets, stopped their projection and let them fall to the ground. Jacob, Aiden, Luke and Emil made short work of the men who rushed them. One blow usually did it. A chop to the neck, a kick at a knee, a jab to the breadbox and it was over.

Moving quickly, they created a trail of injured or unconscious men.

A thunderous sound from the left startled Damien.

"Rocket launcher," Aiden shouted. "Get down…wait, Samuel has it."

A missile whizzed by ten feet from them. It stopped in midair, turned around and sped into the cornfield. Another loud boom and it was raining corn.

"Now," Samuel said. "We will hold here. Go for the barn." The Goddard quartet spread out in a line and faced a group of soldiers.

Damien needed no other prompting. He, David, Jacob and Aiden sprinted forward. Sounds and smells rushed past them but he paid no heed.

Finally, they reached the barn. Aiden threw the double doors wide and the four of them sped in. They took a moment to orient themselves. From the outside, the building had looked like any other barn in this part of the country. Bigger than most but still keeping to the old red barn style. Inside, all such façade disappeared. It could have been any urban office building. The large reception room had a low ceiling with fluorescent lights. One long hallway let off to the left, another to the right. Doors lined each of the halls.

"Which way?" David asked.

Damien concentrated and felt the children. "Left," he said and moved for the hall.

"Wait," Jacob and Aiden said together. They both pulled a gun from behind their backs. "Stay behind us," Aiden added and led the way.

Ten steps in they heard Emma scream.

"Damien, stop," David shouted.

Damien ignored him. Every instinct pushed him forward. Emma was in danger. His mate, his love, called to him. Nothing could hold him back.

He reached the end of the hall and turned right. Emma and Dr. Alphonse Lambert stood in his path. The gun at Emma's head stopped him cold.

"You killed him," Emma sobbed. "My God, you killed him."

Neither of them had seen him. He sensed the others behind him and raised a warning hand. Alphonse Lambert. What was he doing here? The last time Damien had seen him, Samuel had been wiping his memory. That had been months ago back in Michigan. How had the old man ended up here? More importantly, what was he doing with his Emma?

"Stop struggling," Lambert demanded.

Emma didn't obey. If anything, she increased her efforts to pull away. "Get that gun away from me before you kill me too. I'm not much good to you dead."

She twisted in his grip and caught sight of Damien. Her eyes widened and she let out a gasp. Lambert, sensing a change in her, turned. Fear and hatred shot at Damien.

Lambert pressed the gun harder against Emma's head and moved behind her. "Stay away," he shouted. "You come one step closer or try any of your tricks and I'll kill her." He ground the gun into her temple.

Damien raised his hands. "Dr. Lambert, I am surprised to find you here."

The old man let out a gruff laugh. "I'll just bet you are. Outsmarted you, didn't I? Didn't think a mere human could best the mighty Dyads, did you? But I did."

"What do you want?" Aiden asked.

He sneered at them. "I want my life back. I want the money you stole from me."

Damien took a step forward. "Let Emma go and you have my word. I will give you anything you desire."

Damien. David's voice rang in his head. *We cannot give him what he seeks.*

I have given my word. Emma is worth any price he names.

"You think I'd take your word?" Lambert shouted.

"What then?" Damien asked.

"I'm leaving and she's coming with me. Once I'm safely away, I'll contact you with instructions on where to wire my money. I want fifty million. When I've confirmed the money is there, I'll let her go. Maybe." His lips curled in a cruel grin. "How does it feel, Dyad? To be under my power." He moved the gun to Emma's abdomen. "I know about the babies. What if I give her back after she has the babies? Maybe I'll hold on to one of them. I'll let Mom here choose which one."

Damien's stomach twisted. Hopelessness threatened to paralyze him. The man was mad. Emma stood so close he could almost reach out and draw her into his arms. What were the chances of getting her back if he let Lambert take her? On the other hand, if they tried to overpower him, one squeeze of the trigger and Emma and the children would be lost forever. He had never tried to stop a bullet before it left the gun. This was not the time to experiment.

He had no choice. "Jacob, Aiden, put down your guns." He turned back to Lambert. "We will see you safely away from here."

The sight of Damien standing ten feet away, so calm and collected, filled Emma with hope. She drank in his familiar handsome face with a sense of wonder. How was it possible he was here? When she'd left the Diarchy, she thought she'd never see him again. A part of her had already started grieving his loss. Where would she find the strength to walk away from him again?

Lambert moved the gun back to her head. "Let's go," he ordered.

No way in hell was she walking out of here with this madman. Emma fingered the scalpel she'd kept carefully hidden. One chance, that's all she needed. If Lambert let his guard down for a second, she'd cut his fingers off. Let him try to pull the trigger with a bloody stump.

"I'm not taking one step with that gun at my head."

"Emma," Damien urged. "Please do what he says."

"You heard him." Lambert squeezed her arm until she thought it would break.

She locked her legs and refused to budge. "Remember what happened to Ward? I can't trust you not to shoot me from sheer stupidity. Point it at the floor and I'll go with you."

Lambert grabbed the back of her neck and shook. "I'm calling the shots here. I'm in control now. This is my time."

The slightly hysterical tone in his voice chilled Emma. How do you reason with someone who's lost his? Besides, all the jabs to her head with the gun barrel had brought on a monumental headache. Thinking past the pain was becoming difficult.

"Dr. Lambert," she began in her most reasonable voice. "You are in control. I agree. All I'm asking is that you be careful where you point the gun. Think about it. If it goes off by mistake, you'll kill me just like you did Ward. Once I'm dead, the Dyads will be on you in seconds. You'll be under their power again. Helpless again."

Behind her, Lambert stilled. His rapid breathing sent a rush of vile-smelling breath every two seconds. Her gag reflex kicked in and she took a deep breath and held it. The seconds ticked by as Lambert thought over what she'd said.

Suddenly, the pressure against her temple eased. Emma let out the breath she'd been holding.

"Feel this," Lambert hissed.

A sharp pain exploded in her lower back. She cried out. Damien took a few steps toward her before Jacob and David pulled him back.

"In this position if the gun goes off it will miss all your vitals. You won't die but I can guarantee the pain will be excruciating. Understand?"

"Yes," Emma gasped.

"Now, get us out of here," Lambert said to the Dyads.

"This way," David said. He started back down the hall. Jacob and Aiden turned and followed. Only Damien remained immobile.

Emma locked eyes with him and tried to interpret what she saw. Anguish, pain and helplessness flashed across his face. If only she could link with him. She tried to send reassurance, tried to send her love to comfort him. It didn't work.

Damien's gaze moved to Lambert. His expression hardened to absolute hatred. This couldn't be her Damien. Dyads didn't hate.

"If any harm comes to her, human, I will kill you," Damien promised.

"Empty threat," Lambert chided. "Dyads don't kill."

"This Dyad will."

The look in his eye left no doubt. What had happened to him? Had she done this?

David grabbed Damien's arm. "Focus, brother. We must get out of here."

Damien nodded and allowed David to pull him down the hall. His attention never wavered. He didn't turn but instead walked backward, keeping his eyes on Lambert. His head was slightly lowered and he looked up at Lambert through dark brows. Like a lion marking its prey. Emma was positive that if Damien got the chance, he would kill Lambert. Not just kill him, tear him apart.

She couldn't let that happen. If there was killing that needed doing, she'd be the one to do it. Lambert had used up any goodwill right about the time he'd shot Ward. He wanted to experiment on her children. If she killed him, she wouldn't lose a moment's sleep over it. If Damien killed him, it would alter his existence.

They turned a corner and Emma saw the front doors of the barn. If she was going to make a move, it had better be soon.

"How do we do this?" Aiden asked.

David pulled Damien back to join Jacob and Aiden. "I have alerted the others," he began. "They are creating a safe corridor to the woods on the right. Once we reach the woods we will backtrack to where we left the vehicles. We will give Dr. Lambert a vehicle to make his escape with Emma."

Damien growled. The sound sent shivers up Emma's spine. Lambert's odds for making it to the car alive took a nose dive. She couldn't let Damien kill.

"They are ready," David said. "Aiden and Jacob, you will lead the way. Damien and I will go next followed by Emma and Dr. Lambert. Stay close. The others have been expending a great amount of power. The human partners need replenishing but the battle prevents it. The quartets begin to weaken. We must hurry."

Emma's time was running out. She had to act now. But how?

Jacob and Aiden went to the double doors and pulled out guns. David, with Damien in tow, joined them. Lambert kept back a safe distance. Maybe Damien's constant growling and murderous looks were getting to him.

Emma looked around and saw a bucket and mop next to the door. The mop had a metal handle—perfect.

"Stay inside until we call you," David told Lambert.

The two Dyads and their partners dashed out the door.

Lambert moved Emma closer to the doors, the gun still pressed to her back. She took a deep breath, gauged her moment and then pretended to stumble forward. Lambert had to use both hands to steady her. For a moment the gun left her back. Steeling herself, she brought her elbow into Lambert's midsection. His woof of surprise as all the air left his lungs filled her with a savage satisfaction. With her other hand, she swiped at Lambert's gun hand with the scalpel and was rewarded with a howl of pain. She rushed to the door, grabbed the mop and pushed the long handle through the barn door handles, effectively locking them in. More importantly, locking Damien out. She engaged the dead bolt for good measure. Then she turned and faced Lambert, scalpel at the ready.

He cradled his right hand against his side. Blood dripped from a long gash that started at the knuckles and disappeared into his cuff. Her heart sped when she saw the gun in his left hand pointed at her.

"Drop the knife or I'll shoot," he shouted.

Behind her, someone banged on the door.

"You shoot me and Damien will kill you." She moved away from the door looking for an opening in Lambert's defenses. The gun shook in his hand. Blood had made a path down his shirt. She must have cut deeper than she realized. Good.

"Haven't we been through this already?" He took aim and before she could move, fired.

Emma screamed. Pain exploded in her left arm. The pounding on the door intensified.

"The next shot goes in the other arm. The one after that in your right leg. I've got bullets to spare. I'll put all of them into you if I have to."

"Give it your best shot." As fast as she could, Emma rushed Lambert. He swung the gun too late and she crashed into him, sending both of them to the floor. It turned into a desperate wrestling match. She swiped at him with the scalpel and heard the gun skitter away. He managed to pin her hand. She dropped the weapon. He reached for it but she swiveled and kicked it away.

Weaponless, it came down to brute strength. For an old man, Lambert was unusually strong. To make matters worse, her left arm stopped working.

Lambert screamed and got off a jab to her jaw. For a moment, stars appeared before her and then the pain hit. Big, beefy fingers closed around her throat and squeezed. She couldn't breathe. Lambert's body pinned her down. She scratched at his hands but knew it was useless. Lambert screamed again but she could no longer hear the words. She couldn't even hear the pounding on the door anymore. The light started to dim.

Suddenly, Lambert's body flew up in the air. Was she hallucinating? As she gulped in air she watched him dance above her, arms and legs flailing.

The Browns came into view over her.

"Is this man bothering you?" they asked.

* * * * *

Damien threw himself at the barn door, willing the hinges to break. This time the door flew open. He rushed in, sure he would find his love dead. Four steps in, he stopped. Lambert floated close to the ceiling, screaming unintelligible ramblings. The Browns stood over his Emma who lay splayed out on the ground. The hospital gown she wore was covered in blood.

"No," he cried and rushed to her. He collapsed to his knees, anticipating her lifeless eyes.

She turned her head and smiled up at him. "Didn't you read my letter? I told you to stay away."

Alive. She was alive. He reached down and gathered her up in his arms. He took a moment to drink her in. Her smell, the feel of her body, her rapid heartbeat against his chest. Alive. Thank the Balance, alive.

"Brown," Emma croaked.

"We are here, Little Emma," the Browns said. Damien sensed them behind him. Why had she felt the need to address the Browns?

"Mrs. Ward and the baby." Emma looked past him to the Browns. "Did you do it? Are they all right?"

"Yes, the woman and her child will endure," the Browns replied. "She will need to sleep for many days but she will wake healed."

Emma tried to sit up but couldn't manage it. She sank back into his arms. "And Mr. Ward?"

"The man is dead. We could find no spark of life to sing to," the Browns said. Damien heard a hint of sadness in their tone. What had happened to make the Browns mourn a human's passing?

Tears fell down Emma's cheeks. "I thought so but I'd hoped..."

A hand clamped down on his shoulder. Damien growled and shot up with Emma in his arms. "Nobody touches her except me," he snarled. He moved quickly, taking Emma to a room down the hall and kicking the door shut. No distractions, no sharing. It was an un-Dyad thing to do but he didn't care.

Chalkboards lined the walls. Ten rows of chairs faced the front of the room which housed a large desk and had a movie screen behind it.

"Oh, look," Emma said. "This must be where they teach introduction to terrorism."

Damien smiled. Only his Emma would find the humor in this situation. He chose the nearest chair and sat, cradling her in his lap. "Where are you hurt?" he asked gently.

"My arm," she croaked.

He pulled the gown off her shoulder and examined the wound. The bullet had gone straight through the meaty part of her upper arm. No permanent damage but it must hurt. He linked with her and took the pain away. She relaxed in his arms.

"How could you leave me?" he asked quietly.

"Don't talk now please," she whispered. "Just hold me, Damien. Let's pretend for just a little while."

He pulled her close and savored the feel of her. Finally he was at peace. His whole world lay safe in his arms. "I love you, Emma," he said against her hair. "You must never leave me again."

"Shhhh," she said and put a finger to his lips. "I thought I'd never see you again." She kissed him lightly on the mouth. "This time together is a gift. Let's not waste it arguing about things that can never be."

"You are wrong, love. I will not allow us to be parted again."

Tears filled her eyes. "That's a beautiful wish, but…"

"No, wait. If you won't take my word for it, I'll call in my secret weapons."

He sent his mind reaching for hers and formed a strong link. For a moment, he simply enjoyed the sensation of feeling whole again. He sensed her doubt, her sadness about their future apart but he pushed all that aside and reached for their children.

The little beauties were sleeping. He nudged them awake.

Father is here, the little boy thought. *Did you help Mother? She was so sad, so alone.*

His daughter's consciousness hid behind her brother's, tentative and shy.

Yes, he thought back to them. *I am here. And look who I have brought with me.*

Mother, his daughter cried and reached for Emma's mind. Astonished wonder came from Emma. Wonder, joy and unending love flowed through their family link. The delighted child minds fed on her love and shot it right back. Could there be a more perfect union than this?

Much later, Damien broke the link and looked at Emma. Her dreamy, contented expression made him smile.

"They're perfect, aren't they," she said. "Such sweet little things. The boy already looks out for his sister. He'll be just like you, Damien. Protecting everyone around him. When he's older…" She trailed off and her expression darkened.

"Nothing's changed," she said flatly. She stood and moved away from him. "We still have the same bleak choices. I won't let the Elders take our children. I won't let them steal my memories." She turned to him with fire in her eyes. "And above all, you dying is not an option. We are right back where we started. What choice do we have?"

"An excellent question, human," a voice from the doorway said.

Damien spun and found the Salazar and Orchid Elders, in full robed regalia, standing in front of them. The Browns, looking somewhat humbled, stood next to them. David and the others huddled by the door.

Before he could move, Emma dashed in front of him, using her body to protect his.

"Stay right where you are," she warned the Elders. "Not one step closer." When no one moved, she continued. "If you've come here expecting me to give you our children or allow you to wipe my memory, you're wasting your time." Despite her bravado, Damien noticed his brave Emma's knees shaking. What a woman.

"Oh, I know you can force me but I warn you, I'll fight you with everything I've got and in the end, you'll be nothing more than common thieves. I thought Dyads were better than that."

The Orchid Dyad raised their hands in a peacemaking gesture. "Please, Little Emma."

"I'm not finished." Emma cut them off and pointed a shaking finger at Damien. "This man has, for centuries, protected your race from the evils of the outside world. He's followed every order you've given him, even when he knew you were wrong. He and the others have saved both races, Dyad and Human, countless times."

"Emma, stop," Damien warned.

She waved a dismissive hand at him. "And how do you reward him? You threaten to banish him. You would separate him from his mate. And let's not forget you expect him to kill himself if our children upset your numbers. And all the while you tell him it's his fault this has happened. His fault? Well, I didn't see any of you getting off your Elder Dyad butts to help him."

Damien thought it past time to intervene. Although he was tempted to delay awhile. The astonished look on the Elders' faces was priceless.

"Emma," he said and went to stand next to her. "Thank you for defending me but it does not alter the situation we find ourselves in." He brushed a kiss on her cheek and looked at David, who nodded back. Then he turned to the Elders. "David and I have made our decision. We accept banishment. We will live out our lives among humans as humans."

"No, Damien," Emma cried. "Take it back, take it back right now."

Smiling, he put an arm around her. "I told you. I will not be parted from you again."

"But you'll die." Tears formed in her eyes.

"A small price to pay for a lifetime with you and our children."

"But what if we don't get a lifetime? What about the thousand Dyad rule? You can't kill yourself. There has to be another way."

He had no answer for her. There was no way around Dyad biology. If their children plunged the Dyad race into an unbalanced state, David and he would have no choice but to travel on. What were two lives compared to a thousand?

"Elders, the Brown would speak," the Browns said and stepped forward.

"Be silent," the Salazar Dyad snapped. "We have not forgotten we are here because you disobeyed us, Brown."

"No," the Orchids interjected. "We would hear what the Brown have to say."

The Browns glanced at Emma. "This human woman is a worthy being. When we were being held prisoner, she would not leave us. She could have gotten away and yet she chose to stay to help us. We have linked with her and found that we have been wrong about humans."

Damien couldn't believe his ears. The Browns not only admitting they were wrong but also seeing some worth in the human race. What had Emma done to them? And then he realized she'd done nothing more than show the Browns who she was. How could anyone touch his Emma and not see her worth?

"Not all humans," the Browns continued. "Most of them are worthless but we will allow that some." They smiled at Emma. "Show promise."

Now that sounds more like the Browns, Damien thought.

"You ramble like a human, Brown. Get to the point," Salazar said.

The Browns smiled again. Damien couldn't remember the Browns ever smiling. "When we linked with Emma, we were fortunate to meet her children. They are wondrous creatures, pure and perfect. And we think they may be the key to our future. A bridge between Dyads and Humans. They must be given the opportunity to flourish. If they do indeed upset our number, they cannot lose their father. If a Dyad is required to travel on, the Brown will stand in for the Stewart. We will take this burden from them."

Damien's amazement doubled. "Why would you do this for us?"

A touch of the old Brown disdain lit their faces. "We do not do this for you, Stewart." They turned to Emma and their expressions softened. "We do this for your mate and the children she carries."

Emma went to them and took one of their hands in each of hers. "Thank you but the children and I couldn't possibly accept." She turned to the Elders. "You're the big shot leaders around here. Get us out of this dilemma."

The Orchids laughed. "That is why we have come. We suspected Damien would never bring you back to the Diarchy. The Chaldean came to the conclusion that the children will never threaten our number. They are only half Dyad and therefore no danger to us. So your offer, Brown, as noble as it is, will not be needed.

"Moreover, the Elder council has rethought our initial rulings involving Emma and the Stewarts." They shot a pointed look at the Salazars.

"What do you mean?" Emma asked.

The Orchids opened their arms in the formal welcome gesture. "We ask, no, we invite you to live among the Dyads within the Diarchy."

Emma crossed her arms. "Will you take the children away from us like you do your own? To be raised by the community?"

The Orchids shook their heads. "No. You may raise your children in the human fashion. We would like to have you with us. We believe it would be safer for you and the children. However, if you prefer to live in the human world, the Stewarts will not be required to accept banishment. They may come and go as they see fit. It is your choice."

Emma turned to Damien. "Are they serious?" she asked, disbelief warring with hope on her face.

"As serious as a heart attack." Damien pulled another of Emma's grandmother's sayings from their shared memory. She giggled.

The Orchids moved to the door. "Take as long as you require to make up your minds. The battle outside is over but it will take quite some time to clean up the mess. We will leave you for now. Come, Salazar. Let us offer our aid to the groups outside."

The Salazars fell in behind the females. "We would hurry the process," they said. "The air here is…vile. How do they stand it?"

Once they were gone, David and the others rushed to them. Damien watched as Emma was passed from one man to another. Each gave her a bear hug except for Luke, who lifted her in the air and twirled. Even shy Emil joined in, giving her a kiss on the cheek.

David linked with him. *She is a remarkable woman, your mate. I will never forget the look on the Elders' faces when she told them off. Your lives together will never be boring.*

Our lives, David. You will always be a part of us.

Other quartets started to drift in. Each man waited his turn to hug Emma. Damien endured it as long as he was able and then ushered them all out. He wanted her all to himself for a while.

When they were finally alone, Emma threw herself into his arms. "Does all this mean what I think it does?"

He took her by the shoulders and looked into her excited eyes. "Yes, love. We can be together forever, never apart."

"And we can raise our children?"

"Wherever you want. Diarchy or human world. It is up to you."

"No," she cupped his cheek. "It's up to us and I think David should have a say in this as well."

"The important thing is I will have you next to me forever. Dear Emma, doesn't it frighten you, even a little, an eternity with a nonhuman like me?"

"The only thing that frightens me is a life without you."

"Emma, I want to make something right between us. You asked me once how I felt about you and I never answered."

She bit her lower lip and looked away.

"No, don't turn away." He took her face in his hands. "I have your answer. I love you, Emma. It is my love I feel, not the echo of yours for me. There was something about you from the moment we met. Something I always dismissed as impossible. But it was there just waiting to bloom. If there were no children, no mating mark, you would still have my heart."

"Oh, Damien." Her tear-filled eyes gazed up at him. "I love you so."

He kissed her and put the promise of a lifetime together in one little kiss.

Epilogue

Emma adjusted Wulfgar's tie. "You look wonderful, Wulfgar." She smoothed his lapels and took a step back. "Very distinguished."

The Viking grunted. "I feel like a turkey trussed up for a feast. I swear, that damn Scotsman fussed over me for hours. Measuring places no man should ever be measured. I'm wearing more layers than a nun."

He leaned down to Emma's level and continued in a conspiratorial whisper. "He's getting back at me for besting him in that stupid game of his. He called it beginner's luck. Why, any man worth his salt ought to be able to hit that small white ball onto the green every time. Still don't see the point of the game."

"I thought we agreed never to mention that again." Luke appeared from behind a statue of John the Baptist. He sauntered over to Emma and shrugged. "The wind was in his favor that day. It did most of the work for him."

Wulfgar snorted. "The wind blew the same for you and your balls ended in the sand most of the time."

"Enough." Luke held up a hand, demanding silence. "Never mention that day again. Off limits, remember. Just like the time in Italy when you mistook the store mannequin for your date and—"

"Agreed," Wulfgar cut him off. "I…ahh…agree. Off limits."

Emma made a mental note to corner Luke later and get the whole story of Wulfgar and the mannequin. But that could wait.

She looked up at the Viking. "Thanks again for doing this for me. I know it's not exactly what you were offering when you said I could call on you."

Wulfgar took her hand in his beefy one. "It is a noble undertaking if a bit unusual."

"You better get to the front of the church," Emma suggested. "It looks like they're ready to start."

Luke grabbed his forearm, halting him. "Remember, no matter what happens, no swearing. It wouldn't do." He smiled. "Trust me about this."

Wulfgar adjusted his tie and shook his head. "Trust and you don't belong in the same sentence." He patted Emma's hand. "I'll try to do right by you."

"I'm sure you will." Emma watched Wulfgar make his way down the aisle.

"I think I'll go with him," Luke whispered. "In case he forgets his lines. We went over them a hundred times but you know the big guy. He'll get nervous and freeze. See you after." Luke kissed her on the cheek and followed after Wulfgar.

Strong arms circled her waist and Damien's mind brushed up against hers, filling her thoughts with his love. She was still getting used to this Dyad form of greeting. Physical touch wasn't enough for Damien. He needed a more intimate connection. He kissed her neck in just the right spot.

"I should not be thinking what I am thinking in a church," he whispered in her ear.

The answering rush of desire made her sigh. She would never get tired of this. In the five months since the events in Iowa her need for Damien seemed to grow rather than diminish. Each time he touched her, each time they'd made love it cemented him deeper into her heart. She wasn't the only one at the party anymore. At last she knew Damien's love for her was as strong as her own for him. He proved it to her every day.

"How long do we have to stay?" he asked, nibbling on her earlobe.

"For the whole thing." She turned to face him. "But I'll make it up to you later."

"It is a deal," he said and grinned lazily. "Do you want to make it a spit bargain? Those can never be broken."

Emma giggled. "Why on earth would I want to break it? If I had my way, I'd spend all my time alone with you."

"I think the Browns would have strong objections if I kept you all to myself," Damien teased.

Much to everyone's surprise, the Browns had insisted on teaching Emma about Dyad culture. In exchange, Emma was educating them about Humans. She still thought the Browns tipped the pompous scale in a bad way but they were growing on her. Besides, when it had mattered most, they'd offered their lives to save Damien and David. For that she could put up with a little pompous.

"Wulfgar is nervous," Damien said.

Emma smiled. "I know. He was more comfortable fighting off Reisdorph's men than up there as godfather to Alexander Ward Jr."

She looked at the small group surrounding the baptismal fountain and tried not to cry. Alex Jr. was safe and sound in his mother's arms. Jenny Ward beamed down at her son and reached for Wulfgar's hand as he approached her.

A lump formed in Emma's throat as she thought of the man who was missing from this picture. Alexander Ward had made this happy day possible. It was gut-wrenching that he wasn't here to share in it. He had done many terrible things to get what he wanted but she couldn't fault his reasons. Dr. Lambert would spend the rest of his life in jail for murdering Ward but so what? Lambert could spend three lifetimes behind bars but that wouldn't give Alex Jr. his father back.

She'd done everything she could think of to honor her promise to him. With the Elders' permission, Jenny Ward had been told about the Dyads and what they had done for her. She'd also been told about her husband's quest to save her life. Emma would never forget the look of pain and grief on Mrs. Ward's face when she learned of Alex's death.

Emma shuddered in Damien's arms. It so easily could have been her. Like Jenny, she could be facing the rest of her life without the man she loved. Raising his children all alone.

She'd offered Wulfgar as godfather and Jenny had jumped at the chance of having such a positive male role model in her son's life.

Through Wulfgar, Jenny and Alex Jr. would have the protection of all the human partners and their Dyads. It wouldn't replace his father, nothing could do that, but it was the best Emma could do.

"You have done all you can for them," Damien whispered.

"Stay out of my head." She turned to him. "A girl has to have some mystery."

"It is still a mystery to me that you chose to live at the Diarchy." Damien kissed her forehead. "After everything I put you through. After everything we all put you through."

Emma put a finger on his lips. "I love you, Damien." She smiled up at him. "Besides, the babies would never forgive me if I took them away from all their Dyad friends."

He put a hand on her extended stomach. "Only a few more months and you will be able to hold them."

She put her hand over his. "Let's hope they get your height."

"And your laugh," he added.

"As long as they're safe." Emma thought of all the unknowns in her children's future. "Tell me again everything will be all right."

Damien's arms tightened around her. "Reisdorph and all his men have had their memories modified. They are no longer a threat to us."

"What about the men Ward talked about? The men in the dark room. Have the partners found them yet?"

"No, but they will. And when they do, we will deal with them. Do not worry, love. What does your grandmother always say? Do not borrow trouble."

His faced softened. "We have one more thing to do before they are born."

Emma thought of the long hours with the Browns and groaned. "Don't tell me there are more Dyad rituals."

Damien laughed quietly. "No, love." He put his hands on her shoulders. "You must introduce me to your family. I want to know our children's grandparents."

The bottom fell out of Emma's stomach. "How are we going to work that out?" She had a horrible suspicion. "I don't want my family's minds messed with, Damien."

He raised an eyebrow. "You take me to your parents' house and introduce us. I have asked Jacob and he assured me that is how it is done."

"Yes, but…" She trailed off. How could she bring Damien home to her family? What would she say? "Hi, Mom and Dad, not only can I walk now, but look what I got, a gorgeous, non-human man who loves me. Oh, and by the way, I'm expecting semi-human twins."

"Of course we will have to marry before we go there."

Emma choked. "What? What did you say?"

Damien looked down at her and smiled. "I could not face your grandmother otherwise."

The End

Also by Ann Hinnenkamp

eBooks:

Dyad Chronicles 1: Dyad Dreams

Dyad Chronicles 2: Dyad Quest

Dyad Chronicles 3: Dyad Love

Print Books:

Dyad Chronicles 1: Dyad Dreams

Dyad Chronicles 2: Dyad Quest

About the Author

ℌ

Born in a decade that starts with an F, Ann now finds herself in an age decade beginning with the same dreaded letter. Her plan had always been to accept aging with the same effortless grace as any movie star with the last name of Hepburn, but now that her forehead is sliding down around her nose and her neck attracts every rooster in the yard, she's given up on grace and put her faith in a good moisturizer and turtleneck sweaters.

Ann has a B.A. in theater and went to graduate school at the U. of M. in the M.F.A. acting program. She freelances as an actor and director in the twin cities area and has played everything from Eleanor of Aquitaine, to the third extra on the right with the gap in her front teeth.

Taking the advice from her father to heart, she never quit her day job. She works at a messenger service where the motto is: If you got it, a courier brought it. Her years in the business world have taught her a few valuable lessons: When designing a floor plan, never put your own office across from the bathrooms. All it has to do is snow to turn a great day to shit. It's impossible to pick up a monkey at the airport, look him in the eye, and then deliver him to a testing lab. And transporting caskets, even when they're empty, is just plain scary.

ﻙ

The author welcomes comments from readers. You can find her website and email address on her author bio page at www.ellorascave.com.

Tell Us What You Think

We appreciate hearing reader opinions about our books. You can email us at Comments@EllorasCave.com.

Why an electronic book?

We live in the Information Age—an exciting time in the history of human civilization, in which technology rules supreme and continues to progress in leaps and bounds every minute of every day. For a multitude of reasons, more and more avid literary fans are opting to purchase e-books instead of paper books. The question from those not yet initiated into the world of electronic reading is simply: *Why?*

1. ***Price.*** An electronic title at Ellora's Cave Publishing runs anywhere from 40% to 75% less than the cover price of the exact same title in paperback format. Why? Basic mathematics and cost. It is less expensive to publish an e-book (no paper and printing, no warehousing and shipping) than it is to publish a paperback, so the savings are passed along to the consumer.
2. ***Space.*** Running out of room in your house for your books? That is one worry you will never have with electronic books. For a low one-time cost, you can purchase a handheld device specifically designed for e-reading. Many e-readers have large, convenient screens for viewing. Better yet, hundreds of titles can be stored within your new library—on a single microchip. There are a variety of e-readers from different manufacturers. You can also read e-books on your PC or laptop computer. (Please note that Ellora's Cave does not endorse any specific brands.

You can check our website at www.ellorascave.com for information we make available to new consumers.)

3. ***Mobility.*** Because your new e-library consists of only a microchip within a small, easily transportable e-reader, your entire cache of books can be taken with you wherever you go.
4. ***Personal Viewing Preferences.*** Are the words you are currently reading too small? Too large? Too... *ANNOYING*? Paperback books cannot be modified according to personal preferences, but e-books can.
5. ***Instant Gratification.*** Is it the middle of the night and all the bookstores near you are closed? Are you tired of waiting days, sometimes weeks, for bookstores to ship the novels you bought? Ellora's Cave Publishing sells instantaneous downloads twenty-four hours a day, seven days a week, every day of the year. Our webstore is never closed. Our e-book delivery system is 100% automated, meaning your order is filled as soon as you pay for it.

Those are a few of the top reasons why electronic books are replacing paperbacks for many avid readers.

As always, Ellora's Cave welcomes your questions and comments. We invite you to email us at Comments@ellorascave.com or write to us directly at Ellora's Cave Publishing Inc., 1056 Home Avenue, Akron, OH 44310-3502.

ELLORA'S CAVE
ROMANTICA PUBLISHING

CPSIA information can be obtained at www.ICGtesting.com
Printed in the USA
BVOW072347281011

274765BV00002B/3/P

9 781419 965203